KV-398-233

TEN DAYS OF CHRISTMAS

Ten Days of Christmas

G. B. Stern

ISIS
LARGE PRINT
Oxford and Orlando

First published in Great Britain 1950
by Collins

Published in Large Print 2001 by ISIS Publishing Ltd,
7 Centremead, Osney Mead, Oxford OX2 0ES
by arrangement with The Society of Authors

British Library Cataloguing in Publication Data
Stern, G. B. (Gladys Bronwyn), 1890-1973
  Ten days of Christmas. – Large print ed.
  1. Large type books
  I. Title
  823.9'12[F]

ISBN 0-7531-6530-9 (hb)
ISBN 0-7531-6531-7 (pb)

Printed and bound by Antony Rowe, Chippenham and Reading

FOR
ELIZABETH HASSARD

*The author is indebted to Messrs. Frederick Muller
Ltd., for permission to reprint extracts from
"Christmas in the Market Place," by Henri Gheon,
translated by Eric Crozier.*

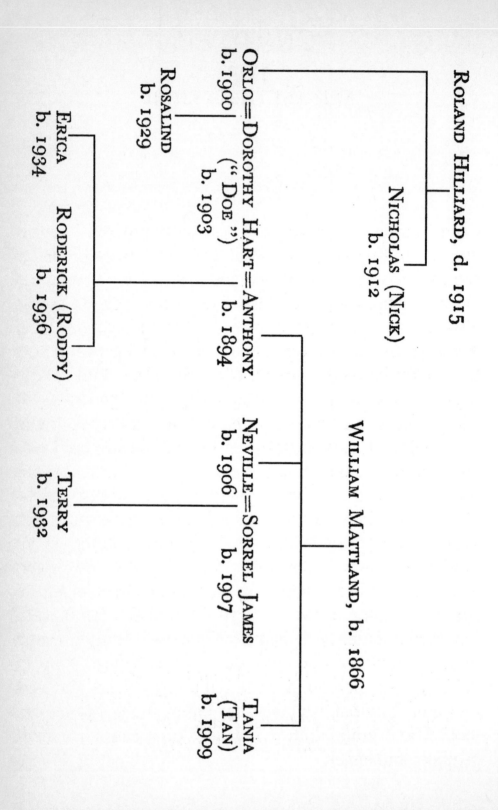

ROLAND HILLIARD, d. 1915

NICHOLAS (NICK)
b. 1912

WILLIAM MAITLAND, b. 1866

ORLO=DOROTHY HART=ANTHONY
b. 1900 ("DOE") b. 1894
b. 1903

NEVILLE=SORREL JAMES
b. 1906 b. 1907

TANIA
(TAN)
b. 1909

ROSALIND
b. 1929

ERICA   RODERICK (RODDY)
b. 1934   b. 1936

TERRY
b. 1932

CHAPTER
ONE

Clare Barnett had come straight to Brambleford on her arrival in England; the Maitlands had invited her to spend Christmas with them, and she had no relations of her own whom she need visit first, as her cousin Lal was also due at Brambleford in a few days, and their Uncle Ted directly he could get away from the theatre, though that might be only to spend Christmas Day with his old friends at the Manor. For the children, the appearance of Uncle Ted would be the high spot in what Clare found they were already beginning to call our Even More Glorious Christmas; eight years ago, in 1938, the last time they had all been together, was our Glorious Christmas. Then, as now, the rest of the grown-ups had been of no account beside Uncle Ted; though they were kind, of course; Anthony and Dorothy Maitland were still as kind as they could be, but Clare was a little shocked with herself at finding that she hardly remembered them; she had expected each familiar figure to have remained diamond-clear as she had tenaciously held them in her mind during the eight years she was living in San Francisco with her father and her American mother and grandmother and her American-born small brothers and sister.

And she had been afraid, terribly afraid, that Lal and the Maitlands might point the finger of scorn at her — Clare's vocabulary expressed itself dramatically only on this one point — for having obediently suffered herself, at the age of seven, directly the "phoney war" had ceased being phoney, to be led away from danger, her own wishes not consulted, and planted with her Granny in California. To her intense relief, however, no fingers of scorn were forthcoming; it really did seem to have occurred to the Maitlands that Clare had perhaps been too young to take up an independent stand on the matter when Mrs. Kenneth Barnett not unnaturally preferred to have her second child in an atmosphere of peace and quietness, with her own mother to look after her.

Now Clare was fifteen, and memory had not served her with any dependable precision. She wished Lal were already at the Manor to enlighten her as to who everybody was. *Everybody*: not alone those already assembled for Christmas, but the scattered members of the party only lately drawn in from their war-time jobs, who were spoken of as liable to turn up at any moment.

Lal, always lucky, was even now staying with Uncle Ted; he had been prematurely sent back for the holidays because of an epidemic at his school. Clare had preceded him at the Manor because she had crossed the Atlantic with the younger van Buren boy in charge of a van Buren aunt; the old van Burens, friends of her grandmother, lived less than twenty miles away from Brambleford. They had promised to meet Clare and Miss Esther Stone van Buren at Southampton, and actually appeared with a car. Mrs. Barnett had thought this arrangement far safer for Clare than letting her knock about with that harum-scarum boy, Lal, in what she still looked upon as a country stiff with blackness and bomb-craters . . .

"But Mother, Uncle Ted can look after us both beautifully and surely we'll soon all three be going down to the Maitlands'?"

But that cut no ice with Louise Barnett: "Your Uncle Ted's acting every night and matinees; he's a big success in his new play. And as for Lal, mercy me, I haven't seen him since he was seven, but even then he was wild as a young steer; a grand little fellow but no sense of preservation — running out and getting himself hit in raids! Not what I'd choose to chaperon you all over the Continent of Europe."

"But Mother, it's not all over it nor over any of it. And girls don't have chaperons since the war; they didn't even before the war."

"This girl's going to have one, or two or twenty, if I say so. Look, Clare, you're not usually an arguing daughter — not like Sadie —"

"Mother, we can sit with Uncle Ted every night. He'd have the star dressing-room, and so we'd be quite safe there."

Clare's father, Kenneth Barnett, intervened with a gentle suggestion that if his daughter's longing to see England again worked out at Nine Nights in a Dressing-room, she really might as well resign herself to the misery of going straight away under comfortable escort to their good friends the Maitlands . . . "And it might perhaps be a little more convenient for Ted," he added, cleverly using her infatuation for his famous brother; "though he'd be the last to say so for fear of hurting your feelings — you don't want to put him in an Awkward Predicament, do you?"

No, Clare certainly did not want to put Uncle Ted in any awkward predicament, though she was crazy to see his new play, "Pearl of Great Price," and sadly disappointed at hearing that Rosalind and Erica and Roddy had been taken to see it before she came to the Manor. Roddy, who was only ten, strangely enough had liked it best. Rosalind, aged seventeen, remarked gently that perhaps it was a little childish, though of course a huge success, but then everybody enjoyed being childish at Christmas, didn't they? Like going to the pantomime and Peter Pan, where you always saw just as many grown-ups as children.

It struck Clare, not for the first time, that Rosalind talked a lot about "children," using a funny voice, not exactly as though they were a species unknown to her but rather as though they no longer offered any personal connection. Rosalind had certainly been the eldest child at the Manor (by two and a half years) in 1938, when Uncle Ted had coached them in a fairy play written by another man whom they had called Uncle Nick, though he was no relation of either Clare or Lal. She had heard the name again recently, in casual reference at the dinner-table: "Is Nick back in England yet?" "Wonder if Nick will get here in time for Christmas?" "I expect Tan would know, but she didn't mention him in her last letter." "When's Aunt Tania coming, Mummy?" "Not till Christmas Eve, Erica darling, they're keeping her too

4

busy up in London; and we want her here, don't we?" "I doubt if Nick will be demobilised in time to get down for Christmas."

Clare decided at last to ask Rosalind about "Tan" and "Tania" — were they the same person? And about "Nick," and where he hitched on to the Manor folk? It was easier to approach Rosalind, with just a touch of deference and an apology for memory gone haywire, than to ask questions of Erica, who though only twelve, was much too aware of knowing all the answers.

"Are they married, Nick and Tania? Or are they brother and sister?" (You can't be saying uncle and aunt all the time, when you don't even recall exactly of whom you are speaking, except vaguely as two people, laughing and benevolently disposed, who were around long ago, helping to distribute toys and parcels and fun!) Then, so that Rosalind should not exclaim in surprise at her ignorance, Clare added remorsefully: "I know it's awful of me to forget, but you can't imagine what a difference it makes, stuck thousands of miles away from you all and having to get the hang of a whole fresh lot of people."

Beautiful Rosalind was never to be able to imagine anything; she lacked the power of swift identification with others. So she simply could not see how Clare was groping in the dark, ashamed of having ceased to belong. Nevertheless, she had formulated an idea, when she saw Clare after eight years in America, tall and well-groomed with a wholly deceptive air of arrogance, that the girl would attach herself to her, Rosalind, sighing over the harsh intervening two and a half years that

5

separated them; and this rather touching appeal seemed to corroborate a not ungratifying theory. So she explained graciously and in detail:

"It is a little difficult, I know, dear, about Uncle Nick and Tania Maitland. You see, they're not even related, and though it was natural for me when I was a child to call her Aunt Tania, she really isn't my aunt at all ... just as *my* Uncle Nick isn't really Roddy and Erica's uncle, though of course till they're grown up they're expected not to call him by his Christian name."

Clare's brain whirled ... She picked up a pencil and a large tolerably clean sheet of blotting-paper from the desk — for they were sitting in the schoolroom — and handed them to Rosalind:

"Maybe if you could draw a sort of family tree, I mightn't be so dumb. Like Whiteoaks, you know."

The Whiteoaks of Jalna formed a happy point of contact with the Maitlands of Brambleford; and Rosalind consented to become genealogical instructress to poor little Clare Barnett.

In a handwriting strong and full of character, usually bestowed by a perverse twist of nature where there is no character to speak of, she started on the blotting-paper with the central fact that Dorothy Maitland had been married twice — ("I'm going to underline the names"). Her first husband, Orlo Hilliard, was Rosalind's father, he had died when she was quite tiny; and presently her mother had married Anthony Maitland, many years her senior, and they had had two children, Erica and Roderick.

"Now," said Rosalind, her pencil hovering and potential as though it were about to perform a conjuring trick, "*now* look: my daddy — we'll call him Orlo for the moment —"

"Orlo's a kind of corney name — you don't mind my saying so, do you? Was he a foreigner?"

"No; I believe he was named Roland after his father, Sir Roland Hilliard, my grandfather; then it somehow got itself into Orlando and then Orlo. Well, Orlo had a much younger brother, Nicholas — there must have been other sisters and brothers between, but I expect they died. And both parents died too, while Nick was still a schoolboy. So his elder brother Orlo, who was very brilliant and Mother always said he would have a great career at the Foreign Office, he became Nick's guardian as well as his brother. And that's all about Hilliard for the minute," said Rosalind, crossing right over to the other side of the blotting-paper, to her mother's second marriage. "*Here's* Anthony Maitland, and here's *his* younger brother, Neville."

"Where?" Clare looked around the schoolroom, startled. Neville was a completely new name to her, rousing not even a tinkling echo from the Glorious Christmas of 1938.

"Nowhere. I've never seen him; nor has Mother. Nobody ever has" — one of Rosalind's rare exaggerations. "He's not dead, he's disappeared. The main thing I'm trying to show you is that old Mr. William Maitland — you must remember Grandpa from last time, don't you? He's coming down for Christmas — he had three children, a long way apart: *Anthony*, *Neville* and *Tania*."

7

And Rosalind triumphantly bestowed the blotting-paper on Clare, to study at her leisure next time her memory played the idiot.

Next time, however, proved to be at once:

"I still don't quite — How does that make Nick and Tan — how are Nicholas and Tania related?" for Rosalind had formally given them their full names on the family tree. "They're way off from each other, right on the outside edges, farther apart than anyone else. And folks always talk of them *together*?"

"You can't altogether judge by how things look on the blotting-paper," Rosalind smiled indulgently at Clare. "They've always been the greatest friends, that's why. In fact, it may have been through their being such friends that Mother met my stepfather."

"Maybe so. Then Nicholas is your mother's brother-in-law one way, and Tania is her sister-in-law the other way, and if they ever married, that would double it all, wouldn't it?"

"Clare dear, you do have such funny little fancies. Now I must go and change. You see, I needn't do anything about you and Lal because none of us are related to you, so you don't come into it — not on paper — you mustn't feel, all the same, that you're not one of our family," Rosalind finished, getting a little muddled herself in her efforts to set Clare at her ease.

"But there ought to be *another*. There ought to be Terry. She acted best of all of us."

Rosalind had been caught out in a serious omission, and went a little dignified in consequence, blaming it on Clare: "Oh, I see; you've forgotten Terry, too? That is a little strange, when you were such friends. They used to call you Terry's Little Champion . . . "

"I hadn't *really* forgotten her, of course. I remember her face and voice more clearly than anyone's . . . But I don't know whose she is — on the blotting-paper," she added, with a crinkle of dry humour.

"Wait, I'll put her in. She's Erica and Roddy's first cousin; not exactly mine, though she's a dear little thing and I'm very fond of her. She stayed here all through the war."

"She's *Neville's* daughter!" Clare guessed, excited as at some spectacular revelation.

"Yes, that's right . . . Neville equals *Sorrel.*" And Rosalind obligingly added this fresh name, and the marriage strokes connecting it with Neville Maitland. "You've heard Erica and Roddy talk of their Aunt Sorrel? — I don't know what her name was before she married him, so I can't fill it in, but it doesn't matter. Anyhow, he left her, and we don't even have a photograph, so that's that. Except that I think he's the reason why Mother gave Sorrel the best bedroom whenever she came down during the war. Mother's so sweet and sensitive about those sort of little ways of cheering people up; and I believe," modestly, "that Erica's growing up the same. Terry's sharing your bedroom, by the way, so it's just as well, isn't it," gently teasing Clare, "that you should know who she is!"

"Couldn't we do a Nativity Play?"

Lal said at once, though amiably: "Of course not," because the suggestion had come from Erica, therefore the negative slipped out automatically before he even considered the proposal. Erica must not be encouraged; for though she was only twelve, the youngest present except for her brother Roddy, she took her part with too much confidence in this meeting of the children's entertainment committee assembled in the Manor schoolroom on that Friday before Christmas. Their first real "Peace" Christmas together; last December, four months after hostilities had ceased, Clare had still been in America; and, among the grown-ups, Nicholas was abroad with the R.A.F., and Tania had some important command with the A.T.S. in the Far East; Sorrel, Terry's mother, was not able to leave her job in London, so Terry had not been there either; and Uncle Ted was rejoicing the troops stationed in North Africa.

Anyhow, this collection of friends and relations and half-relations who had chosen obstinately to adhere against the wash of tide and the years, could not have been housed last year when all the rooms in one wing of the Manor were still requisitioned for army convalescents having treatment at the Ruston hospital, a few miles off.

And last year had not yet any true feeling of peace, secure and inviolate, when they could sit lazily making plans beforehand to do golden things and be sure it could all happen as they had planned it. For instance, acting a play that Uncle Ted could see when he came down for Christmas Day. Eight years ago, he had been free to spend a whole week with the Maitland family, and his niece and nephew, Clare and Lal; his friend Nick Hilliard had specially written a children's play on a nursery rhyme gaily inverted: "*I, said Cock Robin*" — ("with my bow and arrow, I killed the Sparrow!"); and he and Uncle Ted had produced it with riotous success. And the children had said, "We'll do this every single Christmas, whatever happens . . ."

"Whatever happens" had had the laugh on them.

On this Even More Glorious Christmas (because of all the darkness and turmoil and incredulity and lonely suspense which had rolled between 1938 and now), they were naturally able to choose their own play without grown-up guidance:

"I should say we were fifty times too old now for a fairy play; it ought to be something tremendously more important than that." And Roddy thrust in his wish for a pantomime, Ali Baba and the Forty Thieves — "because then we could have forty huge jars on the stage and a man inside each of them and Lal for our Captain."

"Too easy," remarked Lal. "*You* find the forty oil jars and the forty men, and I'll do the rest. Judy, you're our best comic; haven't you an idea to make them sit up?"

Judy was the local doctor's daughter whom Erica called "my great friend"; and though two years older, Judy let it pass; they were not at the same school, where age mattered; and during the holidays, Erica's force of salesmanship, with modest demeanour presenting herself as the only true and perfect specimen of an Erica to be found anywhere, left an easy-going Judy with no option but to take her at her own valuation. Erica could see no flaw in Erica, which added wonderfully to her poise; her round little cherub's face, seen in profile, always seemed to be slightly lifted as though she were listening, not to the commands of her elders, but to celestial music only audible if you were Erica enough; and her soft little pleading voice, a voice from the Home for Waifs and Strays, gave an illusion that please, *please*, although all the other children had had a big tea and lots of cake, and please she didn't mind a bit being left to the last when the plum-cake was finished, please might she have one tiny little bit of bread with the butter scraped off, because please, she was so hungry?

Since her suggestion for a Nativity Play had been rejected, she was silent, planning how they should do it all the same. So Judy, not aware that Erica was quietly settling it all, answered Lal's call for a brilliant new idea with:

"Wouldn't it be fun to do 'I, said Cock Robin' again?"

Lal protested that doing anything *again* was much too unexciting and not in the least memorable:

"This is eight Christmases rolled into one, and we want to remember it all the rest of our lives. Dickens is the most Christmassy writer. And I heard Uncle Ted tell about an old actor his father told him about, who used to play all the parts himself in the 'Christmas Carol', and when he came to the bits where Scrooge laughed, he laughed and laughed and *laughed* and went on laughing till the audience couldn't help laughing too, and then *they* laughed and laughed and went on laughing . . . I'd like to make an audience do that." He broke off from his casual pipe-dream and threw away the pipe: "Except that suppose they didn't, I'd be left up there on the stage laughing for hours alone; nice fool I'd look!"

Clare had lost her foothold in the discussion; were they going to perform "A Christmas Carol," after all, with Lal in a somewhat hysterical hyena rôle?

"There are no big parts in it for women," she pointed out; "there's the Ghost, and Tiny Tim for Roddy, but he wouldn't fit it because he looks so well fed in spite of the rationing" — then she stopped, wishing she had not mentioned rationing, because of her own exemption from hardship, peril and starvation; especially in front of her cousin Lal who had been wounded in one of the London raids; a glory of active participation which had left him with a slight but not incurable limp. The older she grew, the worse she felt about it; even if Daddy had a weak lung, he needn't have stayed out there, need he? "But he's afraid not to do what Mummy tells him," and that was partially true. Girls grow up faster in America than in England; and Clare, no bobby-sox type, was tall for her age; her hair, conker red, had been respectfully treated by talented hairdressers; she was experienced in using rouge and lipstick as a matter of course, though these had been dropped within an hour of noticing that girls in England usually waited till they left school. Clare had had in many ways a wonderful time, with really good boasting material which she never used among the others at the Manor; yet far from feeling travelled and sophisticated compared with them, she tried to serve them with touching humility by every sort of offer and concession; which puzzled them, not realising Clare was drenched and drowned in gratitude to all of them for not scoffing at a companion who had perforce spent the war outside England and two thousand miles away; it seemed to her they must be showing marvellous control. Actually Lal never thought about it at all, and nor did any of the group; it simply did not occur to them to hold her either in scorn nor, worse, in pity; for they took it philosophically that as grown-ups had had to conduct the war, they must be conceded full emergency powers. So Clare was given an affectionate, quite uncomplicated welcome: "Oh good, you're back! Now we'll be complete" — an attitude that hardly called for all that supernatural control with which she was crediting them.

The play project was a slight flaw to her perfect happiness; she had no inborn gift for acting, but would hope for a very small part, as when eight years ago she had been submissively pulled through by Terry and Lal; fair weather enough for her just to be in England again, at Brambleford with Lal and all of them, Uncle Ted coming down in a few days, and the prospect of being taken to London to see him in his play on New Year's Eve. Between Christmas and New Year's Eve she was due for a week-end at the van Burens' house-party; she did not even bother to mention that the sons had enthusiastically urged their parents to invite her for Christmas as well. The luxurious atmosphere they somehow carried with them, even now in England, dancing and cars and all the rest of it, could not offer glamour and thankfulness to compare with that curious blend of both which came from being here and at home in the old schoolroom, sprawling with the other children — (but what *was* the matter with Rosalind?) — and helping them choose a play. On this, Clare's deference might stand aside for a moment, for she honestly could feel that by opportunity she knew more of the subject than they. Ali Baba? The Christmas Carol? — But Gran had taken her to most of the modern productions that touched San Francisco, hoping to swerve her thoughts away from the other side of the Atlantic.

"We could do 'Our Town'," she proposed. "By Thornton Wilder. It's *lovely*; it ran for years. Besides, the way they fixed it, we wouldn't need any scenery or windows or costumes or props —"

"Tell us about it," Lal advised, "instead of a catalogue of all the things we don't need in it. Is it a specially Christmasy play?"

Clare's confidence collapsed over "Our Town" being exactly what they needed. It was a heavenly play, certainly, but nearly all the characters were dead in the last act, sitting up in chairs in the churchyard; and where would be the hilarious Christmas spirit which Lal and Judy declared essential?

"I've thought of the best thing of all," cried Judy. "Let's do a Revue and call it 'The War Is Over' or something like that, and bring in *everything*."

"Tall order," Lal laughed. "Bring in *everything*? — And we've only got from now till Wednesday night to write your Revue, and all the lyrics and songs, and rehearse it and arrange the dances and costumes — I believe we'd do better to choose a play that's been written already. Friday till Wednesday isn't all that long, even if we keep at it; and I'm the only one of you who can sing in tune, and then I can't dance with this leg of mine. Rosalind, you haven't coughed up one idea yet, and we must get it settled this afternoon. No good waiting till Terry comes to-morrow."

In spite of being the eldest, Rosalind had kept silent all this time. Her refusal to collaborate was due to being the eldest, not (as it equally well might have been in her case) a natural outcome of having no ideas. Eight years ago, when all were gathered here at her home for the Glorious Christmas, she had, of course, belonged with the children. Now, although she was seventeen, still those unaccountable grown-ups had made no reasonable suggestion that her natural place was downstairs with them, leaving "the children" to their own juvenile games. And if the grown-ups had not thought of it (what did they think about, if not that?) neither had it occurred to the younger group; Lal had asked her quite casually what play she thought they should do, accepting as a matter of course that she would like to be in it. The only play which might have tempted Rosalind to postpone for a little while longer her withdrawal into emancipated regions, was "The School for Scandal," because she had a fancy to stand pale and guilty behind a screen in a rake's chambers, to be revealed to the audience in all her loveliness and distress when the screen dramatically crashed to the ground. But what was the good? The others were too little. "The School for Scandal" was no play for children.

Rosalind was prepared to be perfectly amiable towards "the children" when viewed from an incredible distance, tiny and complete as though through the wrong end of a telescope: "I'm very *fond* of children," she told herself; fond of them in spite of their limitations and general foolishness. The little speech in which she was to take the opportunity of withdrawing gracefully and for ever from their company must be couched so tactfully that it could not possibly hurt their funny little feelings; for she remembered that even noisy romping children could be hurt very easily.

Lal's direct question was Rosalind's cue for explanation and farewell. But a mobile mind had never been her strong point, and Judy broke in first with some quite ridiculous nonsense about a Nigger Minstrel show:

"We blacken our faces and sit in a semi-circle and make up jokes as we go along, and pretend to be as rude to each other as we can."

"That hasn't gone over big with Erica," Lal surmised, content to lie low and await Erica's ostensible excuse to reject any idea of wilfully blackening that exquisite little pear-blossom face.

"Rude to each other at *Christmas*? Oh, Judy!"

"As if we'd mean it! This is a *show*."

"I'd like to black my face," said Roddy, "and never let it go white again."

"It isn't so very white now," Lal kindly informed him. "I say, we haven't got far, have we?"

"I've thought of the best idea," Roddy announced. And with a conquering air he began to march up and down the threadbare carpet. "And then he can see it when he comes down. He's never *seen* it yet. P'raps it's the only play in the world he's never seen. Me and Ros and Erica have seen it once each. And Clare not even once. And Lal lots and lots and hundreds of times."

"Seven times," Lal struck in, guessing without being told. "Rod, you don't seriously imagine *we* could do 'Pearl of Great Price' — and in front of Uncle Ted himself?"

"Yes, I do," with the dogged persistence of a racehorse that goes on running for the week-end when the race was over on Saturday.

Clare asked her cousin: "Have you really seen it *seven* times? Without getting sick of it?"

Lal laughed at the mere possibility.

"Then of course you won't be coming when I go on New Year's Eve? Not *again*?"

"Of course I *will*. Uncle Ted's giving us the stage box; and I'll let you sit bang in front with Terry. But I wouldn't not come. It's been on for three weeks, and I hate any evening I've missed going. It's so popular I expect it will run for years; three or four years, at least. And when I leave school, I can just go on seeing it as often as I like."

"But now you must know exactly what's coming in it all the way through," Erica objected. For she had not been moonstruck as Lal on the queer new play in which Ted Barnett was scoring his sensational success.

"Makes no difference."

"But what is it?" Clare could not bear even her temporary exile from the cause of her cousin's strange excitement. "I wish they'd let me go directly we landed, before I was rushed over here. But I thought — Tell me, Lal; don't be so cagey. It's a kind of fantasy, isn't it? But a lot of plays in the States have been that way. What makes you — and not only you, I've heard other folk say the same — but seven times in a fortnight — Do tell me, what special thing *is* it?"

. . . Lal's whole body vibrated with a strange conviction that he could pour out through his skin *what* it was, even without coherent words; somehow conveying to them by some form of physical intensity, his passionate love of sitting there alone in the packed theatre, wherever Uncle Ted could squeeze him in . . . till presently the magic would steal over him . . . Could he bear it down here from now till New Year's Eve without a chance of sinking into that state of intangible deep satisfaction at the last scene between Ceddie Conway and St. Cedric? Suppose meanwhile he forgot half a line or an inflexion? Lost them from his private treasury? Lost them and needed them, like that time when he lost his watch and yet had to look every few minutes at his bare wrist . . .

The play had intoxicated him with some ardent secret of which he was too little conscious to be self-conscious; and especially certain rare moments that glowed like the pages of an illuminated missal sprung into life. The story would sound too lame in his mere telling, without the illusion of a stage set to help it along, and without the intervening scenes which he had barely heard in his impetuous desire always to let memory rush on towards his favourite speech importuning him for release before its due time. And without Uncle Ted himself. Yet even without Uncle Ted, his pent-up longing for Clare to share at least that one speech at the end, without further waste of the empty hours till New Year's Eve, burst out in an offer to repeat it and let her from that try and pick up what "special thing" it was:

"I know it almost by heart, except that however hard I always lean forward and listen, determined to remember all of it this time, and carry it out of the theatre so carefully . . . it slips away before I can get it home. It comes in Act III, when Ceddie hears that his Saint isn't going to stay with him on that bare island the whole time, as he'd thought, but will come for certain once a year for twenty-four hours. And at any rate he'd have that to look forward to . . .

"'You have to look forward to just one thing, clear and fresh and cool in the heat, warm when you're chill to the bone. Looking forward — isn't it all the difference between thinking fat and thinking thin, thinking full and thinking empty? All the year I'll go down into sleep filled with looking forward to your coming, and so each new day there'll have been a night swallowed easy in the dark, and you here beside me will be that much nearer when I wake, and by the end of the next day nearer still. Even on the very day after you've gone — I can begin at once looking forward again, as if it was a fire burning through smoke from a long way off. For I swear by St. Cedric — that's a compliment, see? — I swear I'll not look back to say, "Wish it was yesterday and him still here," because already it'll be only three-hundred-and-sixty-four days more . . . Looking forward tastes sweeter than wish-it-was-yesterday, only we've none of us the sense to know that. But it's all in the bag now, happy and glorious, same as in the National Anthem: happy in being so sure you'll come; glorious while you're here. Being *sure* — ah, that's where I score by you being a saint, kind of, and differently placed, shall we say, from the rest of us. Repine's a footling word and a mug's game; not only to pine but keep on *re*-pining; I've seen 'em at it, boys and girls, men and women, and I've laughed. Never cared enough for anyone myself — 'tisn't safe. But now that I do — I'm safer than ever, because of what you are.

"'Only one snag, if you'll forgive me for mentioning it? No need to look grave. Just . . . Well, it's natural for you to have forgotten by now how it might feel, dying alone. Nobody could blame you for forgetting when it was all those hundreds of years ago, and you've had so much foreign travel ever since; I know whenever I'm back from a long tour, my memory's gone quite wonky. Besides, chaps that get martyred *don't* die alone.

"'And there's the snag, as I see it. If you could, so to speak, put a clause in our contract that unless I died *too* sudden — No, no, what am I talking about? Makes no odds to you, of course, *how* sudden — that you'd promise not to wait and look up in your diary how long till the date of our day, but come along at once? At *once*. Will you?'

"'No, Ceddie, I'm afraid I can't promise. That's the one thing you have to take on trust. It's in the book of the rules. Do you want to call the whole thing off? You can, you know.'

"'If I did . . . to whom should I go? No-one else but you has got the hang of it all.'"

Roddy broke the silence: "*Let's* do it, instead of some silly other play. Lal knows the best part, so he wouldn't have to learn it."

Lal skimmed down from the heights, not flushed and embarrassed and stammering, to pick himself up as best he might, but like a champion skier landing without jar or shock. He laughed good-naturedly at the small chunky figure of his admirer . . . .

21

"You don't give up easily, do you, Roddy?"

Still doggedly set on his intention, Roddy said: "There's no part for me, but I don't mind. The dresser with a bad leg could have a son my age, and he could come in with her and say: 'Yes, Mum's leg *is* bad.'"

Clare had sat with hands clasped round her knees, her rapt attention fixed on Lal — (all the more attentive, to compensate for that shocking moment during the speech when Rosalind had interposed: "Lal, dear, none of this is very amusing for poor little Judy." "Oh, I don't mind a bit. But it's funny for a *funny* man to play that part, isn't it?") Though Clare divined that Uncle Ted's play needed Uncle Ted himself before one could hope even remotely to understand its enchantment, she had been searching her mind for comment that Lal might think adequate. So she asked if the title came from Shakespeare?

"No; my Shakespeare has a Concordance at the end, and I looked it up under 'pearl' and 'price', but it isn't under either."

"What's a Concordance?"

Lal tried to define it, gave it up, and seized a dictionary from the shelf:

"'Concord: the state of being concordant; agreement; accordance; an index; the principal words in a book, with references to the passages where they occur, such as in the Bible or Shakespeare.'"

"Concord," Clare repeated dreamily. "Little Women lived at Concord; the Alcott family. It's the right peaceful name for a small town, I think. And 'Pearl of Great Price' sounds as if it came out of the Bible."

. . . An embarrassed suggestion was made that perhaps they could look it up in Grandpa's when he came to-morrow, on the vague assumption that old people, nearer death than the young, would be more likely to keep such an old-fashioned reference book handy.

"Anyhow," Erica covered up the deficiencies in their nursery bookcase, "it's not a bit likely to come out of the Bible because it's not a religious play *at all*; there isn't one single word in it from beginning to end about going to Church."

"All the same, the title must be a quote;" and Lal wondered why he had never been curious enough to ask Uncle Ted; "because that's not how characters talk in a modern play; they'd say instead: 'This pearl's going to cost me a damn sight too much!'"

Taking her cue from all this unwonted Bible chatter, Erica repeated her former plea: "*Couldn't* we do a Nativity Play?" for that delicious hope had revived of hearing once more an audible comment from the front row: "Who is that perfectly *lovely* child?" . . . as when she was chosen for an Angel in some Nativity Tableaux three years ago, a very simple affair for the kiddies and the tots, in aid of National Savings. The audience had been ecstatic, and Erica had had no trouble in identifying who *was* that perfectly lovely child. . . . Naturally she wished she could hear it again; such phrases create an appetite.

"Master Lal, you're wanted on the phone; it's your uncle."

Lal slid down the broad balustrade, not in defiance of etiquette, he was a little past that, but it was a quicker way of getting to Uncle Ted than limping downstairs, each time bringing one foot to join the other, like the toddlers' brigade. He certainly had been warned not to slide down for fear of breaking adhesions that might have formed, but no-one could expect him to take any notice. Roddy whizzed down the same way, so by the time Clare joined them, the first "hellos" were over.

"Don't ring off before he's spoken to me," she begged.

Erica hesitated whether she should also go to the telephone; she was fond of Uncle Ted — who could help it? — but he was not actually *her* uncle. Then curiosity overcame her; she had better know exactly what was going on, always, in every part of the house.

"Coming, Judy?"

Judy turned to Rosalind: "Coming, Ros?"

Rosalind smiled and shook her head. "It hardly needs six of us to take one call for Lal, does it? But you go if you like, dear."

How funny Ros had been lately, thought Judy, the last to leave the schoolroom. Everything with Judy was "how funny"! It simplified both thought and conversation.

Left quite alone, Rosalind walked over to the window looking down on the neglected garden sparsely scattered with snow . . . When they came back, she would tell them . . . The time for pretending was over. Lal, Clare, Erica and Roddy were all dear little things, she was always ready to pet them, but she did not belong any more to this exuberant schoolroom gang, chattering of impossible plays they wanted to do, tearing in a body to

24

the telephone to chatter to their most popular uncle. Presently they would be rushing up again, full of something new and a tiny bit silly. But downstairs in the lounge and sitting-room and library would be men, not just boys . . . Rosalind's musings on men, stirred and rippled, a blue lake placid in the sunshine, as though already they were beside her to cause the ripple and the stir. Men and boys, in her mind, were not within shouting distance of one another; as far apart as children and grown-ups; when you became one, you stopped being the other, that was all; no gradual merging or overlapping; a sharp click and it was done.

"Not coming down for Christmas Day? Not till the Sunday after?" Lal was keenly disappointed; but as Ted Barnett had just explained how he had let himself be booked on Christmas Day for a big party at one of the London hospitals for children, he could hardly plead or complain, but instantly said: "Oh well, that's all right; we'll put off our play till you're there on Sunday night; it gives us more time to rehearse."

"Good," exclaimed Ted, genuinely delighted at not missing the play. "What are you going to do? Have you chosen?"

For the rest of his life Lal never knew what had made him answer without the smallest hesitation, as though it had all been signed, sealed and settled:

"A Nativity Play."

It might have been simply that it was uppermost in his mind as the last suggestion made by Erica just before he was called to the telephone; or it might have been that subconsciously he felt that it *sounded* better than any of their other ideas and proposals during the last hour; more original, and yet more in the Christmas spirit . . . peace on earth, goodwill to men (not that he had any clear notion exactly how much of that would come into a Nativity Play). Anyhow, there it was; he had said it; a gasp from the others clustered round him testified to his bold leadership; and Erica, gratified, put in a rapid: "Tell him it was *my* idea" — of which Lal very properly took no notice.

Yet the reception of his news was amazing. No going back on it now, certainly, after Uncle Ted had said it was the grandest idea they had ever had, and of all plays what he would most look forward to seeing them act. He sounded really excited at the prospect, not just putting it on with an avuncular sort of heartiness. Lal grinned in happy recognition of the Ceddie Conway note in his voice when he said he would be "looking forward" to it . . .

He did not forget, all the same, to cede his place to Clare and not ring off.

She caught them up on the second flight, all talking together, glad to have committed themselves even to something so strange and so difficult. Until his two minutes on the telephone, Lal had been in a pleasantly indolent state; now he had woken up to a sudden onrush of quicksilver vitality. Elated and impudent, he had an irresistible quality as of daring to fly his kite higher and higher, racing along with it, careless of anything that might bring it down, for nothing possible could. The grown-ups had lately marvelled at Lal in these moods;

had even been a little troubled that the 1944 raids over London, and especially the raid which had changed his speed into a limp, had had so little apparent effect on his spirits. And since he had said, "We're going to do a Nativity Play," this coming Christmas appeared to him, heaven alone knew why, more than ever shining and crystalline and indestructible. Peace was declared, victory was declared, and Lal was declaring it for all he was worth, as in a mood of celebration he burst into the schoolroom at the head of the noisy band:

"We *are* going to do a Nativity Play!" they all shouted together at Rosalind, the only one not yet knowing the great news.

"Uncle Ted's thrilled!"

"He'd rather we did it than anything!"

"He can't come down till the Sunday afterwards, so we're going to act it then instead of on Christmas Day!"

Rosalind made no comment on their choice, which naturally did not concern her any more, though in truth she thought a Nativity Play highly unsuitable for the little ones: "The School for Scandal" would have been "better" for Christmas; different, but *better*; one wasn't meant, after all, to be miserable at Christmas; but she only said quietly:

"Not till the Sunday after Christmas? Then Clare can't be in it either."

They did not notice her "either."

"Why ever not?"

"That's the week-end you're going to stay with your friends the van Burens, isn't it, Clare?"

None of them had remembered except Rosalind, to whom the van Buren week-end was of high social importance; she had been quite impressed that Clare was invited to surroundings of such opulence, to a family where there were no juniors at all; the van Buren sons were about the same interesting age as Judy's brother Jonathan, nineteen or twenty. Clare's advantages did not make Rosalind envious, only her disregard that they *were* advantages.

But Clare at once dismissed the van Burens, their opulence, their dazzling week-end and their young men, to a limbo of unimportance. She did not even renounce them as though she minded, or as though, for instance, she were being unselfish for Lal's sake. She merely said: "Of course that's off now, if our play's not till Sunday." Yet she made one odd stipulation: "That is, if you're *sure* I need only have a small part, like the last time?"

Rosalind decided that the moment had come for her valedictory speech:

"Darlings," she began, interrupting babel, "I've something to tell you, and I'm afraid you're not going to like it very much, though it isn't really bad," she added quickly. And then with her arm flung round the nearest shoulders (they happened to be Erica's) she gracefully made her announcement: not only that she had decided not to be in their Yuletide play, but that she was dissociating herself from all future participation in schoolroom life, and from all juvenile company and juvenile pleasures. For the bell had rung; she was seventeen; her place was not with them any more, but with the grown-ups:

"But you must always come and tell me everything, or I shall be really hurt. You see, this is just a thing that has to happen to us, one after another. Clare and Lal will be next, and then Terry; and it isn't as if I were going right away where we'd never see each other; it means chiefly that instead of sitting up here, I shall be sitting downstairs."

"So we'll have more room up here!"

. . . After a moment's pause, Rosalind decided that it would be best to cross over to her little half-brother and give him a warm hug for his last remark. She could not help feeling that her hail and farewell had fallen a little flat; and accounted for it by telling herself that they were stunned and would feel it more later. "Breaking it" had been unnecessary. Preoccupied by the magnitude of their decision to do a Nativity Play and all the problems involved, they had pretended to look attentive; and Judy even said politely: "What a pity you won't be in the play." But Rosalind was already at the door when Roddy suddenly made things worse by calling out "Good-bye" . . . not meaning it impertinently, but *she* had been saying "good-bye" to *them* for the last seven minutes.

"That's quite all right, Ros," called out Lal, reminded by Roddy that she had actually been talking about something, and not nothing. "We'll manage."

The door closed behind her. Now they could plunge!

"We ought to get hold of it at once."

"Get hold of what?"

"The Nativity Play."

"Where do we get it?"

"Is there only one?"

"Yes, I think so."

"There isn't," Erica taught them from her superior dais of knowledge. "There's lots of them." A search through her memory brought forth: "The Ann-un-ci-ation comes into all of them, though."

"You'll choke if you use such long words," Lal laughed.

"I know about Nunciations," Roddy declared unexpectedly, "because I saw Erica do hers. But I wish someone would tell me what a Nativity is?"

Clare did her best: "It's a birthday, Roddy; a most terribly important birthday —"

"Like your grandpa's," put in Lal wickedly. And they all burst out laughing; because old Mr. Maitland's birthday was on Boxing Day, and he never let anyone forget it.

Nevertheless, their first elation at the prospect before them was somewhat quenched; they had become a little tentative in their questions, a little afraid of their own ignorance. It had to be faced that in planning to act a Nativity Play, none of them was on familiar ground. Lal was the first to confess it aloud:

"Look here, we can't manage this show among ourselves. We're sunk if we try. We'll have to get in a producer, after all; probably a grown-up — Yes, I know it's frightful, but we can't let down Uncle Ted, of all people; he's expecting something good; revues and pantomimes and fairy plays are all very well, but we're right out of our depths over Nativity Plays." He added, gravely: "Except, of course, Erica."

Pleased at the concession, Erica was willing to admit that she could not quite undertake the whole production.

Lal went on, coping not only with their unwillingness to let in a grown-up, but with their pretty trust that once they had the book of the words in their hands, the rest would follow automatically: "You see, it's going to be so different; even the sort of parts and the properties and the scenes and the lighting —"

Erica contributed: "Yes, there's the shepherds and the star and the ox and the ass and the inn and the sheep and the Angel — the Angel of the Annunciation — that was me in the Tableaux, so" — a little anxiously — "perhaps it would save a lot of time and trouble and rearrangement, wouldn't it, if I played the same part again?"

"That's for the producer to say."

"Uncle Nick?"

"Too late. We don't know for sure if he'll be here even by Christmas Day."

"Aunt Tania?"

"She mightn't be, either."

"Mummy can't produce, I'm sure."

"Daddy could, but he wouldn't want to," said Roddy, putting his father in a higher category.

Hearing them rummage in vain among their relations, gave Judy an idea: "Jonathan's home; he came down last night. He helped produce — oh, I forget what it was — for the O.U.D.S. He's not interested in plays or acting or anything to do with the stage unless it's *terribly* modern, but he goes on about that all the time; it sounds awful, but he says that's because I don't know the first thing about it."

"Is it worth asking him, d'you think?"

His sister was suddenly a little dubious; she could not quite see Jonathan and a Nativity Play settling down happily together; but it would do no harm to try.

"Let's," said Clare. "He'd be better than a proper grown-up."

"Oh no, he wouldn't; he'd be worse; you don't know Jonathan. Besides, he *is* a grown-up. He's nineteen."

Lal chuckled: "Ask Rosalind! Oh God, I suppose Rosalind will want to come back into it if we have Jonathan producing!"

"Lal, I think you're very disloyal and very unkind, considering how nice Rosalind has always been to you. She said last week 'We must make special allowances for Lal, when he comes'."

"Did she now?" Lal remained sunny and unhurt by Erica's reproof. "Why? Because I've been brought up in the gutter?"

"No, Lal, of course not. She meant because of being lame."

"Oh, *that*!" He dismissed it as a trivial matter not essential to the evening's business. "Come on, we'll all go round and ask Jonathan, and if he says 'no', we'll come home crying loudly, and everyone in Brambleford will dash out of their houses to see what's the matter."

"He's going in for it when he's done his call-up," Judy added to her presentation of Jonathan as an eligible producer.

Somewhat overburdened by their problem and inclined to wonder if they would have done better to abide by Nigger Minstrels, they all trooped round to the doctor's house not five minutes away. And found

Jonathan at home, smoking a very adult old pipe which smelt.

Lal was spokesman; in his preliminary lay-out of their urgent need for a producer, he mentioned a play but concealed its Nativity, afraid that Jonathan would not listen, after that. But Jonathan, lordly and rude, hardly bothered to listen now: "a bunch of kids wanting to act and make fools of themselves" was written in every contemptuous line of his lounging body, and in his eyes wandering to the book-shelves . . . Feeling they might as well be done with it and go home, Lal confessed:

"The reason why we're stumped is that we mean to do the Nativity Play."

Jonathan brought down his long thin legs with a jerk from the mantelpiece. From expressing boredom and indifference, they had suddenly become the most alert legs in Brambleford. "*Which* Nativity Play?"

"Is there more than one?"

"Dozens."

"Lal, I *told* you," put in Erica. "You ought to attend."

Jonathan grinned: "Of course you know Henri Ghéon's 'Christmas in the Market Place' by heart, don't you, Erica? And agree with me that it's absolutely the only one worth doing?"

Erica nodded emphatically.

Jonathan dispensed with sarcasm. "Right. We'll do 'Christmas in the Market Place', and I'll produce it for you. Far more scope in that than in some ghastly pantomime which I thought at first you were after: 'Special engagement of Ed Watson and Ted Barnett as the Brothers Knockabout!'"

"Ted Barnett is Clare's and Lal's uncle," Roddy reminded him.

"I know." But Jonathan never fussed round over unimportant issues to do with politeness and family feelings. He went straight on: "I've always wanted to tackle 'Christmas in the Market Place' on a sort of oblique shaft, keeping it as stark and angular as possible. No props, of course; I can convey it all by the lighting." He half-closed his eyes, visualising oblique shafts on to a stage; then opened them again for a keen scrutiny of his raw material standing in front of him, grateful but bewildered. "Where's that other kid? What's her name — the beautiful one?"

"Rosalind," they supplied in chorus; Judy adding: "You *know* Rosalind, Jon; but she's not a kid — she told us so to-day."

"She gave us notice and went down to sit in the drawing-room with her feet tucked in," said Lal, nonchalantly scornful.

Jonathan had a trick of not hearing anything except what was necessary for his immediate purpose: "I've remembered: *Terry*. Where's Terry? Coming down from London to-morrow? Good. We can phone her presently and tell her to go in to French's and bring down four or five copies of 'Christmas in the Market Place'. She lived with you during most of the war, didn't she? I used to say to myself, 'That kid's got a sort of Emily quality'."

"Emily?"

"David Copperfield," said their universal source of supply. But Erica was wrong for once; Jonathan only stared at her, and gave a slight shudder as though the mention of David Copperfield had been too noxious even for comment.

"Emily in 'Our Town'; Thornton Wilder's play; you wouldn't know."

Clare broke in: "But I *do* know; I went twice. Oh yes! I haven't seen Terry for years, but I see what you mean; I believe she *would* be right for Emily. Not till she's older, because of the way Emily has to look in the last act; but she has it all kind of lying underneath."

"Potential's the word." Jonathan liked Clare for having seen 'Our Town' twice; so he actually addressed her direct: "The American Army Unit did it here at the Scala; no props at all; nothing to divert your attention; it's the only technique; all that old-fashioned fiddling about to have exactly the right period of pictures on the wall —"

"They didn't have any walls in 'Our Town', but you saw them all the same."

"You saw them even more; suggestion's a terrific force and cheaper than scene-shifters. And that's more or less how they did 'Christmas in the Market Place'; I went when they produced it in that church off Regent Street; Blake took me — he's at Merton too — or nothing would have made me set foot in it, but he insisted and he was justified; they were first-class." Jonathan had forgotten he was talking to "a bunch of kids": "By the way, I suppose we'll have to get the Vicar's permission? One of your people had better attend to it; we're in bad odour with him because of my old man being an atheist and refusing to pipe down on it when a patient's dying."

"Get permission *from Mr. Crichton?*"

"Does everybody have to, when they do a Nativity Play?"

"Can he say no?"

"Well, it's his church, so it would be rather churlish to say 'no'; but sometimes they've got bats in the belfry about public performances. The best way to make sure is to promise him a Silver Collection in aid of any old rubbishy cause he may be keen on."

Lal suddenly arrived at what was in Jonathan's mind: "But we can't do our Christmas play in the *church*!"

"You'll do it in the church or nowhere, if I'm to produce it."

"B-b-but — but we acted our last play in the billiard-room; we had a stage built. Don't you remember? You were *in* it." Lal just checked himself from saying: "And Nick said you were about as much use as a sick headache."

Jonathan preferred not to remember; he over-rode their protests with a final assertion that Brambleford Church was the right and proper place, the only place as far as he was concerned, for them to perform what was also the only Nativity Play as far as he was concerned. Nobody could deny that Jonathan Reed knew not alone his own mind but everybody else's he could lay hands on. However, he had a certain amount of trouble in convincing these babes in the wood that a church could be used for any more informal purpose than organs and sermons and people kneeling on a Sunday. They had all been brought up in a slack indeterminate sort of way by parents who had no actual objection to religion and were not averse from announcing cheerfully "Church this morning" on conventional and preferably national patriotic occasions, such as when ordered by the King and the Archbishop of Canterbury; parents influenced by the post-war younger set of the nineteen-twenties, their impatient fling-aside of all forms of what they deemed mere policing for insufficient and unproved reasons; though not so far swirled away into convictions of atheism as to forbid nurses or teachers to encourage their offspring into irregular spurts of "saying their prayers" if it pleased somebody and shocked nobody. And of course weddings often happened in church; and funerals. But as for acting plays — Lal was beginning to regret the impulse by which he had let them all in for a Nativity Play; and to wonder a little why Uncle Ted had been so keen?

Jonathan had it in him to become an excellent producer; and he sensed that a half-hearted company would never do him credit; Lal and Clare, Roddy and Judy and Erica, had ceased to be in his eyes "a bunch of kids"; from now on, they must be professionally handled; so as though carelessly, he let fall certain attractive items about "Christmas in the Market Place", and where it scored over the more direct form of Nativity Play; for instance, that it began towards midnight with a band of strolling gipsies shivering over their supper in the market-square of a small foreign town, with no money and no fire and little to eat; and how the locals gathered to stare at them; and how Joey, the scornful young gipsy who didn't care a hoot for anyone, jumped up and announced they would act a Nativity Play and cash in on that, with himself as Joseph and his young wife as Mary . . .

"Then there's old Melchior: I suppose I'll have to stick on a beard and play it myself; it's a nuisance; I hate acting when I'm producing; but it can't be helped. Gipsies are supposed to be descended from one of the Three Kings, you know, or the Magi, whichever you like to call them —"

Lal suddenly took fire. Gipsies in a little foreign town at midnight — it sounded exciting. He exclaimed: "Bags — I the Three Kings."

"You can't play all three," objected Erica.

"Well, then, I'll play the black one."

Judy giggled. "We're back at our Nigger Minstrel show."

They were all perfectly at ease again now; the tension had been shattered; too much at ease, their producer thought:

"It's *my* business to say who's to play what, and the Three Kings don't come into this version." Rapidly Jonathan cast Lal as Joey the Gipsy, who was also Joseph in the Nativity, Clare for Colomba and Elizabeth — "although I don't know yet how you can act —"

"I'm not good, honestly I'm not. Is 'Elizabeth' a big part?"

"One good scene."

"Aren't there any smaller parts that I can't spoil?"

"Yes, but we're not enough, so I think we'll have to cut them out; 'Sally' and 'Pat' won't matter; they're two young girls of the village who've been singing carols, and they came running down to see the gipsies, and Joey rakes them in to make animal noises for the Ox and the

38

Ass. Judy's our best comic, but she'll have quite enough to do as the Neighbour and the Roman Lady."

"Need I be an anything lady?" Judy protested.

"Oh, you'll like her. She gets all the sheep under her skirts; hundreds of sheep."

"Sheep in a *church*?"

"They won't actually be *there*, you little ass; not real sheep — it's Roddy's business to make the audience think they see them. Roddy's the Shepherd-boy. And Erica —" Jonathan looked amusedly at Erica, and she smiled back at him, and he decided there was no help for it, the producer was not born who could fight against the pointing of such a golden aureole of curls and big blue eyes. "Erica, will you accept the rôle of the Angel?"

"If you're sure I can do it? and if none of the others want it?"

To tease Erica, Lal reminded Jonathan that as yet he had not cast Terry for a part: "In a way she looks more angelic than Erica. But a different sort of Angel."

Jonathan grinned, but for discipline's sake took no notice of the sacrilegious suggestion that Erica's appearance was too bloody obvious. (Had Lal whispered this, or was it floating on the air of its own accord?)

"First rehearsal to-morrow evening. What time is Terry arriving? Before tea? Right, I'll be round at five o'clock. No, not *in* the church; one rehearsal there ought to be enough if you're intelligent. But you needn't imagine, any of you, that you're going to have one of those sweet sentimental Yules with snapdragon and carol-singing and a silver star on top of the tree and feeding robin redbreasts and a bran-tub full of pretty presents . . . I'll allow you one hour off for all that nonsense on Christmas Eve, and the rest of the time we never stop rehearsing except when you're learning your parts. This performance has to be good or nothing. Word-perfect by Tuesday, and all throw away your books from then onwards."

His tone rumbled with such menace that Judy had to remind him meekly that they had not yet got their parts. Jonathan dialled TRU, asked for Terry, and had the luck to find her in: ". . . at Samuel French's in Covent Garden. Five copies ought to do. And don't let them put you off with any other Nativity Play or I'll brain you. By the way, it's Jonathan Reed speaking." It was plain from his voice that she was a favourite.

The others had been whispering among themselves while he telephoned. After he had rung off, they asked him if he could please now come along and talk to Rosalind?

Blankly he demanded: "Whatever for? I don't want to talk to her."

They repeated the news that she had recently withdrawn herself from schoolroom circulation and refused to be in the Christmas play. "Only you see, it might make a big difference when she knows you're producing it."

"But I don't need her."

"Then who's to play the Madonna?"

"Terry, of course."

They were dumb with astonishment; not in opposition to Terry's promotion, only at Jonathan taking it for granted; for he did not condescend to explain that essential quality which he guessed Terry had, and knew Rosalind had not.

Then suddenly Clare exclaimed again in a satisfied way: "*Yes!*" — and Jonathan sent her another look of shrewd approval:

"Remember that scene at the end of Act I in 'Our Town', where George and Emily are sitting at their windows in the moonlight doing sums about wallpaper, and they talk across from one house to the other?"

Clare nodded: "I can imagine Terry in that scene. And where Emily says good-bye to the butternut tree, after she's dead at the end: 'Oh earth, you are too wonderful for anybody to realise you!'"

Roddy was still young enough not to hold back when he was out of his depth; he preferred firm ground beneath his feet: "*We* can't build houses with windows and wallpaper and butter-trees, in church; and you said we were going to do without any walls at all, though I think that's a bit silly."

Jonathan lightly smacked the little boy's buttocks: "Clear out now, and don't forget about getting one of your people to speak to old Crichton. See you tomorrow. You'll have read the play by then, and I expect most of you will need shock treatment. Anyone under ten can ask me six foolish questions, not more; the rest not any at all; I bite heads off when I'm producing. Roddy's had two of his questions already."

"I was ten last month," Roddy informed him with dignity; and they all trooped out, with a polite: "Thank you very much indeed, Jonathan, for consenting to help us," from Erica.

It was dark in the country road, and the church loomed as a mere shape with a squat Norman tower. Nevertheless, in silent unanimity for which they could have given no coherent reason, they stopped outside and solemnly contemplated it as though they had never seen it before. Until now, it had existed in Brambleford as merely an edifice interesting to archaeologists though not to themselves; and used at punctual intervals by punctual people for worship, though again hardly ever by the Maitland family. But now, since Jonathan had spoken, it had definitely passed into their personal possession; now it was *their* church, the church in which they were going to act *their* play . . . Still a little awed at its incredible impact on their familiar interests, they stared, fascinated, reluctant to move on.

CHAPTER
TWO

No-one at the Manor expected Nick and Tania to walk in
together on Friday evening, for Tan had said she would
certainly be working right up until Christmas Eve. Nor
had they known when Nick's leave was due to begin; his
entrances, always unpredictable since he joined the
R.A.F., had become more than ever a somersault from
joy to disappointment or vice versa. Dorothy Maitland
had hardly time for surprise before delight conquered
her at noticing that both had laid down arms in a more
personal sense than the laying down of arms all over the
world. A soft radiance seemed to emanate from the pair,
different from their tingling years of boy-and-girl
companionship, when, as Dorothy complained half-
humorously, you could never tell if they were just
recovering from battle or preparing for another. Now she
could hardly hold back her warm congratulations till
they should actually announce their engagement; delay
which perhaps was fortunate; for they were not engaged
at all; only by some miracle neither had any desire nor
zest in quarrel since they had met again, not three hours
ago. "Why, they're positively *mellow*," thought
their hostess; "it must be Christmas!" . . . But then wonder
was sucked down into the general hubbub that even four

people can create when two have arrived several days in advance of any preparations made for them:

"I ran into Tan, and killed her conscience. There she sat under an avalanche of work slowly sliding down on her; so unlike our Tan; submission used not to be her strong point —"

"It isn't now. But 'ran into Tan' nix; suddenly Group-Captain Hilliard stormed the office barricades and put on a film cowboy act — the old-fashioned stuff: throw the girl across your saddle and gallop like mad! I've got to dash up again on Monday, while he stays here and lazes."

"Darling, you can both laze all over the house by day, but I can't imagine where I'm going to put either of you to laze at night."

"I'll give up my old room to Nick, and turn in with one of the children."

"But Sorrel comes to-morrow, and I'm giving her your old room, as you call it! It's our best spare room and — oh well, you've had a better war than Sorrel!"

"That may be true, darling, but I can't bed and breakfast on it."

"I've fixed up for Doctor Reed to house you, but not till Tuesday. And Ted and Nick will both be at the Cock and Feathers — I must let them know about Ted not coming till Sunday week, by the way. I'm terribly sorry, Nick, you'll have to shake down in the summer-house among Anthony's books for a couple of nights; there's no room at the inn, for the moment; I booked you from next Monday on the off-chance, and I know they're packed until then; streams of visitors."

44

"How seasonable!" laughed Nick. "Of course there's no room at the inn; the taxpayers are come to Bethlehem for the census."

Taxpayers? Census? — He always contrived to puzzle Dorothy within their first five minutes of contact. Anthony, her husband, a silent man, put in a dry:

"Don't shame our vicar's teaching, my dear. One thousand, nine hundred and forty-six years ago, everybody in Judea had to return to their native town or village for enrolment so that not one should escape paying their taxes."

"No-one can escape now," Dorothy remarked ruefully; "but how queer of them to have taken a census just at Christmas!"

Anthony left it at that. But Nicholas drew his sister-in-law tenderly into his arms: "I adore you, Doe; especially for the bland milk-white thoughts you fish up from the Land of Chumperie."

She smiled at him with serene tolerance, for she had always declared they remained such good friends, she and Nick, because from the first she had used tolerance for her only weapon.

Nick remarked to Tania at the time when he was Dorothy's schoolboy brother-in-law, unable to shake off the legend of his young-squirish devotion to her: "Doe never wonders what I'm talking about; she simply takes it for granted that I don't know myself. But I do know, don't I? Considering my age, I'm usually thought rather bright."

"One day she'll discover you're too bright, and then the fur will fly."

"My fur or hers? Tan, why does she get so distressed when we quarrel? *We* don't mind quarrelling."

"Because it comforts her to think of us as Beatrice and Benedick — she's hoping that when we're both grown-up we'll fall in love and get married."

Nick shot her an odd look. He was sixteen and she was nineteen; and he was in love with her already; and also aware she was lost in love for Orlo, his elder brother. . . . That was their story, compressed into a nutshell. Dorothy, Orlo's wife, realised neither that Tania was grown-up and that Nick loved her, nor that Tania loved Orlo; though somewhere in the unexplored regions of her mind, she did wish Nick and Tan would cease from endless fighting and brief truces and enthusiastic renewals of hostilities — "For the queer thing is," she remarked to Orlo, "they're never happy away from each other; that's why Tania comes and stays with us so often during Nick's holidays."

Orlo was an eloquent and over-talkative man, but sometimes (like his successor, Anthony Maitland) he had merely listened indulgently and attempted no comment while Dorothy let one psychological deduction lead to another. She prided herself on her psychological deductions:

"D'you know what Nick and Tan remind me of? 'The Taming of the Shrew'"(a snub to Tania's Beatrice-and-Benedick theory).

"Which is taming which?" asked Orlo. Eleven years older than Nick, he flashed on to the same truth: "You hope they'll settle down in holy wedlock when Nick's old enough, don't you, my dear? So you tell yourself that all this rough-and-tumble must be a sign of love. It needn't be."

"Shakespeare —" Dorothy began.

"If you go into collaboration with Shakespeare, I can't hold out. But Tania is too young for Nick."

"*Orlo!*" in amused expostulation; "she's three years older than he is. That's the one thing not quite right about it."

"There's nothing right about it, my sweet, just as there's everything right about us; even our beautiful placid little daughter Rosalind looks like you and not like me."

Yes, Dorothy knew that, and contentedly accepted the tribute. Everything was right about her and Orlo, as right as her charm and understanding and selfless endeavour could make it.

— Just as now, fifteen years later, everything was right about her and Anthony; even that their beautiful placid little daughter Erica also had the grace to resemble her mother and not her father.

. . . And at last, during this shining Christmas that lay ahead of them, Nick and Tania appeared to have been infected by the goodwill in the very air; each flippancy was a caress, not any more the clang of metal on metal. Nick's supple audacities bent aside of their own accord before they touched her throat; the points of their rapiers wore buttons; gay retort was swathed in kindness lest the edges should do damage, instead of sharpened on the stone to make sure they did. Dorothy's doubts were laid like dust after the passage of a refreshing watercart; her instincts were invariably to sum up the cosmic by the personal instance; so she told herself happily for the hundredth time, smiling secretly at the spectacle of Nick and Tania in their new rare mood of gentleness: "The war is over!"

"Nick can have father's room till he comes down with Philpotts to-morrow," Anthony suggested.

"Of course; I'd forgotten. How clever of you, Anthony. You *don't* mind, do you, Tania," on a lingering doubt as to Tania's reception of having been supplanted, "that I'm putting Sorrel in what used to be your room instead of sending her to Doctor Reed? Because —"

"*I* know," Nick thrust in, with his brightest-boy-in-the-third-form air. "Because you're a nice woman with a nice nature, and it's up to you to make atonement to Sorrel for having married the bad younger son of the Maitland family, while you've married the good elder one."

Rosalind slipped unobtrusively into the room. Her mother said, "Hallo, darling," and signalled to Nick to drop all question of bad younger sons.

After prettily greeting him and Tan, Rosalind took a seat among the grown-ups in their pleasure-park, hoping that by unofficially placing herself among them as though it were a matter of course, none of them would recollect that until five days ago she had belonged to the schoolroom. Half-way downstairs to join the house-party, it had occurred to her that as yet there would be no house-party at all, and that she was tamely going down to join her mother and father; and then usually her father was away at the other end of the garden where a summer-house had been adapted as his study. So she was well pleased to find Tania and Uncle Nick, and prepared to bask in whatever adult glamour they might have brought with them. To remove the subject from the scapegrace Neville, Dorothy continued mapping out details of her sleeping arrangements for when they should all be assembled, till Nicholas, ragging her, checked the enumeration:

"You know that Doe has a Châtelaine complex? She loves to imagine she's distributing her guests into the Peacock Room and the Blue Room and the Haunted Room in the East Wing . . . And ignores that nowadays it remains just a case of who's to muck in with whom."

"Never mind, the spirit's the same; and I'd like to see Grandfather's face if *he* had to 'muck in' with anybody! Tania, you will remember, won't you, darling, to get him a Christmas present *and* another for his eightieth birthday?"

Mr. Maitland's virtuous daughter nodded and looked smug.

"Cripes!" exclaimed Nick. "My knapsack is bulging with Yuletide gifts, but I'd forgotten about the old man's inconvenient birthday on Boxing Day."

"How can you, after the scene he made last time when you only produced one present for him instead of two?"

Dorothy laughed: "Oh, Tan, he *didn't* make a scene."

"No, he closed his eyes and suffered and forgave."

49

For the date of the old man's birthday, December 26th, had been for years a strain on memory and invention. A veteran whose character was entirely sweet and unselfish, on the outrage of "This is to count for your birthday, too", he was transformed to a sabre-toothed tiger. Child and boy and man, he had been compelled to put up with it until he reached an age when he could exact scrupulous observation of two distinct festivals.

. . . "It's so ageing having to eat and drink and toast each other and give a party all over again on Boxing Day, just when we're in a mood to slack off and be surly on weak tea and a boiled egg!"

"Poor Grandpa!" said Rosalind; "he always enjoys his birthday so much, it's worth our making a little effort, isn't it?"

Even Rosalind's mother felt this demure contribution to the conversation marked some odd intangible change which had recently taken place in the family metabolism, though she could not quite lay a finger on it. Nick might have, but he was too busy helping himself and Tania to the much-needed drinks that Anthony had just fetched in.

"Where are the other children, Rosalind darling?"

"Oh, up in the schoolroom," in an off-hand tone. "At least, I believe I heard them all trooping out on one of their busy little errands, after Lal had spoken to Uncle Ted."

Nicholas swung round, on the name of his friend: "Ted? When did you say he was coming down? Not till Christmas Day, I suppose?"

"Not even then; he phoned this evening; not till the Sunday after, and that's only one day before we all have

50

to break up again; such a disappointment." And Dorothy explained about the Christmas show at the children's hospital. "His new play is such a tremendous success, we'll hardly ever see him at all."

"Do you like it?"

"Like not seeing him?"

"Like the new play in the new style? Saxon Saints and Ted Barnett don't strike you as a bit incongruous?"

"Oh no, Nick, *Ted* doesn't play St. Cedric. I forgot that you haven't seen it yet. Or have you?"

"He sent the script out to me to read, before he accepted the part. I advised him strongly against it; so I suppose I should be feeling pretty foolish now. But we can't all like the same thing, can we, Rosalind? Come and kiss your uncle. Aren't you the colleen bawn, as we used to say in bad Irish plays? I suppose you simply *lerved* 'Pearl of Great Price'? No? Have I gone wrong?" Nicholas was genuinely amazed; he did not often go wrong in guessing Rosalind's point of view; her thoughtful comments on life and art and human nature were pasturage on which he could browse happily for hours . . . So it was disconcerting to find her on the same side as his caustic self over Ted Barnett's renunciation of straightforward vaudeville.

"I thought he gave a very clever performance, considering." Rosalind was flattered at being asked her opinion; generally Uncle Nick waited until she volunteered one, and then played merry pitch-and-toss with it. "Of course, it's a little ambitious, and one prefers him in parts where he's more at home."

Nick turned inquiringly from Rosalind to her mother. If the latter also agreed with him, his heart would break.

"I loved every minute of it" — (he gave a sigh of relief) — "though I suppose we must own that it's rather sentimental."

"I want a bath," announced Tania. "And it's the least sentimental play I've ever seen; you've mixed up sentimental and religious."

"I want a bath, too. Before you or after you," Nick added magnanimously, "or simultaneously, if there's a hot-water shortage? I don't care."

"There's a coal shortage. I don't think I'd call it a religious play, Tania; aren't you a little misled by a saint being in it? But calling him a saint was only a *façon de parler*, wasn't it, Nick?"

"I wish I'd learnt French," sighed Nick. "And it was certainly too religious for an out-and-out unbeliever like myself."

"I've been three times, and I may go again on New Year's Eve with the children." Tania smiled mischievously at the out-and-out unbeliever: "Come too?"

"Not on your life. Have the tots seen it yet?"

"Clare hasn't; she came here straight from Southampton. Lal has beaten Tania; I think he said he'd been seven times."

"Good Lord, the boy must be mental! He did put himself in the way of a doodle-bug, didn't he?" Nick's light tones altered to genuine concern. "How d'you find him? Nervy?"

"Not a bit; I've never seen Lal in such high spirits. But Rosalind can tell you more about him." Nevertheless,

Dorothy was rather sorry that Rosalind had planted herself in the lounge that evening; there were so many things one could not say in front of even a modern *jeune fille*, and even in French — ("Nick was odd about that; I thought he spoke French fluently"). Among them were a few pungent criticisms of Lal's father for neglecting his only son and letting him take his chance in the 1944 raids on London during the boy's school holidays. Ted's sister Susan had forgotten to look for kindness when she made a love match with Norman Meredith, always referred to in the press as a "brilliant legal luminary"; both Sue's brothers, Ted and Kenneth, were exceptionally kind men; she thought it could be taken for granted, like breathing. Apparently this brilliant legal luminary had regretted his far from brilliant match, directly his career began to rocket up into the skies. Sue died at Lal's birth, maybe from discouragement, and Norman went on rocketing. Transferred to the S.O.E. in 1939, he became one of those distinguished figures seldom to be found even on the telephone, because he had always flown for a night to Conferences at Madrid or Lisbon or Cairo . . . Ted took affectionate charge of his nephew's welfare whenever he was himself in England, but Meredith cold-shouldered him, resenting too much interference from his late wife's sub-human relations.

"And Clare? What d'you make of her? Bobby-soxer type with a twang you can cut with a knife, I suppose?"

For the third time, Dorothy wished in vain that Rosalind would take herself out of earshot; not yet had the awful truth occurred to her that even without an orthodox pre-war coming-out dance, her elder daughter had come out, and was with them for keeps.

"Only a surprisingly slight American accent, and a few stray words like *corney* and *cagey* that I'd like to weed out. And she was surprised that we were surprised that she used lipstick. Apart from that, I should say Clare was a little too diffident. She's a tall, handsome type, for those who like red hair."

"Red hair and diffidence from her father; tall and handsome from her American mama."

Rosalind leant forward, interested . . . And Dorothy hastily interrupted: "Didn't you want a bath, Nick? It's so lovely to have you here."

"And didn't you say I couldn't have one, Doe, and it's so lovely to *be* here. Why, here comes our little Goldie Locks."

"Hallo, Uncle Nick. Mummy, I want to ask you a favour; it's from all of us, but they sent me. Mummy, will you please go to the Vicar for us? Please."

Even Nick, whom few things could astonish, was somewhat winded by Erica's "favour".

"Does our heathen maid desire to be christened?"

Erica gave a trill of laughter:

"Don't be silly, Uncle Nick; of course I've been christened, haven't I, Mummy? Or I shouldn't be called Erica."

"Something in that."

"Do be quiet, Nick," Tania whispered; "I'm dying to hear what's on her mind."

"Begin at the beginning, darling," her mother suggested. "I'm sure my going to see Mr. Crichton comes at the end."

54

"No, Mummy, it doesn't, honestly; it comes now, but I can make allowances for your surprise, because even I was s'prised at first when Jonathan told us. It's our play, you see; we can't do it like last time on Christmas night, because of Uncle Ted only coming down the Sunday after, and he must be there to see it."

"I didn't know you'd chosen a play yet."

"We chose it this afternoon." And then, legitimately proud: "It was *my* idea. We're going to act a Nativity Play."

Nicholas sat down very suddenly and buried his head in his hands.

"Is Uncle Nick ill?" Erica asked, always ready to be unselfish and put aside her own concerns.

"No, darling, just very tired." Dorothy looked round helplessly: "A Nativity Play? But will it still be all right to act one *after* Christmas?"

Nick raised his head again: "Sunday week will still be within the Christmas Octave. But why don't you postpone it until the Epiphany?"

Erica waited, her petal lips parted, for further information. If you gave grown-ups enough time, you often did not have to betray your ignorance. Sure enough, Tania enlightened her:

"Twelfth Night, my babe: January 6th. But that won't do if you're set on Uncle Ted being here for it."

"Lal's set; *I* thought all along it would be better to wait for the 'piphany."

"There's my little fibber," said her mother, kissing her fondly. "Well now, if you've really settled to do a Nativity Play, I suppose the stage will have to be in the garage . . ." The connection vaguely floating in her mind became apparent: "I wonder if any of the old mangers are still there, as it used to be the stables?"

"The garage, Mummy? *No*. We're going to act it in church. Jonathan says so. Only he wanted us to ask you or Daddy if you'd go and see Mr. Crichton and get permission, and" — impressively — "we'll have a Silver Collection for any cause he likes to name. And that ought to make it all right. But Jonathan would rather not ask himself, because he's not in a very good smell with the Vicar."

"Doe, are *you* in a good smell with the Vicar?"

Dorothy Maitland became a little hysterical. If only her husband would come to her aid. But she perceived that in his usual style of never mentioning his going from the room, Anthony was just not any more present.

"You will go, won't you, Mummy? Could you go this evening? Now? You see, we have to be sure it's all right because Jonathan's going to start us rehearsing to-morrow. He says we'll have to rehearse like mad to be any good."

Rosalind could no longer bear the suspense: "Erica, what has Jonathan got to do with your play?"

"Weren't you there?" chirruped her little sister. "Oh no, I remember now, you weren't. He's producing it for us. Mummy, would you like me to fetch your hat and fur coat and your fleece-lined boots? I don't want you to have to go upstairs just on purpose. Shall I, Mummy?"

"Oh dear," sighed Dorothy, when Erica had run off on her errand; "do they *have* to, just at Christmas?" She was genuinely embarrassed at the children's choice of a play.

Tania laughed: "What could be more appropriate 'just at Christmas'?"

"I don't know," doubtfully. "Surely it's less fun for them than a normal sort of play?"

"Doe, my sweet, I'd so love to know what you mean by 'normal'?"

"Do you take us for heathens like yourself, Nick?"

"Not heathens; nothing so distinct; you merely loiter at the church porch."

The word "church" brought Dorothy back from abstract discussion to the literal problem that confronted her.

"Do you suppose the children would go all stiff and offended if we suggested the billiard-room where they did their little play years ago instead of the church? Now, we've made it the Darts Room, it would be even easier, we needn't move any tables. I hardly know Mr. Crichton; he's a sweet old man, and we've seen him on National Days of Prayer, and when we pray for rain, and of course at Christmas and Easter; but that's not really knowing him. He'll be so astonished if I suddenly — I wonder whether Anthony would go instead?"

"Anthony going wouldn't be at all 'normal' or 'appropriate'. This is your cue for the charm act. Let me see, grave and maternal, I think, and sweetly serious, as if you had realised at last that life wasn't all junketing and plum-pudding. Go *on*, Doe, nobody can do their stuff as you can. Better get it over."

"All very well for you, Captain Hilliard, lying back warm and cosy, and sending me out into the snow and frost. And I thought we were going to have such a heavenly evening, relaxed and happy and mellow . . . "

"You can be mellow with the Vicar, and relax and be happy when you come home. And there isn't a frost to-night."

Rosalind heard none of this, for she had been pondering on whether she should climb down and consent as a temporary measure to become a juvenile again, and to accept a part — the Archangel Gabriel, for instance? — now that Jonathan, over nineteen and an undergraduate of Oxford, had mysteriously been won over to produce the children's theatricals. Had she made a mistake? Then, on a comfortable conclusion that after all she had been quite right (ever the best way to deal with disturbance and doubt within), she decided that Jonathan would probably become impatient with the children and throw it up before the actual night of the performance.

CHAPTER
THREE

A corner seat in a fairly full railway carriage provides an excellent opportunity for Meditation. Or in lay terms, for Terry to have one of her good thinks.

The carriage should be fairly full so that you are separated from your mother, to make conversation impossible . . . Terry went into further details of perfection just for the fun of it: Nobody must know anyone else, so that they could have no impulse to talk either, but stare stolidly in front of them; and not too full or you would have elbows digging into you; and everyone must get in at Paddington for the duration of your own journey, just under two hours, so that they need not rouse you from your good think by stumbling over your feet or lifting down heavy cases from above your head. Was there anything else? Oh yes, a stern elimination of children as travelling companions, and furthermore of colds in the head with their noisy interruption of coughing and blowing. Terry had almost reached the stage of hanging a few good pictures on the walls and choosing a pattern for chintz window-curtains . . . when the whistle blew, the train jerked, moved past the guard waving his flag, and drew out of the station. And she realised that just on this one special journey, though it was the Saturday before Christmas, all the conditions were exactly fulfilled.

First finish reading "Christmas in the Market Place"; there had been no time yesterday evening. She found her place; the Shepherds and the Angel:

MELCHIOR: And suddenly there was with the angel a multitude of the Heavenly host praising God, and saying,
"Glory to God in the highest
And on earth peace, goodwill toward men."
SHEPHERD: Peace, goodwill toward men . . . !
(*He rises, stretches out his arms, then prostrates himself.* MELCHIOR *goes back to his place. A pause. The* SHEPHERD *stands again.*)
I did not dream it? They have gone . . . (*To the sheep*) Sleep! . . . Sleep! The Angel will watch over you. I must go! I must run! He that shall come. He that shall be born — it is He! It is HE!!

— and then it broke off for one of those funny little scenes where the strolling gipsy players discussed among themselves how the Nativity Play was to go on.

At first Terry had been greatly puzzled at this totally new technique; then she grew used to it; and by now she liked "Christmas in the Market Place" better than any other play that had ever come her way.

MELCHIOR: Is the stable ready? — Can we go on?
VOICES: No! — No! Wait a moment . . . I'm not ready! — Yes! — No! (*Confused noise.*)

MELCHIOR: What is the matter?

MARIA: Horatio doesn't want to be Jesus.

MELCHIOR: Then take Edward.

MARIA: He has been playing with the tin of boot-polish and it's all over his face!

MELCHIOR: We will have the baby, then . . .

MARIA: He is asleep.

MELCHIOR: All the better . . .

MARIA: He is sure to cry if he wakes up.

MELCHIOR: Never mind. Don't you think Jesus ever cried as a baby? It will be more realistic. (*To the public*) Excuse me, ladies and gentlemen. You can't always do what you like with children. (*To the others*) Ready now?

BRUNO: No, not yet! The donkey is holding us up —

MELCHIOR: Give him some hay.

COLOMBA: We have run out of hay.

MELCHIOR: Well, let him be. We'll make do without a donkey. We haven't got an ox, anyway. (*To the public*) Excuse us, ladies and gentlemen —

DONKEY: Hi-han! Hi-han!

MELCHIOR: You will have to be satisfied with his voice.

DONKEY: Hi-han! Hi-han!!!

MELCHIOR: Don't overdo it! That's enough for now. (*The* DONKEY *stops.*) I am beginning!

THE OTHERS: All right, Grandpa. Off you go! (*Bell.*)

MELCHIOR: Now the young shepherd, having met with the others, soon found himself near a cave in which he saw a candle burning.

Terry looked up and her lips moved . . . Had she been alone in the carriage, she would have liked to experiment with that donkey noise, try it out to hear if it really sounded like braying; usually she had seen it spelt as hee-haw, hee-haw. Which way was best?

From the far end of the carriage, Sorrel wondered what Terry could have possibly found to laugh at while reading a Nativity Play? Five copies at five shillings each; that young man who had ordered her to bring them down, Jonathan Reed, son of the Brambleford doctor, owed her over a pound. Extravagant! but she remembered hearing that he was in control of his own money inherited from his mother.

What part would he give Terry? Sorrel stole a sideways look at the rounded innocent curve of cheek, half turned away; and was reminded again of the grave attentive beauty of the child in Renoir's picture, La Première Sortie; the same readiness to be absorbed, to offer herself up; touching, because it left her so exposed to disillusion. All this was not a fond maternal partiality, but a fact; when Terry was much younger, you could beckon visitors into her bedroom to see her sleep; and then their soft exclamations at her beauty were enough to satisfy your pride and catch at your heart, while you imperilled the very name of sincerity with your light: "Oh, do you really think so? Yes, I suppose she's quite pretty, but it would be absurd for parents to try and put every quite pretty child into films, wouldn't it? I shouldn't dream of making Terry self-conscious!" . . .

And now that she was thirteen, you had to pay even more severe attention to certain matters of serious import, conforming to their wordless pact that Terry was *not* to be spoilt. It was Sorrel's constant danger, this obstinate longing to spoil her, pet her, admire all she did, keep her away from any imagined danger, tuck her into a warm bed on the slightest provocation, always take her side: "My daughter, right or wrong!" So she sent her away from herself for the duration; not to America, but to her uncle and aunt in Brambleford; dignity and self-respect, these ungenerous sisters to soft sweet sentiment, again demanded it should be taken for granted that mothers did war work in London while little daughters were heartlessly banished to the country.

Other rules . . . They were endless, and all difficult, all the time. Never embarrass your daughter by tasteless remarks about her appearance, especially not in front of people. Remember that her room is her inviolate castle, and not just part of your own flat. Never be demonstrative, but arrange it so that she may think neither of you are not demonstrative by nature, thus warding off suspicion; control yourself, hold yourself back, keep a vigilant guard on even the look in your eyes and the inflexion of your most casual remark. Be interested in her life, but not curious, giving an impression of a separate life of your own which equally you refuse to share. Never, never — and this was the final, most important rule — *Never* say "You're all I've got!" . . . Try and not even think it. Be decent; be a stoic.

Terry had finished the play; it lay in her lap while she gazed out at the foggy December landscape racing backwards, darkening under a half-hearted threat of snow. Now she could surrender to a good think about Rosalind . . .

Of course Rosalind would play the part of the Virgin Mary. Were she not already the most lovely person Terry had ever seen, she could imagine her even lovelier in this play, wearing a cloak of deep blue like pictures of an Italian sky. One's mother did not quite appreciate Rosalind — "You think she's too reserved, don't you, Mummy?" — Rosalind *was* a little silent; Terry did not mind; she preferred it; for then she could always imagine for herself the depth of feeling behind the full tender curve of Rosalind's smile, the sweetness of Rosalind's eyes. If only, Terry reflected, letting her meditations follow any stray path that led aside to fantasy and nonsense and nowhere, if only they were going to do "As You Like It" instead of this Nativity Play, and she herself could be Orlando! She had lately acted Orlando at a school performance, to an awful great lump of a Rosalind — (how *dared* she have the same beautiful name!). But by fastening your memory on the *real* Rosalind, you had just been able to manage to feel romantic . . .

> "From the East to Western Ind,
> No jewel is like Rosalind . . .
>
> All the pictures, fairest lined
> Are but black to Rosalind.
> Let no face be kept in mind
> But the face of Rosalind."

And then had come that idiotic bit, spoiling it, where the fool Touchstone had mocked romance in jingling couplets —

> "If the cat will after kind,
> So be sure will Rosalind.
> Sweetest nut hath sourest rind,
> Such a nut is Rosalind . . ."

Terry supposed that Jonathan, that self-contained lordly young man who always made her feel a little shy, had consented to produce their play because he had fallen madly, helplessly in love with Rosalind, and rehearsals would give him a chance to be looking at her all the time. Was he good enough for her? Certainly not. But perhaps when he was famous ("and everyone says how clever he is!") and perhaps if a Prince of the blood hadn't turned up by then . . .

Nevertheless, a curious sort of play for him to have selected when there was Shakespeare, for instance, or the Sleeping Beauty. Terry picked up her copy again and tried to hear Rosalind in some of the Virgin Mary's speeches. Yet it remained strangely impossible to bring streams of heaven into the dank crowded compartment by merely visualising Rosalind. They were not "speeches" anyhow; not like Portia's "The quality of mercy" — that was a "speech"; though all the same, if you took it slowly and sentence by sentence instead of in one solid chunk, and if you turned the Elizabethan English into how we talk now, all that Portia said was quite true. Yes, but what the Virgin Mary said in this Nativity Play felt true to begin with; even if it could not have been what she had *actually* said, because she must have actually lived and spoken according to her own how-we-talk-now, even longer ago than Queen Elizabeth's reign.

Terry mused a little on whether they ought to be acting a Nativity Play at all? Then came to the conclusion that it would be all right because "they", Rosalind and Lal and Erica and all of them, would not be acting it, but only acting the gipsies acting it; and the gipsies were quite ordinary and not particularly good human people, rather like themselves; jabbering on more or less in the same way. And that seemed to remove them once off from the Virgin Mary and Joseph and the Angel . . . "Like cousins once removed."

Mummy had a cousin-once-removed, whom they called the Awful Warning, because she too had no husband and one daughter, and together they did all the things that made one feel hot, especially up the back of one's neck and behind the ears! That Jeepers-how-*can*-they feeling! The Awful Warning mother was always hugging and kissing her Awful Warning little daughter, pushing back her hair or her hat or pulling them forward, and then sighing: "Take your spectacles off, my little bud of spring, and let Auntie Sorrel see your big brown eyes! "And her ghastly dialogue with other mothers at the dancing-class: "Belinda is so highly strung that sometimes I wonder if I ought to let her dance at all? She puts All She Has into it, and when I get her home she just cries and cries and won't eat any supper and lies

66

awake for hours. But then I've only got to say 'My darling babykin, *please*, you hurt Mummy's heart with your tears; Mummy's heart is like a little boat, it can float on a calm lake, but your tears call up a great storm and the poor little boat is tossed about till it begins to sink, so won't you please stop crying and save the little boat?' . . . And she's so brave, she nearly always manages to control herself; her love for her Mummy is a very powerful — a very powerful —"

— "Life-belt," Terry had supplied, to Sorrel's rather overdone impromptu. "Go *on*, Mummy. When it's my turn, I've got a new one that'll make us quite sick!"

"Mine's nearly finished: We're such *kum*rads, Belinda and I, it's as if we were the same age; having no father, you see. And for fun, we've given my heart a name as though it were a little yacht: 'La Belle Coeur de Maman', and made it into a chansonette . . . "

"I don't think I'll do mine to-day, after all," Terry's tremulous recovery from La Belle Coeur de Maman paid a compliment to Sorrel's invention; "it isn't quite as awful as yours, so I'll save it for a time when we're left without. It's about Belinda being so delicate, and having to be kept in bed 'just in case'."

And this too passed into their special idiom whenever they talked of the Awful Warning pair: "Poor Belinda, she couldn't go to school to-day; she's got just-in-case again: 'Whenever she doesn't feel well, she becomes my baby, I pop her into my bed instead of her own, and I sleep on the sofa, and it's a treat for both of us. Funny treats we mothers have, don't we, Sorrel?'"

. . . All that hugging and kissing and hand-holding and nestling-up-tight. How glad, how *thankful* Terry was that her own mother not only never petted nor fussed her in public, nor pulled her hair forward from under her hat, but did not even want to in private. She really was an excellent specimen of a mother; and they had so many jokes about the Awful Warning pair that it was quite fun when they came to tea and supplied fresh material, fresh evidence of their shameless, unblushing Awfulness. When Auntie Myrtle and Belinda really excelled themselves, she and Mummy could keep on telling each other about it afterwards with unholy delight at the horror of the performance they had just witnessed: "Terry, *stop*. I can't laugh any more; it hurts too much; it's not true, I don't believe you." . . . "It *is* true! They did, they *did*! You weren't in the room for that bit." Longing to stop laughing because the muscles of her belly, too, ached so badly, Terry would sometimes be overcome by uncertainty (though never by remorse) as to whether the latest anecdote of the Awful Pair may not have sprung out of her intoxicated imaginings? Not that Auntie Myrtle and Belinda were not capable of it; they were undoubtedly capable of anything; but being scrupulously addicted to truth on other matters, Terry was a little surprised at her one excess, as for instance an almost total abstainer might be surprised to find he could never refuse Clos du Roi. All the same, though the pair tempted her to sin, she must not forget to be grateful to them for showing up in such atrocious shape what you must never do and never be yourself, if (like the Little Bud of Spring) you are also an only daughter of a father who abandoned your mother because he was a Bad Lot.

* * *

. . . Be a stoic. For dignity's sake, and not to offend that fastidious quality born into Terry's delicate bones, Sorrel had put herself under a régime of non-indulgence in sentimentality, as rigorous as the training of any young neophyte of the old Imperial Ballet. She reflected ruefully that girls who believe one must never by any single sign betray one's love to a man for dread of losing him, have set themselves an easy task; let them try and keep to the same hard astringent code with an only beloved little daughter! In the spirit of comic irony, but not so comic and containing a deal too much irony in the dose, it was a pity perhaps that this same beloved little daughter was now pouring out her evident capacity for worship into a Rhapsody on Rosalind. There were moments since the schoolgirl rave began, when Sorrel's opinion of Rosalind had led her to wonder whether it might be advisable to have a medical test on Terry's sanity? Not that Rosalind was the first to occupy the romantic altar; not wholly the first, but decidedly the worst. And no silent sentry-guard could save Terry from being hurt; fools could hurt more cruelly than sadists . . .

Or was that not true? Sorrel thought of Neville. None of the Maitlands were fools; not Anthony nor Tan; and Neville combined brains with a bonny talent for cruelty. Luckily Terry was hardly three years old before he abandoned the home-and-domestic role altogether, and disappeared into that nebulous place of no fixed address or country, having thought up nothing new to add to the orthodox behaviour of the bad lot, the black sheep of the family, the waster, the scapegrace, the prodigal son.

He merely rang the changes on all the old lucrative platitudes: the horse that was "certain to win"; a spot of embezzlement — "I was so sure of putting it back next month"; a prey to sirens or soubrettes. Whenever Anthony successfully arranged to send him abroad as many thousand miles as was geographically possible, Neville turned up again double-quick (too quick nowadays by air) to cadge for enough and a spot over, "if convenient," to cover the fare he had borrowed; and promised on his honour to repay.

Once indeed, lapsing into a Belinda child, Terry had overheard her grandfather's man allude to Mr. Neville as "a bad lot" — before he caught sight of Mr. Neville's infant daughter listening wide-eyed . . . "What's Daddy a bad lot *of*, Mummy?" And Sorrel, an opportunist where Terry's peace of mind was involved, rapidly seized the chance to make the whole undignified business of being deserted, into an unpainful joke; she did not intend that Terry should wince for the rest of her life every time that fathers were mentioned; nor leave a door open for self-pity to enter and settle down on a juicy diet . . . So let's plump for the Bad Lot, and be free and heartless about him . . . Neville was, after all, a bit of a joke; carry on from there! No alternative except that cloudy pretence stuff Sorrel hated, about a daddy who was neither dead and an angel, nor alive and a nuisance, but somehow dematerialised into a "perhaps one day he'll come back and bring us lovely presents" sort of person; or on the other hand, a stony vengeful blotting-

70

out, once and for all; "Never mention his name!" — Treatment somewhat bleak for Terry, whose look-out over the horizon was anyhow too serious, as though she had coastguard blood in her . . . I wish I'd married a coastguard, mused Sorrel. I suppose that's whimsical, but I do like their flagstaffs and clean gardens with white chalk edges, and the way they *don't* keep on changing their job. In contrast with Neville, who did.

Their train was outrageously late, as might have been expected on the Saturday before Christmas; several taxi-drivers had shrugged their shoulders and departed half-an-hour ago, but theirs, ordered from the Manor, had waited — a lovable man! — so they bundled in with three stranded people for Brambleford, leaving Terry again at liberty to finish her good think . . . for now they were only five miles away from Rosalind . . . four-and-a-half . . . four . . . Terry thrilled as she visualised a Christmas present carefully packed in a bundle of so many scarves and woollies that Mummy, who usually asked no questions, had inquired: "What *is* this monstrous balloon, crowding out all your shoes?"

"Oh, just a parcel," in an off-hand voice; "never mind my shoes if there's no room; I can do without."

It was a present that seemed to fit in perfectly (though Terry did not quite know why) with Rosalind and with what she felt about Rosalind; and with this special and most glorious Christmas, even more glorious than eight years ago, for the war was at last over, and they were all to be together again.

The black-out had disappeared from London eighteen months before; you had been even more aware of it in the country, how you had to grope right up to the gates of the drive and to the house itself . . . walk into its very walls before you could distinguish it from thick darkness. Oh, the excitement now of seeing light stream brilliantly from every window! And when the hall door was flung open at the sound of the car, more light pouring out in true Christmas-card style . . . And Rosalind, actually Rosalind, was the very first figure Terry saw in the welcoming group; with a little behind her in the background (though perhaps they were not really behind her, not really in the background) Uncle Anthony and Aunt Dorothy and Aunt Tania and Uncle Nick. Rosalind was wearing her green velvet dress made for her from Aunt Doe's pre-war evening cloak: "I'd *hoped* she would be wearing that one!" — Terry jumped out and ran up the steps: "And she must have guessed I was longing to see her first of all."

. . . From the road, the thin nostalgic sound of little boys singing "I saw three ships a-sailing" drew nearer and nearer. All things combined in magic.

And Rosalind kissed her. She did not only say "Hallo, Terry!" and smile. She kissed her.

Only . . . it was a puzzling sort of kiss . . . the bending-down sort. Rosalind was taller than herself, but all the same . . . something not quite right about it. And when the others, led by Lal and Roddy, all shouted from the landing above that Terry was to come up *at once*, Rosalind did not come up too. One pang of disappointment — Terry had no time for more. For rapacious as young bears whose normal diet was drama, not buns, they crowded round her: "*Where's the play?* Oh, never mind about stopping to hug Clare. Have you got it?"

"Here's one copy; I was reading it in the train. The rest are in my suitcase. It's frightfully good, and not a bit like any other play; what made you choose it?"

"Jonathan," said Roddy.

"Me," said Erica.

"Me and Uncle Ted," said Lal, capping both claims.

"I say, Terry, Jonathan will be here in an hour — no, your train must have been terribly late; in about five minutes, to start rehearsing —"

"So you'd better get out all the other copies, quick! There's not a moment to waste."

"Though we're not doing it till Sunday."

"*Sunday?* To-morrow?"

"You ass! Sunday week."

"Not on Christmas night?"

"The Sunday after is still Christmas," Erica swaggered, remembering what had been said downstairs; "at least, it's in the Christmas Octave."

Even Lal was impressed; but could not wait to inquire further into octaves.

"Uncle Ted can't come down on Christmas night. He's at some Children's Hospital."

"Besides, a play like that needs hundreds of rehearsals. And —" a long pause for effect, till they could hold their secret no longer — "we're doing it *in the church*!"

Terry was not quite as staggered as they had been when first told by Jonathan; for a printed note in front of the play had stated that "Christmas in the Market Place" had already been performed "by the Pilgrim Players of Canterbury (in association with C.E.M.A.), in August, 1943, and on Christmas Eve, 1943, the production was given in the Crypt of St. Paul's Cathedral." But that such audacity should have no limits even at Brambleford —!

"Have you asked?"

"Of course! We couldn't just break in and act it."

"Aunt Doe went down to the Vicar —"

"*I* went down and asked Mummy to ask —"

"Jonathan told us to promise him a Silver Collection, and there's going to be one —"

"And Terry, what d'you suppose it's going to be in aid of?"

"Can't suppose. It would have been War Weapons while we still needed them."

"It's nice that we don't," remarked Clare contentedly. And it was nice that she no longer had to wonder if she should say "you" instead of "we"; nice that Terry had hugged her first, even before she had answered all their eager questions.

"Let *me* tell. Terry, you've been to church while you lived here, haven't you?"

"Yes, of course. At least three times."

"Well, do you remember" — long-drawn-out suspense — "shut your eyes and sort of pretend, you're seeing the altar straight in front of you; and behind it —"

Roddy grabbed Erica's revelation from its elaborate build-up, and blurted out:

"— An ugly, hateful, hidjus picture; the most hidjus picture in the world. The Vicar thinks so too. And our play's going to buy a piece of brocade stuff to cover it up so that no-one who goes to church need ever see it no more," he finished triumphantly; you had to hurry to wrest the story from a sister who had been told at her silly school that she was an excellent little narrator. ("What's a narrator, anyway?" "A story-teller." "Ha, ha, Erica's a story-teller, Erica's a story-teller, Erica's an awful storyteller!")

"A Silver Collection makes our play sound frightfully important."

"It *is* important," put in Lal quickly. "And Uncle Ted's looking forward to it a lot; and Clare's given up a week-end with some posh American friends of hers where she'd have had her own bathroom, to be in it."

"As though I wouldn't!" threw in Clare, scorning her posh friends and their bathroom.

"But why don't they — I mean, we'd act our play anyway, of course, but why don't they — why doesn't the Vicar just take down the picture if it's so awful?"

Erica's turn had swung round again:

"Because there's been a Faculty."

("Erica's had a faculty, a facul-ackle-lacklety —")

Very gently, not to smother him completely, Lal laid Roddy on the floor, and sat on his face. He enjoyed Roddy; but as a narrator almost equal to Erica, he badly wanted to explain about the picture:

"It's one of those dark heavy old paintings nobody looks at, and yet it's rather frightening for women and children if they're the timid sort and do happen to notice it stuck up there bang in front of them while they say their prayers. It's the Sacrifice of Isaac, and Abraham looks as though he's going to be sick at any moment. I mean, it's not the sort of picture you need be reverent about. The Vicar himself can't bear it; Mrs. — I forget her name — a rich widow who used to live round here and rather lorded it over everybody, presented it in aid of her husband's death, or in gratitude or something like that. And because she'd always done a lot for them, the Vicar couldn't refuse, and they had to get permission from a Faculty, and I don't know any more than Erica or Roddy what a Faculty is."

"I *do* know!"

"— Except that once they've allowed you to hang up a picture in a church, you have to get another permission from another silly old Faculty, or the same one, to take it down again, and there's a lot of fuss, and it's much simpler to cover up the picture and be done with it; you don't have to have a Faculty for that, and the Vicar told Aunt Doe about a shop in London where they sell gorgeous pieces of brocade, and it would cost about ten or twelve pounds."

"And I heard Mr. Crichton say he didn't think it com*para*ble with his conscience to spend that out of any other fund, especially during the war, unless it was from such an outside extra that he never dreamt he'd ever get it at all. And now here it is, or it easily will be as soon as we've acted our play and made a collection."

"A Silver Collection." Red in the face, but still breathing, Roddy reappeared from his sojourn beneath Lal. "No good them putting in pennies or halfpennies; we'd throw them out again and say 'You're a mean old stingy pot! Can't you read? S-i-l-l-v-e-r spells *silver*!'"

76

During Roddy's fantasy, Lal had been racing through the first pages of "Christmas in the Market Place."

"This is grand stuff. Joey's a grand part. It's nearly all Joey at first, while they're still being gipsies. I have to eat soup and cheek the villagers — oh, and steal a chicken. Did you read it, Terry?"

Terry nodded; "Joey the gypsy-boy is Joseph a little later; the Virgin Mary's husband. You'll have to be quite different then. Joey's like you are yourself already."

"You haven't told Terry about *her* part yet," Erica spoke mysteriously. "Wait, Roddy; let *me*! Terry, Jonathan says —"

At that moment, followed by Judy, Jonathan walked into the schoolroom five minutes before time.

"Good, Terry's here; now we can start." He grabbed the play from Lal. "Where are the other copies? Packed? Well, you should have unpacked them; one's no use."

"I know where they've put Terry's luggage; she's sleeping with Clare. I'll get them. May I?"

"Don't keep on saying you'll get them; get 'em first and say it afterwards. We'll read it through now, and by to-morrow you'll all know your parts. Terry, you're to play the Virgin Mary."

Terry did not quite take it in at first. Impossibilities were not announced in such a business-like tone.

"But isn't Rosalind —?"

"Rosalind? Good heavens, no. You've got to have a mind as well as a face for that part." ("And a soul" did not occur to him.)

"And anyhow Ros is never coming upstairs again; she told us she wasn't, yesterday; she's gone to the grown-ups — you know, like going to the dogs; like Nanny told Grandpa's Mr. Philpotts we have an uncle who has."

All that was human in Jonathan, and there had never been very much, was now entirely submerged in the producer. He was already moving the furniture to get a rough indication of a village market-place, a caravan, a platform, etc.

"No, Roddy, never mind about the drum now; it'll do next time."

Terry had remained stunned at the swift revelation of a Jonathan emphatically not prostrate and adoring before Rosalind. Dismay succeeded incredulity . . . until the world which had flown into bits gradually pieced itself together again, for a reasonable solution flashed into her mind: Jonathan must have gone too far, and Rosalind had very sweetly told him there was no hope, or else told him he must wait for her for five years, and he was still feeling cold from the snub. Now that Terry had settled this, she could pass on to joyful realisation that as she herself was to play the Virgin Mary, Rosalind would be among the audience in the church, watching her, seeing her in a blue mantle . . . Gradually she began to remember that it was a wonderful part; and so after all (and even though Rosalind was remaining downstairs for life) this was going to be an Even More Glorious Christmas than any that had ever been before, or would ever be again.

Jonathan was refreshing his memory, half aloud, from volume he had already efficiently marked "Prompt Copy."

MELCHIOR (*excited*): Then — then — I will explain my book to them — tell them the story — and you shall act it for them.

THE OTHERS: What? Us? Act it?

MELCHIOR: Don't you remember the year when it rained all the time down in Cornwall, and you acted it in the crypt for our Saint Colomba?

"Yes, a whole lot of this will have to be cut." The company watched their producer in awe, while he pulled out a pencil and used it with professional ruthlessness on the text.

"In honour of the Child Jesus? It will be a magnificent gesture, Joey! We owe Him something . . ."

CHAPTER
FOUR

Jonathan reflected, after rehearsing his company on Saturday evening and all day Sunday, that it was wonderful what a little terrorising could do. To his astonishment, he saw unmistakable signs that they would really prove excellent if they kept it up. The fact that they had no more than a remote notion what the whole thing might be about, lent a curious sort of zest and innocence to their performance. Even that girl from California, Clare, who had begged in vain to be given only a very small part for fear of spoiling the play, even she, as Elizabeth in the Magnificat scene with the Virgin Mary, forgot to be diffident and self-conscious, and spoke her lines as though a deep sincerity had inspired her:

"Whence is this to me that the mother of my Lord should come to me?"

And Mary's reply: "Receive her quite simply, she is your cousin and your friend."

Those two youngsters, Clare and Terry, might have been rehearsing together all their lives: "If they go at it like that on the night, it's going to bring everyone up out of their seats." Clare had taken the trouble, too, to learn the whole of her part between Saturday evening and

Sunday morning. Jonathan was distinctly pleased with her, and with Terry too; he almost told them so. Lal's acting in Joey the gipsy was more convincing, so far, than his acting in Joey's rôle of Joseph; but no doubt his Joseph would come on presently. In fact, the producer's one minor headache was Erica's somewhat too smug Angel of the Annunciation. Erica found this play's version of the Angel rather unorthodox, and said so, fearlessly. Jonathan replied to her criticism by simply cutting down her speeches to half their length; she had already learnt it all, but as Jonathan was a formidable person when he bared his teeth and growled, Erica wisely decided to argue no more, but to acquiesce in the Angel's unorthodoxy.

By about half-past five on Sunday, they were so elated at their success as to have soared miles above the solid ground, almost out of sight in the stratosphere.

"I'll let you off now," said Jonathan briskly, realising that seven hours of rehearsing except for an interval for Sunday dinner had squeezed them of their last drop of available energy. "You're not bad, but it's no good getting you tired."

"Tired" was an understatement, for they had dropped exhausted to the floor and lay in limp heaps.

"Take a short rest and then go on learning your parts till bedtime. You especially, Erica."

"You especially, Erica" should be heard only when linked to "amaze me by your beauty and talent." . . . But her limpid smile forgave him for not having quite learnt the rules. He stared at her coldly, and went on:

"Rehearsal to-morrow morning at ten. Roddy, stop imitating donkeys or I'll flay you alive. Oh, it was a sheep, was it? Well, sheep noises aren't your business, nor Judy's; the rest of us will do them off-stage; you're the Shepherd-boy. By the way, Judy, you may as well be here half an hour earlier to-morrow morning, to run through the shepherd-and-lady scene before I come. I'll take you in it this evening after supper."

Jonathan was single-minded in all he undertook. In his production of a Nativity Play the stress fell neither on the play nor certainly on the Nativity . . .

"He thinks we're going to be frightfully good," remarked Lal, prone on the rug. "He'd rather die than say so, but he does."

Terry agreed: "I never dreamt it would all come so easily, did you? I meant to try very hard, but somehow it feels as though I weren't trying but being better than if I had. Do you think it's anything to do with acting a Nativity Play instead of the ordinary kind?"

No-one dared expand on a speculation so tremendous. They were relieved when Lal continued on slightly more material lines:

"I've written reams to Uncle Ted and told him all about the Vicar and the picture and the Silver Collection and everything."

"They won't put twelve pounds into the Silver Collection unless we're good *enough*. There's nothing silver smaller than sixpence, but if we weren't good, they might each only put in sixpence instead of a big fat heavy half-crown. A sixpenny bit would fall so lightly into the plate," Erica mused, "we'll either hear a lot of little tinkles, or we'll hear clonk, clonk. What I mean is, that if the Vicar simply can't bear any longer to have that dreadful picture not covered up —"

"Is it really all that corney? I suppose I must have seen it when I was here for the Glorious Christmas years ago, but I can't remember any picture."

Erica and Roddy at once volunteered to take Clare to the church and show her Abraham and Isaac, so that she too could gloat over their imminent disappearance behind a fall of handsome brocade supplied by the company's genius and generosity.

"Can we get in?"

"I'm not — yes, it's Sunday; open all day; and listen, there are the bells; I think it's for Evensong. Nanny went sometimes during the war; because I remember her saying: 'It do seem uncanny, to be sure, not hearing church bells on Sunday evening when it gets dark and snow on the ground, though what with them meaning an Invasion we wouldn't want to hear them, would we, madam?'"

"You can take me to see the picture some other time; we needn't go just on Sunday-aft." Clare shrank from the nakedness of a public appearance at Evensong. But Erica insisted it would be even more fun when people were there, and they the only ones of all the congregation to know — ("Except the Vicar." "He's *not* congregation") — the only ones to know that the picture spoiling the church would soon spoil it no more.

Such a dramatic and unusual reason appealed to Clare; and Roddy, too, was feeling dauntless as though

Brambleford Church were now under his protection and dependent on his personal efforts.

But Terry and Lal, more worn out by Jonathan's unflagging "Come on now, we'll take that through again," continued to lie just where they had flopped. And sent impudent messages to the picture via Erica and Roddy, who bore off Clare between them.

Mr. Crichton was *very* surprised at seeing three attentive young faces staring up at him (and even towards a spot a little beyond his shoulder) where certainly those three attentive young faces had never appeared before at Evensong.

". . . Lal, if I show you something, now, while nobody's here, will you promise you won't tell one single soul about it?"

"Promise," murmured Lal, lazily rolling over on to his back, hands comfortably clasped behind his head. "As long as I needn't move."

Terry scampered off to fetch whatever it was she wished to show him. It lay hidden at the bottom of her suitcase, swathed in scarves and woollies like a monstrous balloon. She carried it upstairs still with the scarves round it, in case she met someone; and before unrobing it, she locked the schoolroom door.

"Dark conspiracy. Do I hear an ominous ticking inside that round parcel? Put it down carefully between us, Terry, and we'll die together."

"It's a Christmas present. For Rosalind."

"Oh . . . I see."

"So it's very, *very* special indeed. I couldn't risk anyone coming in."

Lal watched to see what would emerge, as she lovingly unswathed the mufflers and displayed a transparent ball, half full of water, with two little painted celluloid ducks floating inside it.

"You can hold it if you like." Terry yielded up her treasure to the boy, who slid her an odd look beyond his years, ironical rather than inquiring.

"For Ros?"

"Yes. You don't mind, do you, Lal? I'd love to have bought presents for you and all the rest, but I was so broke this Christmas that besides this one I could only just afford them for the grown-ups; you know how they mind about not getting presents; it means an awful lot to them. And there had to be two for Grandpa; I haven't finished doing his birthday slippers yet; Mummy will have to. But this somehow *looked* like Rosalind."

Did it? Lal was shaking the ball about gently so that the ducks moved on the water . . .

"What does it do?"

"It doesn't exactly *do* anything. It's for when you're doing nothing; you just sit and hold it and shake it and watch the ducks behave like love-ducks. Look!" She took it from him again. "Now they're beak to beak; now the yellow one is chasing the blue one; now he's following her round. D'you remember that time — oh, no, you weren't here; it was when we went over to the family who gave Grandpa a birthday lunch, and they had ducks on their pond, and Rosalind said they were so

85

funny she could sit and watch them for hours. Don't you like it, Lal?" anxiously. "Don't you think Rosalind will?"

"Sure to," he lied; for in truth he thought the gift more appropriate for a child than for the new-born débutante of Brambleford Manor. "You're right, Terry; one can get quite hypnotised watching them; they're jolly good time-wasters. But they don't look to me as if they were love-ducks. Lord love-a-duck," he chuckled . . . and twirled the ball rather more violently so as to create a storm within, "they're quarrelling; shut up in this ball and quarrelling like mad."

"That's because you've got them back to back."

"I haven't got them anything; they got themselves like that and won't break away. Now they're cutting each other in the street — on the water, I mean. And when you said the yellow one was following, it wasn't for love, it was to tell the blue duck exactly what he thought of her. There now, they're tail to tail again, terribly haughty." Lal put the ducks through all the possible movements and permutations of a quarrel, within their clear tough unbreakable globe. "Where on earth did you get it, Terry?"

"I found the shop on one of those queer days when things happen because the day's stronger than you are. Till then, I simply couldn't think what to give Rosalind that anybody else might not have thought of as well. You remember that thick fog last week? I was out with Sally Freeland; we meant to stay in and paint, but she had to fetch Johnny from school as they can't get a nurse; and he ran ahead and got lost in the fog, quite near home; it swallowed him so quickly that we were frightened, till we saw he had fetched up at the window of a little shop I hadn't known about though it was at the end of our road . . . That's what made it seem so magicky; it was a Post Office too, and people streamed in with parcels to send off, and two scarlet mail-vans were drawn up outside with postmen throwing more parcels around; and red lights smouldering through a blur of fog; I suppose all that Christmas importance had something to do with my noticing the shop for the first time. And there were toys in the other window where Johnny was staring in; not many, but *real* toys, the kind we used to have before the war; most of the windows have looked awful this Christmas, making the best of what are hardly toys at all. And then suddenly I saw the duck-ball. So I went in and bought it; I didn't hesitate for a moment; it was as if something inside me whispered 'Get it!' The girl told me they had inherited some pre-war stock which her grandfather had had put away. I could have simply hugged her and Johnny and the fog and the red mail-vans —"

"What other toys did they have?" Lal was still idly playing with the duck-ball.

"I saw a diver, but of course that would have been too childish to give Rosalind."

(And again ruled by kindliness, Lal checked his comment before it was spoken.)

"I had one when I was little," Terry went on; "you blow through a long rubber tube, and he comes very slowly up in your bath, or dives very slowly down, I forget which. And then there was a round box with a sort of tight transparent top — the same stuff as this ball is made of —"

"Talc," said Lal. "I think it's talc. Car windows have it."

"— And two little clowns inside, and if you rub lightly on the top with your fingers, they spring up and begin to caper about and dangle upside-down."

"Because you shake the box?"

"No, because of the electricity in your fingers, the girl said; it happens sometimes when you brush your hair, or when you pull your knickers off and they're full of sparks, and crackle. I liked the clown-box, but the duck-ball was Rosalind and the clown-box wasn't, so I didn't even argue with myself. But it's got to be a secret, Lal. You won't divulge it?"

"Now you've turned into Erica."

Terry laughed at her own grandiloquence. "Promise all the same that you won't divulge to one single person one single word of any single thing I've told you?"

"S'welp me. Word of honour."

Footsteps, and someone rattled at the door: "Who's been and locked it? You, Roddy? How often have I told you I won't let the nursery door be locked?"

"It's all right, Nanny, Roddy's not here; he's gone to church. What do you think of that?" And Lal kept the old woman talking, teasing her because she still said nursery instead of schoolroom, teasing her for being so surprised at Roddy's sudden piety. . . while Terry swiftly slipped out and sped away to put her duck-ball back into safety until Christmas Eve.

* * *

Lal wished he could have found Tan by herself in the library, but she and Uncle Nick were always together now. He asked very politely if he might speak to her alone for a moment?

"Yes, Lal, of course. Speak to me as much as you like."

"Have a cocktail?" suggested Nick.

"No, thanks. If you could come outside for a moment?" He said it as politely as he could; Nick was fun and awfully good-natured and a war hero and Uncle Ted's greatest friend; Nick was clever and famous and free with his tips and had never made the mistake of treating you like a small boy but always casually as his equal. Yet granting all this, Lal did not absolutely trust Nick not to blab.

"He put me neatly in my place," laughed Group-Captain Nicholas Hilliard, three minutes later. "What was all that about?"

"Wild horses wouldn't drag it out of me, so don't wheedle."

"Something to do with their Nativity Play?" he wheedled instantly.

"No, Master Nick, nothing to do with their Nativity Play."

"Rosalind told me to-day she had wondered whether she should perhaps offer after all to take on the Angel Gabriel, but had decided against it. And what reason do you suppose she gave?"

"That it was too childish!"

"Tan, how *did* you guess?"

"I've been watching Rosalind disassociate herself from the children; she obviously thinks it better not to expose herself to infection by being too much with them."

"On the same theory as measles? But I was rather winded at the idea of the Annunciation being too childish for her to have anything to do with it."

"Our other niece is playing the Angel Gabriel, so we're keeping him in the family."

"I'm fascinated by the spectacle of a Nativity Play acted by children brought up not to know a thing about religion. The Victorian generation used to lead illuminated-text lives, while yours —" Nick loftily excluded himself from belonging to any generation whatsoever.

Tan took up the theme on "illuminated-text lives": "I remember that Nanny —"

"Same Nanny as now?"

"Yes, Nanny Curtis; she gave me 'I am the Good Shepherd' to hang on the wall over my cot, but at the same time she used to impress on me how 'self-praise is no recommendation'; one cancelled the other, so I didn't bother with either."

"What a logical infant! 'I am the Good Shepherd' — if you'd been told the surrounding text, you wouldn't have read it with such a sanctimonious flavour: 'good' here does not mean self-praise for exceeding virtue and merit, a holy freedom from wickedness; it means simply 'efficient' or 'expert' — a shepherd knowing his job; a shepherd familiar to his sheep because he has always treated them with skill and knowledge, as his own; he comes in by the right door and they have no hesitation in following him. A good shepherd will give his life to

90

protect his sheep from the wolf, while a hireling, a bad shepherd to whom the sheep mean little or nothing, will fly and leave them."

Tan remarked that for a valuable unit of Lucifer's Own Brigade, as he obviously supposed himself to be, he was remarkably well up in the Scriptures.

"Oh, one has to know the disposition of enemy forces," said Nick, lightly excusing himself.

She reflected on how sad and gaunt his face had come to look in repose. Repose was a word seldom to be used about Nick. Why did he *care* so much? To console him, she brought him back to a subject he always found oddly irresistible:

"Rosalind hasn't read their play, of course, but she believes the idea of doing it is a *little* unseasonable."

Nick cheered up instantly: "I revel in Rosalind; she's a superb specimen of a chump. Chumps drive me mad if I have to talk *to* them for a long time, but they have a provocative quality that makes me long to talk *about* them; to draw them out and wonder what they can be made to say; it's usually so characteristic that it simply can't be true." He rattled on happily. And Tan lay back, content with her success.

Nicholas was perfectly aware that she had skilfully drawn him away from dangerous ground. Years ago, she would have sprung on the defensive in a moment, barely giving him time to lay hand on a weapon before she was already attacking him. Strange that a war should have made her gentle. He could not imagine what had become of her old zest in their mimic warfare. Did she now compare it with the real thing and all its weariness? But it had always been a weariness to him, loving her so much, to wrangle and jangle and clash steel with Tan; she had provoked him into it, flicked his pride, dared him, taunted him with being her junior by three years.

Then . . . was there now no further need for him to watch and be agile in defence and counter-attack? Was any subject that might drift to the surface no longer precarious, in this new quietness between him and Tan? Following the wider armistice of nations, was their hateful fee-fo-fum business blessedly over? Could he put away flint and tinder-box as Tan had done herself just now? During hostilities abroad, he had forgotten his girl sometimes for weeks together; yet directly he was demobilised, he had come straight to her and to no-one else . . . to find that here, too, peace was declared.

"I'm looking forward to 'Christmas in the Market Place', aren't you? They're being so careful this time about not letting the grown-ups in."

"I wish we didn't have to be 'the grown-ups' ; at least, I wish they didn't refer to us like that, in an indistinguishable lump, as though we didn't exist at all except in those books for juveniles where 'the grown-ups' are always sad and shadowy and kind."

"Or else misusing their powers of administration to thwart whatever the children want to do. But nobody could say *we* were misusing our grown-up powers," Nick reassured her; "grown-ups aren't like that any more; it gives me quite a shock when I hear your old Nanny giving out-of-date orders: 'Come along now', or 'Change your wet shoes at once', or 'You're not to have your tea standing up and running round the room, I won't have it'."

"And do you remember, Nick, when we used to walk in after one of our quarrels, belching flame from the nostrils, and Orlo always said: 'Hallo, trouble in the Balkans *again*?'"

They had been in such perfect accord ever since he had brought her down to the Manor, that he dared allude to their quarrelling days as though they were vivid but bygone as a mediaeval legend. And she dared in reply to quote "A Midsummer Night's Dream":

"'And they do square, that all their elves for fear
Creep into acorn cups and hide them there'."

"The elves had nothing to fear," he mused; "the quarrel lay between their king and queen." He had not understood so clearly, in his careless twenties, how even in fairyland itself, horror was more subtle than fear; horror that harmony should have been killed from the very air and the din of angry voices was hammering love out of existence. Their little lives had hitherto skipped the dreadful discordance of war; but had fairyland been fairyland too long? Their happy immunity was forfeit, and they had to hear of threats and fury . . . Nick imagined them crouched down at the bottom of their acorn-cups, shuddering that unkindness had broken loose into words like stinging nettles. How could Puck deride mortals for being fools, when his own royal Oberon and Titania had bartered all tranquil delight for the jealous sake of snatching at one little native boy to be their exclusive property? If war could break out over that, if war could break out in fairyland itself —

"'Ill met by moonlight, proud Titania.'

"'What, jealous Oberon? Fairies, skip hence, I have forsworn his bed and company.'"

"Have you, Tan?"

"No, Nick."

". . . You're too alike," Doe used to say, with her air of having straightway solved the deepest mystery (only it happened not always to be the right solution). "You're too alike, you two." Was it indeed as simple? Were they two identical fools, both worn out by war's endurance and content to be at peace? Nick could still hardly believe in the rush of joy which had come to him just now when he recognised that Tan of all people had twice softly led him away from quarrel, back into safe quiet places.

The entrance of Sorrel with her sewing-bag did nothing as violent as breaking the gentle spell, for she was too gentle herself; she merely did as superstitious people do when they lay a finger on a glass and the strange musical note hangs a moment in mid-air . . . and is still.

"What were you two talking about?"

"Titania," replied Nicholas promptly. "Did you know that Titania, not Tania, was Tan's real name?"

"No, I always took Tania for granted. Titania! How pagan it must have sounded at your christening."

"'I name this child Sorrel'," mused Tan. "That doesn't sound particularly Christian either."

"My father was a trainer, and I had bright red hair when I was born. You wouldn't think it, would you?"

94

"So your name came straight out of the horse's mane? But my dear, you're the dark horse of the Maitland stables, not a sorrel at all. I've often said that I'd nominate you as the most likely murderer, if we had a murder on the premises."

"Nice of you, Nick," she dimpled at him. "At the age of ten, I suddenly announced I was going to change both my names 'by deed poll'. I'd heard my parents discussing someone who had, and it seemed to me a sound idea. I wanted a *thin* name, not round and podgy like 'Marjorie Sorrel'; Dad used to call me Polly."

"That's a tea-kettle name," Nick chaffed her "Can you remember what you suggested instead, when you were going to change it by deed poll?"

"It's funny, I *do* remember: I wanted a mermaid name, or a Maori name, or to be named after a warrior —"

"As it might be Montgomery or Hannibal? Hannibal Fishtail Weiora — what other species was to be included? — Oh, I think we'll go on calling you Sorrel; Sorrel the Dark Horse; and then literal people can have the fun of pointing out to us that a sorrel is a *red* horse. Is your father dead? Do you mind my asking? I really know awfully little about you, you know."

Sorrel nodded, and said: "Ask any questions you like." So of course Nick could think of none, and it looked as though she would go on being a Dark Horse . . . except for what he already knew about her husband Neville the Bad Lot. He knew about that engaging younger son of the Maitlands from Ted who had once hoisted Neville out of a pretty sticky mess, its exact nature unspecified; Ted did not dwell on it; and certainly it had been hardly worth while hoisting him out, considering the speed with

95

which he fell into another mess; this time it was not connected with a Revue Touring Company, so Ted could do no more for him, or he would certainly have gone about the job with renewed good heart, hopefully as though he had never been let down.

The Maitlands did not fail in gratitude, though their thanks expressed itself in terms of practical hospitality rather than eloquence. For Ted Barnett had his own family problems: a sweet foolish sister who had died when Lal was born, her sentimental heart flogged by her husband's cold adhesion to a brilliant legal career; and a brother too subdued to resist his American wife's firm if natural preference to reside in America. Lal and Clare accepted the fact that they could always look on the Manor as a second home during times of emergency, in the careless fashion of children who are given a warm enough welcome. And Sorrel apparently never babbled to Terry of her most unsatisfactory father, nor left him a name dramatically shrouded in sable, a name that festered in the dark. Nice woman, Sorrel! On an impulse of rewarding her for her good behaviour all round, Nick offered to thread her needle, for she seemed to be in difficulties.

"Are you really going up to-morrow, Tan?"

"Afraid I must, till Tuesday evening. Pre-Christmas rush and all that. Nick darling, hadn't you better give that back to Sorrel? Manly men can't thread needles; womanly women can."

"Sounds like a slogan: 'Manly men can't thread needles'. Here you are, Sorrel; I meant well, and I've sucked both ends. Who's it for?"

"Thank you, Nick. For Father; his second present from Terry."

"Then Terry ought to be working it with her own little pricked fingers; you spoil her — Well, as a matter of truth and justice, you don't."

"Terry hadn't counted on such a long part to learn; Jonathan's a slave-driver; he ought to do well if he takes it up professionally."

"How's the play going?"

"Wonderfully well. I've never seen Terry so confident."

"They're all in a state of auto-intoxication. I've gathered that their triumphant performance down here is only the beginning; after they've raked in the silver shekels, amounting to a beggarly two or three hundred pounds to buy the Vicar his damask and rebuild his church with what's over, they're looking ahead and light-heartedly planning to perform their play in St. Paul's Cathedral and be publicly thanked by the Pope . . ."

Tan repeated: "'Looking ahead and light-heartedly planning'— isn't that what we've missed almost more than anything else? And now we can do it again."

CHAPTER
FIVE

"Not a nice tree," sighed Doe, "but better than no tree at all. War Christmasses! — our last here was in 1940, but with only our own kids."

"And Terry."

"Yes, and Terry; you must have missed her; that was the bleakest Christmas. Sorrel, can you give me a hand with these rusty old candle-clips?"

Sorrel begged her to wait; she was on her knees, not praying, but on the contrary, separating her father-in-law's birthday presents from his Christmas presents; and she feared if she stopped now, she might have to begin all over again:

"Let me see, here's yours for his Christmas heap, and Anthony's for the birthday heap; and here are my two, *that's* all right. It's getting more and more difficult, isn't it, to find him something that isn't books and isn't smoking and isn't on coupons and that he hasn't had already and which doesn't look cheaper for his birthday than for Christmas? 'Many happy returns Sir from respectfully Philpotts — so that goes into the birthday heap; but where on earth did I put his Christmas present from Philpotts? I've had it in my hand because it felt so queer through the paper and I remember wondering — oh yes, here it is. Doe, is it my fancy, or does it *smell*?"

Doe came off the ladder and sniffed at the parcel:

"It doesn't smell at all."

"You've picked the wrong one."

"The other doesn't smell either."

"Not like a bit of old cheese? Then I'm a victim to auto-suggestion."

"'For Major Maitland, with respectful good wishes for Christmas, from Emily Curtis.' Catch, Sorrel!" Doe threw it over to her.

"Biscuits; they crunch. You must have broken several by throwing it."

"But what a good thought of Nanny's! Anthony's a night nibbler, though nobody would think it to look at him."

"A card of kittens peeping from a basket stuck outside *this* neat parcel; feels like a book: 'A Christmas Hamper for *You*', printed, and then written, 'Major Maitland with best wishes from Philpotts hoping you will excuse the liberty'. Is a book a liberty?"

"I've had a job convincing Philpotts it isn't a liberty for him to give Anthony a present at all. Something to do with precedence. If he were Anthony's own man it would all be in order, but being grandfather's" — Doe imitated with some success: "'Mrs. Curtis might think — well, you know what she is, and I wouldn't upset her for worlds. You and I can put up with anything, Madam, but Mrs. Curtis does hold so to her rights, belonging here as she has for so many years'."

Having had this same problem in delicacy laid before her, Sorrel was able to carry on with the impersonation:

"'It isn't as though Mrs. Curtis didn't give *Mr.* Maitland his two presents regular every year; though him being my own gentleman, I'd have just as much right as her to get upset over that, especially when we had both wondered about handkerchiefs for both gentlemen, anything on coupons being welcome with them having to go short as us; between ourselves, Mrs. Neville, I've made it *tea* this year for Mrs. Maitland —'"

"*Has* he? Good old Philpotts!"

"'— which not even Mrs. Curtis could take offence at, both of us over seventy and getting extra, but she drinking all hers, and tea, when you come to think of it, not being like handkerchiefs. And then, Mrs. Neville, what did Mrs. Curtis do but *drop* the handkerchiefs and get the Major a Boer War loving-cup, and if that isn't making free —? You could have knocked me down with a feather when she told me! Now Mrs. Edwards, 'oo is rightfully entitled, one may say, having been with my Mr. Maitland Senior before she settled down here for the war, she said she'd like to consult me over what I'd consider *suitable*? And we agreed that a few nice flowers from her nephew's greenhouses near Reading if he could get them over in time, they hardly count as a *present*, as they have to be thrown away. And yet Mrs. Edwards could take precedence of Mrs. Curtis if *she* chose to insist on loving-cups for Mr. *and* Major Maitland, having been in service with both as a cook-housekeeper, but she has more savwah of what's right and proper, and no hard thoughts between me and Mrs. Edwards ever, but Peace on Earth and God Rest Ye Merrie Gentlemen —'"

100

"Sorrel!"

"Verbatim. Every single word."

"I don't altogether believe you. Do hurry, my lamb, it's nearly five o'clock; we told them we'd be ready by five, and they'll all come trooping in."

"We *have* left it a bit late." Sorrel swiftly threw old Mr. Maitland's birthday present into a basket, and hid it till required on Boxing Day. "Tan hasn't arrived yet, has she? Aren't we going to wait?"

"It might mean waiting till midnight, as she isn't here yet; the 2.20 must be in hours ago; I sent a taxi to meet it, but if she missed that, the next train crawls. Roddy was a problem this year; he makes such devastating remarks over his presents. We've paid the earth for a magnetic blackboard; look!"

They played with it happily for an all too brief period.

"Once Roddy gets near it, we shan't have a chance. Rosalind's easy; something to wear, at her stage of growing-up."

"I've given her my old opera-glasses, mother-of-pearl —"

"She'll look nice in those," said Doe absently, fidgeting with a pre-war tinsel fairy at a tipsy angle on top of the tree.

"Tan's for it; only a birthday present 'for darling Dad'. Shall I suppress the card and call it her Christmas present, as that comes first?"

"Heavens, no, girl! Don't dare do anything like that; you'll upset the *balance*. Tan has probably sweated blood over getting them exactly right. She'll bring two or three last-minute things down with her, I expect."

"And there's nothing from her to me," complained Sorrel.

"Come to that, there's nothing from *you* to me, but you don't hear me make a fuss, do you? After all, it's the thought that counts."

Sorrel went off into gurgles of reminiscent laughter: "That was old Carpenter!"

"Is, not was."

"Don't say she's still with you? My dear, she must be over ninety."

"She does light kitchen work for Mrs. Edwards; and all our staff are over ninety, except Angela; Angie's thirteen and a great help with the shoes. How do you imagine we'd have any staff otherwise, these days? They're really rather a gallant remnant. You'll see old Carpenter; she'll come toddling up with the rest; she likes money better than presents."

"So do I, but —"

"Listen!"

A hubbub of voices, gay and confused and expectant; and as the clatter of footsteps on the parquet drew nearer, Dorothy Maitland was rapidly transformed to the perfect Châtelaine of the Old Manor on Christmas Eve; a rôle, as her husband had guessed, far closer to her heart than she pretended. Gratitude was hers that they were *all* there instead of two or three missing, as might easily have been, from their group of family and kin and near friends. No reason to hold back on Yule in all its merriest traditions. She made a sign to Sorrel to turn on the gramophone concealed behind the curtains of the bay window . . . and waited till the plangent strains of:

"Come, come, come to the Manger,
  Children, come to the children's King"

were well under way, providing an extra dollop of atmosphere. Then she flung open the double doors:

"Come in, all of you. Come in, children; come in, Nanny; come in, Nick and Mrs. Edwards . . ."

(Fortunately she did not hear Nick's soft parody, calling up the cows at High Tide on the Coast of Lincolnshire: "'Come up, Lightfoot; Come up, Cusha' . . .")

"Mr. Philpotts, you should give Mrs. Carpenter your arm, the parquet is so slippery — I've told you, Angie, not to be too zealous with the polishing, bless your heart! — and it doesn't help, Roddy darling, if you slide on it; in fact, it does just the other thing."

"What *is* the other thing from helping?"

A scream from Sorrel; they had forgotten to switch off the electric lights, although candles, the first for many years, were to be a triumphant feature of the tree.

"Go *back*, children — only for a minute — back, all of you!" Doe shooed them away from the threshold; they scuffled and giggled and pressed forward again; "No, we're not *quite* ready . . . Yes, I know I called you in . . . Roddy, don't be such an obstreperous little hound . . . All right now, Sorrel? Good! Come along, infants . . . Isn't it a lovely, lovely tree, with all those winking candles — Never seen candles on a Christmas tree before, have you, my son! Nick, will you cut down the parcels that are too high for me, and hand them down to Sorrel? And she'll call out the names. Anthony, move the armchair a little this way for Father; he's going to sit down and have his parcels brought to him."

Old Mr. Maitland was heard to say with diffident charm that nobody ought to have bothered about presents for *him* at *his* age . . .

. . . The second stage of the ceremony had been reached, when the lights were switched on again and the candles blown out; when torn paper lay in drifts on the floor and all over the chairs and sideboard; when most of the parcels had been burst open and examined, the first spontaneous chorus of surprise and gratitude had died down, and: "Let's look at yours" was heard from everyone except Anthony, who, oblivious of his surroundings, was leaning up against the wall, gravely reading his new book presented to him by Philpotts: *Gems Chosen from the Classics.* Having a peculiarly direct approach to life, he took it for granted that that was what one did with a book.

Mr. Maitland had also subtracted his voice from the general hilarity, and sat quietly grieving; not angry, but just grieving . . . A crony whose memory one could only charitably suppose was suffering from malnutrition and lack of proteins, had sent him as combined Christmas-and-birthday present, a photograph handsomely framed.

"Hallo!" exclaimed Nick suddenly. "What have you got there, Rosalind?"

"Terry gave it to me. Isn't it *sweet* of her! I've never seen one like it before."

"I have — but that was fifteen years ago!" Nicholas seized the duck-ball from Rosalind, and began throwing it up and catching it again.

"Where on earth did you get hold of this, Terry? Are there any more about?"

Terry replied, demure and proud: "No, it's from pre-war stock." . . . She could hardly speak for the wonder and happiness that had begun when they were first summoned into the big room, dark save for the glow and sparkle thrown out from the enchanted branches of the Christmas tree . . . Conscious of her own little duck-ball for Rosalind still hidden so snugly among the gifts piled up round it . . . The words of the carol sung twice over and now died away, reminded her of their own lovely little play, waiting suspended during this interlude of an hour, till presently they would rush upstairs again to rehearse . . . Acting in a Nativity Play somehow made her feel more *involved*, caught up into the very essence of Christmas, its core and reason. And she was perfectly satisfied for the moment with Rosalind's charming little speech of thanks (Rosalind had vowed she was going to keep it on her dressing-table where she could *always* see it while she did her hair) . . . And that was only a start; there had been no time yet, with her many other gifts to examine, for the peculiar spell of the duck-ball to creep over her, as later on it must; you could scarcely expect Rosalind, who had such beautiful manners, to say in front of everybody: "I like all my presents, but Terry's by far the best!" — Could you?

Nicholas shook the little blue duck and the little yellow duck till they spun round madly on the water, tail glued to tail.

"It's much more in my line than yours, Rosalind. I'll swop it with you for — what do you most want? A lipstick?"

"Of *course* not," his niece shook her golden head; "as though I'd part from My Duck-ball."

"Garn! You could just as easily say: 'As though I'd part from My Lipstick'."

"What's all this about a lipstick?" inquired Rosalind's mother. For one of those lulls had occurred as though somebody had torn a hole in the solid shout of voices which had been going on ever since the doors were opened for Christmas Eve to have its way with them; and attention was focused on Nicholas; he appeared to have a practised way with duck-balls; the little painted birds were giving an extra lively performance.

"Here you are," he said at last, reluctantly handing it back to Rosalind. "Mind, my offer's open, so — *Tan*!"

"Have I missed all the fun? What a shame! Paddington was like a madhouse. Here you are, Father; it wasn't ready till I went to the shop to-day and frightened the pants off 'em. Rosalind, this is for you; an extra and a queer sort of present, but there's a special reason . . . I'll tell you about it some day."

For Rosalind was beginning to disclaim any right to another gift: "Your scarf was so lovely, Aunt Tania; just what I wanted; thanks ever so much." . . . But she put down Terry's duck-ball for a moment, to open Tan's "extra."

Another duck-ball.

. . . Complete silence. The grown-ups were aware of tension swelling the air. Nicholas, glancing quickly at Terry's face and then away again, saw the suspense in her eyes, and whispered a soft "Damn!" He had no faith whatever in Rosalind's charm when it came to dealing with a situation.

Roddy said: "I say, you've got two now!"

Rosalind felt ridiculous with duck-balls multiplying in her hand, and everyone staring at her; especially as she did not care for toys, though of course to please the child she had had to pretend to like the first duck-ball, because children always mind so much if you're not pleased with their funny little presents . . . remembering an awful box made of shells she had once given her father, the same sort of present as the duck-ball, and how disappointed she had been at Orlo's involuntary grimace.

She said to herself: "I *must* think of the right thing to do, quickly." (Nicholas would have said she was incapable of it, even slowly.) Should she keep them both and pretend she adored having two? Or give them both away — "and then nobody can mind"? But somehow there was nobody suitable to give them to. Uncle Nick had pretended to hanker for a duck-ball — should she give him one? No, he *could* only have been pretending . . . Besides, it might look as though she wanted the lipstick he had offered her in exchange! It had been nice when she and Uncle Nick, adults both, had slipped into playful alliance to please Terry and heighten her childish gratification at having chosen such a wonderful present.

Then — a brilliant flash, a genuine inspiration: it would be terribly rude, out of the question, in fact, to return Tan's; if either had to be sacrificed —

Luckily there was no need to sacrifice anyone.

"Terry darling," — and to Nick's real horror, in a voice suitable for coaxing a backward child of seven,

107

Rosalind proceeded to make the most tactful, charming, graceful little speech of her whole grown-up career . . . Ending with: "So now, you see, we'll *each* have one, and that'll be much more fun, because we can do them together, can't we?"

And she gave Terry's duck-ball back to Terry.

("That's torn it!" Nick was able to guess that as far as Terry was concerned — and this time he dared not throw so much as a glance at her face — Rosalind had committed suicide.)

"Thank you very much indeed, Rosalind." Terry spoke quietly and steadily. She laid the duck-ball back on the desk . . . It rocked a little before it stood quite still, as though in discarding it, her hand had trembled. Hypnotised, they all stared at it. Even Nicholas could not think of any possible thing to say quickly, before any of Doe's kin, Erica or Rosalind herself, oblivious of peril in the air, uttered the unspeakable; instead of functioning intelligently, his brain perversely threw up a series of ghastly examples of what *they* were likely to say, each so characteristic as to be hardly a parody. Then he drew a long breath of relief: "By God, that good-looking niece of Ted's can be quick on the up-take!" For —

"Please," said Clare, rather anxiously looking at the clock, "if no-one minds, we'd better go upstairs now, because Jonathan's coming to rehearse us this evening, directly the presents and the tree are over; and he'd be so angry if we were late; so please, Auntie Doe?"

Nick sent his blessing after Clare, as she flung Terry across the pummel of her charger and galloped with her upstairs; the rescue was effected so naturally that he could not even be certain she had been conscious of picking up an S O S.

"What went wrong just at the end?" Doe asked, while she and Sorrel and Tan threw themselves energetically into the herculean task of clearing up: dragging the furniture back to its proper place; gathering up coloured paper impatiently crumpled, glittering oddments of tinsel and string, discarded lids of boxes, jolly little cards of greeting, half burnt-out candles — "I didn't notice how the trouble started; I was too tied up with reassuring Nanny that Philpotts' book simply couldn't compete with her digestive biscuits and loving-cup. I do hope Philpotts didn't hear me."

"There was no trouble and nothing went wrong," said Sorrel placidly. "It was a huge success. You're splendid at that sort of thing, Doe."

"Sorrel *is* a dark horse! Signed: Nick the Merry-monger. Anyway, Doe, why don't you ask your elder daughter who's been and gone and made that glorious mess-up?"

Rosalind answered with dignity:

"It was a very difficult situation, Uncle Nicholas; but I think you'll find it will be quite all right now. Terry loved that little toy she gave me, and she's delighted to have it back."

"Hear her!" groaned Nick. "Hear my beautiful niece!"

His beautiful niece went on, turning to Tan:

"And it was awfully sweet of you, Aunt Tania, to give me the dear little ducks in a ball; and I'd love some time to hear the story behind it. I'll look on it as an old-world souvenir."

Exuding sweetness, and carrying one duck-ball, Rosalind made her exit.

"Well, my sweet," remarked Nicholas lightly to Tan, "a nice situation you've created, with your sentimental adhesions to the past."

"Oh . . . so you *do* remember?"

"Certainly I remember, even though I was 'only a little boy' at the time."

"What *is* all this?" asked Doe, again mystified.

"Just something that happened years ago."

"About a duck-ball?"

"A duck-ball of no importance."

"No importance whatever," Tan agreed. "Only I wish Rosalind had given mine back to me, instead of Terry's to Terry; I only gave it to somebody because it would have been too indecently sentimental to buy one to give myself."

Nick nodded towards the duck-ball on the desk: "Pinch that one, then; it looks rather forlorn. And they're both alike."

Doe wondered: "Do you think she'd better? After all, Rosalind gave it to Terry, and she may —"

"She won't."

"Nick dear, aren't you making rather heavy weather of all this?"

"Am I? Did you notice Terry's weather . . . hearing sleigh-bells and seeing the bare world in a mist and a silver glitter . . . before her Christmas was ripped open?"

110

"Yes, I thought she looked specially pretty to-night in that leaf-green dress. Green suits her. But I still can't quite understand. Was it coincidence that Tan gave Rosalind a duck-ball too? Where did you buy it, Tan?"

"Lal wanted something from a special little toy-shop in Chelsea, and when I went to get it for him, I happened to see the duck-ball; the last they had in stock. I suppose Terry must have told him about the shop, though he didn't say so."

"But Tania, my beloved Tania, where's your sense of character? You could have guessed that even though Rosalind was Orlo's daughter, she was the wrong age, wrong type, wrong everything to whom to give an amusing piece of childish nonsense like that. She hadn't a clue what to do with it. I had the clue, so considering everything, why didn't you give it to me instead?"

Tan considered everything. She had to go back nearly twenty years . . . till she touched an episode flavoured, in retrospect, with the half-bitter yet delectable taste of green almonds.

Nick was sixteen, and she was three years older; so naturally and by right of those three years she took the lead; with the result that they scrapped like mad, for Nick was not acquiescing tamely in his schoolboy status. "Trouble in the Balkans blowing up again?" Orlo used to inquire, amused. Orlo was in the Diplomatic Service; so he recognised when trouble was dangerous with her and Nick, or when it was a perfectly normal state of affairs which no more threatened the solid alliance of their friendship, fast and loyal against the world, than thunderstorms could dispel all the gay advantages of summer.

Nick was Orlo's junior by some twelve years; both their parents were dead, and the boy had his home with his grown-up brother during school holidays.

"Home," at the time of the incident of the magic duck-ball, was a suite in an hotel in Paris. Tan and Nick arrived to stay one night en route for a careless holiday in the Salzkammergut. Orlo happened not to be in the *salon* when they turned up in company with two more of their youthful party, also on their way to the mountains. "Hope he'll arrive soon" — because they were thirsty and hot and wanted cocktails before he took them out to dinner, as of course he would do; being taken out to dinner in Paris by a distinguished young member of the Foreign Office belonged to glamour when she and Nick went abroad together; an evening of style and elegance at the very beginning of the rough and tumble. It was understood that Orlo belonged to them on that evening, devoting himself, without rival, to their sole entertainment.

(Oh God! thought Tan . . . for heart and memory could still check suddenly on their retrospect of those evenings; of Orlo's lazy teasing voice; of the things he said, ironic, affectionate, at one moment treating them as though they were a couple of nice ridiculous children, and the next, advancing them, but always both together, he had never separated them by the girl's seniority, to a grave sophisticated companionship in all his most cherished disillusions.)

112

"Hallo, what's this?" On his rambles round the stiff *salon*, Nick had discovered a toy which had not been there before. "Why on earth has Orlo got this?"

"Let's see!"

"Some kid's been here and left it, perhaps?"

"I don't think so;" Tan squatted on the parquet, her hair falling loosely over her flushed face as she bent over the transparent ball, half full of water, two little painted ducks afloat on it. "Somehow I can imagine Orlo liking it for himself; it's *fun!*"

Nick knelt beside her, and Jim and Marigold pressed up to them, each demanding the duck-ball, wanting to see what it did?

"It doesn't *do* anything," said Nick. "It isn't mechanical; you just shake it. Give it here for a moment, Tan."

They passed the duck-ball from hand to hand, the four of them huddled into a close circle. Jim was the eldest; he and Tan were both grown-up, formally speaking, and Marigold only a year younger. But Tan imagined afterwards, corroborated by the three visitors who in a moment were to break in on their moment of absorption, that they must all have looked much the same age: not *her* age and Jim's, but Nick's; the girls dressed for travel, in pullovers and thick tweed skirts and brogues; clothes crushed and untidy from the train; all four badly in need of a wash and brush-up . . . Tan threw herself sprawling across Marigold's knees to snatch the fascinating toy away from Nick . . . In one moment they would be tired of it, get up from the floor and shake themselves, and again impatiently announce their

113

intention of giving Orlo just five minutes more and then on their own initiative order cocktails to be brought up.

. . . In another wing of the hotel, and in a much more sumptuous suite, Orlo was saying to his friends:

"I simply must rush off to this conference, John. I know the old Wallaby when he summons me in that voice; it means he's terrified out of his wits to face them alone. But I've booked a table for four at the Cascade, and we'll have the whole evening together; it's hot enough to dine on the terrace. And meanwhile — oh, by the way, I've got a lot of awful children, my baby brother among them, waiting for me upstairs; they're just over from England and I haven't had a moment for them; you might in a noble spirit see that they aren't quarrelling and that they get a good tea."

Ostensibly he was addressing John and Virginia Samson, but his eyes were most of the time on their visitor from England, Dorothy Hart. She had been staying with them for less than a week, and she and Orlo had been engaged for less than a day.

So that was why, when the *salon* door opened and Tan shook back her hair and looked up, hoping it was the waiter — (had it been Orlo's step, she would not have needed to look up) — she saw a tall, fair, beautiful woman smiling down on her; a golden gracious woman, tranquil, self-possessed, amused, benign — oh, all the things that roused Tan's antagonism. What had she to be benign *about*? Scowling like a cross child confronted with strangers, she turned her eyes away from the unnecessary intruder, to the accompanying well-dressed pair, and spoke a polite: "How do you do?"

114

By that time, the juveniles had all scrambled to their feet.

"Were you looking for Mr. Hilliard? I'm afraid there's only us. But won't you have cocktails?" For at that moment the waiter really did arrive, and stood hovering for orders.

"Isn't she *killing*?" whispered the well-dressed woman to her husband.

The Beautiful Gracious One (Nick was to find a better name for her presently) went on smiling down at the curly-headed child standing there with a toy in her hand, aping grown-up manners, offering them cocktails.

"You mustn't bother about us, dear, though it's very sweet of you. You see, we're staying here and you've only just come. And you must be starving. Orlo — Mr. Hilliard had to go out, but he said we were to look after you."

And turning to the waiter, in faultless but very English French — (Tan's was fifty times more fluent and colloquial) — she ordered a sumptuous tea to be brought up ("*aussi vite que possible, s'il vous plaît*"), with stacks of cream buns and other *pâtisseries*.

Tan and Marigold and Jim and Nick listened in silent protest. *Cream buns*, when their throats were lusting for the sharp bite of an iced martini?" Do they take us for children?" — And then, more or less simultaneously, the quartet realised that indeed and under spell of the duck-ball, these ignorant people *did* take them for children. Feeling that appearances were against them, their own appearances, they decided in silent consultation to play up and not attempt to rectify the mistake. The waiter had left the room, swollen with orders for the type of food that would at the same time fill up and be a treat for a band of healthy youngsters let loose for the holidays; so it would have been quite a job to cancel and re-order. Nevertheless, they felt slightly hysterical, and when Nick had an opportunity not to be overheard, he quoted a line in Tan's ear:

"'Lord Ronald has brought a lily-white doe, to give his cousin, Lady Clare' . . ." which made her chuckle joyously at the apt description; from that moment they re-named the Beautiful Gracious One: Orlo's lily-white doe; then and now and for always, that was her to the life; that was Doe . . .

Not till Tan and Nick came back and lingered again in Paris after their holiday, were they casually told by Orlo that he was to marry Dorothy Hart.

A first impression sticks, however wrong. And even when Doe's idea of Tan as one of Orlo's "bad children needing tea" was replaced by the sight of Tania Elizabeth Maitland "being her age" in London at a highly sophisticated cocktail party, hair and make-up and costume unassailably right, she still went on for ages thinking of her as "about Nick's age" . . . Nick, her impudent little brother-in-law, must be made to feel from the start that his home with Orlo and Orlo's wife would still be his home, his favourite little friend as welcome as himself: "Those wild youngsters are always quarrelling, and yet they're devoted, in a way. Perhaps when they're both a bit older . . ." She only really caught up with it all when seven years later she married Tan's elder brother Anthony. Then perforce viewing this

116

wilful pretty tomboy suddenly from a different angle, part of her new family and not inseparably associated with Nick and a duck-ball, Doe was at last jolted out of her first impression. Tan was then twenty-six, and nobody in the Maitland family ever said, "This is our baby."

As though then it could matter to Tan one way or another! As though anything could matter, since Orlo died.

Scoffing at herself for a sentimental ass, Tan simply could not leave a duck-ball among the old pre-war stock dug up again in December, 1946, and put for sale on the shelf of a little shop in Chelsea. She *had* to buy it. But as for keeping it herself — well then, why not give it to Rosalind, thrown in as an extra besides her expensive gift of a Jacqmar scarf? By giving Rosalind the duck-ball, Tan felt she was still sharing a characteristic joke with Orlo; Orlo, like Nick, would have known from the start that Rosalind would not care for it: "A pity about my daughter, but give it to the wench, all the same. . . ."

And the two-duck-ball situation must be Orlo functioning — one might as well say "from heaven". Much better have given it to Nick, who could have been trusted to know in a flash what she meant by her Old-World Souvenir, her "*recherché du temps perdu*". Orlo's brother would have appreciated the significance of duck-balls . . . visualising four "children" in a charmed circle on the floor of a *salon* in a Paris hotel, rolling the water in the clear little globe to animate the painted ducks into their duckish equivalent of billing and cooing. For Tan, that had been positively a last performance of being so happy that she simply could not be happier without dying of it . . . for Orlo would be coming in at any moment. Even though in sheer mischief she played up to Dorothy Hart's conception of her as a child with an exuberant appetite for cream buns . . . it *should* have been Orlo who came in. And he could have said: "Hallo, infants!" till all was blue, and all would still have been splendour of carmine and gold.

And he did not take them out that evening; he gave Nick a generous supply of cash to treat them, instead. And as for their holiday in the mountains of the Salzkammergut — "Yes, thank you ever so much, we've never had such a wonderful time" . . . Nor had they ever, she and Nick, quarrelled as fiercely. Once or twice she really did rather marvel how they could set it right again?

Perhaps they never had, quite. Until at last this Christmas of universal peace and goodwill. . . . Christmas of 1946.

Doe and Nick were still amicably discussing how Rosalind should have coped with the situation:

"She might have said she would keep one downstairs and one upstairs, and feed them separately."

Doe smiled at Nick's flippancy; he was joking, but it showed that the problem, small as it was, remained so far insoluble, even to adult wits.

"She couldn't keep two duck-balls. And she couldn't be so rude as to give back the one Tan gave her, could she? I think Rosalind did the best thing, under the circumstances," Doe finished. And Nick put in a post-script:

"Anyhow it's what you would have done, isn't it, Doe?"

"More or less. Perhaps on slightly more mature lines."

"Candida, I'm sure, would have thought of exactly the right solution." For Nicholas had always contested that Doe subconsciously modelled herself on Candida, her favourite heroine . . . Though even while he spoke, he shot a quick glance at Tan, half guilty, half challenging, knowing she would remember having said to him as recently as when they were together in the train last Friday: "Nick, you've only worked up a case against Candida because she reminds you of Doe. You're very fond of Doe, but because she irritates you, Candida does too. We're always more unfair about people who irritate us than about people we really hate!"

At which Nick gaily contested every single point, and then gave in on them all, so then Tan also gave in on them all, both curiously thrilled by their strange new game of surrender without quarrelling.

Afraid, therefore, that Tan might now feel he was backsliding on good behaviour, Nick poured out a stream of semi-comic suggestions as to what Rosalind *might* well have done with the duck-balls: "The line of Brutal Frankness, such as chucking them out of the window, saying, 'I've absolutely *no use* for duck-balls'?
—" (and that would have hurt Terry far less, he reflected); "or the line of Whimsical Persiflage, giving back Tan's to Tan, saying Duck-ball the First had already ascended the throne, so Duck-ball the Second

was an intruder, and as she was now sole guardian and protector of Duck-ball the First —"

"I'll be sick in a minute," murmured Tan. And even Doe laughingly adjured him to be sensible.

"Very well, I'll be sensible. As it happens, I gave Rosalind her cue quite by accident, just before Tan came in; I asked her to give me her duck-ball, and offered her a lipstick or a phantom beaver coat or the Crown of Scotland instead. Any fool could have seen I meant it. There was her chance to give me Tan's and keep Terry's."

"Perhaps she felt, Master Nicholas, that it would be bad for your character to be given at once whatever you ask for; there *are* things in Heaven and earth, you know, that even the offer of a phantom beaver coat can't get. It would be funny, wouldn't it," Doe teased him, "if a duck-ball were one of them?"

Silently Tan prayed that Nick would remember his manners . . . It was a bit of a toss-up when Doe adopted that special nauseating line of hers. But he only said, good as gold, and apparently irrelevant:

"With her tact and playfulness and wisdom, her ineffable condescension in the bestowal of her rare self on the 'man who needs me most', Candida comes from the same smug cabbage-patch as Irene Forsyte. The Reverend James is far and away the only character in that play whom one could possibly respect. Eugene Marchbanks had insufferably bad manners and never stopped showing off — rather like me."

Doe was a little nonplussed at Nick's point of view, but as he had made a special point of the fact that

120

Marchbanks was insufferable and very like himself, she dismissed the whole tirade as another of his jokes. So she appealed to Sorrel, who, after all, was Terry's mother: "Sorrel, do you think dear little Terry has been hurt? Rosalind is seventeen, but in many way she's still a sleeping princess, you know."

("Young people must have their sleep out," muttered Nick, "even if it's for a hundred years. But someone at the Palace ought to have set that alarm-clock.")

Surprising them all, Sorrel took up the cudgels — (swathed cudgels, hardly cudgels at all) — on behalf of Doe's daughter, not her own:

"There's really nothing whatever to fuss about; Rosalind acted just as one would have expected; it was a very sweet idea of hers that Terry would enjoy both of them having duck-balls." After a pause: "Terry has to learn."

And if Sorrel took Rosalind's part, Doe felt she could do no less for tolerance and understanding than come in equally generously on Terry's side; so much more civilised than two partial mothers flying at each other's throats, each with the war-cry: "My daughter, right or wrong!"

"Poor Terry," very gently. "You know, Sorrel, I don't quite agree; one can't *learn* not to be hyper-sensitive. My own experience is —"

Nicholas interrupted coolly:

"Sorrel didn't mean that Terry had to learn not to be hyper-sensitive. She meant that Terry must learn at what altars she may safely plunk down her capacity for worship and not have to pick it up and trudge on again."

121

Doe smiled at him:

"Yes, it's always safer to worship dead heroes of long ago. But all the same, it's fairly natural for a romantic girl of Terry's age to have a rave on an older girl, especially as attractive as Rosalind. You know, Nick, I think you're a *little* unfair on Rosalind."

Tan's Paris reverie broke for a second time . . . a warning of brittle weather in the atmosphere:

"I wouldn't worry about that, Doe, because luckily Rosalind herself isn't aware of it; she told me she and Nick were such friends, they weren't like uncle and niece at all; a sort of rival establishment to Lal and his Uncle Ted."

Nick flicked her a grimace — (you wait, my girl, till I get you alone!) — "Oh, we're tremendous pals! I tell Rosalind *everything*."

Doe said lightly: "I hope not!" She was a little puzzled, taking this at its face value.

"Rosalind is always sweet with the younger ones," remarked Sorrel. "Terry will get over it now they're rehearsing; nothing is so absorbing as to be in a play."

Without preamble of any sort, without even raising his eyes from *Gems Chosen from the Classics*, Anthony interrupted them by reading aloud, having no apparent bearing on the subject under discussion, a Gem that had taken his fancy. You never could tell with Anthony whether he had or had not been listening.

> "If you strike
> Upon a thought that baffles you, break off
> From that entanglement and try another.
> So shall your wits be fresh to start again."

Seated at her dressing-table before going to bed, Dorothy Maitland often found that the long steady strokes of the brush on her fair hair, as recommended by hair specialists, promoted not only circulation and growth, but also stimulated the profounder processes of psychology. At about the twentieth stroke, her deductions were usually ready to share with her husband; thirteen years of marriage to an impersonal thinker had not yet taught her that to gain his attention she would do well first to lop away the personal foliage.

A few silvery hairs, not enough to disturb her pleasure at the reflection of a handsome woman in her prime, with two (consecutive) husbands, both devoted ("they needed me in such different ways"), three attractive children, the war over, all those she loved best under her own roof . . . Yes, undoubtedly she was a very, very lucky woman. She would remember it again thankfully and, so to speak, officially in church on Christmas morning. Meanwhile: "I've always said one can pray just as well in one's own home."

. . . The strokes of her brush grew slower, her mind preoccupied by something a little out of the normal which had been said downstairs. Often, before the war, she had had to brush her hair at night for quite a long time before she succeeded in banishing little clouds of perplexity dimming the lucid sun; usually from something that Nick had flung forth, detrimental to the general peace; or Tan, influenced by Nick. Doe never let herself be angry with Nick or Tan; she did not believe in stinging ripost; they had required wise handling, those two fiery young mortals; but the war had improved and mellowed them both; and they had now learnt to be light-hearted without hurting one another or themselves. Nick, of course, had been silly about Candida, but Bernard Shaw could look after himself.

No, it was *Sorrel* of all people who had puzzled her this evening. Surely it was odd that Sorrel should not have stuck up for her own child, but had seemed to think Terry was making mountains out of molehills.

. . . "Anthony, I've been wondering whether deep down in her subconscious, Sorrel really hates Terry?"

No reply.

"Anthony, are you listening?"

"Yes, my dear. I'd ask her if I were you. It comes cheaper in the end."

"Cheaper than what?"

"Cheaper than wondering."

"She'd deny it, naturally," said Doe. "Probably she's not aware of it herself. It was just something she said gave me a clue . . . Not exactly *said*, either, but I don't need it in black and white; it was her *attitude*. I've an idea she really may hate Terry because — well, Terry *is* Neville's child. And she looks so like him."

"Good thing too; Neville's looks were the best part of Neville."

At moments Doe wondered if Clever Men were disappointed when they ran into the blank wall of her husband's limitations, as she was disappointed when he would not join her in a chase down among the Freudian rabbit-warrens of maternal instinct . . .

"One can't blame her for hating Neville, after the way he's treated her; I can't even *blame* her if her reactions deflect from Neville on to Neville's daughter; probably in her subconscious she confuses them. Tonight is the first time I noticed anything."

"'You can begin our thrilling new serial now'" . . . But far from beginning it, Anthony retired into the bathroom, still with *Gems Chosen from the Classics* in his hand.

Doe went on brushing and musing . . . "I'm glad they've given Terry such a nice part in their play . . . Of course Candida could have put things right about the duck-balls; in a mature way that would hurt nobody. Would she, I wonder? I'm afraid poor little Terry *was* a bit hurt . . . "

Having cast herself temporarily as Candida (in despite of Nick's hasty and ill-judged opinion of the lady), Doe felt she should not give up too easily, or Candida herself might never trust her prototype again.

. . . To give away the second duck-ball, Terry's, yes, all right so far. But not give it *back* to Terry; doing her best, Rosalind had failed here. A more subtle, equally generous idea might have been . . .

(Yes, it was coming now.)

. . . Mrs. Curtis had a little grandchild, eight years old: "just the right age for duck-balls." She was so patient with her asthma, poor kiddy, and suffered from not being nearly as pretty nor as bright as Mrs. Curtis's other grandchild; and received hardly any presents except from Doe herself (Ivy worshipped Mrs. Maitland). Supposing Rosalind had suggested to Terry that a duck-ball would delight little Ivy, but that Terry herself, not Rosalind, must certainly have the pleasure of giving it to her?

Anthony wandered in again, ready for bed.

"Doe."

"Yes, dear?"

"'Nothing in human life is more to be lamented, than that a wise man should have so little influence' — Herodotus."

CHAPTER
SIX

Lal was secretly dismayed at the blaze of fury which leapt in a scorching fan towards him, directly they were back in the schoolroom. He never dreamt that Terry, a quiet kid on the whole, had been banking down such flame; she hardly seemed to care how she seared and shrivelled his self-esteem: he, her friend, her husband in the play, he, Lal, who had actually been wounded in an air-raid, Norman Meredith's son, Uncle Ted's Nephew, already fourteen and a half, more than a year older than young Terry and fifty times as brilliant; not that he had ever condescended when they were together; all these superiorities would never for a moment have occurred to him but for her burst of uncontrollable temerity. Staggered and blinded, he had to collect himself . . . And directly he began to speak, she attacked him again, with the rummest language to hear in the Manor schoolroom; he had hardly understood until now what people had meant about people when they said: "She's beside herself." Terry had been such a little while ago rather pretty, rather fun, rather different from the usual run of girls, knew how to think; but here, beside herself, stood this other Terry, storming, raging . . . while the rest of them stood round, shocked at how suddenly peace could be destroyed.

"You're a traitor; a d-d-damnable traitor. Traitors are the worst of all; they get pushed down into the point at the bottom of hell; they're Judas Iscariot; and you're a Judas too. In the war, they don't even shoot traitors, it's too good for them, too good for you. You promised me you wouldn't tell, and then you went off and told her to go and buy another duck-ball for Rosalind exactly the same at the same shop, so that you could laugh and *laugh* at the joke, your beastly rotten horrible joke. I hate you; I could kill you; I can't bear even to look at you; you're below looking at; you're dirty and mean and hideous. You've ruined Christmas and ruined everything. Like one of those b-bombs that shouldn't ever have fallen. And it makes it a million times worse that you said, 'I promise' and 'So help me' —"

"But Terry, *listen*: it wasn't a joke. I'd never for a moment have thought up a foul joke like that. And I didn't promise either; I said, 'Swelp me'; that was just fun and not a bit like 'So help me'; I wouldn't have used 'So help me' over a toy; that's what people have to say when they're taking the oath on their honour."

"Honour," muttered Terry.

Lal flushed. Nevertheless, he was feeling better for her piled-up scorn and unjust invective against him. Downstairs, when the second duck-ball had appeared from Tan's parcel handed to Rosalind, and at the ridiculous sight of Ros standing there obviously wondering what she could do with the two when one of them was bad enough, he *had* felt a guilty qualm; suspecting himself of having omitted to ask Terry whether she minded Tan going to the shop and getting

128

him the clown-box? . . . Well, girls could be such asses; suppose Terry should say, look here, she did mind, it was *her* shop, *her* discovery, *her* secret, so, why should he cash in on it? Yet if he had risked a refusal — (but he wanted those clowns!) — probably she would have said, "All right, Lal, I don't mind" — and this catastrophe need not have happened. So Lal had intended to say to Terry the instant they got away from downstairs: "I say, Terry, I *am* most frightfully sorry it's happened, though of course I'd no idea Tan would put her foot in it like this! "And then Terry would have said that of course it simply couldn't be helped. Or even granted she might lose her temper a little, till he had explained — People ought to lose their tempers *reasonably*, not bring in a lot of melodrama about traitors and Judas and the bottom point of hell! As for saying you broke promises — why, good Lord, it's as bad as saying you give mean presents! the sort of thing you can't possibly allow anyone to tack on to you; and in front of Roddy and Erica, brats hardly out of the nursery who had to be kept in their place anyhow. So: "I'm damned now if I'm going to apologise to her at all." Taking his chance on Terry's hoarseness putting her temporarily out of action, Lal's voice sounded cool and biting and sceptical, even faintly amused; an it's-a-shame-to-take-the-money voice . . . the voice and manner of Norman Meredith, K.C. hardly bothering to pulverise his opponent in a much too easy case:

"Will you kindly listen, instead of raving hot air: I did *not* betray your secret, as you call it. At least, I did not mention one single word about either you or your duck-ball. And that was the part that mattered."

"But you did! You did! Nobody else knew. How could Aunt Tania possibly have known what shop to go to or how to get to it if you hadn't told her what I told you? You can't put it right again by a lie." Again Terry choked on her own vehemence; and again Lal was able to show off how quiet he could remain under injustice, how logically he marshalled his arguments, how he scorned people who could only storm and stammer without effect or coherence:

"I certainly informed her of the exact whereabouts of the shop, because I wanted her to go there on my behalf and buy something, as she was to be in London on Monday, and as it would hardly have been convenient, while we were rehearsing all day, for me to go up and buy it myself. I was specially careful not to breathe one syllable concerning a duck-ball; nor did I mention your name. I promised I wouldn't tell a soul you'd bought a duck-ball for Rosalind. I myself don't particularly care for people who break promises. So kindly apologise."

"You're telling lies again. If you told her exactly where to find the shop, my secret shop, you must have told her to go there and buy a duck-ball just like mine, or why should she, if you hadn't told her to give it for a joke to — to the s-s-same person" — A great raw gash inside her where "Rosalind" had once been written in flowing gold; she could not bring herself to utter the name aloud.

"You're making me tired," murmured Lal. He was doing so well on his side of the quarrel, so indisputably well compared with Terry, that he could even feel superbly sorry that she of all people should expose

130

herself in such a pitiful fashion. "I've already told you twice that I did *not* mention you or that silly toy you bought. I'd promised I wouldn't. It was by the sheerest chance that Tan saw another duck-ball and chose to purchase it for Rosalind as well. If you can bring yourself to shut up for a minute" — he lapsed slightly from his lofty vernacular — "I can *prove* to you that ducks had nothing whatever to do with it, and that I'd forgotten all about them. But I *did* remember something else you happened to tell me they had in stock, because it sounded so jolly: a sort of round box with clowns jumping about inside when you rub the top."

"What makes them jump?" put in Roddy, interested. It was the first time since they came upstairs that anyone except Terry and Lal had spoken at all, and Lal was rather relieved. He turned to Roddy with a charming air of man to man: "I'll show you — if Terry will kindly allow me to go and get it? I suppose you won't deny," turning back to his opponent, "that while we were here alone and the rest were at church, you did describe that clown-box, as well as the fog and the shop and the duck-ball, after that parade of locked doors and everything wrapped round fifty times in your old woollen jackets?"

"Who's got to be wrapped in a woolly jacket?" inquired Judy, who usually ran ahead of her brother to announce him.

Terry had begun by hurling herself too far into her appalling belief that the second duck-ball had been Lal's wicked Christmas joke against her . . . and she could not now reverse the impetus:

"I didn't divide up what I told you into 'You can tell this bit' and 'You mayn't tell that bit'. You're just trying to wriggle out of the awful terrible thing you've done, so that we should all respect you again."

"Respect me? Good Lord, as if I cared — I was quite capable of judging for myself which part of my promise mattered and which part didn't."

"I trusted you never to let out *any* of it. You're twisting it round and round because you think if you twist enough you won't be a traitor any more; but you will, you will, for the rest of your life! If you live to be eighty, you will."

"I imagine in your rather babyish way you're trying now to accuse me of sophistry. Will you allow me to fetch the clown-box?"

"No. I mean I can't stop you. But it doesn't make the slightest difference over what's happened."

"That's true," nonchalantly cruel; "if she had one or two or a dozen given to her, Ros still wouldn't have wanted that duck-ball; so you're right, it doesn't make any difference."

"Was the clown-box for you to keep, Lal?" Erica, non-combatant, was not defending either Terry or Lal; because she was already making busy little dove-coloured plans in her head to approach each of them afterwards, separately, to assure them they were half right, half wrong, so *please* would they stop quarrelling and make it up, and if they liked, she, Erica, would bear the olive-branch from one to the other, and then from the other back again to the one. But she was really curious to know why Lal at his age would possibly want a toy, however special, that sounded too juvenile even for Roddy?

For the first time Lal hesitated. Then: "I'm not particularly keen on telling," he confessed frankly; "but if it's going to bring Terry to her senses . . . I wanted that box with the little jumping clowns in it — and it isn't as infantile as the ducks because it works scientifically; your fingers generate electricity when they come into contact with — Oh well, never mind for the moment; I bought it to give to Uncle Ted for Christmas."

And at that, Clare, his cousin, entered the arena for the first time since she had borne Terry off from the massacre downstairs:

"You bought a box with little performing clowns in it, to *give Uncle Ted?*" She spoke as though she could hardly believe it as a statement of fact.

"Yes, shall I get it? Would you like to see how it works? It's really an awfully clever contraption; they skip about and chuck themselves up to the ceiling — the talc — and hang there upside down, and kick a little ball about, and sometimes even go on twirling after you've stopped rubbing the top of the box; it's uncanny when you see them doing the knockabout act on their own like that."

"And you were going to give this to *Uncle Ted?*"

Lal stared in astonishment: "What *is* the matter with you, Clare? Have all you girls gone bats? Yes, I *am* going to give it to him."

"He was a clown himself when he first went on the stage. Can't you see that he's the last person in the world to give it to? Clowns are terribly sensitive; it's not their fault they've had to be clowns, but that anyone should be thick enough to give them on purpose something that would remind them — Haven't you ever been hurt yourself in a place where you're raw? — a place you keep covered up? Haven't you heard Pagliacci sing about wearing the motley when his heart is broken? It's — it's — oh, I can't understand you, Lal! You pretend to love him — *I* love him and I'd rather die than even mention a clown in front of him. It's just as bad as what one couldn't ever do about hunchbacks."

"Thanks. So I'm thick and stupid and insensitive, as well as a traitor and a liar? Perhaps I'd better cut my throat before I do anything else?"

Clare's wish was deadly earnest, to protect Uncle Ted from this agony that Lal had in store for him. Luckily it was not too late. She pounded on:

"You must promise, Lal, that when he comes you won't give him that clown thing of yours. There'll be time to get him something else when Christmas is over."

"I wonder you waste your breath wanting me to promise anything," said Lal, swaggering. "You've forgotten, I don't keep promises; I promise for the fun of it, and then I spill them at once. Ask Terry; she'll tell you."

"You shouldn't talk like that, Lal darling." Erica went up to him and affectionately slipped her hand into his. "You know how miserable we'd all be without either you or Terry, though I do understand how Terry feels as well."

"I don't," Roddy put in bluntly. "Not one bit I don't. If you like something, you don't mind having two or

134

three or four of it; I wish they'd given me two torches instead of only one. But I wouldn't even once have liked that ball with ducks inside; it's an awfully babyish toy, and I'm not a bit surprised Ros gave it back to Terry."

Clare scored a cool point:

"And what about your Aunt Tania having given it to Rosalind, if it's so babyish? Rosalind didn't give it back to *her*, did she? Only to Terry. You haven't the faintest idea what you're talking about, Roddy, so you'd better keep out of it altogether."

"You see, Roddy dear," Erica spoke in her most motherly voice, "it isn't about whether Ros likes duck-balls or not; it's about if Lal should have broken his promise even for the sake of a joke, when Terry told him as a secret?" She turned to Clare with a gentle aside: "It's always much better, you know, to explain to the younger ones instead of losing our tempers with them." She was careful to say "our tempers", not "your temper", because she was anxious to make things better and not worse.

"Damn it, Erica, shut *up*! Damn it, I've told you all, I don't think up filthy jokes like that. I didn't suppose it mattered mentioning the shop, as long as I kept mum about the other idiot things that Terry wouldn't have cared tuppence about if she hadn't got this idiot rave on your sister."

Suddenly Terry smashed all pledges with justice and reason. She had struggled to keep hold of them, not to lash out wildly beyond. Now she did not care any more if she were in the wrong; in fact, strangely, perversely, she wished to stand alone, to lose all support, to seek

135

voluntary exile, forfeit sympathy from the other children, throw away Clare as her ally. Nothing mattered, so one might as well let in all the devils; truth and heaven had broken-faith with her, romance was a cheat, Christmas a wilderness, and no help could come any more from anywhere . . . except that it might help a little to think of frightful insulting things and say them and hear herself saying them:

"If you'd been killed in that air-raid, I'd have been glad. It's dangerous to have people alive who don't know the difference between what's funny and what hurts, between what they've promised and what they think afterwards in their own heads they might just as well do because they want to. If you'd been killed — instead of being so proud of yourself for getting a little splinter in your leg — pretending you have to limp —" She stopped dead. She had meant to go to the utmost limit of beastliness, but this was somehow farther . . . and she could not call it back.

Oh, but what had happened? Only an hour ago they had all been waiting breathlessly expectant outside a door with Christmas behind it . . . Aunt Doe standing there smiling to welcome them in . . . all the lit candles twinkling on the tree . . . carol-singers . . . And Rosalind forgetting in that splendour and high excitement that she did not belong to the rest of the children, forgetting she belonged with the grown-ups, standing beside her to gasp: "O-h-h!" with the rest of them. Rosalind . . . she too had been a candle, a flame, and someone had blown her out . . . Rosalind's name did not hurt any more; and what Rosalind had done to her, that did not hurt any

136

more either; Rosalind, an empty parcel, a song gone flat; the gold was off the gingerbread, and the gingerbread itself without honest taste; Rosalind was a girl turned to cardboard as she so sweetly gave back her present to the giver. Purged of illusion, Terry could only stand and listen to the sound still hanging in the air, of what pain had driven her to say to Lal.

Lal looked at her . . . slightly shrugged his shoulders, and turned away. His attitude indicated clearly that it was hopeless to argue or reply, at any rate while this whirl of insanity was on. They heard Jonathan running upstairs. He entered in excellent humour:

"Here already, all of you? Good." He approved of their keenness. Really they were an unusual troupe, not to assemble late for rehearsal even on Christmas Eve; comparing favourably with many adult companies he had known. Then his face clouded:

"Why are you standing about, when you haven't set the stage for Act II. yet?"

Erica said brightly: "We're so sorry, Jonathan, we've only just come upstairs," and willingly set about preparing the room as he had bidden. Clare, after a pause, began to help her. Only Roddy, literal-minded, thought of answering Jonathan's question and contradicting Erica's fictional excuse:

"We haven't; we've been up here for ages." It seemed important to him that their producer should know exactly what had occurred . . . But Jonathan, inattentive and already studying the script, merely heard a jabber of "Terry said" and "Lal said" and "Ros" and "Clare" and "Aunt Tania" and "duck-balls" and "clown-box —"

"Look here, I don't want to be shown your mechanical quack-quacks, or your monkey-on-a-stick, or your tin soldiers and box of bricks and toy fort and pretty dolls' tea-sets that you can *almost* drink tea out of; you seem to have done pretty well." His gaze raked over the presents, irrelevant to the matter in hand, that were heaped about on table and floor. "It's all very nice, I'm sure, and I'm glad you were pleased, and Merry Christmas to all of you! And now, if you don't mind, I was under a sort of impression we'd called a rehearsal. So shut up, Roddy, and stop whispering to him, Erica; you're the world's worst whisperer. Where did we leave off? Part II., Scene 3: 'Elizabeth mounts the platform and goes to sit on the left' . . . We needn't do all that again. Clare, get a move on; you're sitting there: 'She takes her head in her hands. The Angel arrives and stands behind her' Erica! — 'Mary and Joseph come on from the right. Joseph is tenderly supporting Mary'. What in the name of — What *has* happened to you all?" For Jonathan became aware of such tension that even he, for all his determined authority, was nonplussed.

Roddy inquired with deep interest: "Which side are *you* on, Judy?"

"Well, I'm not quite sure," Judy began. "You see, I came in late and haven't nearly heard it all yet; I rather think I'm going to be on Lal's side because —" She was sternly quenched by her brother:

"Nobody's going to be on any side. This isn't a war. In case you haven't heard, the war's over. This is meant to be a rehearsal. Terry! Lal!"

Terry and Lal stood still, not side by side, Joseph tenderly supporting Mary, but facing one another . . .

138

CHAPTER
SEVEN

Doe would have gone to the eleven o'clock service as a matter of course on Christmas morning; but this particular Christmas, inclination offered an arm to duty. She had hoped to bring most of her house-party in a troop to please the Vicar, with whom she had so recently been brought into a more benevolent relationship by her mission on behalf of the children and their play, and by the impending Silver Collection which was to provide a damask curtain (he called it a dosel) to cover that really somewhat unfortunate reredos presented by the Hon. Mrs. Haviland (who, thank heaven, had left the neighbourhood some time ago!) Not unlike her daughter Erica, Doe was to-day conscious of the picture and of herself as one of its rightful executioners; she brimmed over with pleasant juvenile pride: "The Vicar and I have a secret" . . . (Once or twice she thought he looked at her.) He was such a dear man; and had confided in her so touchingly the low state of funds at his disposal, that it leant an extra gusto to the naturally devout mood of Christmas morning and the choir's lusty singing of "Come all ye faithful". Well, she *was* faithful, and she *had* come; sitting here, large as life, Sorrel and Rosalind with her, and Nanny Curtis; not such a large party as she had visualised, but of course Anthony would not join them, and even more, of course, nobody would suggest it to Nicholas. Doe thought that Tan had indeed wavered between church and a long tramp with Nick through the bad weather; had even looked a little ruefully at Doe and Sorrel when they came downstairs in their best clothes, almost as though she wished they would take her by force, not leave to her a decision too difficult with Nick standing by. It was curious, mused Doe, how Tan's independent spirit, usually whipped out stiff in the wind like a flag on top of a high building, had been so little in evidence ever since Nick had reappeared on the scene. What excuse had she given for not coming to church? Easier to have remembered if Tan let it depend on one reason only, and a good one; it was unlike her to have fetched up three at least and then a fourth, more plausible than the three others, that had only occurred to her a moment later and was hastily thrown in to thicken the gravy . . . She's in love, smiled Doe, well pleased. What a handsome dark pair they were; handsomer now than when they were a mutinous boy and girl.

As for the children, certainly they should all have been at church; but Erica, acting as spokesman, announced at breakfast that they were rehearsing with Jonathan.

"What, on Christmas morning as well as on Christmas Eve?"

"Jonathan said he was fed up with all our silly business of Christmas making a difference . . . Because, you see," Erica added, "it didn't go very well yesterday."

"All your little heads stuffed too full of presents, I expect," suggested Erica's grandfather.

140

Clare, still standing sentry at Terry's side, drew away the talk from presents which might lead to duck-balls and so right over the cliff of destruction . . .

"Jonathan has to waste most of Friday anyhow, he says, going up to London to hire our costumes. Tomorrow's Boxing Day, so the place won't be open."

"Ah, Boxing Day — and what else, I wonder? But I expect you've all forgotten!"

"*Father!*" (as though you'd let us!).

Nanny Curtis *was* shocked at the children's absence, but Doe affectionately reassured her on their way to church by telling her a little about "Christmas in the Market Place", and how it was not at all the same as rehearsing an ordinary play or pantomime, and that, indeed, the project had brought the Church and the Manor much nearer together than they had ever been before.

"And I haven't had a minute yet for you to show me your Christmas cards, Nanny. I suppose, as usual, you had more than all the rest of us put together?"

And probably had they been able to add up their Christmas cards in figures, Doe would have been proved right and Nanny's column would have put to shame the sum of all the rest, excluding old Mr. Maitland's birthday haul still to come.

They assembled in full family force for the ritual goose and plum pudding. Tan and Nick had returned from their walk grandly hungry and hilarious. The children's end of the table could not match the grown-ups for continual gaiety and laughter; Terry hardly chattered at all, and Clare was also a little silent; Lal, on the other hand, put on an act with terrific gusto, badly overdoing his exuberant role as jester of the party; Roddy and Erica, their mother thought, were in much their usual form . . . Yet she was not sure; tired, perhaps; a pity Jonathan had not allowed them this one morning off from rehearsal. After all, nobody expected perfection next Sunday night.

To cheer them up, she started flinging round crackers rather early in the proceedings, before the dessert. Tan had contributed them, quite a feat; though they were slimmer than the unstinted jolly old Yuletime crackers, and carried a faintly apologetic air for being in existence merely to be pulled apart and wasted . . .

"Air-raid warning!" remarked Grandpa, making his grisly little joke as the separate bangs were organised into one simultaneous big explosion, everyone standing up, linked by crackers gripped from hand to hand . . .

"One — two — *three*!" from Doe, giving the signal. Nobody could possibly be sunk in melancholy while crackers were pulled, mottoes read, caps unfolded and perched at an absurd tilt on sober grown-up heads. Perhaps she had only imagined a feeling of strain among the children during the earlier part of lunch?

But Erica lingered behind afterwards, and followed her elders into the lounge . . .

"Mummy."

"What is it, darling?"

"I think you'd better know."

So serious and troubled did she look, that Doe unconsciously removed her flamboyant paper crown, the flushed and festive hour was obviously over.

"Would you rather tell me alone, my lamb? We'll go up to my room if you like?"

Erica shook her head.

"No, it isn't private, and perhaps when you all think hard together, you'd be more likely to think of something to do about it all. Except that if she doesn't mind, please, I think it might be better if Ros didn't listen."

Not moving from where she sat, Rosalind smiled across at her Uncle Nick: "Erica doesn't mean it."

"According to you, my pet, nobody ever *means* anything, which makes for a totally meaningless world, doesn't it?"

"Besides," Erica put in, borrowing for once some of Roddy's bluntness, "I do. Mean it, I mean."

Nick perceived that Rosalind was undecided, at this, whether to quit the room in high dudgeon or very naturally to smack Erica's head and stay. Good-naturedly he gave her a cue:

"Are you sure, Erica, that you wouldn't rather get rid of me instead? It's always the most important person who's requested to leave, isn't it, Rosalind?"

His twinkling glance enlisted her as his equal, ready to humour a baby sister's solemn conspiratorial airs. So seeing it would not appear at all adult to be cross at her banishment, Rosalind pretended she was immensely injured, and went off on a mock-haughty line of thank you, she never stayed where she wasn't wanted . . . but she pulled one of Erica's curls indulgently as she passed her, children-and-their-funny-little-secrets written all over her exit . . . hoping, nevertheless, that one of the grown-ups would have the decency to tell her presently what all this nonsense was about. So far, this was certainly not Rosalind's Even More Glorious Christmas.

Erica drew a long breath:

"You see, all the rest are taking sides, and I'm the only one who isn't, because only I can see there's a lot to be said for both sides, Terry's *and* Lal's, so if I try very hard and go on seeing that, I'll be of much more use while it's all going on, shan't I, than if I was right in it with my eyes tight shut and calling out 'Lal's as wrong as he can be', or — or 'Terry hadn't any right to say what she did'?"

"Well spoken, little Switzerland!" remarked Nick.

Erica looked at him in limpid inquiry: "Switzerland?"

"*Erica!*"

A prompt and obedient child, she switched her attention on to Anthony:

"Yes, Daddy?"

"If we have any more of this circumlocution, I'll fetch Roddy; then we can be sure of a direct statement."

"But Roddy's on Lal's side, heart and soul; he *is*, daddy. So if you asked him, you wouldn't hear Terry's side at all, and that wouldn't be fair, would it? And it's no good you asking Clare either, though she's the eldest, because *she's* on Terry's side. There is only me."

"That being the case, little Switzerland, we won't interrupt any more. Let us in on the brawl. War broke out when you all went upstairs after the tree yesterday evening, didn't it?"

"How *did* you know, Uncle Nick?"

"Instinct, little Una, instinct."

144

"Una?"

"Go on, Erica darling. And in spite of your father's advice, put in *all* the circumlocution; I like it."

Encouraged by her mother, Erica set forth on a well-rounded narrative of the scene preceding Jonathan's arrival, interspersed by exemplary comments of her own:

". . . And then Jonathan came in and said, 'What *has* happened to you all, for the love of Mike? Nobody's to be on any side; this isn't a war'; but all the same he simply couldn't make Terry and Lal rehearse the next scene; they just stood and looked at each other and hated each other. So at last Jonathan said, 'All right; we'll skip that scene for the moment. You'll have come to your senses by to-morrow morning'. And after he'd gone, I ran after him and tried to tell him exactly what had happened, and how Lal had broken his promise and said it wasn't breaking it; and Terry had called him Judas Iscariot and wished the bomb had killed him so that he couldn't break any more promises because promise-breakers were dangerous; and Jonathan said, 'I couldn't care less. I'm not standing for this sort of thing at rehearsals. *You* seem to have kept your head, Erica, so you'd better tell them that from me'. So I went back and told them that from him, but not all together, because Terry and Lal weren't either of them there any more; they'd gone. So I had separate talks, first with Judy because she's still my greatest friend — but it isn't quite fair of her to be on Lal's side as he's already got Roddy, and Terry's only got Clare, so it would have been better for Judy to stay like me; and then I talked to Roddy, and

145

I'm sorry to tell you, Mummy, but Roddy was just the littlest bit rude; I put it down to its being so over-exciting for him to get such a lot of presents; I believe he had more than me this year, but of course I didn't mind a bit, and then for him to hear Terry and Lal not caring what dreadful things they said to each other. But my longest alone talk was with Clare; I called her out on to the landing . . . but I still don't think she's ready to help me, because this morning was the worst rehearsal we've ever had except in the one scene between Clare and Terry, when they're the Virgin Mary and her cousin Elizabeth, you know. Terry and Lal won't rehearse with each other at all, and not even Jonathan can force them. It doesn't matter so much about Lal, he has such a lot to act as Joey the gipsy, and he was funnier than ever in all his funny bits; but whenever he and Terry met in the play-inside-the-play, where it was Nativity and not gipsies, it all sort of stopped running, and Jonathan shouted at them — well, not exactly shouted, because he doesn't shout, he gets biting and sarcastic and his voice sends shivers up and down one's back; I'm the only one that doesn't mind, because I know how to — how to — yes, that's right, thank you, Uncle Nick, I know how to disarm him. But he said, 'I'm not here to conduct a rehearsal of wooden marionettes. Clear off the stage if you can't do better than that, and I'll take the Lady and the Shepherd, — that's Judy and Roddy. And it was a little better then, because one has to laugh over making sheep noises, though I had to make most of them. But I simply don't know what's going to happen about Terry being the Virgin Mary; she was so good in it up till yesterday

146

evening. And oh dear, it *had* been such fun before, and the play was going so beautifully —" Erica broke down into a genuine wail of sorrow for lost delights. "It's the worst quarrel we've all ever had, and it isn't like us to be quarrelling at all — it's like strangers. Oh, and now I'm nearly as bad —"

("I almost thought for a moment she was going to say 'quite as bad'," reflected Nicholas.)

"— I hurt Rosalind's feelings to get her out of the room while I told you about it being her and the two duck-balls beginning it all. I'll go and tell her I'm sorry."

Exit Erica, breathless and penitent, but glad she had shifted the responsibility; her diplomatic mission on behalf of peace could not fail to achieve a true and a happier state of affairs: "And then they'll all thank me — even Terry and even Lal; they can't not; and we've still got Thursday and Friday and Saturday to rehearse properly again."

With his characteristic tendency towards conversion of personal and domestic issues into a summing-up on general lines, Anthony Maitland remarked: "When one adjures another person earnestly and by every binding oath not to tell, and still feels uneasy, it isn't usually because one can't trust that other person, or one would hardly risk telling them at all. It's because one's hinterland is aware of having oneself a potentiality for betraying confidences, and one is therefore conscious of a final lack of safety in any promise whatever."

"As though you'd ever given away a secret, Anthony!"

147

Anthony replied that he had not said "I"; he had said "a person" and "one". His tone defied them, as it always did, to draw up their chairs cosily round a subject already profoundly interesting him if kept at a distance, and from a psychological point of view; "Secret is a woman's word."

"You can't really expect Terry and Lal to say, 'This is in strictest confidence'; they're bound to say, 'This is a secret'; there *is* no other phrase except the old-fashioned sentimental 'keeping faith'."

"'Keeping faith' is lovely, but it isn't exactly the same," said Sorrel. "What you mean is 'keep this dark'."

(Keeping it dark . . . as she, Sorrel, dark horse of Nick's amused suspicions, was keeping dark her fear, her heartache over Terry, that had sprung into life at Erica's revelation: "Terry and Lal won't rehearse with each other at all, and not even Jonathan can make them . . . I simply don't know what's going to happen now over Terry being the Virgin Mary; she was so good in it, up till yesterday evening.")

Yesterday evening . . . when Rosalind had so sweetly given back Terry's duck-ball to Terry. Sorrel could have half killed Tan for bringing in that present of a second duck-ball, and Doe for having ever in slow complacent childbirth brought forth Rosalind, and Nick for trespassing on Terry's childish dignity by daring to see the stricken look on her face. Nevertheless, Terry's disillusion, her black hour, had been bound to come. As Sorrel herself had already remarked, a penalty was always exacted sooner or later for worshipping false gods. Fortunate, then, that when it came it should have coincided with the child's new breathless happiness over the part she had been allotted in "Christmas in the Market Place". Excellent Jonathan, when he cast the play, for having the sense to realise Terry's quality. And excellent Ted, for approving of the play so heartily that Lal would be content with nothing less ambitious. Above all, at that crude moment of impact when Terry stood there exposed, stunned by what had just been done to her, thrice excellent Clare for so swiftly removing her upstairs to rehearsal; if Terry's ship had foundered, at least a lifeboat was at hand. Thus Sorrel had surrendered her anxiety, thus she had comforted herself through the night and this morning at church; surely that play of plays must have some mysterious healing property, during the Christmas season, to render it even more efficacious? She could do nothing for Terry herself; their code forbade it; but it would be all right . . . Don't be a fool, Sorrel, it's bound to work out! Imagine if Terry had been left empty-handed and forlorn! Perhaps, thought Sorrel, this was what Christmas meant, that no child need be left forlorn. And then involuntarily her mind nimbly staged a very funny scene of the Awful Warning Pair, with Mummy doing all her stuff to "make it up" to her Belinda-sweet for the unkind thing that had been done to her . . . A whole day of Very Special Treats, culminating in having Belinda to sleep with her in her bedroom so that they could hug each other *tight* . . . and of course Myrtle would say, "You've still got your ownest mother, darling pet, and she's got you."

. . . Terry had not been anywhere near her ownest mother since she ran upstairs with Clare. That was to be expected. Never mind, leave it to the play, trust in the play . . .

The first twinge of doubt had come to Sorrel during their Christmas dinner; difficult to pretend, by what she could glimpse from the far end of the table, that the child was carefree or making a quick recovery.

And then Erica had appeared, little Switzerland, little Una, little angel of peace, with her tidings of Terry gone haywire: not only Rosalind had collapsed; Lal, too, had betrayed her secret; had not kept it dark; had not kept faith . . .

"You didn't really suppose," asked Tan of Anthony (her conscience warm and guilty with duck-balls, with Orlo, with a thousand intimate adhesions deplorable to her brother), "that when Terry made Lal promise not to tell, she had all those complications piling up behind? I don't. Let's simplify: she said, 'Don't tell' because she didn't want him to tell; and he *did* tell because he wanted me to find the shop for him; and now he's trying to argue himself out of it because he's stung up at being accused in public of being the sort of boy who can't keep a secret."

Nick agreed, and added:

"Didn't you hear Lal's objectionable father in every line of his defence, as Erica repeated it? Wonderful memory *that* little horror's got — saving your presence, Doe!"

"You needn't save it," laughed Doe. "I thought your nickname for her was marvellous: Little Switzerland! I'm afraid it will stick."

150

It was remarkable that so far none of the grown-ups were being grown-up enough to attempt to solve the situation on behalf of the children, despite Erica's trustful assumption that they would seriously get down to it. Tan was still trying to be honest about herself and secrets:

"If I'm told a secret, and sometimes if the one person I most long to tell happens to be not too far away, something inside me makes a small reservation in favour of telling him and nobody else . . . even while I'm earnestly doing all that s'welp-me business. But *that's* not exactly telling, is it? When I know I can trust him not to pass it on — or her — rather too hastily."

Nick grinned at the amendment.

"And suppose, Tan my sweet, that he or she also makes that small inward reservation over just one other person? It can go on like that in single file till there's a crowd. Anyhow, that's not Lal's defence; which was, I gather, that he could judge for himself which half of the secret was important: not to divulge Terry's name nor say anything about the duck-ball; and as he kept to his word *strictly* on those points, it couldn't matter if he told Tan the address of the shop which was the unimportant half. Norman all over!"

"The perils of ratiocination!" Anthony went on to deliver a brief homily on the human tendency to ratiocinate in justifying their quarrels; a tendency that reappeared from war to war; showing more than ever man's fundamental need, which was agreeably to assert his ego without forfeiting his self-righteousness. He relaxed so far from his rule never to let the cosmic be overcome by the particular, as to mention examples of various famous quarrels in history and literature and in the general conduct of the world down the ages between Henry II. and Thomas à Becket, Wordsworth and Coleridge, Stevenson and Henley, Gilbert and Sullivan —

"One might imagine," Tan interrupted, after the impudent fashion of younger sisters, "that nobody was ever a woman, and nobody was ever alive; which about sums up your world, doesn't it, Anthony dear? And extremely desirable, I'm sure, only not quite true."

His answer startled them all; it was so irrelevant to the date and time:

"I'm going to work. Is there a fire in my study?"

"Darling, no. I never dreamt you'd want to work on Christmas Day."

"All right; I'll see to it." Anthony left them with an air abstracted yet decisive, as though only politeness kept him from saying: "And I hope I don't set eyes on any of you again for weeks."

"And what's that in aid of?" Tan demanded of the rest. Her astonishment was natural; he had not removed himself to his study since 1939. Of course the master of the house sat in the library every day when he was not out or away at his A.R.P. Headquarters, working as Chief Warden for the district. But the summer-house study was a different matter.

"He must be powerfully stirred! What started him off? Just the children's quarrel?"

And this brought Doe from a wifely interest in Anthony's speculations on the psychology of quarrels down the ages, to a local and very living problem to be solved upstairs in the schoolroom of her own house; involving not Sullivan nor Coleridge nor any contingency more remote than the children's performance scheduled for the following Sunday evening:

"I do feel it's a pity — oh, they must squabble sometimes, and ours are quite a peaceable lot on the whole, so I do feel it's rather a pity they should be quarrelling just while they're rehearsing a religious play. I should think that would somehow make it so unlikely."

"Ever heard of the Crusades? What a quaint superstitious 'think' of yours, Doe, that the subject of their play should have been enough to avert trouble; religion and superstition, when you get down to their bare bones, aren't the same bones at all."

Doe gently maintained that one should be tolerant and not scornful of people who believed in touching wood and so forth: "I'm not superstitious myself, but I can see it's better than having no religion."

"Your 'tolerance' will be the death of me, my darling. Give me an atheist every time. And *of course* you're superstitious, out and out. Every woman will deny like mad that she ever does anything more than take a few elementary precautions, but all the same . . . Look at the time when you and Orlo had a snowball letter with your breakfast."

Doe remained peculiarly unruffled, smiling as though he had unwittingly entered a plea that would score a point for her instead of for himself.

Sorrel perceived that Doe was not merely amused by Nicholas's reminder, but was munching over some secret satisfaction of long ago which Nick did not know yet. "Look-at-that-time-when-you —" did not sound to her as though it would lead to any good; she was exasperated as only that trio of Doe and Rosalind and Erica had power to exasperate her, though she had kept it under control for years, among the hundred and one things her code dictated must never run amuck. Glad of her somewhat unholy curiosity, glad of anything that led her away from silent worrying over Terry at this juncture, she idly asked:

"What *did* you and Orlo do about a snowball letter? I remember the period when they were going round and round and everybody had to copy them, but I don't think I was in on yours, was I?"

"No, of course you weren't; it was long before I married into the Maitland family. Orlo and I had only just moved into a rather jolly little house in Kent, after Paris and Stockholm. Nick was staying with us during his vacation — you were already at Cambridge, weren't you, Nick?"

He nodded.

"So I imagine," Doe added with an indulgent smile, "that Nick's girl-friend was staying with us too. Tan wasn't my sister-in-law then," she explained carefully; to be sure the whole lay-out was accurate and in good order . . . (Nick and Tan carefully refrained from exchanging a glance.) "Rosalind can't have been more than about a year old; I think sometimes she was even lovelier at that age than Erica — oh, I don't know, they were both lovely."

"Spittin' image of you," Nick conceded gracefully.

"Thank you, Nick. It's true, they're not like Anthony."

"Funny if Rosalind had been!"

"Well, we were at breakfast, and Orlo received one of those snowball letters: 'Copy this out nine times in your own handwriting and send them to nine different people within nine days of receiving this, or your luck will break'. You'd have supposed, wouldn't you, that Orlo would laugh at it and throw it away? Instead, he worked himself into a state of really violent indignation at the nuisance. D'you remember, Nick?"

"Two tubs and a plank," Nick agreed. "Something usually set him off about once in three years, and strangers were always surprised."

"You could hardly call his wife a stranger. Yes . . . I *was* surprised." It seemed as though she were again hearing Orlo fulminate at the type of mind which under a semi-religious guise started the ball of superstition rolling, rolling, benefiting no-one, putting it over on large sections of their impressionable fellow-men, subjecting them to this absurd compulsion, this lunatic fear of "breaking the luck." He swore he would take up the matter in a big way; show this letter to the P.M., the Home Secretary, have questions asked in the House about stupid people who have either a power complex or a perverted form of humour, so that they're tickled to death to think of all that time wasted.

"And you said: 'But Orlo, don't you think there might be something in it? I mean, I'd willingly copy it out for you, only it has to be in your own writing'."

"Did I, Nick? How you remember! Still, it's quite probable; it sounds like sense to me."

155

"It sounded like nonsense to Orlo. Tolerance in the wrong place: either there was nothing in it, as he said, or everything; never 'something'."

"How like him you've grown, except —"

"I'd skip that 'except' if I were you," laughed Nick . . . and a growing tension was relieved.

"Do go on with the snowball story," Sorrel begged.

"Orlo absolutely forbade me to carry on this tyranny, as he called it. He very rarely forbade me anything, but he was so eloquent — Orlo *could* be eloquent, he'd have made a wonderful politician — that he convinced me he was right, and that superstition meant dangerously submitting yourself to unorthodox dominion . . . That was his phrase."

"I preferred my brother's lighter vein, but I dare say you're right, and that if he'd stuck to the polysyllabic thunder, he might in time have become one of England's Grand Old Statesmen."

"Everyone knew he had a brilliant career in front of him as Foreign Secretary. Only he died."

Doe spoke simply, with a regret from which all pain had been drained off. She was one of those fortunate women who, marrying twice, could truthfully say that she loved both her husbands alike, and both her daughters. It may have been that Roddy was the only one of her family, past and present, who had not come in on this happy equality of affection — ("And yet Roddy's likely to *need* me more than the girls.")

"But Doe, his death so long afterwards — you couldn't possibly have put it down to his breaking the luck of a snowball letter? Oh, is that why Nick accused you of being superstitious?"

Doe smiled.

"It was . . . just a little unfair of Nick. But then, you see, Orlo never knew I knew" — she paused for effect — "that he secretly copied out that letter himself, and sent it round."

Pleased with the impression she had made, and certainly relishing herself as a raconteuse, Doe continued feeding her attentive audience . . . (She could hardly guess that her complacent style of narrative was irritating Nick to a frenzy.)

"About six weeks later, while I was staying in London with the Stantons (Vera liked to have me to herself every now and then, and Orlo never minded), I received the same snowball letter. Yes, Sorrel, the very same. Only it was addressed to me this time, instead of to Orlo. Of course they were spreading into hundreds by then, all along different tracks, but as it happened, I recognised the writing; one had to think of nine friends, you see, to whom to send it, and this was from a friend of mine, Lydia Waterson; she hadn't disguised those Greek E's enough. So through her, I traced it back and then back again to — who do you think?"

"Orlo," from a sombre Nick. "You've already told us."

Doe had forgotten she had already made her dramatic curtain line before it was actually due. Her creamy calm was a little ruffled, though Doe-like, it only showed in a gentle amusement too kind for triumph, directly trained upon Nicholas . . . to whom it was now for the first time revealed that *she* was not superstitious, but that his adored brother, like so many men of genius, was no

157

more than a poor deluded sweet to those in his own home who had loved him best!

"I was thunderstruck at first, of course. *Orlo!* After all his speechifying at breakfast, all his rage against the snowball letter menace. And then I thought it over, and I remembered . . . A few days after he'd made such heavy weather at breakfast, he had to stay in bed with a sprained ankle and a feverish chill he'd caught lying out with it in the rain in Groton Wood, before anybody heard his shouts and came along to carry him home. We had to nurse him carefully, because it was absolutely imperative he should be well by the end of the week when he had to speak at the by-election, an important one; they were counting on him. And we *did* get him well. A great many people said that but for Orlo his man would never have got in; he won every waverer on to his side; made them laugh. Orlo could always count on making people laugh, and that's what they like best."

"But how on earth did he come to copy out and send round that letter?" Sorrel asked.

"Now that was where I had a flash of illumination; I do get these flashes, as though something quite outside me comes along . . . I always say inspiration has very little to do with brains, for I don't pretend to be clever. Having an accident just then when it was imperative he shouldn't be ill for that by-election obviously set him off wondering — (he must have been fundamentally more superstitious than I'd ever guessed) — had his luck broken because he hadn't copied the letter and sent it on? 'Have I broken it myself?' And lying there, I expect it came to him that perhaps even then it wasn't too late, and if he copied the letter quickly, nine copies, copied it very, very secretly so that I need never know he'd gone back on his tirade: 'I forbid it, Doe,' and all the rest of it ... No, you mustn't laugh at my Orlo, he was only human, and he *was* a little vain, the darling, it would have mortified him too terribly to realise I ever knew he'd caved in. There was only one thing for me to do. If two people are really in love, in love in the right way, any form of cheap triumph doesn't mean a thing to them. So I burnt that letter — oh, of *course*, without copying it nine times. You'll take it back, won't you, Nick my lamb, over me being foolishly superstitious? One in the family was quite enough! I made up my mind to keep it an inviolate secret. And I did as long as he lived. I never meant my Orlo to guess that anyone had ever stumbled on to his one little moment of weakness, and thank God, he never did."

"But Tan knew all along," said Nicholas.

CHAPTER
EIGHT

Sorrel had an impulse to spring up and cry, "Was that lightning?" as it forked through the darkening room . . . and was gone before one could be sure.

Bewildered, Doe repeated:

"*Tan* knew? *Tan? Knew* I'd found out what Orlo had done? But I can't see how?"

Nick made a brusque uneasy movement, twisting his chair so that he could not see Tan's face. "Your finding out was only a side issue." He was furious at the humiliation to Orlo's prestige: even after death, to have had to go on accepting Doe's kind bounty . . . "What Tan knew all along was that Orlo had written nine copies of the letter. You see, he called her upstairs to help him, and then she delivered them just in time. He trusted Tan."

"Damn!" muttered Orlo, thirstily reaching for the glass of milk diluted with soda water that Doe had left beside his bed, and upsetting it. He stared gloomily at the thin white puddle spreading on the carpet; no doubt of it, he had broken his luck, broken it four days ago. To be laid up with this beastly ankle, feeling rotten and feverish, every bone aching, with that by-election just coming on

160

and Harley relying on him to ginger up the whole thing — Oh *damn*!

Suppose one were to capitulate? He twisted a wry grimace at the thought of stooping to propitiate those devils that from somewhere pulled the strings: right for luck, left for bad luck . . . Funny how you used a qualifying adjective over luck only when it was the reverse of good.

As usual he had been too arrogant, and now look at him, a fool crying over spilt milk.

"Doe, I've spilt the milk!"

No answer. Then he heard the two-seater scrape to a standstill at the gate; the door slammed; Doe's voice calling for Nick. Thought she was giving the boy a treat, did she, letting him drive her into Rye to do the shopping? As they drove off, he heard young Tan's voice calling a gay good-bye. Orlo reflected, with a certain sardonic sympathy for his young brother's predicament, how Nick would have preferred to spend the morning with that attractive child Tania . . . And as he thought of Tan and himself left alone in the house, he suddenly made up his mind. His window was wide open; he heard her step crunching on the gravel as she came back from the gate: "Tan," he shouted, not too loud, but she heard him and sang out:

"Hallo! Shall I come up?"

. . . Amazing how quickly she understood his sudden capitulation, without any irritating protestations of understanding; no fuss, no argument, no do-you-think-you-ought, or, on the other hand, not too much sycophantic agreement: Oh-yes-Orlo-I'm-psychic-as-well-

161

and-I-*do*-think-you'd-better-not-go-upsetting-them. A wonderful kid, Tan; her businesslike: "Yes, of course, it's plain silly to take risks when there's a political issue ahead" was just on the note; his heart warmed to her.

"I couldn't even get up to fetch *la plume de ma tante* and all the other implements. This infernal ankle —"

"Don't try and move. I'll rootle round in your study and bring them up. But if there are crooked rules, one had much better not tamper with them, so I mustn't actually write any of the letters for you or the thing might still go wrong."

They agreed that by this unpredictable tyranny it was a good thing his foot and not his right wrist had been injured. Halfway downstairs, Tan came running back:

"I say, we quite forgot — the letter itself — the one that has to be copied — in which suit do I find it? You put it in your pocket, didn't you, to show the P.M. and the Home Secretary?"

And again he could have kissed her in his gratitude for her instinct of taking for granted that he was serious in his tirade the other morning at breakfast; serious while it lasted; Orlo knew his own mental processes pretty well; recognised that working himself up to such over-eloquence on the subject he had really meant what he said, really would have shown that maddening letter to the P.M. — or the whole blessed Cabinet — had they chanced to walk in during breakfast that morning: "This sort of trading on nerves has gone too far; it ought to be thoroughly sifted — the people exposed —" Then (little Tan guessing right again) he had completely forgotten all about the footling thing.

Scribbling his nine copies was easy, with Tan sitting on the end of the bed and keeping him amused; but once accomplished, nine envelopes had then to be addressed to nine suitable acquaintances; not friends; they must not recognise his writing — or might he disguise it? They discussed earnestly whether a disguised handwriting would also militate against a full free chance of the thing beginning to work now in his favour and allowing him up in time to be driven to Sanbury the day after to-morrow and hobble on to the election platform? Tan advised him to use his natural handwriting, but to eliminate his intimates from the list.

"Then who's left? I don't know nine people *not* intimately."

"I do, hundreds. Would it be allowed, do you think, if I supplied two or three names and addresses?"

With anxious brows they debated this further delicate point of snowball etiquette . . . Simultaneously both became aware of the ridiculous aspect of what they were doing, and laughed so much that they grew hysterical . . . All the same, by unspoken pact they remembered to keep on the alert for the sound of the Hillman-Minx returning.

When Orlo declared that he could address no more envelopes without a drink, Tan ran downstairs again. He felt more optimistic already; nothing like these practical remedies! Tan appeared with a cocktail shaker — trust her not to suggest a nice pure draught of milk! He kindly let her lick the stamps and stick them on; stick, he said, was not good for his complaint. The whole job neatly completed, and his fever rapidly abating, he lay back

163

against his pillows, and with the satisfaction of a good boy who had done his duty to the nation, inquired what was nine times nine?

"Eighty-four," replied Tan promptly. "No, forty-nine."

"Forty-nine, my sweet, is seven times seven. I do know that, because *if* I were superstitious, it would be my lucky number." "If I were superstitious" came out in his gravest tones, looking Tan steadily between the eyes. She chuckled . . . and had another shot at nine times nine:

"Sixty-four. That's right. I *know* it's sixty-four."

"How do you know? You're an ignorant little girl."

"I'm not an ignorant little girl, and I do know." She started in a sing-song voice: "Nine nines are sixty-four, nine tens are —"

"Ninety. You can't deny that?"

"Beast! Oh well, as nine tens must be ninety, nine nines are nine less than ninety. Eighty-one. That still doesn't *sound* likely. Why do you have to know?"

"Eighty-one additions to the snowball to-morrow. Eighty-one stamps. Nine times eighty-one the day after to-morrow."

"Orlo, stop; it's making me dizzy. And we can't be sure they'll all do it at once; some of them may wait four days till the last possible —"

He stopped her with a look of frozen horror: "Tan, what were you going to do with these letters?"

"Post them, of course, at once, before the 12.30 collection."

"It's no good. They won't arrive till to-morrow, and to-day *is* the fourth of my four days. Midnight's the limit. Bang goes my candidate." He laughed, still carrying on his lapse as a huge joke . . . but his worried eyes betrayed him.

Immediately, directly it was needed, Tan became his business partner again: "That's all right; nothing could be easier; I'll buzz up and deliver them by hand."

So might Jaggers, messenger boy of their grandparents' generation, have casually volunteered to cross the Atlantic on behalf of his employers.

Orlo felt weak with relief. Had he not fallen in love with her before, he would have loved her now.

(But he had loved her always, from the moment young Nick brought her home, except for that one hour of his life when he had been blandly bewitched to a bed of Durable Domesticity, all satin and cream.)

"My blessing," said Benedick the married man who had failed to recognise his girl born beneath a dancing star, "two of the fortunate nine don't even live in London; one's in Devonshire and the other at Broadstairs."

"Couldn't do it in the time, I'm afraid. Oh well, we'll have to scrape up a couple more of our London pals; only, Orlo darling, do hurry up if I'm to catch the 1.10."

A wild gay chase after two more victims; and then Tan swept up the letters, removed all debris of their guilt including the cocktail shaker, and refused Orlo's offer to finance her expedition by car the whole way there and back.

"You can't afford it; nine stamps you've already squandered. Do you think they'll be puzzled to get stamped letters that haven't been through the post?"

"No, because each of them will only get one, so how can they know that the other eight have been stamped too?"

"Orlo, England needs men like you with brains like yours . . . If I should expire from heart failure, you'll remember all the rest of your life, won't you, that I died faithful to my solemn trust?"

". . . He called her up to help him, and then she delivered them just in time. He trusted Tan."

Sorrel could hardly believe Doe was not possessed by some stranger from the underworld, her reply was so harsh and brutal:

"*Trusted* her! Such a dear little pal . . . And then I suppose she went straight off and broadcast it to the boy-friend, when you came home from Rye that morning. You must have laughed your heads off, you and Tan; I can just hear you: *Poor* Doe, she hasn't a notion of the merry parties that go on when she's safely out of the house!"

Tan could not bear it; she would deal later with Nick's wickedness; but meanwhile Doe had been hurt. In one impetuous movement, Tan was across the room and kneeling beside her:

"Darling, darling, *don't* look like that; don't listen to Nick. We didn't laugh, of course we didn't; why, there was nothing to laugh at. Orlo's reason for not wanting you to hear was to save his face where you were concerned; your good opinion mattered so terribly to him, and he was being a bit of a donkey. Wonderful of you, when you found out, not to score over him as any other wife —"

166

But her eager sentences could make no headway against Doe's solid wall of antagonism. It was a shock to realise, as she had certainly not realised before or she would not have flung herself across the room on a fool's errand, that her sister-in-law actually hated her:

"You needn't explain my husband to me, thank you very much, Tan. All that child-about-the-house business. . . . I should have guessed long before . . . I *did* guess, from that first moment when I saw you at the Morlands' cocktail party, after you'd tricked me in Paris by sitting on the floor playing with a toy and stuffing cream buns like a schoolgirl — how old were you already? Twenty-one? Twenty-two? But you had a pretty shrewd idea of how you could manage to keep close to Orlo when you heard we were going to be married and your time was up: 'Nick's little playmate' . . . tearing round in shorts with your curls tumbling over your face — that's how you wormed yourself in, and never mind dignity or even decency . . . What did they matter, when you were so crazy on Orlo that you had to scheme and plot and act and disguise yourself and tell lies for the sake of being free of the house, free of his bedroom, the moment I was away for an hour?"

Better now, the pain and the soreness, for having uttered at last what had festered in some stagnant backwater of her mind for so long: conviction that it would be safer for Orlo (strongly and tenderly as he loved her) if young Tan and young Nick, the children about the house, not *their* children, not quite children, were to fall in love and marry and go right away and be for evermore absorbed in one another.

. . . Tan still knelt stiffly on the floor beside Doe; she could not get up and walk across the room to the door or back to her chair, being hated; *she*, not Nick; that was the strange part of it — or was it perhaps not so strange? And high time someone paid a little attention to Nicholas son of Satan.

He felt Tan looking straight at him. Oh, all right, if she wanted a row, he was prepared to stand by what he had said; he did not regret one single word; Doe had asked for it.

"Yes, my girl?" with his sunniest, frankest smile.

"Nick, please tell Doe that 'Tan knew all along' did *not* also mean that Nick knew all along; and that I was hardly likely to run round blabbing out Orlo's secrets. Tell her that I can keep my word, even if you can't."

Obediently, Nick informed Doe, who barely listened, that not till after his brother died had Tan spoken of that episode when a potential Foreign Secretary, his untimely end deeply regretted by all the Obituary Notices, had lapsed into a rueful, adorable, human idiot of idiots. After Orlo died, Tan would surely have been stingy not to share with Nick such a tender memory of him, in the course of their long sorrowful talks which had seemed to heal grief at its rawest. Nick had had need, then, of all the help Tan could give him.

Of this, naturally, he said nothing to Doe; he merely testified in brief telegram language that Tan had not told him till after Orlo's death.

"I can't see that the date of publication matters," Doe remarked, still in the aloof mood which had succeeded the astonishing vehemence of her outburst against Tan.

Absently seeking an object on which they would expend their restlessness, her fingers lifted the duck-ball from the desk beside her, where Terry had gently set it down on Christmas Eve . . . Could that have been only yesterday? — decorating the tree, lighting the candles, all the party trooping in to the strains of "Come to the Manger", her little speech of gracious yet sincere welcome ("You do these things so well, Doe!"), Terry's duck-ball that Rosalind gave back because Tan had mysteriously elected to buy her another . . . Tan had not given it to one of the other children, no, but to Rosalind, when already she had given Ros a rather specially extravagant present. Why, Doe had wondered? Yet that, too, was now stupidly easy to understand.

"You gave it to Rosalind because she was Orlo's daughter. I imagine it was part of another little intimate joke against me, when you and Orlo — you and Orlo — you and Orlo — "And she hurled the duck-ball into the fire.

There was no flame; the logs were sulky; and Sorrel, leaning forward, was able without even scorching her fingers, to pick out the ball and lay it back again quietly on the desk, with a touch of contempt for the melodrama that found relief in throwing things about.

"The room's getting colder every moment; do help me build up a proper fire, Nick; it's never any good *poking* logs."

"Leave them alone; they're too heavy for you to lift. Haven't you got any bellows?" He saw the bellows quite clearly, for they were over on Tan's side; at least he could give her this chance to move from where she still knelt. But she handed them to Nick in silence.

169

"Yes, that's better; there's a through draught now; blow just here, Sorrel, and we'll soon get a flame; my tender skin will be up in blisters presently, but nobody cares."

"I don't think your tender skin will suffer," said Tan, with a note in her voice that made Sorrel think: Oh, God, we're off again!

"Now what exactly do you mean by that?" Nick's eyes were bright and hard as he challenged Tan not to make inscrutable statements in his disfavour.

("'I'll met by moonlight, proud Titania.'"

"'What, jealous Oberon! . . . I have foresworn his bed and company.'"

"Have you, Tan?" softly.

"No, Nick.")

"A tender skin? Yours? Have you ever tried to penetrate the pachyderm of a rhinoceros?"

"I see. And may I ask, dear Lady Disdain and all that, how you came to the conclusion that I was so thick-skinned?"

"Either that or inconceivably cruel," Tan answered, not directly but on an oblique shaft. "Which would you rather?"

"What have I done?" bluntly.

And equally bluntly: "Hurt Doe and broken your swear."

That was what they had always called it, and Nick dropped back twenty years with his heated: "I haven't broken my swear. What swear?"

"After Orlo died and we couldn't stop talking about him, when I told you about the time we'd copied those letters."

170

He interrupted hotly, to ward off what he saw was coming: "Yes, I did swear that I wouldn't tell. And I wouldn't have, ever. It was *not* breaking my swear to tell Doe just now, because she knew already."

"You told her that *I* knew."

"That's quite different." Nick went on plugging his defence. "She knew already that he'd carried on with the snowball letters, or wild horses wouldn't have made me betray him — or you. You can't possibly accuse me of breaking a swear when a person already knows a thing, to say that another person had known all along. Even *you* can't, and God knows you're unreasonable!"

"Sophistry!" exclaimed Tan, utterly scornful of his clever trick-work. "I've often wondered if Judas had a Counsel for the Defence."

Sorrel thought Tan was wilfully exaggerating. That Doe had not been able to control her fishwife reactions hardly justified both of them turning on poor Nick as though he were Public Enemy No. 1. He had fought in a real war, after all, and on achievement alone was entitled now to peace and gentle treatment:

"Honestly, Tan, I can't see where Judas comes in. You can be dead sure Nick would never break his sworn word. And he and I may both be sophists, but it does strike me, too, that it's quite different from a crude betrayal, simply to say that someone knew all along."

"The ancient pastime of splitting hairs. But this is between Nick and me alone, so keep out of it, Sorrel."

Far from Sorrel keeping out of it, Doe now came into it, and to Sorrel's astonishment, on the same side as herself:

"Anyhow, for *Tan* to lash herself up into a state over treachery — Tan who sat on Orlo's bed when he was helpless and couldn't get rid of her, pretending to be still a dear little schoolgirl, laughing and urging him on into a plot against me —"

Nick was in a quandary. He did not want allies; especially he did not want them when he and Tan were so dangerously at loggerheads again; even more especially, he did not want Sorrel and Doe as allies. What were they thinking of, to rush in to support him and not Tan, leaving the poor kid to fight her battles alone? Unsure enough of his audacious plea, he felt that anyone convinced by it could not be much use, anyhow. Here he was, outwardly defiant, inwardly guilty as hell, backed up by Sorrel and beyond all sense by Doe, making it more than ever difficult to put himself right with Tan again. Doe was being quite unspeakable . . . how could she have *known* that Tan had sat on Orlo's bed? Nobody had shown her a photograph.

(Jealousy always guesses right.)

Though come to that, how could *he* be so sure it was true? Nick searched his memory: Tan had told him how they had laughed in choosing the victims for the letters, and about Jaggers and nine-times-nine . . . But no, she had never said: "*I sat on Orlo's bed*". Well then . . .

(Jealousy always guesses right.)

Was nobody ever going to break this brooding silence that had fallen on them all?

"I've had a nice rest," remarked old Mr. Maitland, entering still mellow with Christmas, chatty and genial, "and I've been wondering which of you has been resting

172

too? And whether our Dorothy had decided, after such a Christmas banquet, that tea would be an unwelcome superfluity? Dear me, what long words I use: Unwelcome superfluity! What do you say, Doe, my dear? A cup of China tea, perhaps, and nothing to eat? — at least, they call it China, but it's nothing like our old favourite Lapsang."

He settled himself happily in the armchair vacated for him, and beamed with approval at his daughter and his two daughters-in-law, and even at his daughter-in law's first husband's brother, hardly a kinsman at all, though they had all counted themselves for so long as one united family.

"That'll do, my boy, that'll do; not all the cushions in the room, though I suppose I must expect to be treated as a veteran from to-morrow onwards; I can hardly believe this is my last evening of being a mere lad of seventy-nine. Are all the windows shut? It feels a trifle cold. Ah, I see, you've let the fire go down. What about a little bellowing? No, no, not bellowing, bellowsing; we've all had enough bellowing, haven't we, during the war, to last us a lifetime? Tell me, Dorothy, my dear — I know you won't let me off from some little celebration of my birthday to-morrow — and of course I'm not asking any of you to betray secrets —"

Tan was wondering: "How the *hell* did she know I sat on Orlo's bed?"

CHAPTER
NINE

Lord, I am just a poor man. You have shown me that, I might say, in everything about me. Oh! I am not complaining! You say "Go!" and I go. I go — I stay — I don't try to understand. I know now that You are with me. You hold me by the hand . . . *in* Your hand. Don't be afraid — I obey You.'"

Listening, Terry thought: Lal can't do that speech; he's terribly bad in it; he doesn't mean his humility. Lal's wonderful as Joey — so amusing and so sure of himself, just like a gipsy boy who steals chickens and gets away with it. But — doesn't Jonathan see? Isn't he going to say something?

Jonathan did say something, coldly: "You always forget your cue, Terry. If you don't call Joseph at that point, he can't get his exit."

"Oh, I'm sorry, Jonathan. I was thinking. I —"

"Your scene with Elizabeth is all very fine, but you needn't get above yourself; you're rotten lately in all the rest. Now then, we won't rehearse the Shepherd and the Lady over and over again. Start 'Enter Joseph supporting Mary. Stops near the young Shepherd.'"

As always since Christmas Eve, Lal and Terry looked obdurate and did not budge from where they stood.

174

Terry dreaded too much the tenderness, the confident trust with which Mary would have to turn to Joseph a little farther on:

"'Joseph, I cannot stand.'"

"'Lean on me, lean on me, Mary!'"

Lal did not dread it, he simply did not wish to do it, after the way Terry had blackguarded him. He enjoyed more than ever, since then, swaggering through Joey; but from this scene onwards, his part was nearly all Joseph. He suggested carelessly to the producer that the Joey half of it was ever so much more important: "Can't we cut out some of Joseph?"

Joey more important that *Joseph*? More important than Mary's spouse? And Lal had actually dared to say "Cut out some of Joseph"? . . . Terry held her breath and waited for a thunderclap from an ink-dark Heaven.

Only Judy, who had several times after rehearsal heard her brother speak strong and straight on the subject of his company's deficiencies, their ruddy obstinacy, their infernal conceit in refusing to accept direction over scenes — only Judy knew how he felt over the deadlock of Lal and Terry; how helpless in face of their black antagonism. Helpless was not a word usually to be found in Jonathan's vocabulary, but their hate was stronger than he; he could do nothing except rehearse unnecessarily the scenes of the play where they did not appear together, and hope from day to day that the cause for this lethal hold-up might disappear as mysteriously as it came. Had he listened to Erica's wisdom from the very beginning of trouble, had he listened to any of them but particularly to Erica (who had done her best to bring about a council of appeasement) then at least nothing would be mysterious, and he would have known what he was up against. But from first to last, Jonathan had not a remote notion, not a glimmer of why Terry and Lal had stiffened into wood. Secretly he was astonished how inflexible they remained alike to his threats and to his commands.

Erica now reminded him that since the first day (when they had been allowed to read their parts) not once had they gone through the last scenes of all, with the three kings bringing their gifts, and the rejoicing and the dance and the final shout: Noël! Noël! Noël!

Officious little beast, Erica! She *would* remind him of that, in her angel efforts to keep the peace. Jonathan could not bear the showy side of the theatre, the acting side; and although he had had to play Old Melchior, the veteran gipsy who to a certain extent was also the commentator in "Christmas in the Market Place" and held it together, he would have given much to eliminate the long monologue where as in a vision Old Melchior describes the visitation of the Magi. Any born actor would have described Melchior as a "fat part" largely owing to this monologue; but Jonathan disliked it, avoided rehearsing it. Apart from anything else, memory was not his strong point. *Dear* little Erica, how exactly like her to drag it up!

"I can rehearse that by myself at home without wasting our time. I'll just give the Shepherd his cue. Ready, Roddy?" He mumbled: "'Gold of my faith, frankincense of my hope, and myrrh of my charity. Will

You have them, precious babe? You will forgive Joey, won't you, dear Jesus?'"

"Look here," Lal burst in, "I've got an idea. Let's do the three kings properly. I mean, let's have all three of them. This is an awfully dud scene — the scene, not you, of course — where you pretend to lead them all on and they're not really there. Wouldn't it be ever so much more fun if they actually did come on in a sort of procession, bringing their gifts? You're so good at lighting effects and all that, and it wouldn't take us a moment to write in some appropriate lines for each of them. I'll be Baltazar, the black one," he added in a great hurry, in case anyone else should try and claim it.

Terry cried in horror, addressing Lal for the first time since the outbreak of hostilities:

"You can't possibly change the play and write in new scenes; not *this* play; you simply can't!"

"Why not?" retorted Lal, laconic and at the same time impudent. "It isn't Holy Writ, it's just a play written by a Frenchman, and we can damn well write in any scenes we want."

"You can't, you can't; it's all wrong; it's different. You've got Joseph, the loveliest part; can't you be content with that? *He* didn't want glory; *he* would never have tried to push himself forward and show off in a whole lot of other parts."

Lal shrugged his shoulders. "What about it, Jonathan? Terry seems a bit hysterical on the subject, but we needn't mind that. The fact is," he flashed her a tentative look — should he say it? Yes, why not, after all the things she had said at him?" The fact is, she's not thinking of anyone but her precious self. And she's putting on all this religious set-up simply because she doesn't like the idea of sitting there to accept gifts from me; she's still too fed up over her silly old duck-ball that was her 'gift' to Ros. Look here, Jonathan, what about letting me throw up Joseph and only do Joey and Baltazar? Then our poor Terry needn't have the misery of letting me even touch her in the play. I couldn't care less; I'd prefer it."

Jonathan told him curtly to stop talking hot air: Who was there at the eleventh hour to play Joseph? And anyhow the part was a natural extension from Joey the gipsy:

"But your notion over the Three Kings *has* got a spot of sense in it. We needn't have many lines, only where they offer the gold and myrrh and frankincense, the rest I can work out in mime, seeing the star, following it along and so forth." He was tempted, for it would release him, as Old Melchior, from the long monologue.

Lal sent a triumphant look glinting towards Terry.

"Baltazar, Melchior and Caspar; the only thing is," Jonathan went on, "who can we have for the third of the Kings?"

"Clare's tall. She could do it in robes with a beard."

"But I don't want to. I don't want to be any of the Kings to please Lal. Terry's right; Lal never sees why about anything; he's too thick-skinned."

Lal swept her a mocking bow. "Thank you, Cousin Clare. Back we go all the way to our clown-box."

"*Let's* have all three kings, and Clare with a beard and Lal with a black face — let's! Why shouldn't we?" Roddy took up his stand firmly as one of Lal's henchmen.

178

"Roddy darling, I don't think you should interfere. We're much the youngest, you know, you and Judy and even me, and if Jonathan doesn't want to write in a new scene —"

"*Please* don't, Jonathan. Do let's leave it as it is. The play is so beautiful, and it's a Nativity Play, and what Lal wrote in couldn't possibly sound the same —"

"Terry, stop making fusses about your potty personal grievances, opposing everything, and saying we can't do this and we can't do that. Who do you think you are? Leading lady at the Old Vic? Swelled heads aren't going to get us anywhere." Jonathan went on lashing himself up and being unfair towards Terry, because originally she had been his favourite; he had hoped most from her. "Has it penetrated your infant mind, by any chance, that this is Friday morning; I've got to see about getting the electrician to fix up the portable switchboard and all the flex, *and* spend the whole afternoon up in London hiring the costumes and bringing them down with me for the dress rehearsal to-morrow? We've been all mucked up with Christmas and Boxing Day and things being closed, and now the week-end's on top of us, *and the play is on Sunday night*. And yet you stand there with a white face and big eyes, babbling all sorts of sentimental loyalties that don't even exist."

Terry tried to say something to defend herself. Coherence toppled and crashed. She rushed out of the room.

* * *

But how could Lal think, how *could* he, that she still minded about Rosalind having given her back the duck-ball? His jibe had so taken her by surprise that she had no breath to refute it. And then Jonathan turned on her for making a fuss. None of them would have believed her, not one of them except perhaps Clare, if she had declared then that nothing, nothing mattered except the play; that her gift to Rosalind and what Rosalind did with it had shrunk and withered to a dry speck she could hardly see any more. The play possessed her wholly, all her faith and all her service. Surely the others — Lal — must feel the same? Must feel, as she did, that it had miraculous properties exerting their influence during those wonderful rehearsals before she herself had — No, don't think of Christmas Eve for a moment; it hurt too much; try and forget it. Those lovely early rehearsals were real; and all this horrible jangling and noise and hate with which they were spoiling the play now, no more real than when you looked back on all the horrible war things, air-raids and rumours of invasion and the black-out, before the radiant stillness of peace . . .

"Did you want to come in, Miss Terry? I thought we'd give your room a proper do-out this morning, as it's had nothing but a lick and a promise, as you might say, during Christmas."

"No, it's all right, thanks, Nanny."

Terry walked slowly away. She was not exactly crying yet, although her eyes stung and her throat was swollen, but all the same she simply had to be by herself in case of suddenly remembering small things from their first rehearsals that did make her cry before she could control it . . . How sweet Lal had sounded just before the Angel appeared to him in a dream, when as Joey he had had to announce: "'I am playing Joseph this time, a very dignified man'."

Where could one possibly go, in winter, to be quite alone in a houseful of people, and everyone you met saying —

"Hallo, Terry. I thought you children were rehearsing? Not much time left before Sunday, is there?"

"We *are* rehearsing, Auntie Doe. They sent me to fetch —"

What could they have sent her to fetch? A blank white spot spread over her mind . . . How queer Auntie Doe looked! Quite different from her usual sort of nice-all-throughness. "I couldn't find it," Terry added lamely.

"That's right, dear," and absently Doe passed on downstairs.

And downstairs was always the danger of bumping into Mummy; and while Mummy too might have said: "That's right, dear," she would certainly guess it was so far from right that it couldn't be more wrong. Mummy was the last person to meet now when you were alone and defenceless, just because she always knew without having to ask questions, so you would be forced into an extra display of unresponsive coldness. Up till the present, having successfully avoided Sorrel, except at meals, ever since Christmas Eve, Terry thought she had managed not to betray anything of the tumult of unhappiness surging up and having to be sternly pressed down again . . .

The old nursery, now Nanny's sewing-room, *must* be empty at this hour, with Nanny doing the beds, and

181

Roddy (who still kept some of his things there) safe at rehearsal. You couldn't hang about on the stairs; and it was so dank out of doors where all your favourite trees and corners could have given sanctuary any time except in the dead of winter.

Yes, the nursery was empty. Terry closed the door and cast herself gratefully into the rocking-chair. How often Nanny had sat there supervising all their earnest games, their shouts and squabbles, while she sewed and tilted herself backwards and forwards with that slow soothing rhythm . . . like this . . . like this . . .

("Now, Roddy, stop bothering your sister, she's much too kind to you, and you're not allowed to use a penknife. Yes, I know Terry's been given one of her own, but she's a lot older even if she isn't a boy. Oh, very well, very well, my head's splitting with your noise; anything for peace and quietness!")

Anything for peace and quietness.

Anything?

What would be the "anything" that she, Terry, could do to bring peace and quietness back where they belonged, at the heart of a Nativity Play?" Christmas in the Market Place" — if they did it now, if they persevered with rehearsals and acted it as they had planned in front of Uncle Ted and everybody in the church on Sunday evening, it still couldn't be good; any other play might have been acted even while they were all quarrelling; not this one; it had to *feel* sincere. And suddenly Terry felt deeply ashamed on behalf of all of them that they should have boldly chosen a play which had a sort of privilege attached to it, a play all washed in love for Mary and Joseph and the Angel and the Birth of the Christ-Child in a stable . . . and yet dared to oppose the story, not humbly let it have its way with them. Had she herself been wrong to oppose Lal when he wanted to change the scene of the Three Kings? No harm in that surely? No, but in Lal's *way* of wishing it, grabbing at the part of Baltazar for the fun of blacking his face and wearing the robes of a king, when already he was playing a part finer than any king: he was Joseph, the quiet man who stepped back and without fanfare of trumpets acquiesced in yielding up all his "rights". And Lal had preferred the boastful cocksure part of Joey the gipsy, saying it was worth a lot more than Joseph — Oh, *what* had happened to Lal? How *could* he care more for any fun or any dressing-up, when he was to say to the shepherds: "'Enter, and worship. He is here.'"

Rosalind entered in a great hurry, and stopped short at the unexpected sight of Terry in meditation . . . as though she had nothing else to do, as though she had not a care in the world.

"Hello, Terry. I thought you children were rehearsing?"

"They are; they'll want me; I was just going!" Not very convincingly, Terry sprang up and made a dash for the door.

"Do you know where Nanny is? I must have my dress ironed for this evening."

"She was in my bedroom just now," Terry called out from the stairs.

The bathroom? It was a lavatory too, and the only place where one had a right to lock the door. There, at least, was immunity from people chivvying you up and down stairs and all over the house, chivving you back to rehearsal before you had *settled* anything . . . Yes, her glorious Rosalind had just become people-who-chivvied-you, and that showed what an utter fool you had been to flare round on Lal and destroy their Christmas play on account of a goddess who didn't exist except as a tiresome girl who could easily have waited to get her silly old dress ironed.

Terry sat down on the edge of the bath and meditated anew on St. Joseph, who would never have made such a song and dance over a duck-ball! She had fallen about a million miles short of St. Joseph, in wanting hers to be the only duck-ball. "If we — I — we — any of us had been more like him —"

From the very start, he had held a strange fascination for Terry, more than the other parts in the Nativity, more even than the part of the Virgin Mary, though she was playing that herself. Only rarely did she speak of him to herself as "Saint" Joseph, because in the play she had come to know him as a real man in real trouble, before he became a bearded saint in churches; a living man and Mary's husband, sheltering and protecting her and the Infant Jesus. He was so good, her Joseph, so gentle and humble; he looked after everybody and asked for no reward; never drew attention to himself; he simply didn't bother about importance; he was the least important person in the story, willing to efface himself and keep in the background. Terry could not have shaped into words, even without having to utter them aloud, what she dimly realised gave St. Joseph his true claim to her impulse of worship: that in faith and for love's sake he had accepted a scheme of things whereby he would have to surrender importance for the rest of his days: "How could he bear never even to think Yes-but-where-do-*I*-come-in? —"

Someone rattled the door handle . . . And refusing to believe the bad news that it was locked, rattled it again more impatiently. At once Terry turned on the bath.

"Who's in there?" shouted Roddy above the noise of running water. No need to answer. She sat quite still. When she heard him stump away down the corridor, she turned off the water because the torrent kept her from thinking. Then Roddy's voice from farther away:

"But I *can't*. Someone's having a bath. I'll have to go down to the kitchen lav."

"Ought to be more in a house this size," grumbled Nanny Curtis. "Who's in there?" she demanded, as one having the divine right over soap and sponge and the cleansing of the inner ear.

This was persecution. Quickly Terry turned on both taps again, and shouted through the roar: "Me. Terry."

"This ain't your right time for the bath," shouted a baffled Nanny through the door. "Eleven in the morning indeed! What next!"

Terry did not in the least know what next, so she remained silent. With the persistence of Love Locked Out, Nanny went on rattling handles and badgering her ex-nurseling: "Lying there for hours as idle as you please, and I'll be bound covered in scented soap —"

(What *did* she mean? — Oh, of course, Nanny's invariable Christmas present to the older girls. Terry had forgotten.)

185

"— not caring who does the bedrooms on this floor and needs to come in. You get out now in a jiffy, Terry, and dress. I'll give you ten minutes."

Terry gave herself seven minutes sitting on the rim of the bath, remembered to wet the (scented) soap; then unlocked the door, leaving it wide open, and fled downstairs.

Anything for peace and quietness. Roddy and Nannie between them had left her with a slightly hysterical need for escape. She recognised her mother's old fur coat on a peg in the hall, slipped it on and ran outside into the air with its wet blowy threat of more rain. Nobody saw her pelt across the garden to the gate that led into the yard and towards a group of barns. One barn, she knew, would be deserted because it leaked badly and had never been repaired. If only you had your own sitting-room — withdrawing-room they used to call it — where you could withdraw till all was blue and never be bothered! While you were still in the children class, you had no right to sit anywhere or to take a bath or to think or — You had to carry your enormous Think about with you till it had gone all glazed and shrunken . . . "Oh damn," whispered Terry, penitent, not angry as before; "I'm being important *again*."

For what rocking-chairs, what withdrawing-room had Joseph and Mary when they came to Bethlehem?

Crackle of straw beneath her as she sank down on to it, the subdued light trickling through a hole in the rafters, a faint musty scent of old fodder, oxen lowing from their stalls across the yard . . . Terry was glad she had taken refuge here, though she shivered a little . . .

186

Nice to feel sweet and spicy with tenderness again . . . to feel even as though she might be on the verge of surrender.

Through darkness, the Nativity glimmered with a real reason for Christmas, beyond mere contemporary celebration by presents and rich meals and the chime of bells at unwonted hours, the excited unwrapping of coloured paper. And now she knew what she had to do to achieve peace and quietness, so that in the heart of them the play could come to life again.

For when you said "anything for peace and quietness", that meant *anything*; it meant atonement, making amends for her personal responsibility at having hurled Christmas, not into a market-place, but on to a battlefield.

Lal would never confess he was sorry; he would become more and more defiant and swaggering, less and less like his prototype Joseph who could be a saint before he became a saint.

And if Lal went on refusing to act with her as Mary —

No, I can't. I can't. Why should I? If I do, he'll believe he was right all along about telling where my shop was, breaking his faithful promise. If he had owned up on Christmas Eve that he *was* sorry and that it was breaking a promise, I'd have stopped in a minute, and we wouldn't have quarrelled, and all our scenes together in the play would be going beautifully as they did at first.

Unless we both stop being right at exactly the same moment, it simply wouldn't be fair. Unfair that I should have to do all the difficult part and Lal none of it.

("It takes two to make a quarrel" . . . Again Nanny Curtis and her ready-made old saws and sayings.)

187

Oh, shut *up*, Nanny! None of those things you were always saying means anything at all. You just said them to keep Roddy quiet, or any of us, while we were still in the nursery. Besides, if it takes two to make a quarrel, it jolly well takes two to stop it.

Wrath died down again; though it was Nanny who used to say it, it was she, Terry, who alone in the twilit barn, once and for all recognised that the power lay with her to make peace. Literally to make it; to be active, not passive; the one of the two who stopped so that then the other would naturally stop as well: — "he couldn't not" — and the quarrel would come *un*made. She could go to Lal — no, it would be *too* hard to have to start her apology while that mocking sparkle was still in his eyes. Easier to write to him, as they were not rehearsing this afternoon anyhow. Leave it on his pillow, and she needn't see him any more after bedtime, and then he would have read her letter before they met again to-morrow for rehearsal. And he would say in his old warm affectionate style: "I've never heard such utter nonsense, Terry! Give up playing Mary simply because we both behaved like a pair of idiots? As though our quarrel mattered compared with the play. Why, I've almost forgotten what it was about, and I bet you have too?" (I have, Lal, honestly I have.) "Come on now, it's ages since we've done our scenes together. We'll get Jonathan to plug away at them the whole morning, and then we shan't be so bad for the dress rehearsal. We've got Sunday morning, too. Oh gosh, Terry, I'm glad you wrote me that letter!"

Yes, well, but meanwhile the letter still had to be written. No half-measures either, if she let herself feel resentful inside, or even worse, self-righteous and strongly conscious that she had been the one in the right; if giving-in were conditional, her surrender wouldn't be true, wouldn't link, wouldn't make sense. "Peace and quietness" — she had a flying glimpse of the phrase illuminating space as it rushed through towards a now believable heaven . . . with all mankind at one with Terry and Lal in their atonement of declaring they would do anything for peace and quietness, all mankind acting by Nanny's axiom that it takes two to make a quarrel.

Terry got up. The church clock chimed. She counted the strokes: twelve. Her legs ached; it would be nice to soak in a hot bath before lunch, to take away this stiff cramped feeling in all her limbs. Plenty of time later on to write the letter. Her secret intention, as unseen she slipped into the house by a side door, was not altogether free from mischief . . . They would have finished now doing the bedrooms; those old fuss-boxes who called themselves so grandly the Staff, always had their dinner at twelve o'clock.

A few minutes later, the bathroom door was locked again and the taps turned on, while Terry stripped. A nice *full* bath, and let the consequences rip! She lay back contentedly in wreaths of steam . . . *Good* Terry, doing the sensible thing so that she shouldn't catch cold! The grown-ups would be pleased with her . . . perhaps. And more than perhaps, they had better not know.

What a strange long Think it had been, and in all sorts of funny places, since she had dashed away from rehearsal. She hoped that with the weight of their feud lifted, Lal would rapidly work up the Joseph and Mary scenes. Beginning from to-morrow.

Yet in spite of the letter preparing itself in the genuine spirit of sacrifice and abnegation, it did not occur to her that by this time to-morrow, she might not be playing Mary at all.

CHAPTER
TEN

Flushed from her nice hot bath, and feeling deliciously clean inside and out, Terry devoured her lunch with a relish that she certainly had not known for several days. Good luck was eating out of her hand, so to speak; for going downstairs, Erica delivered a message, in her capacity of go-between from producer to leading lady in partial disgrace, that when they had stopped rehearsing that morning —

"After you ratted," put in Roddy.

Jonathan had gone up to London by an earlier train than he had intended, taking Lal with him, to see about the hiring of their costumes; and that their one rehearsal in the church to-morrow afternoon was to be for lighting and positions only.

"Not a dress rehearsal?" For the moment Terry had forgotten she had stepped backwards into unimportance and might no longer be arrayed as the Virgin Mary; or perhaps she did not really believe her sacrifice could lead to any such definite result; it was just a sacrifice swimming in a haze; someone had to lay down self for the sake of the play, and she had elected to be that someone . . . And of course her letter to Lal had still to be written; one more horrid and actual thing not yet done; there had been no time before having her bath. Once written and delivered and read, her "sacrifice" accepted, the future was blurred in a sort of golden smoke ascending to heaven —

So she was able to ask Erica about the dress rehearsal so naturally, in a voice so free from overloaded emotion, that Erica looked at her in surprise at the startling change, remembering the recent trouble, before answering:

"The dress rehearsal is to be here, not at the church, Jonathan says. We've got to parade in front of him to-morrow morning, and he'll tell us if we're all right. But he said our costumes didn't matter nearly as much as where we come in and stand and move and all that part of it. Judy told me that production was all he really cared about; for instance, how the lights are shone on me and you in our Annunciation scene, which is really the big scene of the play, isn't it? And as one of us is an Angel, the lighting would have to be sort of extra-special."

By this time they were at table; and with Lal away, and Terry in this sudden happy mood, Clare on her side and Erica a tactful little neutral, the children chattered away — about the play and their costumes and the "ambers" and what Judy reported of her brother's intentions and what it would be like actually doing their parts at last in the church itself — under no restriction from the grown-ups perpetually bidding them give their elders a chance to be heard. Though apparently the elders did not very much desire to be heard; it was their turn to be oddly silent; silent, and, Roddy reflected, horridly grumpy except for his father whose taciturnity

192

was always normal and kindly, and Grandpa chattering away with Rosalind about their tea-party yesterday at the Kennedys'. Roddy debated whether he should say aloud: "What's the matter with you all?" Would it help? He pulled Erica down so that he could ask her in a whisper.

"Roddy, of course not," she whispered back. "We pretend to take no notice."

Roddy whispered again, rather more audibly. Erica nodded:

"Yes, I expect it might easily be that, so go on taking no notice." For her brother had wondered if all the grown-ups, every one of them except perhaps Auntie Sorrel who had started looking quite cheerful, were suffering from having drunk too much at Grandpa's birthday dinner last night, after the children had withdrawn? Terry was on Roddy's other side, so with a broad grin of pleasure at his discovery, he had to whisper his theory to her too . . . Before Doe, looking martyred by a sick headache, reminded him that whispering at table was extremely ill-mannered, besides being a very irritating habit.

"Well, but you wouldn't like me to say what I've been saying out loud either," Roddy argued. "You'd say it was making remarks. So what am I to do when I've got a special thought about something?"

"Wait till you can put it in a book," his father advised him.

"What? When am I to?"

"After lunch."

After lunch, Terry had meant to write her letter to Lal; but now he was away in London till late, she need not write it till after tea. She would *for certain*, then. And lay it on his pillow before he returned, so that she might hear no more of it till to-morrow morning. And by that time . . . oh, by that time . . . the golden haze once more descended. The immediate future was a gift; her time between lunch and tea was her own; she could use it as she pleased; lie on the rug in front of the schoolroom fire and read an enticing new story "Party Frock", which Auntie Tan had given her for Christmas.

And at that moment Nick decided his existence here had become intolerable since Christmas Day when he had been fool enough to quarrel with Tan — (I didn't quarrel with her. I haven't quarrelled with her. I can't help it if she minds so terribly just one thing that perhaps I ought not quite to have said to Doe!). So he threw out an invitation to all four children ("I know it's no good including you with the juveniles, Rosalind!") to come in with him to the pantomime at Fordingbridge, their nearest town.

"If I can get a box, that is; there wouldn't be an earthly chance to-morrow; but perhaps as to-day's between Boxing Day and Saturday, we might."

A clamour of delighted acceptance from Clare, Terry, Erica and Roddy, was checked by Doe saying:

"Roddy and Erica can't, I'm afraid, Nick. They're going to a party at The Chestnuts."

"Mummy, we're *not*. After you'd accepted for us you let them know we couldn't because we'd be rehearsing every single afternoon. You told Mrs. Lambert-King, and we told Pamela and Dick directly we began the play, that after all we couldn't come."

194

"Yes, but you see you're not rehearsing this afternoon as Lal and Jonathan have gone to London."

"Yes, but then we can go to the panto."

"No, Roddy, that would be very rude to Mrs. Lambert-King. As you *are* free, you and Erica, and I had originally accepted for you, rehearsing was your only true excuse not to go."

"But we'd rather go to the panto. We'd a million times rather."

"Rather's nothing to do with it, Roddy. I've already rung up Mrs. Lambert-King."

"Without consulting us?" shouted Roddy furiously. And even Doe had to smile.

"Yes, my son, without consulting you. You always enjoy parties, and this, I hear, will be a specially nice one with a tree. Erica quite understands. And even at your age, you can't play fast and loose with invitations."

"It can't be playing what-you-said-just-now not to go because we're rehearsing, even if we do go to the pantomime instead because we're not."

"You've got something there," remarked his father, *sotto voce*.

Nick and Tan, somewhat relieved that this strong breeze had sprung up between Roddy and Doe to divert their own treadmill of thinking, waited attentively for Erica's choice of behaviour in the matter, good or bad:

"I do see what you mean, Mummy, in a way; but wouldn't it be even ruder, when you first accepted and then unaccepted and Mrs. Lambert-King has filled our places because it isn't a very large dining-room, and I expect there'd have been a present for each of us on the

195

tree, so she'd have to get two more quickly if Roddy and I came *after* she'd asked two other children instead of us — mightn't it be perhaps a bit more considerate to go to the pantomime and not embarrass her by coming after all at the last minute?"

Anthony nodded approval: that was quite ingenious, too; both his children, he considered, were putting up a good show. He was not going to interfere, but he hoped Doe would let them get away with it.

But Doe was not feeling benevolent; and Erica's sweetly reasonable arguments exasperated her almost as much as Roddy's open wrath.

"You'll both go to your party," she decided. "And I'll take you to the pantomime next week or the week after, which will be just as good. You're all getting too overexcited with this play, and I'll be glad when it's over."

Frustrated, and aware from her tone that there was no more to be said, Roddy nevertheless said it. Wherefore Anthony sent him out of the room. He appreciated his son's point of view that it would be not at all the same, tamely to be taken to the pantomime with his mother and Erica the week after next, as being taken by Nicholas, a man and a hero, this very afternoon, in a box. But perhaps it would have been better not to have said so.

("That means I shan't be able to write my letter after tea, but it doesn't matter, because home by about six o'clock will give me plenty of time. It needn't be a long letter. I expect it will be quite a short one.")

Going to the telephone, Nick paused in the doorway, and looking at Tan, asked humbly:

"I suppose — you wouldn't care about joining us?"

196

Tan shook her head.

Oh, all right; sorry I asked. He did not say this aloud, and tried hard to keep himself from thinking what fun the expedition would have been had she remained in that enchanting mood which had so surprised and delighted him on his return to England, only a week ago to-day. Oh well . . . how could he guess she would fly off the handle simply because his careless tongue had upset Doe, who anyhow had always been jealous of her? Controlled jealousy; not even honestly acknowledged; the very worst kind . . .

Nick called out to Terry and Clare that he had fixed it all up and the local taxi would be fetching them in five minutes; so they pelted upstairs to get ready, carefully not looking towards Roddy kicking the hall-table as though it were the social world he was learning to loathe:

"Hell blast! hell blast! hell blast! hell blast damn —"

("Or there might just be time before supper, or tonight after I've gone to bed — no, because I'd have to get up again and put it in his room, and Clare would ask me about it. Never mind, there's plenty of time, plenty of time, plenty of lovely time!")

Time was sparkling again and running swift; a stream in the sunlight, dew on the grass, freshness in the parched air.

And when they came home, exhilarated and talkative, they were even later than Terry had expected; for doing the thing in style, Nick had treated them to a sort of hybrid meal at the hotel after the show; and because it was still difficult to get proper cakes and ices, ordered all sorts of fascinating adult things that one did not usually have for tea. Meanwhile, Jonathan had telephoned from London with a brief message that he needed Lal who would therefore be spending the night with him, as they would be back late with plenty to do and a new scene to write in.

From Terry's point of view, nothing could have been nicer; once more with a clear conscience she could postpone writing her letter; that letter which was going to be so perfectly easy to compose and would only take a minute.

Clare remarked while they were undressing:

"You know, Lal's simply adoring all this."

"What, the play?" Terry felt a little self-conscious over Lal . . . But there was no point in confiding her purpose in Clare whom it did not directly concern; except that like all of them, she would be relieved and happy at the result, when they could swing back again into rehearsing with all their hearts instead of with just a few shreds of it for "Christmas in the Market Place" and the rest occupied with their own wars.

"Not exactly the play. But being suddenly so thick with Jonathan, as though they were both grown-up fellows and all of us only kids. Swell for him. Going up to London together, and I suppose being consulted over our costumes, and coming back late, and sitting up with Jonathan to write in a new scene; having all three kings was Lal's idea, anyhow. You see, he'll be mighty shot with himself when we all meet at the church."

Terry hugged her secret tighter. Clare was her ally against Lal because of the clown-box, but soon there

198

would be no more alliances and no more against. Soon the nightmare would be over.

"Is it your bath or Erica's or mine to-night? I forget."

Terry laughed and went on laughing.

"Well, honest, Terry, I don't see what there's to laugh at in that?"

"It's between you and Erica."

"Are you sure? I had a sort of an idea —"

"I don't want a bath."

"What are you being so sacrificing about, all of a sudden?"

And that set Terry off again.

"Dirty little pig," remarked Clare amiably, as she went off with her exotic American sponge and American bathsalts.

Terry had been sleeping so badly since Christmas Eve, that her rested mind allowed her to over-sleep; so her letter to Lal was not written, as she had intended, in a leisurely contemplative fashion between six and seven-thirty on the morning of Saturday December 28th; but scribbled frantically on the corner of the dressing- table after Clare had already gone down to breakfast with a warning:

"You'll be late!"

She should have given herself more time to write a Really Wonderful Letter; and it only just occurred to her that she had omitted last night to think up a way of getting it to Lal, now the pillow-delivery was off, leaving only the one means she had hoped to avoid: personal delivery.

But when Jonathan came striding in with his usual look of menace (just in case anyone should deserve menace) Terry was saved again; for he had left Lal at the church competently carrying on with a weird bewildering business professionally referred to as "batons", "spots", "floats", and so forth. ("A week's work at least," said Jonathan.) It was plain, however, that he was pleased with his assistant and trusted him to be intelligent even without supervision. Terry realised thankfully that here was yet another reprieve, and that there would be time for her after lunch to write a *proper* letter, that Really Wonderful Letter moving in slow elaborate circles round and round in her mind. So the dress parade proved plenty of fun; and their Biblical costumes modified or rather gaudified by ramshackle gipsy notions of Biblical probability in a French market-town, were not too solemn to cumber their high spirits. Sorrel was called in as needlewoman to do a quantity of hasty alterations on the spot; chosen as less likely to be maddening than Nanny; and they were all pleasantly, because legitimately, late for lunch.

When Terry managed to settle herself down afterwards to chase a mood of pure composition, the mood would not be chased; and her many attempts at a Really Wonderful Letter proved far more inadequate than the unlaboured missive she had scribbled in a tearing hurry before breakfast. So she finally decided in despair to use that one, and tore into tatters all her elaborations of remorse.

It was about half-past four when she laid hold of Roddy:

"Look here, Roddy. Will you do something for me?"

"Depends," said Roddy, playing for time.

"Will you take this letter round to Lal? At once?"

"Who's it from?"

"Me."

"Well, but what d'you want to write letters to him for? You'll be seeing him in half an hour."

"Half an hour won't do. I want him to have it *now*. Please, Roddy."

Roddy took the letter reluctantly, for Terry and Lal had quarrelled, and he was on Lal's side. Nor did he share his sister's trotting passion to act as go-between, nor her unappeasable curiosity either. The grown-ups were always picking on him as a convenient bearer and messenger, but Terry was no grown-up; and Terry had gone to the pantomime yesterday while he had been despatched to a silly old party where there was dancing, dancing with little girls, and no conjurer, and no candles on the tree, just silly little dogs and lambs and horses and things that shone a bit in the dark. So why should he be in a hurry to run errands for Terry?

But he did not want her to see him hanging about, so presently he dawdled forth. And met Nicholas returning from a long solitary tramp over the Downs.

"Hallo, Roddy, where are you off to?"

"Church," replied Roddy, a statement both true and strange. "We're rehearsing there, but I'm early. Uncle Nick, how much are you going to put in our silver collection to-morrow night?"

"Sixpence."

Roddy was shocked.

"Were you expecting more?" Nick inquired innocently.

"If each person only gives sixpence, the Vicar won't be able to buy his dossal."

Nick was speechless at such erudition. Roddy grinned, quite aware of the sensation he had produced by echoing, via his mother and Erica, Mr. Crichton's exact term for the rich drapery to be hung over the reredos.

"Uncle Nick, have you seen that picture? Come and see it now and then you'll know it's simply *got* to be covered up; it's frightful. Uncle Nick, if you saw it, you'd give more than sixpence; I shouldn't be surprised if you didn't give four half-crowns."

"I'll settle for three," said Nick, walking along with him, "if you're not exaggerating about the picture."

The church was empty of worshippers; Lal and Jonathan, sweating in a tangle of flex and trouble, were too absorbed in their spasmodic dialogue on such mysteries as baby spots and dimmers and amber and steel-blue jellies, to notice the entrance of one airman and one minor member of the company. Nick and Roddy stood in the centre of the aisle in undisturbed contemplation of Abraham's Sacrifice of Isaac, with a much becurled ram ostentatiously caught in the thicket.

"*There!*" said Roddy.

. . . Nicholas spoke at last: "A noble work of art. Abraham can't have combed his hair for a week."

"Isaac's is all sleeked down and damp, the way Nanny likes mine."

"Yes; and there the resemblance ceases. But I see your point, Roddy; future generations must be protected."

202

"So you *will* give more than sixpence?" Roddy persisted, accompanying him out of the church again.

Nick vowed a heavy subscription into the silver collection — "To-morrow night already? You haven't allowed yourselves much time. Good luck."

Nick strolled off towards the Manor; and Roddy re-entered the church in a hurry, for he saw Clare and Erica approaching, and it suddenly occurred to him that he had been a dilatory messenger (not that it mattered) and Terry's letter to Lal was still undelivered and crumpled up in his pocket.

"Here's a letter for you, Lal."

"Letter for me? Who from?"

"Terry."

Lal did not want just now to be bracketed with Terry in Jonathan's eyes. The latter was already eyeing the envelope with sardonic amusement; for since the rehearsal had been destroyed yesterday morning solely by Terry's idiotic scruples, he had seemed to adopt Lal as an equal in age as well as in sense; a kinship so gratifying to Lal's pride that he would not forfeit one moment of it for any of Terry's nonsense; sending him letters by Roddy as though it were a kids' squabble, a girls' squabble! That journey up to London with Jonathan, their sophisticated lunch at the Ivy, that was the thing; Jonathan knew all the stage celebrities, and at least two of them knew him, and one he introduced to Lal. And then the initiated way in which Lal had helped make their selections at the Costumiers. And in the evening they had visited the church and discussed the production itself from all its angles; Jonathan did not

203

seem to think the acting was important at all "except from the obvious reactions of an ignorant bourgeois audience". The Three Kings scene, for instance, was to be almost entirely a question of production and would take quite a lot of doing.

Lal was convinced (and rightly) that any notice paid him by Jonathan sprang not from capricious favouritism, but along a hard single-minded track of recognition that his ideas were genuinely of use in this production, and that a quick-eyed lieutenant was more than necessary. So he was rapidly advanced to assistant producer and Jonathan's right hand, without the latter concerning himself whether the post might be harmful to a boy's arrogance. What could it matter?

"Has she got over it?" asked Jonathan, standing up and filling his pipe.

Knowing Jonathan had not the remotest notion what it was that Terry might or might not have "got over", Lal was certainly not going to put his own promotion in jeopardy by going into long details of young Terry's apparent attack of penitence. He skimmed the letter hastily, did not believe she could mean it about giving up the part of Mary . . . and as co-producer, went on discussing exits and entrances with his chief till the rest of the company had assembled.

Terry contrived to arrive by herself about ten minutes after Clare and Erica; delayed by nothing tangible except a queer shy feeling about coming face to face with Lal after her letter. She wished that she and he could have already made it up and have just reached her first cue in rehearsal, so that she could slip straight into her part with no more tension or averted looks or hate raging in the air; the torn edges of their feud perfectly healed . . .

For once, Jonathan did not appear to have noticed that anyone was not sharp on the hour appointed. He and Lal were deeply absorbed in a debate on whether the Stable scene with the two girls Sally and Pat — (looped in by the gipsies to do the ox and the ass, and appended at the end of "Christmas in the Market Place" for possible inclusion) — should or should not be done? Jonathan was doubtful, for practical reasons; but Lal, whose ambitions were soaring, argued eagerly in its favour:

"It'll be terribly short otherwise, cutting out the whole of Part III with old Anna and Simeon and all that; not that we want *them* in, but this is a jolly little bit with Sally and Pat, and it says here that in the original production they were put in instead of Part III. Do let's have it, Jonathan; *do*. It's fun where Sally practises donkey noises; and I can manage all the extra gipsy lines."

"I don't see how we can. O.K. if we had any more girls, but we're doubling as it is, and too late at this point to get in anybody fresh."

"I could play one of them," Judy volunteered. "The one that hasn't the most to say, because of learning it. I'd like to."

Suddenly Lal caught sight of Terry. And swinging right round towards her, called down the aisle:

"Here, you, Terry . . . I suppose you were just coming over all grand and up-stage in your letter, and didn't mean what you wrote, about being so sorry that you'd give up playing the Virgin Mary? But if you did, what about being a little sorrier and taking on Sally instead? the girl who makes the animal noises?"

Terry stood still as a stone.

"What the hell is all this about?" demanded Jonathan. "Are you bats?"

Lal shrugged his shoulders. But he dropped his conqueror's arrogance, and sounded quite reasonable the moment he addressed Jonathan as man to man:

"*I* don't care if Terry plays Sally or not; but she said in her letter she was ready to chuck being our leading lady, as a sort of noble sacrifice because she doesn't want to go on spoiling the play and all that; so I just thought it might be rather more noble if she consented to play Sally instead of walking out on us altogether. She'd be of some use then."

. . . Silence sounded even more silent in a church with its vaulted roof. To show that he, at any rate, was not in the least subdued by the situation, Lal remarked to the world in general and no-one in particular:

"People never *really* mean it when they say they're sorry. They're simply putting on an act, and are frightfully disappointed if nobody's impressed by it."

Jonathan addressed Terry sharply:

"Come here. I can't talk to you all the way down there." He waited till she was at the foot of the chancel steps. "Is it true you're throwing up your part?"

"Yes," she whispered. And was surprised that even one monosyllable could pass the rasping tightness in her throat. Desperately she swallowed, and managed to say in that same queer husky voice which hardly belonged to her:

"I'll try and do Sally if you want me to."

(The play, she told herself. Never mind Lal now. The *play*.)

Jonathan remarked caustically that it was all very nice and self-sacrificing, and he was deeply impressed, but that it was just necessary in order to perform a Nativity Play to have someone in the part of the Virgin Mary — "Or am I being too conventional?"

"I'm sure Rosalind would do it," cried Erica. Her voice rang clear and high with excitement. "I'm sure she would, Jonathan, because ever since she knew you were producing us, we've guessed, Judy and I, that she's regretted she didn't accept the part —"

"Though it wasn't ever offered to her." Judy had an inconvenient spurt of memory.

"But she's been sick as mud all the same." Roddy for once bore out Erica's notion.

"Shall I run back and ask her now, Jonathan? I think I know better than anyone how to say it so that she'll understand and come. Shall I?"

She stood poised, an Ariel ready for instant flight, awaiting Jonathan's verdict. Which at any other period of rehearsal would have been an uncompromising: "Rosalind? My God, no!" But he and Lal in their prospecting tour of the church the night before, had found all sorts of marvellous possibilities to make a neo-modernistic producer realise what an asset a church could be to a Nativity Play . . . And he was still in a mood to reckon his actors as a secondary consideration, a necessary side-line but no more. Rosalind as the Virgin Mary was a desperate expedient, but he would cut down

207

her lines, and use her as far as possible as a beautiful lay figure in a series of tableaux. So after brief reflection, he nodded assent to Erica, who sped off down the aisle, hand in hand with Judy.

"It'll mean cutting down the Magnificat scene to a bare minimum, but still —" He was speaking to no-one in particular, but Roddy took it that he was being consulted:

"I don't think Ros will be much good. She'll never act as well as Terry did when we first began."

Nobody dreamt that such a fair-minded summing-up could be the cue for Clare to fling out a sensational declaration that she would *not* play Elizabeth if Rosalind were now to be the Virgin Mary:

"I won't play that scene with Rosalind. I couldn't. She'd ruin it. It was my only good scene. I never knew I could act at all until now . . . But it was such a wonderful scene, Terry and I doing it together. You're more than selfish, Terry; you're a deserter, you're a traitor. Can you imagine playing it with Rosalind standing there like a wooden post? Oh, it was the loveliest thing that's ever happened to me when I found it came without even trying. Nothing in the whole world is going to make me do it with Rosalind. Everything's spoilt. I'll play that other girl, Pat, and you can get anyone you like for Elizabeth."

Jonathan's voice fell like an icy douche:

"Kindly tell me how many more of you think of throwing up your parts? Of course nothing's easier than to re-write the whole play from start to finish, and we can have one dear little rehearsal just before the performance to-morrow night. Only —" finally losing his temper in a big way — "only there isn't going to be a performance. I'm through. This is what comes of trying to do anything decent with a pack of quarrelling, yapping kids!"

And he stalked out, slamming the vestry door.

"I hope you're glad," Clare sounded as though she minded more bitterly than any of them, and her look at Terry was like a blow in the face, "I hope you're glad there isn't going to be a play. That's what you wanted, wasn't it? To kill it for all of us. You might as well have said from the start that you never meant to play it; then I'd have known; then I wouldn't have let myself care so much. I *hate* having been on your side against Lal. I never want to act again as long as I live. Acting's damnable. I'm going to 'phone the van Burens to send their car *now*, this very minute, to fetch me, and I'll have a fine week-end . . . What *luck* not to be missing it for the sake of a rotten preaching phoney old Nativity Play!"

And she, too, stormed out through the vestry.

Terry could bear no more. She collapsed prone across the chancel steps, face downwards, her body shaken and torn . . .

And in horror at finding himself, as he thought, alone with a girl crying more piteously than he had ever heard anyone cry before, crying as though now she had begun she could never stop, Roddy slipped out of the church, his feet stumbling over the grassy mounds of the graveyard, to remove himself as quickly as possible from sight and hearing . . .

Safely beyond the gate, he met Rosalind escorted by Erica and Judy; Rosalind in a sweetly helpful mood, ready to undertake the part of the Virgin Mary at the eleventh hour, ready to acquiesce in any arrangements Jonathan put forward, brimming over with sympathy and understanding of his plight. She intended to take him aside for a moment before he began rehearsing her, and tell him the children did not really mean it, children were always a little un-co-operative but they probably would be good as gold when it came to the actual performance . . .

"Jonathan's chucked it up," Roddy informed them. "He's gone home. We're not going to do our play."

From behind the screen of the transept, Lal limped as far as the chancel steps . . . Paused for a moment, standing beside Terry, looking down at her silently as she lay there drowned in grief . . . Then, still in silence, he went on slowly down the aisle and out of the church.

CHAPTER
ELEVEN

Roddy was never to be sensitive to the moods of other people unless, as in the case of his mother vetoing the pantomime, they directly affected his own will and wishes. In this he resembled his father, equally unresponsive even to his immediate family when they came along expecting him to take an interest in their temperament chart. Where there was need for action, Anthony could and would be swift and kind and extraordinarily efficient, but chasing emotions up and down for the sport of it seemed to him a useless waste of time. The day was not very far off when he and Roddy would smoke a pipe together, and between satisfactory and bulky silences, agree on this subject as on most others.

So the boy received no impression of his encounter with Nick beyond approving that the latter showed such readiness to come into the church with him, see the picture and discuss it without the customary silly postponement of grown-ups: "Presently, old boy"; "Sorry, Roddy, no time now, can't possibly spare a moment"; "Tomorrow, perhaps". On the contrary, Nicholas appeared oddly pleased at being intercepted and delayed. "I'm not surprised," Roddy reflected;

211

"they're all as cross and dull as ditches. I suppose they ate too much trifle at Grandpa's birthday party last night! It *looked* that rich sort, from over the banisters."

Nick had returned from his long tramp over the Downs strangely elated at having decided to take a line which, at the sacrifice of his own pride, could not fail to put things right again between him and Tan; heal the quarrel which was spoiling a Christmas that should have been their Christmas without flaw. Yet though he was braced and tingling at the prospect opening out just beyond his act of humility, he had a natural reluctance to overcome the preliminaries, enter the Maitlands' house and actually start being publicly contrite. Not that he was seeking to postpone it; of course not; not for one instant; he simply wanted to be on the farther side of having done it. *Nothing* should make him postpone it; he knew from his professional war experiences the evils of postponement when an attack was planned. Nevertheless, he was grateful to Roddy for meeting him just then and carting him along into the church: "Can't refuse the little chap." Nick was surprised Doe had remained so obdurate over the pantomime; he understood better than anyone present that her loose promise to escort Roddy and Erica "the week after next" was wholly inadequate. Anyhow he did really want to see this fearsome picture doomed so soon to be eliminated.

He had gone upon to the Downs directly after lunch because like a child who was not wanted anywhere and knew it and yet had nowhere to go, he simply had to put himself somewhere; and where was immunity in a house full of people chivvying you all over the place? Lock yourself in the bathroom, perhaps, or hang about on the stairs . . .? A disconsolate state of affairs now that he was back in England, back again with Tan. A week and a day since he had picked her up in London and they had travelled down here together, joyfully aware that a miracle had happened to their feeling for one another, not by propinquity but even more to be viewed in amaze, while they had been for four years apart.

And now . . . "She won't speak to me, won't look at me, won't even quarrel with me" . . . Yet he was resolved that however desperate his plight, he was not going to quit Brambleford till he could wrest some sense from this too sudden, far too bewildering estrangement. The hours since Christmas Day were crawling grey eternities. He could not very well shut himself up in his bedroom and work on his Revue, polishing and revising it, because he had no bedroom at the Manor where retirement at least would have been less conspicuous than hanging about downstairs, a leper in banishment; his emergency room at the crowded Cock and Feathers had been taken (and paid for) by the Maitlands merely for dossing purposes; his days, they took for granted, would be spent with all of them, a light-hearted member of their Christmas house-party . . . (And at the Manor, as a minor inconvenience, Doe, his hostess, was hating his guts.) Yesterday's pantomime had enlivened three or four hours of what would otherwise have been dragging inactivity, mooching around hoping against hope that Tan at any moment might relent. As for Boxing Day,

213

from first to last that had been a nightmare; though they had all behaved like heroes of a small lifeboat in heavy seas, grimly determined that though Christmas for them had foundered, old Mr. Maitland's eightieth birthday must be saved from shipwreck and disaster.

Nicholas felt better already, striding along high up on the Ridgeway of the Downs, away from those human beings so contemptibly like himself that they could not remain for more than five days in the crystal air of paradise without on the sixth ignominiously being tumbled out, hard and flat. As his mind took this ironic bend, a healthier sign of recovery than just being utterly thwarted and miserable, he sent a rueful salute towards (of all people) his niece Rosalind, conceding her a large share in preserving his sanity all through the long labouring hours of Boxing Day. Had he then been still close to Tan, if they could even have called a truce for ten minutes, they would undoubtedly have discovered a first-class joke against themselves, albeit a joke with a twist in it, in the gratitude they owed (and felt) to Rosalind; honestly acknowledging her success from the moment she stepped forward, golden and smiling, to take complete charge of Grandpa's birthday.

She had happened on Philpotts leaning against the wall outside old Mr. Maitland's room, struggling with some far from abstract emotion, his complexion grey-green: something he must have eaten at his Christmas dinner. He confided in Miss Rosalind that he had been up half the night, and had only just managed not to betray his secret while getting his master ready to be escorted downstairs in triumph to breakfast; Mr.

Maitland would be astonished that he had rushed away, and had not returned to fetch him.

"Oh, *poor* Philpotts!" — Nick could hear her saying it — "you're to go straight back to bed and not worry a bit. I'll look after my grandfather; I'd love to."

They had made a charming sentimental picture, entering the dining-room, the white-haired veteran supported by the fair-haired young girl. (On the following day Mr. Maitland would undoubtedly walk perfectly well by himself; he always did; but on his eightieth birthday he had to totter a little.) Dutifully awaiting his entrance, Doe and Tan and Anthony, Sorrel and Nick, could have hugged Rosalind for providing such a pretty diversion from the normal lay-out; they should have hugged Philpotts, too, for providing the original cause.

"*I'm* looking after Grandpa for his birthday!" she cried merrily, and struck the right note from the start, as though it were no emergency but her chosen treat. And Nick had mentally awarded her at least twice as much as he had ever meant to spend on her wedding-present when that inevitable occasion arose.

His birthday was the only day of the year when old Mr. Maitland elected to get up to breakfast, so they always delayed it half an hour. Unluckily Nick had forgotten this, and arrived from the inn at the usual time, anxious to get breakfast over, so he had to look on while in glum silence Doe and Tan built up a heap of parcels and presents and cards around the birthday plate . . . The whole family must watch Grandpa while he opened them, rippling with bogus surprise. Little Erica, burbling affection, stood at his side helping him undo the knots ("And I've got a new piece to recite to you, Grandpa; you'll like it; it's French. I was afraid with all my Angel part to keep learning as well, I wouldn't be able to, but I have, only you must wait till after breakfast.")

Watching her and Rosalind: "They're a pair," thought Nicholas. The other children made no effort at all to aid in supplying a festive spirit; they had had enough of presents and parcels, and were, besides, tethered to contemplation of their own troubles. Before their release was even decent, they escaped upstairs, without waiting to hear Little Switzerland recite:

"'L'Art d'Etre Grandpére' by Victor Hugo."

("I might have guessed!")

Rosalind had confided in Nicholas that she had had a *little* difficulty with Mrs. Edwards, who on learning Philpotts was out of action for the day, had come forward to offer herself as substitute:

"I had to be *very* tactful, Uncle Nick, when she reminded me she had a right to come next after Philpotts, as she'd once been Grandpa's cook. But she's so old, and it was more fun for Grandpa, I think, for that one day to have me; at least, he told me it was. So I had a good idea: 'Don't you think perhaps, Mrs. Edwards,' I said, 'that Philpotts, when he gets up again, would *mind* much less when he found I'd been looking after my grandfather instead of you? Because if you do, it will mean that Mr. Maitland is bound not to miss him so much; and when people get as old as that, they do sometimes say straight out what's in their mind'. And do you know, Uncle Nick," Rosalind laughed, "I'd

216

completely forgotten that Mrs. Edwards herself was even older. But it was quite all right, and she was very pleased. Have you ever noticed how people never seem to think one might mean *them*?"

And that, reflected Nick, is the most subtle bit of perception that will probably ever come out of this niece of mine.

But Rosalind's star turn was reserved for the afternoon of the Nightmare Birthday, after Grandpa had had a nice long rest, drowsily mulling over the triumph of his little speech at lunch in reply to old General Somebody-or-other proposing his health. She had laid hold of a young man with a car, a young man rich and squat and adoring, and arranged with him that his people, living about twelve miles away, should give a tea-party in her grandfather's honour. As poor Adam Kennedy had been sighing for the smallest sign of attention from this dazzling Princess during two years and more, at once he put at her disposal his parents, their house, their butter, and their accumulated store of petrol for shopping. "Adam and I are going to run away with Grandpa!" Rosalind gaily announced to the others, winding Mr. Maitland into scarves and overcoats. Then, reassuring them in a lower voice: "Don't worry; I'll look after him and get him back in good time not to be too tired for dinner."

Another old general and his wife — or perhaps the same? Nick was beyond noticing — had been invited to dine. And this one too made a speech proposing Mr. Maitland's health on the occasion of his Eightieth Birthday; perhaps the same speech.

It had all been a huge success, and Nick hardly dared think how much more intense their suffering would have been but for the old man's favourite grand-daughter who was not really his grand-daughter at all. "But I'll take damn good care to be in another continent for his eighty first!"

And quite irrelevantly he thought: perhaps by next Boxing Day I shall be married to his daughter; perhaps by then Tan will have forgiven me. Linking up that glory with something small and ridiculous like "*I'm* going to look after Pop all day!" (well, he would be my father-in-law!) made Tan's forgiveness seem more real and possible; made him vow anew that he would find means to melt the frozen stalactites that hollowly dripped from the roof of that inhospitable cavern.

The fatal line "Tan knew all along" had slipped out in an inverted sort of pride on *her* behalf, not on his own; that was another joke he could not share with her, and if not with her, with no-one else. For him to swagger vicariously that Orlo had cared for Tan as deeply as Tan for Orlo — was ever such a fool? Surely she must perceive an exquisite humour in this: that the boy who had given her his single-minded love was still moved, more than fifteen years later, by an irresistible compulsion to bring it home to Doe's complacency that it was Tan who came first with Orlo . . . Tan, Tan, *Tan*! For Doe had never vividly enough realised Tan's attraction; let her hear it now in five plain words: "*But Tan knew all along . . .*" Like a knight in the lists, but a knight of rueful countenance, he challenged all comers to produce a rival to the Queen of Beauty! He was so absurdly proud of Tan, so incredulous that Orlo could even for five minutes have preferred someone else.

"But then . . . what did I *want*?" Nick tried to puzzle it out, bring his madness to some less fantastic conclusion. What I suppose I wanted, Tania, was for Orlo to have paid you the due of his undivided passion; but for you, my sweet, my beloved, to have been my girl and only mine from the start, and a little sorry for my poor pathetic elder brother. And for Doe to have been — shall we say non-existent? *My* arrangements, I grant you, not God's. God's are undoubtedly much much funnier, but have led us at last to a pretty situation: a trio glooming in the same house and not on speaking terms during this Christmas of Peace and Goodwill in the Year of Our Lord 1946 — "And I dare say that's roughly what it will lead to all over the world in the Year of Our Lord 1956, but that doesn't help me with Tan now."

Yet he was conscious of power potential within him, as he strode along the level track where the Romans had once marched; carelessly slashed at the long withered grasses. His blood, sluggish from inaction of the last few days, was once more pounding through his veins. Could he but encounter Tan up here and now, away from the rest.

"'Ill met by moonlight, proud Titania!'"

"'What, jealous Oberon? . . . I have forsworn his bed and company.'"

What was the next line?

Then Nick laughed aloud as it came back to him, not an altogether wise or conciliatory retort: "'Tarry, rash wanton, am not I your lord?'"

Tan, listen. Tan, I *like* Doe. I like her *most* awfully. Often I said to Orlo: My sister-in-law commands my entire devotion. Lord Ronald, I said, this lilywhite doe whom you've brought into the family is the nonpareil of womanhood.

(Like hell she is! Give me a dark woman every time. That breed of blondes, Doe, Rosalind, Erica, you can see them multiplying to inherit the earth.)

Nick could not bear blondes. They existed merely to fill the need of an hour . . . since as a boy of sixteen he had accepted that Tan was not for him. Because if it could not be Tan, he set himself against any substitute dark woman. Blondes! A cheap term for all the Does and all the Rosalinds and Ericas; picture-gallery of blondes; parliament of blondes — (As though he would allow even his innermost thoughts to refer to Tania as "a brunette"!)

What fortune-teller could have foreseen in the jargon of her trade, that he, a man-between-colours returning to a dark woman across the water, should find by a miracle his dark woman not yet married to (for instance) a fair man whom she had met at the cross-roads?

Miracles. According to Nick's unthankful belief, miracles apparently happened of their own volition. A miracle, to him, was the rope-trick: a rope was thrown up in the air . . . and someone, no matter who, pulled it taut for the climber. If the miracle crumpled up and the climber fell, naturally you could blame God for that, yet repudiate God from any successful miracle. If praying had been of avail, he would have prayed to grow more like Orlo in her sight; but he had always scotched the impulse, arguing that as no man could add a cubit to his stature . . . Yet his own sweetest, most breath-taking miracle had happened when he had walked in on Tan a week ago; and not expecting him, she had cried out, startled, before she could check herself: "*Orlo!* . . . You've grown so like Orlo!"

Miraculously she had changed towards him in that radiant moment . . . And they had travelled down together to Brambleford, looking forward to a Christmas more glorious than any that had ever happened before.

And now look at it! Just look at it!

And — (reflected Nick, shedding that unnecessary encumbrance of truthfully seeing himself) — it isn't as though I were quarrelsome by nature. Anybody would think I *enjoyed* quarrelling.

And denying that he could possibly have been the mover and origin of dissension, simply by a mischievous: "But Tan knew all along," he traced the start of it all, the infernal responsibility, to a little farther back: to the duck-ball; to Tan for giving it to Orlo's daughter simply because long ago in Paris they had all been playing with a duck-ball when Doe came into the room. At least *he* had bought no duck-ball; not he; he knew better.

Then where had *he* first come into it? Probably at the moment of seeing that child Terry's face; it had upset him badly; invincible stupidity always did; stupidity was crueller always than cruelty (whatever you may say about me, Tan darling!) Terry, victim to Rosalind's benevolence . . . Rosalind . . . Doe . . . there we go again! Troy's Helen; the blonde and beautiful breed; at any moment Erica, too, might start a forest fire.

He must act rapidly, the moment he got home, at all costs to win back Tan; for if he let her go now without "making it up" — involuntarily he used that childish phrase of desperate exaggeration — he would never, never, never see her again.

Might she have gone already? it was not Tan's way to linger. Then he felt safer as he suddenly remembered Ted was coming down to-morrow morning, and her deep affection for Ted. Ted was her best friend; had been for years; a firm alliance different in essence from her friendship with Nick; she and Ted never quarrelled; Ted could never become in a flash her enemy.

Enemy? "Oh God, I've had enough of this!" *He*, Tan's enemy? He had had a hundred years of combating that preposterous idea, and he was dog-tired. Why had he thrown away, careless as a god of abundance, the miracle for which he had waited and waited, just for the sake of a cheap score over Doe? Yet had not Doe been irritating him for even longer than a hundred years?

Tired of enemies at home and abroad . . . Even when you've scored and scored — what's in it, after all? Scoring on points will never bring Tan to lie still in your arms. So let them have the last word — "Wait, that's the title of a poem I rather like; old Matthew Arnold:

> "Let the long contention cease,
> Geese are swans, and swans are geese.
> Let them have it how they will,
> You are tired, best lie still."

Not quite right, but near enough. Give them the last word then . . . and lie still . . . with Tan. Sleep . . . with Tan — "And I *mean* sleep!" Nick scowled fiercely at whoever might be challenging his choice of a ready-made phrase. For how could he ever hope to know real sleep unless it were with Tan after the strong rush of his love fulfilled at last?

If only he could be sent direct inspiration how to fetch her back to him. Suppose he left it to another piece of miraculous staff-work, since now he had proved that miracles could happen to him as well as to the Orthodox who knelt in pews and prayed in ritual terms? He found himself placing an odd reliance on receiving an order from some sort of . . . headquarters, the instant he reappeared down there at the Manor, ready to surrender arrogance all along the line; ready to say he had been wrong, he was sorry, he wouldn't do it again. Tania could not but relent when a true penitent knelt before her in sackcloth and ashes, peas in his shoes, humility his dwelling-place.

. . . Glinting and vanishing and glittering forth again through the massed clouds, Nick saw their celestial city; a city without battlements.

Towards five o'clock on Saturday evening, Anthony Maitland found himself at that stage of planning a new book when he needed an audience; not to applaud him, nor (heaven forbid) to help him; he abhorred helpfulness; but to clarify his thoughts, which by experience he had always found he could do better aloud, as though justifying them against objective argument, before he began on the actual writing. It was more than anybody's life was worth to argue, though even that was better than too ready, too eager manifestations of indiscriminate approval: his wife's speciality; Doe had never been able to learn that he required no personal collaboration; in fact, that her low appreciative chuckles, even at the right places, could put him completely off. That was why he never dared take the risk of inviting her alone to listen to him at this juncture, when he had a rough lay-out of how he intended to treat his theme but was not yet wholly satisfied. On the other hand, he could not, without hurting Doe pretty badly, invite any of the others instead to be his sounding-board; at all events, not one of the other women, his sister or Sorrel: "Come along to my study while I read you what I've done of my new book "would be enough for Doe to lock herself in her room in one of those incongruous fish-wife rages that on rare occasions had sent vibrations through the whole house.

Nick would be best; Nick was intelligent enough to understand that no alert intelligence was required of him. So Anthony gathered up his notebooks and went in search of Nick. He was not to be found, however, and Philpotts said he had seen him take the path up to the Downs much earlier in the afternoon.

Regretting that his son Roderick was not quite of an age to supply the type of audience required, Anthony sought out Doe and Sorrel and Tan; and without consideration for the separate employments in which they were occupied, mustered them, glum and furious, in the lounge:

224

"The children started me off, gave me the germ for a new book, and a title; I don't know yet how it's going to work out or if it'll work out at all: The Psychology of Quarrels. They'll probably have made it up now, but they *did* quarrel and when they least wanted to, at Christmas, their first Christmas together since war began; peace on earth, goodwill to men — and then some small trumpery thing set them off, Rosalind given a toy in duplicate, wasn't it? A match struck in the dark, flung down — and a flare and a conflagration. The whole world apparently wants peace and rest; the whole world declares itself glad the war's over. Doesn't everyone in the thick of a quarrel always deny any wish on their part to have brought it about or to be keeping it up? I expect even in the War of the Angels . . . Well, can I show an analogy of war by reducing it to the analysis of single quarrels, in embryo and as they develop?

"Quarrels between lovers can, I think, be discounted as part of an unreal state of mind and body; they must occur and they mean little. I find them the least interesting specimen of quarrel, and their similarity is sickening.

"Most of all in family life, the fundamental causes of a quarrel reach back and are lost in obscurity. A family row is hardly ever concerned with — I can't get this sentence finished; my rough note says 'rarely about what they seem to be about'; that's enough for the moment.

"There's a thing every nation at war has to look out for: shedding their nobler characteristics till they

225

become so like the enemy that they're indistinguishable . . . Tweedledum and Tweedledee agreed to have a battle, for Tweedledum *said* Tweedledee had spoilt his nice new rattle!

"A rattle — that's our duck-ball, our small substantial object. Which might bring us to nursery quarrels, schoolroom quarrels, a whole Juvenile Section.

"We're apt to keep children and adults in watertight compartments, but when we come to quarrelling, don't the adults also behave and talk and think in an utterly childish way? Not all the time, of course, but off and on; relaxing too suddenly from some long mental strain.

"*Sharing* as another cause for war. The primitive incapability of human beings to share any damn thing — unless they've made the suggestion themselves and arranged all the conditions; then they like it; then it makes them feel civilised.

"Quarrelling feeds some element in people, some odd craving . . . They can't understand any of their friends standing out and remaining aloof; they demand unreasonable loyalties, and are criminally capable of saying 'So-and-So quite agrees with me' even if So-and-So has desperately managed not to give an opinion at all. Dangerous, that type; quarrels are infectious to an nth degree, but you can't segregate people unless they have leprosy or scarlet fever or something like that. What about segregating the mischief-makers, the incendiaries?" — Anthony paused to scribble a few words in the margin.

"The easiest part, of course, will be actual examples: famous quarrels in history and literature; a whole crowd

226

of them; Voltaire and Frederick the Great; Brutus and Cassius; Stevenson and Henley — an almost perfect quarrel," Anthony declared with the real enthusiasm of a collector. "I'll have to set out one quarrel in detail, and that'll probably be the one; the ashes are still not cold. Capulet and Montague — did anyone ever know *what* those two families were quarrelling about? 'From ancient grudge break to new mutiny' . . . What did old Capulet give old Montague for Christmas when they were boys? Clan and tribal quarrels must have started somewhere, with some visible . . . duck-ball?

"And I can easily devote a whole section to quarrels about property and prerogative, as opposed to the emotional kind. And a sub-section on money and financial dependence.

"Favouritism — now that's a *casus belli* which has been strangely neglected. The horse and the stable — wall psychology: one person mayn't even look over the stable wall, while the other can walk away with the horse.

"*No quarrel would ever be surprising if we knew its previous case-history.*

"People packed too closely together. Housing and Proximity.

"The atom bomb is not, as some think, an equivalent to a change of heart.

"But a change of heart is our only remedy, universal and simultaneous, or it can't be expected to function at all . . . except as a lead to more wars. 'Universal and simultaneous' . . . the coming of the Kingdom of Heaven. But that's not within the scope of the present volume.

227

"Feuds sound out-of-date, like feudal; yet 'feuds' recurred over and over again in old-fashioned stories on the nursery book-shelf. I'll have to look into modern juvenile fiction to find out what Erica and Roddy are reading. I fancy I shan't find feuds; only ponies and speed-boats and aeroplanes and animals of all sorts and sizes.

"A few odd bits and pieces and reminders that I'll have to insert much earlier: a passage on the fatal compulsion in most people, most parties, most nations, to *score*. I'd go so far as to say it's one of the root motivations for quarrel. And absolutely and entirely sterile. Establish a scoring-point over the other person — and what have we got? Nothing. Sterile, as I said. Nevertheless, to see an opportunity to score and not use it, is humanly speaking, very nearly impossible; a losing struggle. Justice, kindness, decency even, remorse, happiness, truth — we'd sacrifice the lot, just to score. What is the inner compulsion, in the devil's name, greater even than a desire for popularity? Because if or when it's proved we're in the right, it definitely makes for unpopularity — and we know it.

"If any one of us could know exactly what any other one of us was thinking about them nearly all the time, most of us would die of surprise.

"After a quarrel between friends, there's little hope that the protagonists, even reconciled, can move back into the main building; though they might make themselves tolerably comfortable in an annexe.

"Look here, if I allow myself to become sceptical and pessimistic at this juncture of my analogy, the whole book needn't be written, and I might as well tear up these notes! My dear Tan, I *know* you didn't say a word; it's all shouting from your face.

"It may be that with the comedians, the clowns, the laughter-makers, lies the only hope of peace for the whole world. In fact —"

Anthony broke off: "I can't possibly go on, with Nick standing there."

"I'm awfully sorry to have barged in," Nick apologised. His entrance had allowed him to hear the last four or five of Anthony's rough notes, and realising at once that something was going on which must not be interrupted, he had remained standing by the door, his own urgent errand suspended. Nevertheless, though silent, he brought in with him from outside such a glow of good purpose, such an irresistible force against which no opposition could stand, that Tan and Sorrel looked across at him in amazement, comparing it with his defiant demeanour of the last few days.

"I'm sorry," he repeated. "I was keeping perfectly quiet and good, wasn't I?"

"Yes, but you were listening."

Nick thought the objection faintly unreasonable: "So were the others."

"Hardly at all. I prefer them not to!" In a testy spirit which accorded ill with his proposed theme of human nature under close impersonal observation, Anthony pushed back his chair, removed his spectacles, and gathered up notes and notebook.

"I seem to have upset the penny-reading." And as Nick spoke the words "penny reading", he perceived his cue, his "orders" how to break through the stiff harsh atmosphere of hostility. He had been right to let it pass out of his own hands, and wait for an illuminated sign on the wall.

("It may be that with the comedians, the clowns, the laughter-makers, lies our only hope of peace.")

"Anthony's had his whack. What about a little light relief? On the old playbills, they nearly always put a short farce after the full-length drama. Would you like it if I read you my new Revue? Some of it, anyhow; the plums. Between ourselves, I think it's quite good fun, and it goes into rehearsal next week. Shall I fetch it? It's over at the Cock and Feathers. Do please humour me and all cry 'Yes, Nick, what a *lovely* idea'!"

His eagerness to entertain them was charming, and especially charming his total disregard of the strife which had been sapping all mutual kindness. Nor was he altogether cheerful and oblivious, which might under the circumstances have been maddening, considered as coming from the prime offender; his look from one to the other pleaded "Let me do this small inadequate thing to amuse you; it's more fun than apologising, isn't it? As long as you'll understand?" And they were compelled to respond without being able to define whether it was art or candour that had won them at least half-way across from the field of war towards his chosen field of the cloth of gold . . .

Sorrel was the only one who actually did pick up: "Yes, Nick, what a lovely idea," but Doe, too, smiled her

230

assent. And he had no need to hear Tan's voice — a swift look between them was enough.

"The script's in a ghastly mess; never mind. I shan't be a moment. Hold everything." He paused on his exit and called back with a grin: "Tell Anthony that he mustn't *dream* of staying!"

For in fact, Anthony had long ago turned out the reading-lamp and gone back to his study, perfectly unaware of lacking in politeness. The same firm will that the three women of his household should be present while he read aloud, rejected with equal firmness any further distraction.

The front door slammed; and Nick's rapid steps receded down the drive.

Tan leant back in the deep arm-chair, her lips curved in a smile at her brother's characteristic behaviour, bracketing him, as she so often did, with his son Roderick. But her smile was tender as well as amused when she went on to think of Nick. She was glad of the brief respite in the dusk till he should return to read them his new Revue. For the first time since "Tan knew all along", she felt able to relax from tension, strangely at peace, though nothing apparently had as yet marked the melting away of their recent unhappy feud: he had been out and he came in, that was all. In the same easy way, after arbitrary command had kept them for over four years missing each other even during their leaves, he had suddenly walked in on her, the Friday before Christmas, not merely Orlo's young brother, but by magic brilliant and unaccountable, grown so like him in the interval that she could not contain herself but had to exclaim in wonder what she had never thought would escape from her to Nick. And he, too, was not prepared for it; she had seen gladness leap into his face like a bonfire on a hillside in the dark . . .

She had been unjust to him during these last few ruined days; he was not fundamentally cruel, she would swear to it now. Tan could not bear cruelty; but it was different, it *was*, when Doe provoked it; Doe had that effect on him. "As though I didn't know, better than anyone else in the world!" Compassion no less than understanding should have kept her from blazing up against him with such intolerance, not only on Christmas Day, but ever since Christmas. She did not deserve his debonair surrender, just now; why had she not surrendered first, instead of leaving that spontaneous grace to an airman weary from the war, glad to have come home? Suppose, while she had been holding him off as a criminal, suppose he had gone altogether. . . instead of just round to the inn to fetch his manuscript?

So Tan resolved that presently, when he had read to them and when the frozen air had melted into warmth and pleasure, she would find an occasion to tell him that she too was sorry. If only they could somehow spend the evening together, she and Nick, apart from the rest. Never mind . . . No hurry . . . To-morrow morning Ted arrived, the darling, for the children's Nativity Play (they had all been selfish as only adults can be when absorbed in their own troubles; but it was not quite too late; probably to-morrow the children would be glad of their help). And so to-morrow would speed towards the evening's performance to give them all, children and grown-up children, another chance not to carry the burden of having betrayed Christmas to another war, infinitesimal but deadly as all wars.

And early on Monday, she and Nick would return to London together.

... Those were Nick's footsteps returning. For all his perception, he could not have guessed that there was no longer any need to read them his Revue; as far as she was concerned, a miracle had already been accomplished for the second time in a week, simply by his coming into the room and being Nick.

Nor had she been as unreceptive as she had seemed over Anthony's terse analysis of the psychology of individual quarrels which lay behind the quarrels of the world. After all, his aphorisms so nearly concerned her, concerned them all, that it was almost comic . . . A jungle hewn down, spaces cleared for sun and light to enter among the intertwining tree-trunks, all from one seed of thought planted by a children's squabble.

Children! Were they all like children, lashing out, slanging one another, past caring what damage they did? (But the real children had been their old selves this morning; perhaps they too had come to terms and were happy again?) Nick would soon know that she had been brushed by the same wing, quickened by the same spirit which had brought him back from the high Downs —

"Wasn't long, was I?" Nick flung himself into Anthony's chair, and switched on the reading-lamp again. "I haven't got a title for it yet, so any suggestions are welcome. As a matter of fact, I wondered if I could call it 'Geese are Swans'? Provisionally, anyhow. How does it strike you? Remember, it's a Revue." His touch of shyness gone, now that he was plunged into actual discussion on his work, he glanced from one to the other, picking up their reactions.

One by one, used to the professional idiom, they tried it out:

" 'Have you been to "Geese are Swans"?' "

" 'I was at the first night of "Geese are Swans." ' "

" 'You simply *have* to see "Geese are Swans"; only they say it's packed out for months ahead.' "

" 'So-and-so asked me what's the best thing on? I said "Geese are Swans" without a doubt.' "

Then, dropping their temporary rôles as casual members of the theatre-going public:

"Yes, Nick, I do rather like it."

"So do I."

"Good. Too many s's, that's the trouble. I don't know — I only just thought of it."

"What inspired you? Us?" laughed Doe.

"Partly." His eyes twinkled; they would have been surprised to hear that it was a meditation on some lines of Matthew Arnold which had brought him a quite satisfactory title for a modern Revue. "People do still say 'All her swans are geese', don't they?"

"No, they don't, my lamb; the other way round: 'All her geese are swans.' "

"O.K. I'll have to write in an opening chorus pretty quick, if that's to be my title. Swan costume; goose costume . . . I think I see it."

"Décor, a pond in a grass circle; farm buildings —" Tan broke off. "Go on, Nick, we needn't settle details for

234

the minute; in fact, they're not for us to settle at all. Who's doing your sets? Joanna Wickham again?"

"Yes. Look here, I'm not going to plug straight through; one can't, with a Revue; not like a play; I'll pick out a few sketches and some of the best lyrics."

The first lyric he read them would without doubt prove one of the romantic song hits of the year when fitted with a suitable tune. Nick was immensely pleased at its reception by his audience of three. Then he read them a couple of sketches. Then another lyric, comic, in quartette form.

"Hard hitting," remarked Sorrel. "England's premier Revue writer is himself again, vain as a peacock and gentle as a sabre-toothed tiger."

"And it's all very well to look as innocent as a whole choir of cherubim, Nick, but where does the Censor come in?"

He looked a little dashed: "I hoped that one would get past; won't it?"

"Not unless he's drugged and insensible."

"I've known him pass worse lines. Oh well, we'll just have to pray he doesn't quite see it. Here's my best of all; my pride and joy. I meant to keep it in reserve till the end, but I'm not sure if I can any longer."

"A sketch?"

"No, a burlesque: 'Take a Pew'. In fact, it's — no, I'm not going to tell you; I want to see how long before you tumble to it." And he repeated on a chuckle: "'Take a pew.'"

"Do stop relishing this pearl of a joke all by yourself, darling. It's so tantalising; let us in."

"You're right, it is a pearl of a joke." And before he could stop himself, he added: "A pearl of great price."

* * *

. . . When there was no longer any possible room for doubt:

"I think you'd better stop there." Tan's voice was hardly recognisable.

(And indignant as Sorrel was with Nick for the heartless parody of Ted and Ted's play, she knew at once that she and Doe could do nothing to avert catastrophe.)

"Stop? But that's not the end. Don't you like it? Is it a misfire?"

"No. A long way from that."

"Well then —" Nick was keenly disappointed and a little impatient. He knew that "Take a Pew" was brilliantly funny.

Tan gave him one more chance.

"You'll *have* to cut it out, Nick."

"I wish you wouldn't be so deadly, ferociously quiet all of a sudden; it's making me nervous. Which lines do you want cut?"

"The whole number."

"The whole — *Why*, in God's name?"

"Your damnably thick place again! Have you forgotten, in the devil's name, that you've a friend called Ted Barnett?"

"I *had* forgotten you're all crazy about that ghastly symbolic muck which he chooses to call a play, so that he can have the luxury of addressing a congregation every night for two and a half hours. Apart from being usual, in a Revue, to burlesque the biggest topical

236

success, I rather hoped it might bring old Ted to his senses when he saw it."

"You haven't been to his play yourself?"

"No, but I read it three months ago, when he sent it out to me. He had no *right* — He's a born clown; when clowns feel they have a message to preach — God, it turns my stomach! I haven't a hope that debunking him in going to shorten his run by even a night, because audiences have a mania for being dumped in pews and made to listen to religious cant; modern reaction from tough stuff. But at least I'll have done my best. The odd thing is that they'll probably laugh themselves sick over 'Take a Pew', all the same."

Flushed with his own eloquence, and still hungering for a little praise, having been given it so abundantly to start with, Nick dropped his rôle of whom-he-loveth-he-chasteneth, and pleaded:

"At least, Tan, you must admit that it's not unfunny."

And Tan gave herself one moment of longing to be back again in that happy reverie of twenty minutes ago, when lazily weaving halo after halo for Nick's head, she had put herself under a spell of believing he was not in reality cruel; only when Doe goaded him into it; exclusively (and justifiably) Doe and no-one else. Pretty rationalisation! Imagine her forgetting, simply because she so wanted to forget, how from the very start of all her frequent quarrels with Nick, they were never isolated quarrels sprung from boy-and-girl high spirits, from refusal to cede this point or that; but could all have been strung together on her protest at an unyielding arrogance incapable of perceiving its own cruelty.

She was aware now that she could do nothing to change Nick. But perhaps she could still intervene to save Ted?

"Listen, Nick —"

"I'm listening."

"I can see you were carried away by the Revue spirit into *writing* it in; but don't, don't *leave* it in."

"Give me one reason why I shouldn't, apart from your personal lech for 'Pearl of Great Price'"

"Never mind my lech — it doesn't come into it. The point is that this burlesque of yours is too cruel for decency. It's not a burlesque, it's a wicked caricature. If Ted goes to see the Revue — and he's sure to, being yours — not only will it hurt him so terribly that I can't bear to think of it, but it may easily shake his essential belief in what he is and what he's doing. He may not be able to play Ceddie Conway any more. That's why you must cut it out."

"I don't *want* him to play Ceddie Conway any more. It would be a damn good thing if he didn't play Ceddie Conway any more. That's why I'm leaving it in."

"Finally?"

"Oh yes. Finally and categorically. And don't suppose, Tan my girl, that you're being tremendously loyal, fighting on the side of the angels or anything beautiful of that sort . . . The nation's brain has deteriorated, and so has Ted's; they flock to bogus sentimental twaddle; it makes them feel good. They need bracing, and that's where I come in."

"I see. A crusader."

Nick shrugged his shoulders:

"I could prove to you that a clown has his own sacred calling, all down the ages. But they grow vain, they betray their clownhood by playing Hamlet; then they lose everything. There are plenty of Hamlets, and we need the clown; clowns bring a necessary cathartic to mankind; the word itself means a purging, a letting-out or release —"

"Take a pew," suggested Tan gently.

At last she had got under his skin. "That's different," Nick defended himself with some passion. "I'm not preaching; I'm stripping a sham. I believe in God right enough; not in your respectful lukewarm way, sometimes picking Him up and sometimes letting Him drop. I don't think He's good, and I'm not going to let Him get away with it. Nor Ted. Nor you."

"Quick and simple, then: if you don't cut out that burlesque from your Revue, I'll never, never, never speak to you again."

. . . And desolation crawled into the room and settled down among them, elated at not being banished after all.

"Forgive me if I appear rude," said Nick, "but you know, I don't call that modest request simple; I call it ridiculously, preposterously and quite incredibly childish."

"Yes." Defeated, Tan pulled herself up out of her chair, and without again looking at Nick, spoke blindly in the direction of where Doe was sitting:

"Forgive me, Doe. I'm a deserter and ashamed of it, but I can't possibly stop here and see Ted. So I'm off home tonight. If I go at once and pack, I might catch the 5.45 up."

Nick waited to see if Tan meant to speak to him direct. Then, without seeming to move in any undue haste, reached the door in time to open it for her. Still nonchalant, he inquired politely of his hostess whether she would prefer him under the circumstances to finish the week-end staying with his friend Major Wimbourne near Oxford?

"I've an open invitation to turn up any time I like. In fact, he particularly wanted me before my Revue went into rehearsal next week; I suspect a pretty sister who will pipe songs for me, in the hope of getting into the chorus."

He was a little curious, though too heartsick really to care as to whether Doe would show up on his side or Tan's in this final phase of their Christmas war.

And because it did not touch any vulnerable spot, she was able to judge the matter true and fair; and told Nick, albeit not with rudeness, that she could well imagine, however much he bluffed it out, he would prefer not to have to encounter Ted . . . So perhaps he *had* better leave at once, and think over the question of cutting out that burlesque.

"But my dear, there's no question of cutting it out. There never was. So it's good-bye, and thank you for my lovely visit. Good-bye, Sorrel —" his brows took an odd twist to match his parting fling: "According to you too, I suppose, exit the devil in human shape. It's nice that some of you have at last found something to agree about."

* * *

Doe and Sorrel were silent for a little while after the discord of this double departure; silent and disappointed . . . it had felt good for them all to be laughing together again.

"It's a shame Tan won't see the children's play," remarked Doe. "They seemed quite in their usual form again this morning. A dress rehearsal, wasn't it?"

"Yes, they graciously permitted me to do a little sewing, a few urgent alterations, before I was hustled out of the way." Sorrel, like Doe, was trying hard to make ordinary conversation with the remnants of normal behaviour still left to them. "Erica looked perfectly lovely as a sort of fair gipsy-in-the-market-place conception of an angel, though I think she herself would have preferred — Why, what is it, dear?" For Erica's sudden entrance alone, at an hour when all the children were supposed to be up at the church rehearsing for all they were worth, was faintly ominous.

She was flushed and breathing hard, as though she had been running: "Please, Aunt Sorrel, could you go to Terry — no, it's all right — I mean, it's not an accident or anything, but she was crying so terribly, and I don't think she ought just to lie there. I've never seen anyone cry like that before."

"Lie there? Lie *where*?"

"On the chancel steps. I was the only one to stay behind when I saw she — You have to forget yourself or nothing's any use; I told her that. But Terry was in such an awful state, I couldn't get her to listen or be reasonable. I told her 'Never mind about me seeing you, but you're years older than Roddy, what do you suppose *he* thought'? And Judy, too. And I told her that she, more than all of us, oughtn't to break down like that."

"Why Terry more than all of you?" Sorrel's tone was stern enough to intimidate almost any child but Erica: "Well it was her fault from the start that they quarrelled and that Jonathan's thrown it up and we're not going to do the play at all."

"Darling, tell us," her mother began, distressed; but Sorrel cut in harshly:

"It might be just as well, don't you think, never to say 'tell us' to Erica, but 'don't tell us'. She's babbled quite enough already."

"But Aunt Sorrel —"

"It wouldn't occur to you, would it, you smug little tinsel angel, that you might try and cover up the fact that an older girl is crying? No, you had to stand over her and say your piece, and then come along here and spill a few more platitudes. Enjoying yourself, aren't you, Erica? There's no pleasure like a really good wallow in disloyalty."

Could it be her kind Aunt Sorrel, this strange woman thrusting at her so unfairly? Erica raised her big blue eyes swimming in tears:

"I haven't done anything wrong. I didn't even take sides. I tried to make them all be friends again. I'm the only one who did."

"You said that before."

Doe put her arm round Erica and kissed her fondly:

"Run away, darling. Aunt Sorrel is a little nervous and upset; she doesn't mean what she said. You were a fine set of pickles, working her like a slave this morning on

242

your costumes. Don't worry about Terry; we'll see she's all right."

Erica hugged her mother and obediently departed; glad, for once, to be off grown-up territory.

It was quite a different Dorothy Maitland, however, who now turned upon her sister-in-law:

"I can't see any need to visit your temper on Erica. She did nothing except bring you a message from Terry."

"She did *not* bring me a message from Terry."

"Oh . . . well!" impatiently.

"Because Terry isn't showing her usual stoic quality, your complacent little daughter had to cash in on it. Couldn't you see, or are you as blind as Erica, that she was delighted to see Terry brought down? There was no need for you to pet and praise her for it, unless you happen to feel the same."

"Sorrel, you're mad. And I won't have Erica frightened and bullied and made responsible for all sorts of petty jealousies that never entered her head. Jumping down her throat like that! She's a very sweet little girl and I wouldn't change her for any stoic. *I've* got no maternal inhibitions, thank God, and so I'm not ashamed of being a natural mother who sticks up for her children. It wasn't normal, on Christmas Eve, when you took Rosalind's side instead of Terry's, over the duck-ball. You don't really love Terry at all . . . I have an instinct in these matters . . . You hate her for being Neville's daughter. If you really loved her, nothing would have kept you; you'd have rushed straight off to the church and taken her in your arms and hugged and comforted her, instead of making Erica cry."

"Would I? You couldn't understand Terry in a thousand years. I suppose you think I don't *want* to rush off at once and hug her and take her in my arms — and do everything she could least bear to remember afterwards when the storm had blown itself out. *I*, hate Terry? I wonder where you fished up that bit of deep deep psychology? You're a fool, Doe, and you're showing yourself even more of a fool than usual. Stay as maternal as you like; it's when you start being profound that Anthony goes off and shuts himself up and works alone. I never knew Orlo, but I'm ready to swear that he didn't stand for much of that, either; he never really talked to you, did he? He was indulgent to you, but he talked to Tan . . . As a wife, you're superfluous. Your second husband is indulgent too, but that's all you'll ever get from either of them."

With every splinter of bone and thread of nerve tugging her towards the front door and the drive dark under the trees, up the deserted road to where Terry lay crying alone across the chancel steps in the dim cold church, Sorrel yet went slowly upstairs, her rage all spent. For there was nothing to do now but wait. You had to be faithful to your code, even when it meant suspense and blind terror. Terry could at least trust her not to yield to the easy instincts of an Awful-Warning Parent with one ewe lamb. "Thank God," Doe had said, "I'm not ashamed of being a natural mother who sticks up for her children . . . It isn't as though you really love Terry at all;

244

you hate her for being Neville's daughter."

Doe — Rosalind — Erica — what a trio when they started creating havoc! As Sorrel paused on the landing, reluctant to open the door and enter the bedroom where she suspected hours of inaction lay before her, she had a vision of Rosalind handing back the duck-ball to Terry, and Rosalind's plausible voice producing her extraordinary form of consolation: "And now we've each got one, so we'll be able to do them together, and that'll be lovely." . . . And next, Erica: "You have to forget yourself or nothing's any use. I told her that. But Terry was in such an awful state, I couldn't even get her to listen. It was her fault from the start that they quarrelled and Jonathan's thrown it up and we're not going to do the play at all."

Someone moved . . . someone who was flung down on the bed . . . Then in an instant Terry had hurled herself into Sorrel's arms; clung there, trembling and sobbing, as though she might never leave go; as though she had never had a mother until this moment.

CHAPTER
TWELVE

Swiftly and tenderly Sorrel undressed a docile little daughter and slipped her into the large double bed, wondering whether she herself had been tossed upwards from a lurching world into a heaven she had never dreamed could be gained upon earth. And meanwhile, still not able to stop crying and hiccuping and blindly stretching out her hand to grope for a clean handkerchief, Terry poured out an incoherent and quite un-Terryish account of what had been happening to her and what had been done to her . . . Jonathan had said . . . and Clare had said . . . Oh, and Lal had said . . . all the way back to the letter she had written Lal after her resolve to discipline self-importance and put things right for the sake of the play . . . Lying on the barn's straw a long long time ago, yesterday morning . . . Sitting on the rim of the bath with both taps turned on and the door locked: "I *must* do something! I must!" . . . Still farther back to their rehearsals, the Joseph and Mary scenes missed out because she had quarrelled with Lal; and back again, right back to Christmas Eve, when she knew Lal must have told where the shop was, her duck-ball shop. None of it mattered very much any more compared with the recent most dreadful moment of all . . . Oh please God, please Mummy, it couldn't be true, it couldn't, that after she had capitulated, laid down arms, laid down her pride, after she had come half-way, nearly all the way, it *couldn't* be true that when she said she was sorry, Lal should not have felt sorry too? Felt it and said it? . . ." I thought the only hard part was to make yourself be the one to say it first. And I hoped we'd have such a lovely rehearsal afterwards, like they were before Christmas Eve, but Lal said I d-did it to be grand and up-stage, and Clare said I thought of nobody but me and had spoilt her one good scene; and Jonathan . . . Oh Mummy, he's *given up the play*! We're not going to have our lovely play! I've never wanted anything so much in all my life, not in that special way, and Erica said it was all my fault."

Yet it was deeply comforting not to have to bother any more about their Spartan code of never giving one's mother a chance to be an ordinary warm hugging mother, but to let her fuss over you as though you were a baby again. So Terry yielded without a struggle. Yielded? More than that, she begged for it with every look, with every movement; decided she need not ever behave well again, never again return to those cold unrewarded regions, but choose to stay in soft feather beds where she could lie at ease, relaxed and imperious. Mothers *ought* to fuss over you and be indignant on your behalf, mothers *ought* to keep on reassuring you that you are good and all the other children bad; that's what mothers were for; an abundance of partisan love expressed in a thousand little physical services. Why, Terry wondered, had she never helped herself from this abundance before?

"I'll sleep here tonight, won't I?" she demanded; "I don't want to go back to my own room with Clare. And then you needn't go down to dinner, need you? Please stay with me up here. Oh Mummy, my head's so hot, I'm going to kick off all these hot blankets and things. Mummy, read to me, read till I go to sleep; not from a *thinky* book; get something I'd like a lot from the nursery. No, don't go away; come back quick. Mummy, I think I'm going to be much too ill for weeks to get up and move, so you're to stay here and look after me, and not go back to work on Monday; I do so hate it when you're away all day at work and leave me alone."

Could any of this be *Terry*? This very childish child, sore and sorrowful, shamelessly articulate, raising no objections to being fussed over? Why, it was the first time she had breathed a suggestion that on her account, Sorrel might stay away even one day from work.

"Of course I will, darling! I wouldn't dream of going up and leaving you behind."

And could this indeed be Sorrel, marvelling as she heard herself speak, who during the War had sent Terry into safety right away from her, down here in the country, their parting treated as a matter of course?

Nevertheless, it was a try-on, and Terry herself was a bit surprised at the way it had succeeded. She was exhausted from crying, her head *did* ache, she *was* hot and miserable, her eyelids swollen, her throat choky and closed up — but she was not quite as ill as all that; not properly ill; Terry knew it, and Sorrel knew it, but the Awful Warning mother and little daughter had receded

248

far over the horizon. And Terry went on denying her glimpse of the astringent truth . . .

("I don't care; they've smashed up all the real things, so I'll just take this instead. It's nicer. And perhaps the real things weren't real at all!")

She wriggled down gratefully into the soft springy hollow in the centre of the bed, and issued a few more orders: Yes, she might manage supper, she admitted, provided her mother went down to fetch it and brought it up herself and didn't stay downstairs more than a minute — "I don't know what I'd like — I think some lovely hot soup — no, some icy cold lemonade — I don't know — a slice of chicken or turkey, the white bits. And not jelly afterwards, jelly's so dull; grapes — or some of Grandpa's birthday trifle — there was a lot left." Feeling suddenly sick at her own food images, she changed her mind again in favour of *fresh* oranges squeezed into a tumbler with *two* lumps of ice "so that they tinkle; and squeeze them yourself, please, or they'll say tinned orange-juice tastes the same. Anyhow, Mummy, don't stop to answer if they ask you a lot of questions; say you're having your supper up here with me."

Left alone for a few necessary moments, Terry failed to hold memory any longer at bay, of Lal's scornful voice ringing down the aisle, when she had entered the church, expecting a miracle . . . "Here, you, Terry, I suppose you were just coming over all grand and upstage in your letter, and didn't really mean what you wrote, about being so sorry you'd give up playing the Virgin Mary?"

Having once surrendered to crying, she cried again; tears not as tight and scalding as before; much wetter, forlorner tears, damping the pillow and her hair . . . She was surprised at the unrationed flow of all this cry-stuff stored up inside her head . . . like the Walt Disney picture of live Broomsticks obstinately carrying along pails and pails of water when the Sorcerer's Apprentice could not stop them. She wallowed luxuriously, aware that when her mother returned with the supper-tray, she could hardly help being impressed not only by the depth but also by the longevity of her only child's premature taste of tragedy . . .

In fact, Terry had fallen so low from her own standards that she did not even mind old Nanny finding her thus swamped in tears. Nanny had heard that one of her war-time nurslings had been put to bed with a touch of fever, when, on the way downstairs, Sorrel went to the nursery to find the right sort of story-book for reading Terry to sleep: "I hope she'll be all right in the morning, Nanny, but one can't be too careful, can one?" It was a pity Nanny had not been out of the way at that moment, for Sorrel was fairly sure that wild horses would not keep her from visiting Terry and prescribing; yet it would have looked too strange if the news had got round among the staff afterwards, and nothing had been said by the invalid's own mother. But she did hope that Terry would have sufficiently pulled herself together to present no more than an appearance of "sickening for something".

"I hope you're not thinking of giving her anything solid, Mrs. Neville? A glass of warm milk, now, or some gruel; and by to-morrow morning, if she's no better, I'll have a look in my chest" — she meant her medicine-chest, not her symbolic pelican chest — "for some beef-tea jelly that I always keep a spare jar of, though it can't compare with beef-tea made at home from the fresh meat. But there, what are you to do these days? No fruit-juice either," she insisted; "warm milk, not to lie chilly on her stomach." And Sorrel, the hypocrite, entirely agreed, and told herself to scout about and make sure Nanny was downstairs having her own supper, before bringing up the tumbler with two lumps of ice "so that it tinkles".

Nanny advanced towards the bed with "Little Women" which she had volunteered to take in to Terry, but still kept out of sight a small object wrapped up in gay Christmas paper while she did her cosy Nanny-patter suitable for a child of six; plumping up the sodden pillows, assurances of affection interspersed with scoldings on the evils of over-eating at Christmas if you had a tum-tum that couldn't stand it — "and no wonder, with the sort of food I expect they give you up in London. Now, now, don't take on so, my precious lamb. But there, you always were one to get into states and cry for nothing" — ("I *wasn't*! How d-d-damnably unfair! I always cried less than any of the others!") "You wouldn't like Roddy and Erica to know you'd been crying, would you?"

But Terry was past caring for that reminder, innocently given, of what Roddy and Erica *had* seen.

"Thoroughly over-excited with all that play-acting and dressing-up . . . I shouldn't be surprised if you couldn't

251

lift your head to-morrow night, and then where will your play be? There, there, no need to start off crying again; be a good girl and do everything your mother tells you, and I expect you'll be able to act as long as I see to it myself that you're properly wrapped up and don't throw off your warm coat, for all churches are draughty, say what you like, and you'd catch your death of cold running round in one of those gauzy pantomime dresses all sequins; sequins never yet kept anybody warm. Now, now, now, stop crying, my blessed, and see what Nanny's got for you. I saved it from Mrs. Lambert-King's party yesterday, and *you* shall have it. Her mother was there, old Lady Fenchurch, eighty-four if she's a day, and she wouldn't allow one candle on the Christmas tree for fear the children set fire to themselves going too near; a very nervous lady! So what did Mrs. Lambert-King do but order three dozen of these that she'd seen in a shop, and hung them all over the branches instead of candles. The things people think of! Lambs and horses and rabbits . . . shining in the dark as if they had little lamps inside them. So directly I heard you were ill — 'Terry shall have the little lamb' I said to myself, and here it is! 'Good night, Terry love,' it's saying; 'I hope you sleep well and wake up such a lot better in the morning'!"

Terry thanked her politely. And her breath still caught by those obstinate sobs that go on and on, asked for want of something better to say: "W-w-what's it made of?"

Nanny replied: "There now, if I didn't ask just the same thing. Smooth and creamy it looks, and almost like ivory, but of course it couldn't be, and Major Lambert-

252

King, he laughed and said 'some sort of luminous composition'."

Then she kissed Terry, adjuring her once more to go to sleep like a good girl; and tucked in the bed-clothes in the capable Nanny fashion which somehow or other always reduced even the most dignified grown-up to nursery status. At the door, she could not refrain from one parting shot: "I thought there must be *something* wrong when you went to have a bath at that funny time yesterday morning."

Directly Nanny had departed, Terry put her lambskin aside on the bed-table, and turned away in tears again at the mortifying thought that Nanny was now considering her such a baby as to give her a baby's toy, something that was hung on a Christmas tree for infants too small to be trusted with candles so there had to be little animals instead that shone in the dark . . . And only a short time ago she had had the most important part in a Nativity Play they were going to perform in a church; the Virgin Mary — "in a lovely mantle like the sky when it's dark blue in summer. I'm *not* going to be bundled up warmly by Roddy's old Nanny-Fusspots . . . I *won't* be . . . I'd rather not act at all . . . "

"Oh, but we're not doing the play anyhow. Oh Mummy, I'd forgotten for a minute. Mummy, you've been away *hours* and Nanny's been simply *frightful*!"

Supper at the Manor that evening was to have been at no specified time, owing to last rehearsals; Erica had warned her mother that they could not be sure when Jonathan would dismiss them from the church. There was hot soup because of old Mr. Maitland, and he and Rosalind were the only two who actually coincided at table at five minutes to eight.

"Where's everybody?" Grandpa asked at intervals throughout the meal. "Are we the only survivors?"

Fortunately Rosalind was not aware that his little joke came perilously near the truth.

Next Anthony lumbered in, wholly preoccupied with mental revisions of his book, and not in the least interested as to where "everybody" might be. He said he had not seen his wife nor his sister nor his sister-in-law since reading aloud to them: "After tea," he added vaguely; "they seemed all right then."

So Rosalind ran upstairs to tap at her mother's door with a cheerful if mendacious:

"We're all at supper, Mummy. Are you coming down?"

And through the closed door, Doe shouted at her daughter yes, *shouted* at her to go away. Her voice was unnatural and suffused with fury . . .

Rosalind went downstairs again, very worried; but always thoughtful for Grandpa, whispered for some moments in Anthony's ear.

Meanwhile her Aunt Sorrel had appeared from upstairs and was scooping up oranges from a fruit-dish on the sideboard.

"Then there's nothing to be done," said Anthony, assimilating the tidings that his wife, for some obscure reason, had been suddenly swept up into one of her fish-wife rages that had only occurred two or three times before, during the period of their marriage. "You can't expect me to turn out the fire-engines. Go and sit down, Rosalind, and don't fuss."

He became aware of Sorrel and her activities, and his tone softened as he offered to carve her some spam:

"That's an odd collection you're making there. Not having a midnight feast, are you?"

Sorrel explained that Terry was in bed with a temperature; and she was going to have supper upstairs with her. "Is Doe ill too?" she asked, greatly relieved at not having to encounter Doe at the table, but at the same time feeling she had to know exactly how much damage had been done? She was the only person present who had a guilty knowledge of the reason why their hostess was not present and looking after everybody at the supper-table with her normal charm and good manners, using all her tact to cover raw places, supplying a plausible weave of excuses for anybody behaving badly . . .

"No, she's not ill; she's in a state."

"In a state?" asked old Mr. Maitland. "What state?"

"State of Denmark," said Anthony.

"*Denmark?*"

Lal came in and sat down in his usual place, but showed no hurry to eat. He was looking desolate and ill . . .

"Rehearsal over for to-night?" inquired Mr. Maitland genially.

Lal made no reply. Sorrel gazed at him steadily; the boy who had been so cruel to Terry. She could not hate him; but for him, Terry would not have given her this amazing fulfilment of all her dreams. Her feelings towards Lal were therefore mixed.

255

Rosalind's encounter with Roddy at the gates of the church had told her why rehearsals were over, not only for to-night, but for all nights; and why Terry was ill; and why Lal so white and silent with dark circles round his eyes; so she immediately became deputy for her mother, and began to talk very quickly and brightly about what people liked best to have brought them to eat in bed when they weren't very well, and what she liked best, and what did Grandpa like best? And had Aunt Sorrel got everything she wanted for herself and poor little Terry? And should she help to carry up the tray?

"Lal will do that," said Mr. Maitland. "Can't have the ladies waiting on each other while there's a gentleman at table."

Lal turned scarlet, but did not move. He was faintly relieved, however, to get this hint that Terry was still alive and eating.

"It's quite all right, Father, really; the tray's not a bit heavy; Terry only wanted an orange drink."

"Give her my love," said Anthony, surprising everyone there. But he had always been peculiarly human about his rapscallion brother's only child.

Sorrel departed, not at all sure whether she should have remained on under Doe's roof for even this one night after she had lost her temper so far as to fling at her an assortment of insults which had been kept under hatches for years. But she could not leave while Terry was ill and needed her . . . *needed* her, clung to her, pleaded to be let sleep in her room and in her bed.

"Where's everybody else?" from old Mr. Maitland. "We aren't all here. Doe's ill and Terry's ill — both must have eaten something that didn't agree with them — but where's Tan? Where's Nick? Where's Clare?"

His son was not attending any more, for the whereabouts of the individual (not only at mealtime) were not deemed by him a matter of the least importance. But Rosalind, with an exactly opposite point of view inherited from her mother, found herself with a Situation in hand and a question of grave responsibility to settle: for if she answered Grandpa's question as regards Clare by saying Clare had gone off in a high-powered car sent specially to fetch her to spend what remained of the week-end with a high-powered house-party of rich American friends, this reply would be bound to reveal that the play had crashed and that there was to be no performance after all in the church to-morrow evening. And Grandpa would be so terribly disappointed; already some discussion as to whether it would be too cold, too fatiguing for him to be present, had been playfully and kindly over-ruled by Doe, several days ago; conviviality was meat and drink to him, and he was looking on the children's Nativity Play the next evening as a subsidiary celebration of his own birthday, which in his opinion had not gone on nearly long enough — (On a trembling echo of seventy-five years ago, he could hear and resent his old nurse's brisk: "You've got to make this last, Master William, for there won't be no more birthdays till next Boxing Day!") He would have to know, reflected Rosalind, but it would be a pity for him to go to bed with something sad to think about; and perhaps by to-morrow, Mummy will be well enough to break it to him herself what has happened.

Rosalind was a little bit envious of Clare; apparently two or three young men of about Jonathan's age were featured in that luxurious American week-end; and the programme, dancing and so forth, would be far more sophisticated than anything Brambleford could offer. In fact, she was surprised, when she went to Clare's room and found her throwing attractive grown-up clothes into a suitcase, that Clare, like Lal, had been looking so desperately unhappy.

("I *am* so sorry, Clare darling, if you're disappointed about not doing the play — here, let me help to fold them — but I hope Erica told you I was quite ready to come in at the eleventh hour as the Virgin Mary?")

". . . I haven't any idea where Aunt Tan and Uncle Nick can have got to, Grandpa. I haven't seen them. Do you know, Father?"

"Gone for a walk, I expect," replied Anthony in a final stage of withdrawal from contemporary events; and he pushed back his chair and walked off to his study.

"Those two are always going for walks," complained old Mr. Maitland; "sometimes together and sometimes not. But this is a silly time for a walk."

"May I get up?" asked Lal. And bolted.

"That leaves you and me, Grandpa," laughed Rosalind. "Isn't it fun?"

"Fun?" a little fretfully, even to his favourite; "I don't know about fun. Where *is* everybody?"

It was past eleven o'clock when Doe had an inspiration how to refute Sorrel's final accusation that stung and smarted beyond all the other wicked things they had all been flinging at her; refute it by the simple means of proving that it was not true: "It's when you start being profound that Anthony goes off and shuts himself up and works alone . . . Orlo never really talked to you, did he? He was indulgent to you, but he talked to Tan . . . As a wife you're superfluous. Your second husband is indulgent too, but that's all you'll ever get from either of them."

How could Sorrel have guessed that she had always longed for both Orlo and Anthony to admit her as an intellectual equal? To discuss his work with her . . . it had slipped into the singular; Orlo, after all, had gone out of her life a long time ago; but Anthony was here, Anthony was in his study at the end of the garden. So Doe spent herself in rage against Sorrel who had found her sorest spot and rubbed pepper into it, rather than with Tan, Anthony's sister, who had only hurt her years ago through Orlo, her first husband.

Sorrel had said "he was indulgent to you, but he talked to Tan. As a wife, you're superfluous!"

A lie! A jealous lie! Orlo had been devoted to her, and so was Anthony. She was twice a golden success as wife and mother. Of course Sorrel was wildly jealous, Sorrel who could not keep even one husband and who hated her own pathetic little daughter.

And Sorrel was a favourite with Anthony. He had always been oddly and specially nice to both her and Terry; had shown the child a tenderness quite unlike his usual dry manner with Erica. Doe had invariably explained to everyone that it was because of Neville having treated Sorrel so badly, and how glad she was that Anthony helped her in making Sorrel feel that the Manor was still a sort of second home whenever she wanted to come down.

"But she's never to come down again; never, never, whatever Anthony may say! I'm mistress here. I wonder she could bear to stay on to-night after insulting me with all those horrible jealous lies. Perhaps she hasn't; perhaps she's gone already; perhaps they've all gone" — All those damnable people, Sorrel and Tan and Nick, who had wrecked her Christmas with their hate when she had meant to give them such a lovely time. And now here she lay stretched on her bed alone, abandoned by everyone, nobody coming to see, nobody caring, utterly forlorn. And bewildered too: "What have I *done*? Why can't they see I meant our Christmas to be so happy, everything going right, everything running smoothly?"

"I'm not going to stay up here, out in the cold. I'll go downstairs, and — and —"

"No, I won't. I'll call Anthony and tell him what they've done to me, tell him Sorrel and Terry must go at once. He's always much, much happier when he and I are alone together; we don't need anyone else; we're all in all to each other — 'And if you imagine, Sorrel — why, Doe is the *perfect* collaborator, I wouldn't dream of writing a line without discussing it with her because I've the greatest respect for her judgment; so if you imagine —'"

("Where was I?")

"'Doe is my ideal mate, and you'll find out one day, all of you (Sorrel and Tan and Nick) that a woman like Doe needn't forfeit her claims as a wife and mother

260

simply because she can be your intellectual companion as well, *and* run your house so beautifully even in wartime that you're sorry for everyone who isn't married to somebody like Doe!'"

". . . I'm going to ask him not to call me Doe any more; it's Nick's name; Orlo never called me Doe until Nick started quoting that silly line out of Tennyson. Dorothea. Dorothea has more dignity. Oh, but I don't want to be dignified with Anthony; perhaps he has his own private name for me that he uses to himself whenever he thinks of me, but he's too shy —"

No, that bit wouldn't hold water even in a fantasy of Anthony, and she discarded it.

"I'm *so* hungry. I wonder if they're missing me downstairs?"

"I hate Sorrel, I hate her, I hate her. Not for any single thing that she said to me, but because she was so beastly to my poor little Erica."

For Doe had been genuinely touched and upset at the sight of Erica's usually happy little face when Sorrel had so vindictively lashed out at her. To visit temper on a child, out of one's own bitterness to have made a child shed tears, was unforgivable; never again might Erica lean with quite the same implicit trust on the fairness and kindness of grown-ups . . .

Wondering therefore if she could find some way of reassuring her little girl, Doe had waited till she knew Rosalind must be down at supper, and then had gone along to their bedroom. With her sensible affectionate disposition, Erica was not adding to her mother's troubles by any display of futile emotion on account of the sudden sad change in her Aunt Sorrel. Lying sadly awake in the dark, she greeted Doe's arrival with enthusiasm and kisses and: "Oh Mummy, *how* nice of you to have come to say a special good night."

Doe turned on the fire, and sat on the bed; drew Erica on to her lap just as though she were a little tiny baby again: "*My* baby, anyhow!" — (she had forgotten Roddy) — and thought Erica had the sweetest character of them all; look how she had not shown the slightest resentment over being deprived of the pantomime — (and here Doe had *not* forgotten Roddy) — And look how the other children staying in the house, all much older than Erica, had quarrelled even to the point of destroying their play, and only Erica had shown a true Christmas spirit and had tried her hardest to heal discord, instead of joining in and making it worse.

"Tell me, darling — I think I'd better know, don't you? — exactly what happened this evening at the church, to make you all have to give up the play?" She did not add "Perhaps together we can think out a way to put it right," because she did not very much desire to put it right for Terry, for Sorrel's daughter. There was a queer satisfaction in recognising that not only her own tranquil heart had been violently assaulted, but everything all round her was shattered to pieces too, all their fun, all their Christmas . . . (And she could somehow make it up to Erica for not playing the Angel this time; plenty more angels for Erica to play all through her life.) "Tell me exactly what happened, darling?"

The next half-hour was jam for Erica, jam of a deep golden hue, apricot jam. She had an excellent memory and her mother's full attention; Doe did not interrupt, but her very silences were mellow with praise. This was the first time that the quarrel which had begun with the duck-ball, and ended with Terry lying broken across the chancel steps, had been told in one long consecutive, detailed, uninterrupted narrative. Erica was even able to reproduce whole sentences exactly as they had been uttered, hurled forth by Lal and Terry and Clare . . . Listening attentively, Doe was struck by the astonishingly adult quality of their phrasing; hardly like children at all; did they mysteriously grow up when they quarrelled?

And it was this queer point which suddenly, nearly two hours later, flashed across her mind in converse to Anthony's dictum laid down in the rough notes he had read them from The Psychology of Quarrels:

"Grown-ups quarrel exactly like children."

Yes, *that* might be true; it *was* true of Nick and Tan, especially in their recent battle. But Anthony's observation should have been lengthened to include a more important observation: that in their recent parallel quarrel, on Erica's report, the children had skipped the intervening years, and had quarrelled not as the young are supposed to do, perpetually dropping the original cause to hurl quite irrelevant accusations simply for the sake of being hurtful, dragging in anything that came into their heads, picking up names that did not fit the context to fling at their protagonist, names without sense or logic or truth or accuracy, gabbling outrageous irrelevant nonsense just for the sake of being outrageous:

263

"Your father went to prison" — just for the sake of hearing themselves say it in their rage, working off steam. When Sorrel had hurled at Doe that as a wife she was superfluous, with what logic could that calumny link on to Doe's natural refusal to stand by and see Erica bullied? But from first to last, enclosed in the Unities like protagonists in a Greek drama, the children had not once let themselves be diverted; the cause of dissension had swelled and swelled, but the duck-ball was still contained in it.

What if she, Doe, were to tell Anthony? Not certainly carping at his work, but in the very spirit of impersonal collaboration which they all denied her; let him know quietly how he had gone wrong in one of his premises; and how his failure to check up conclusions on individual human behaviour had let him down. Cosmic wisdom, even Anthony's was not always enough; here, grasped in her hand like a pebble, she held one small hard result of her own instinctive rejection of the cosmic approach. Suppose, then, she were to take it along to him now? Conquer her longing for his human sympathy and indignation on her behalf? Could she keep the lid pressed down on her boiling kettle of self-pity? Yes, she could, for the sake of seeing Anthony look at her with respect after she had quietly stated her point . . . "Sit down, my dear" — for the first time inviting her to an academic discussion in a temperature without heat or icy winds; admitting, though cautiously and pending examination, "You might be right, Dorothy," for once not merely tolerant at what he deemed her feminine habits of thought. And this attitude would outlast to-night; she would be in on Anthony's new book: "My wife's got a man's brain; you wouldn't think it to look at her, would you?" his voice and smile implying "She's too beautiful." No need then to be lonely and out in the cold through all the long closing-in of winter, all the lengthening days of the reluctant spring.

In on Anthony's new book.

Sorrel was a fool not to recognise perfect harmony when she saw it, perfect companionship between husband and wife, simply because it wasn't obvious to intruders at the Manor.

The house was silent; probably they were the only two awake, she up in her room, Anthony in his study. Doe peered out — yes, there was a chink of light showing between the trees. She slipped into her garden-and-bad-weather fur coat, her fleece-lined boots; trod softly along the corridor and downstairs; unbolted a side door into the garden, and ran happily down the path to the converted summer-house which was her husband's study. She wondered, as she paused on the threshold to gather breath and try to give excitement a chance to subside, whether that car on the main road were drawing nearer and had turned aside up their drive? But then Anthony called out: "Who's there?" And she forgot everything except her purpose.

Terry woke from deep exhausted sleep, in what felt like the middle of the night; woke apparently for no reason at all . . . unless she had really heard a door slam in the silence outside? She could not get her bearings . . . and when at last her mind did grope back to the events of the evening before, and realised there was nothing anywhere except emptiness, such desolation rushed over her that she simply did not know how she was going to bear it?

. . . Then she saw quite clearly the small chunky outline of a white lamb gleaming four-square in oceans of black space.

"So it *does* really shine in the dark."

Oddly, this comforted her a little; only a very little, but it was somehow friendly to shut her eyes — and then open them quickly and still see it there beside her.

Terry sighed . . . turned over and went to sleep again.

". . . And I've tried and tried to make allowances, because of course we know that Neville — but this time Sorrel went too far, and it's no good, Anthony, she's not to come here again, whatever you say. If you hadn't always treated her so that she imagined she was a privileged person, she and Terry — I wish you could have heard her saying things to frighten poor little Erica. Not that I suppose you'd have minded, you've never been fair to Erica, never; you've petted Terry and neglected your own daughter, but if you've any loyalty in you, at least you'll back us up this time and tell that bloody sister-in-law of yours that she's got to control her foul temper. You can tell her your wife comes first, and you can tell her that she's no judge of the sacred intimate bond between husband and wife, simply because we don't choose to be blatant and publish it to the world, but it's there all the same, and she's not likely to understand it in a million years! She's an outsider who's been sponging on you all these years. No, you've never told me, but of course she has, pretending to work so hard and earn a bare living for her and Terry. I can always spot her type, they have a face like a begging letter. Do you *hear*, Anthony? Do you hear that you're to tell her —"

Doe went on and on, passionately denouncing Sorrel, recounting her dire grievances, appealing with sobs for Anthony's chivalrous espousal of her cause and to hell with reason and hospitality — Oh, to hell with it all! "You've got to tell Sorrel to-morrow — to-night! Anthony, don't just *sit* there. Oh Anthony, I'm so unhappy and it's all Sorrel's fault because she said — No, I'm not going to tell you what she said; you'd be too furious with her; I thought she was going to strike Erica, and then she turned on me like a madwoman. But she's always secretly hated me, only you were too wrapt up in her to see it. I shielded her for as long as I could . . . "

Anthony had laid down his pen some time ago. He sat and listened. The tirade beat on his ears, making it impossible meanwhile to proceed with his own train of thought or remember at what point she had interrupted him. Presently, not yet, she would exhaust herself. Then he would pat her shoulder and murmur something non-committal . . . as he had always done before . . . as he had always done before . . . And by and by he would take her back to the house; no hope of returning to-night to his deeply satisfactory state of total immersion.

Lal sat up in bed, taut, listening . . . As a dog recognises by love and instinct one footstep among a hundred, so he knew the sound of that car being driven at that pace up

267

the drive; he had heard it often enough, staying with Uncle Ted. It had now come to a halt outside. In a moment and without waking Roddy, he was at the window, drew up the blind and leant out. It *was* Uncle Ted, who had driven himself down to-night after the play, instead of waiting, as he said, until to-morrow morning. Oh, thank God! Lal snatched out something from a drawer, and sliding down the bannisters for speed, not certainly in the spirit of high cockalorum, arrived in time to unbolt and open the front door (softly, for he did not want them all rushing down) before Uncle Ted could lift the knocker.

"Lal, you young scoundrel! Who cast you for the butler in this show?" Ted was delighted at the apparition of a nephew in pyjamas and tousled hair, but a bit surprised; he had managed the run on nearly empty roads in less than an hour and a half, and the household at the Manor did not usually retire early.

"I heard your window go up. Well, where's everybody? Didn't expect me till to-morrow, did you? I was so keen to get down to-night, I didn't take any curtains — no, no, I wouldn't disappoint them altogether; I just stepped forward at the end and took 'em into my confidence; said I wanted to get here before midnight and surprise you all: 'You see, they're the nearest I've got to a family', I said, 'and I wasn't able to spend Christmas with them, and to-morrow the youngsters are putting on a play, so come now, you don't really want to hold me up any longer, do you?' Always the best way with an audience; they like to be told things. So do I. Here, let's get that fire going again;

you're shivering." He took off his huge fleece-lined overcoat and wrapped it round the boy. "Come on, put your arms in the sleeves; it's warmer that way. What have you been doing to yourself?" with a quick affectionate scrutiny. "Not on top of your form? But I know what last rehearsals can do to a man. How's it all going? I haven't had a chance to see a play for weeks, so to-morrow night's going to be my Night Out in a big way."

"We're not doing the play," said Lal. "It's down the drain." He tried to send up a grin to ward off the compassion which he felt he could not quite bear even from Unele Ted; not just at that moment; disappointment as well as compassion; he had said how he had been looking forward to it, and this was sincere; Uncle Ted never pretended merely to curry favour with the juvenile brigade. It was a shame he should not have had any share in their Christmas down here and now was even to be robbed of seeing their Nativity Play. So Lal brought into the light what he had been holding behind his back:

"It's my Christmas present for you."

Ted dropped the bellows with which he had been urging the half-dead fire to a blaze, and eagerly, delightedly, grabbed hold of the clown-box which Lal surrendered with a pretence of nonchalance. Presently he slid his uncle a wary glance, half defiant, half apprehensive that Clare might have been right about all that wincing . . . yet with still a lingering faith that Uncle Ted might not prove as ready to be wounded to the quick as everyone else during this truly awful Christmas.

Ted was bent over the directions on the little box, absorbed in getting the hang of it, the right trick of his fingers on the talc . . . He had not quite achieved it yet, but he persevered.

Suddenly the little cardboard clowns began to leap and caper and throw themselves about. Ted's shout of triumph brought Lal over to his side.

"Look! Look! Aren't they grand! How's it done? See them kick the ball about! No — wait — don't! Leave it to me." He let them subside for the pleasure of starting them up again. "Look, they go on even after I've stopped. Look, one's hanging from the ceiling. *Attaboy*! You could make them do any blooming thing. Why, they remind me of me! I used to be a clown once, before I went into vaudeville; did you know? Come on now, boys — houp-là! Here we are again!"

Ted's face was a-glow. None of this delight was put on; Lal would have known had it only been done to please him. No, Uncle Ted *loved* his present; he was enchanted with it; the warmth of his enjoyment pervaded the room; worked its way round Lal's feeling of desolation that nothing could ever come right again. His body had been chilled, too, but now the fire was warm, and the big furry overcoat still warm from Ted's wearing. And Christmas over was a radiant Christmas at last!

But then with a shock, watching Ted's face, he was suddenly moved to remember vividly Terry's face when her present to Rosalind, also chosen in breathless hope, was rejected, set aside, returned with pretty thanks. Terry's face! It came to him in an agony of remorse that all undeserving, he, Lal, had had the luck, not Terry. He

270

recalled his arrogant reception of her letter; could even hear his voice ringing towards her down the aisle with that echoing clarity lent by an almost empty church: "Here, you, Terry . . . I suppose you were just coming over all grand and up-stage in your letter, and didn't really mean what you wrote about being so sorry you'd give up playing the Virgin Mary?" Why were reward and punishment so unfairly meted out? Uncle Ted playing with his present, and Rosalind returning Terry's?

Fiercely Lal scrubbed a flapping great overcoat sleeve across his eyes. Ted looked up and caught him at it.

"Look, old boy," very gently, "I've been mixed up in things myself that flopped even before they came on. I know just how it feels. Bad, isn't it? How did all this happen? You'll find it easier to tell an old pro, you know."

It did not take very long, for Lal wasted no time with endless tiresome self-justification; but made a short honest story out of the quarrel which had wrecked the play; and remembered to put in that though, of course, the appearance of two duck-balls had not been deliberately arranged by him for a joke, as Terry at first believed, he *had* nevertheless decided against asking Terry's permission to send Tan to the shop, for fear she might say no: "And when she lashed out at me over breaking my promise, that's what made me argue like blazes that it wasn't actually breaking a promise. And I've loathed myself ever since. I don't think I want to read for the bar and be a K.C. any more. I don't like what they do."

Lal was leaning with one arm against the mantelpiece in rather a grown-up fashion, staring into the fire. Nevertheless, Ted dared not betray what an assault this last item of the boy's confession had made on his sense of humour; he just managed to remain outwardly grave for fear his nephew should suddenly swing round and see him. But Lal had not finished yet; in fact, all the worst was still to come, as in retrospect he showed himself growing more and more cock-a-hoop at rehearsals; contemptuous of Terry, yet goading her on; making a bonfire of her feelings; swaggering in the part of Joey except where it merged into Joseph, husband of Mary, and became negligible; swaggering over his friendship with Jonathan who was nineteen already and almost a professional producer of plays. And then that last ghastly mess-up when they all met in the church to rehearse for positions, and Terry had sent him a letter to say she was sorry, surrendering for the sake of peace, even if it had meant giving up her part; though he could see now that she had never dreamt he *could* be so ungenerous as not only to allow that, but to exact even more humiliating conditions, publicly, in front of them all.

(The only thing which Lal left out was Clare on the subject of their Uncle Pagliacci and hyper-sensitive clowns.)

He pulled himself together after a rather shaky description of the final collapse, and finished on a matter-of-fact summing up:

"And I haven't seen Terry since; she's got a temperature; and Jonathan's walked out on us for good;

272

and Clare's gone off for the week-end to her American pals. So you see that's that."

And he waited, his heart thumping hard and fast, for Ted's comment, wondering just where it would strike. For even the nicest man in the world and the most understanding could not be expected to let him off too lightly.

It seemed as though the clock had ticked away a whole hour before Ted spoke:

"Well, and what about your promise to the Vicar? We can't let him down, can we? What did he say, poor old fellow, when you broke it to him?"

"Good *Lord*!" exclaimed Lal. "I'd clean forgotten. I believe we've all forgotten. I don't think he knows yet."

"There's a nice kettle of fish," remarked Ted; and so completely had he identified himself already with the company's predicament, that his eyes were screwed up tight in an endeavour to force out a helpful solution from the brain behind them.

"It's too late to-night," Lal muttered after a long pause. "It'll have to be to-morrow morning. Perhaps Aunt Doe — unless you think it would come better from Uncle Anthony?"

"I don't think it would come better from anybody. Look, Lal, he's been counting on that — what did you call it? — dossal? — that expensive bit of stuff to hang over an ugly grim forbidding picture and hide it. You told me yourself, in your letter, that he wouldn't be able to afford it from the usual church funds."

"Yes, I did. He can't. But — it's an awful shame and I'm damned sorry, but he'll just have to lump it, won't he?"

"That's a bit too easy, to say anybody can lump a thing." And Lal felt less happy at this note of sternness which had crept into his uncle's voice.

"You promised him a Silver Collection, all of you. Just imagine how disappointed he'll be, after looking forward to getting that picture covered and out of sight. I expect it hurt him every time his eyes went that way by mistake."

"Looking forward" . . . Ted had been thinking so earnestly of the Vicar, putting himself mind and soul into the other man's mind and soul, that he actually had not realised he had been on the verge of quoting from that speech which Lal had heard nine times now, and was to hear again a tenth time on New Year's Eve; speech at which every night a packed theatre audience, rocking with hilarity, were suddenly hushed so that not one word might escape them . . .

("Looking forward — isn't it all the difference between thinking fat and thinking thin, thinking full and thinking empty?")

. . . And the Vicar had been looking forward to what he would do with the Silver Collection.

"Listen, Uncle Ted," Lal burst forth on a medium good inspiration — or so he thought; "he'd worked out from other collections that it would come to about twelve pounds; fourteen pounds at the most. You're quite right, I *did* promise and I *am* responsible. So do you think you could — could you possibly lend me say twelve pounds ten, to hand over to him right away? And I'd give you my I O U to pay you back the minute I was earning. It would probably have to be in instalments, but perhaps in three or four years I'd find some way. *Please*, Uncle Ted, will you?"

But hope faded fast; Ted was looking grave and sorry, and shook his head very decidedly:

"I'm afraid I can't, old boy. This is an awfully bad moment to have tackled me. Twelve-ten — call it twelve quid — it's a lot of money whichever way you look at it, all in a lump like that." He went on with some rather ashamed and therefore not very clear admissions of having dabbled on the market . . . unwisely taken a tip on insecure information . . . and then he'd been let down again on a couple of bad debts: "You can't *trust* people. And coming all at once — you see how it is Lal? I hate saying so, but you won't press me?"

Of course Lal would not press him; he could have kicked himself for having asked and put Uncle Ted to the pain of refusing him. Whatever he did lately made somebody miserable. That broken promise to the Vicar was the last straw. He looked round desperately; one simply could not grow up into the sort of man who let out the whereabouts of little secret shops, who confidently promised Silver Collections to vicars and then mucked it all up . . .

"Uncle Ted, what do you think I'd better do?"

Ted put his arm round Lal's shoulder and drew him towards the stairs.

"I think you'd better go up to bed, Lal. You're tired and so am I. Doe said she'd booked a room for me at the Cock and Feathers; that would be for to-morrow night, but I don't expect they'd be crowded out now Christmas is over, so I'll take the car round without disturbing her and Anthony to-night. Don't you worry about the play. We'll manage."

"Manage?" echoed Lal. "Manage?" He repeated on a sigh: "What are we to manage?"

"To put it on after all."

"But Terry's ill, and Clare's gone away, and Jonathan's chucked it up —"

Ted laughed, and before saying good night, set the little clowns prancing in a final fling; he had never had a present which pleased him so much, and he did not have to assure Lal in so many words that that was true; it was evident from the way he kept on going back to it, perhaps because he had been a clown himself, a long time ago . . .

He realised Lal had had about as much as he could bear. Yet it was essential the children should not carry as a burden all their lives the consciousness of having botched the play through their own failure to keep peace even through one Christmas.

"I'll just come up with you. No hurry."

Lal did not protest, for he was suddenly so weary that even with Ted supporting him, the two flights loomed like a range of the Andes.

"Good night, old man. Sleep well."

And then, as he departed, Lal softly called him back.

"Uncle Ted . . . if you should see Terry to-morrow . . . I don't suppose you will, but if you should, don't play with the clown-box in front of her."

And Ted whistled a little march of victory under his breath, all along the corridor and down the stairs.

276

CHAPTER
THIRTEEN

"I thought I heard a car last night," exclaimed Doe, surprised and delighted at Ted's arrival from the inn for breakfast. She did not quite add in so many words: "Anthony and I were working late, out in his study" . . . though it was somehow implicit, not only in what she said, but in her mental recreation of the sequence of events that had prevented her from being on the spot as châtelaine.

"Oh, I couldn't possibly wait till today to join the Christmas party. I did a bunk after the show;" Ted fell upon his breakfast with a grand hunger, and simultaneously told them about his personal appeal to the audience to let him off on only one curtain-call.

"They said at the Cock that Nick had left yesterday."

"Yes, isn't it a pity?" And Doe added in vague extenuation: "He couldn't stay."

"And Tan? Where's my blessed darling, Tan?"

And again, after a hardly perceptible silence: "*She* couldn't stay, either."

Ted was surprised, but left it at that.

"You see," added Doe, regaining her tranquillity as she realised she had in her possession a perfectly plausible reason to offer, if not for the mysterious departure of Nick and Tan, at least for removing what would have been an essential excuse for their staying; "you see, I'm afraid there's bad news for you, Ted; our play is not going to be done to-night, and I know you'd been looking forward to it tremendously. Or did Lal tell you?"

"Yes, Lal told me. And of course I'd been looking forward to it; busman's holiday." But he did not seem at all quenched.

The next down to breakfast was Rosalind:

"Oh, Uncle Ted, fancy you already! You must have got up long before cock-crow."

"What, me? Oh no, I'm not an early riser; I rolled out of bed about twenty minutes ago. My dear, you look more like a rose than any girl has a right to look at this hour of the morning."

"Thank you, Uncle Ted," dimpling with pleasure. "We've missed you terribly all over Christmas, haven't we, Daddy? When you phoned — Oh dear," she cried in dismay, suddenly remembering the children's choice of their Nativity Play had been because the idea had so delighted Uncle Ted; "and now they're not doing their little play to-night, after all. What a shame!" She did not particularly care herself, but she could sympathise with other people's disappointments.

"Don't you be too sure," laughed Ted. "What'll you bet against the curtain going up?"

"They were going to do it in the church, you know, where there wouldn't have been a curtain," Rosalind kindly explained. "But anyhow it couldn't, Uncle Ted, because Clare's away and Terry's ill in bed."

"Well . . . I may stroll round presently and have a talk

with young Jonathan Reed. Has anyone got Clare's phone number, or at least the address of the people she's staying with?"

"I have. I helped her pack her suitcase. She was in such a state, so I thought I'd better write it down, just in case. It's a good thing, because a letter arrived for her directly after she went, and it's from her mother, I think; the postmark's America."

"Good, I'll get through to her. Not gone far, has she?"

"About forty or fifty miles."

"Oh dear, and I'm nearly at the end of my petrol. Never mind. Here comes the fire brigade!" as a clattering of feet and voices sounded on the stairs. "That's more the Christmas spirit. Which reminds me —"

Roddy burst in just ahead of Erica, whose entrances were always sedate.

"Dad, what d'you think? I can't get Lal to wake up. He isn't dead, but he's awfully fast asleep, and when I pulled him he grunted and swore just like men and went to sleep again. So shall I —" He broke off at an unexpected sight of his Uncle Ted sitting comfortably at the table finishing a hearty breakfast, and rushed at him with a volley of questions.

"But I say, it's no good your having come, because you know our play to-night? Well, there isn't one."

"That's what *you* think," spoke Ted from under a rosebud shower of Erica's kisses.

"But Clare's gone away and Terry's ill in bed."

"You've only got to keep your eye on your uncle; I'll drag Clare home and pull Terry out of bed; nothing easier."

Erica greeted this with silvery laughter, and Doe remarked gaily: "Anyone would think you were a conjurer, Ted."

"I've conjured up a car full of Christmas presents — there, I thought that would make Roddy drop his porridge out of his mouth!"

But Roddy and Erica were already out of the dining-room and down the steps to the car.

"I was afraid they'd arrive too late and stale if I posted them off on the Friday before Christmas, so I decided to bring them myself and be in on the fun."

He hid his perplexity as to what could have happened to the grown-up faction of the house-party? Something had broken loose during this Christmas of peace and goodwill to which no-one would give him a clue. Anthony, he thought, was looking even more reticent than usual. Nick and Tan, his special friends, had gone off, certainly not together, just before they knew he was coming. A hell of a row between Nick and Tan was nothing new, but he sensed that this time it would need something more dramatic than a tolerant acceptance of their warring natures to bring them together again. And he knew Doe well enough to be aware that her air of serenity need not mean that others in her immediate neighbourhood were necessarily serene. Nick had no illusions about Doe, and no affection for her; Ted simply had no illusions.

However, primarily this question of the play had to be tackled. Ted left them all unpacking parcels and enjoying themselves: "Those two are for Grandpa, Christmas and birthday, so don't let Roddy grab a double share. Rosalind, give me Clare's number."

* * *

"Yes, my dear, that's who it is! Happy Christmas! . . . Well, never mind; come back now, sweetheart, and have another one. I cried when I found you weren't here . . . Yes, yes, but listen, dear, we're going to do the play tonight, after all, so I want you back at once. That's all right, isn't it? . . . There's my niece, bless her! I always say you can trust your own flesh and blood . . . Rather, if they can? I'm short of petrol. Besides, I'm wanted here, so if you *can* wangle it from your end? . . . Right, my darling; that's the ticket! As soon as possible and a great deal sooner. Good-bye!"

As he came away from the telephone, Ted's heart brimmed with paternal tenderness for this nearly daughter of his who had not argued nor protested nor stood upon her rights, but quite simply, when he said he wanted her back immediately to play her part in "Christmas in the Market Place," had accepted his request as very few children or grown-ups had ever learnt to accept, merely showing a slight doubt as to how soon she could persuade one of the van Buren young men to drive her back again to the place from which she had so urgently desired them to fetch her only the evening before.

"Well, that fixes Clare. Lal was easy enough, and Clare was easier; she's a grand girl, is my Clare! Now for Terry!" He put his head in at the dining-room door and said:

"Just going to run up and see Sorrel; that all right? I suppose she doesn't want to leave the invalid."

He was prepared to find Sorrel, as usual, with her troubles concealed, not like Doe's beneath layers of cream, but from loyalty to some code that she had never resolved into actual words even to him, though he came nearer to her confidence than anyone. And of course she would be worried with Terry in the state Lal had described her; Terry hurt, Terry ill; not so very ill, but pretty badly hurt. So he was certainly a little astonished — (Ted never went to extremes of astonishment, finding that if you didn't first have to exclaim for hours, you could the more quickly discover what would make the grass grow again) — a little astonished, on his encounter with Sorrel going along to refill a hot-water bottle for Terry, at the radiant happiness which clothed her. "Clothed" was too flimsy; she was armoured in happiness; she was the last paragraph in every fairy-story; she had seen a vision of paradise and heard all the seraphim singing in praise of love. In other words, thought Ted, embracing her warmly (and for about the tenth time telling of his arrival last night instead of this morning) in other words, she's dropped sixpence and picked up a sovereign. Now why?

"And how's Terry? Bit of a bother for you, having her ill like this."

"Her temperature's down below normal, but I'm keeping her in bed for to-day. It's safer, I think, don't you, as we have to travel to-morrow? And Terry's not really a robust child, though she likes to pretend she is. Have you noticed, Ted," bubbling on in sheer exuberance, "how delicate children always like to pretend that they're giant-killers? But Terry for once is

282

being perfectly good and obedient; even when Nanny brought in a basin of perfectly revolting gruel this morning — the stiff kind, you know; we waited till she'd gone, and then Terry looked at me and I looked back at Terry and neither said a word —"

"And you poured it out on the flower-beds? That's right; good for all plants, gruel!"

He carefully made no comment on this new and extraordinarily orthodox attitude of hers regarding Terry; not only maternal but possessive, and not only possessive but exultant and unashamed. Ted did not know why, but he suddenly felt impelled to kiss Sorrel again, holding her stoutly in his arms as though she were threatened by some danger which he could not avert from her. Indeed, his instinct told him that he might presently be the cause of it — "though for the life of me I can't see why!" — Had she not *wanted* Terry to act in the play?

"Can I go in and see the child? I won't do her any harm."

"I'm sure you won't, and Terry would love to see you." She spoke indulgently, yet as though her hands were full of diamonds and she were giving him one as a permit. "In that case, I'll run down meanwhile and get my breakfast. I'm as hungry as a hunter."

And that was odd, too; devoted mothers with their only daughter in bed and probably weak after a temperature, were not usually as hungry as hunters. Hunters . . . "Sorrel's a dark horse," Ted echoed a remark Nick had once made to him. A whole stable of dark horses, and Sorrel the darkest. He sent one more loving thought towards Clare over at the van Burens, as he went in to Terry.

* * *

Sorrel was pretty sure that after all her emotional upheavals of the day, Doe would still be prostrate up in her room. Her own intention was to make an excellent breakfast and then go to Doe, crave for admittance, and make the formal apology which she considered due to her hostess if she were staying on yet one more night at the Manor to give Terry a chance to gather a little more strength for their cold journey home. She was so happy that she did not even mind having this act of grace in front of her; grace from the lips, not from the heart. What did it matter? Terry and I, Terry and I, Terry and I will soon be going home together: "I'll put the child to bed the moment we get in, with a bright fire and a nice little supper, and we can talk comfortably about everything that happened down here. She'll be ready to laugh by then; the hurt and the soreness will have ebbed once she's alone with me. She has the prettiest laugh . . . "

Doe had almost finished her own breakfast, but insisted on sitting down again to keep Sorrel company, for Anthony and Rosalind and the children were already gone. And she inquired after Terry with real concern. Sorrel felt a little dazed. Had she dreamt that nightmare quarrel between them yesterday? Surely even Doe could not have so perfectly smoothed it over, ironed it out and hung it up in the wardrobe? Surely her unembarrassed greeting, her English version of "The top o' the morning to ye" was willed by talent or cunning? could not have sprung from a total loss of memory? Nevertheless, Sorrel failed to see what talent or cunning

284

stood to gain by the display? (Anthony could have told her that it was somehow necessary for Doe to behave like this to lash up the high waves, pile wreck after wreck on the shore, and then after sleep to say with genuine astonishment, when the psychological weather-reports were brought in, that she thought there *had* been a little breeze, hardly any, enough maybe to chase away those few little dancing clouds; but look, lovely blue weather now! I think we're in for a fine spell.)

Fine spell or not, Sorrel responded only as much as was barely necessary; though she laid away her formal apology as being apparently superfluous . . . ("Dar-*ling*, of course I forgive you. Besides, what is there to forgive? We've always understood each other *beautifully*. Apology indeed? so pompous. Now I'm not going to listen to another word!")

"Dar-*ling* —"

(Sorrel started. She had forgotten how much of this had actually been said. Would Doe's next words be "Of course I forgive you"?)

"Darling, when you go upstairs again, do take this to amuse Terry. Ted brought it for Anthony. Such fun; look, when you pick it up, it plays John Peel."

"A bit hearty for Anthony, isn't it?" Sorrel took up the beer-mug cum musical-box with its picture of a man in full hunting regalia; it certainly would amuse Terry. She reflected, in mutiny against Doe's bland assumption that all had gone surpassingly well, that they need not ever come back to the Manor again, not for Christmas nor at any other time; they would make their own Christmases, she and Terry . . .

"But now he has gone far far away,
We shall ne'er hear his voice in the morning."

It was a sad nostalgic little tune, tinkling all the way up the stairs.

Terry was not in bed. She was up and more than half dressed.

"Oh, I couldn't see any sense in staying in bed. Yes, I know I was feverish last night, but I'm not any more. I wish people wouldn't keep *on* reminding one of last night." Her manner became increasingly off-hand. "Besides, there's an awful lot to be done. Has Uncle Ted told you we're doing the play after all?" She was ready now; picked up her brush and comb, her pyjamas, dressing-gown and washing things. "Clare's coming back," carelessly, "so I might as well put these back in our room now. Once Jonathan gets us rehearsing —"

And Sorrel understood . . . that her short ration of heaven was over. Terry had renounced being a sick child, an adorable unhappy baby, appealing to be nursed and petted though not by anyone but her mother. She must never never allude to it unless Terry did so first; and that was not likely either; self-respect once violated and then set up again, would be a fence too high to scale, too dangerous to pull down. Sorrel knew perfectly well things were as they had been before Terry's lapse; as they had always been.

Except . . . she also knew they would not again even have fun together doing the Awful Warning mother and child.

She put down the mug abruptly, and the music jarred and stopped.

286

"Naturally I don't mind. It's no concern of mine any more. Do as you like."

"I'm going to," Ted sounded more amiable than he felt, for Jonathan's attitude towards the production of "Christmas in the Market Place" had set him longing to put the time back eight years, when he and Nick were producing a pantomime at the Manor and both had rather unfairly bullied the doctor's much too intelligent little boy who could not act but behaved as though he were the cat's whiskers. Ted was well aware that he cut no ice with the lordly young undergraduate, who having a taste for ultra-modern experimental technique of production, looked on him, Ted, as a mere Knockabout Comedian, lowest of the low. Ted would have enjoyed playing up to it and being even more of a knock-about comedian than nature and art had already made him; for instance, snatch up the ink-pot and glass paper-weight and one or two other breakable objects, throw them to the ceiling and fail to catch them again, give a hoarse laugh and ejaculate: "That's not a lady, that's my wife!" . . . in obliging confirmation of Jonathan's scornful estimate. However, this morning's visit was not merely for enjoyment:

"The play's going on to-night, whatever happens. It would make things a bit easier, that's all, as you've been rehearsing them all this time —"

"No, thanks. My point is that they're under-rehearsed, and I can't afford to be associated with a failure, even a tin-pot affair like this. I'm going in for it professionally.

287

To tell the truth, I'm browned off with the whole set-up; the children were amazingly good at first, I wouldn't have believed it, but then they just went to pieces for no reason at all."

"Does anyone go to pieces for no reason at all?"

Jonathan shrugged his shoulders: he was really not interested, so Ted wasted no more time on abstract discussion.

"Take my advice and drop it," said Jonathan kindly. "When things have slipped so far, they can't be hauled back into shape at the eleventh hour. Kids don't realise, it's not an easy play to present: it isn't as though it were all modern gipsy stuff, or all New Testament, but sliding from one to the other —"

"Oh, I expect we'll make a hell of a mess of it!" Ted agreed cheerfully. "Look here, about the costumes?"

"All over at the Manor already."

"You hired them, I suppose? Price's?"

"No; I tried Price; no good. Newsomes. See they get sent back safely on Monday, won't you?"

"O.K., I'll be responsible. What's the damage?"

Jonathan mentioned a sum far in excess of the twelve pounds ten which Ted's unfortunate investments had by no means allowed him to lend Lal for the Vicar's dosel. The investments must have recovered in the night . . . for Ted merely nodded and showed no perturbation. Just as he was leaving, he stopped and asked:

"By the way, your sister; she's in it, isn't she?"

"Oh yes, Judy doubles two fairly big parts: I don't know where she's got to. Wait a minute."

Jonathan laid hold of a servant, but his inquiries were of no avail; Judy was not in the house and had left no word of her whereabouts or the time of her return.

"She needs one of these cruel stepmothers," Jonathan remarked; but affectionately; for Judy's movements, free of all control, seemed to him as good as any other method of bringing up a young sister.

"Send her to the Manor as soon as she comes in, will you? Say it's urgent."

"Right. She'll be fairly glad, I expect. She quite likes acting."

Ted wondered a little irritably if the young man had to modify every sentence he uttered with "quite" or "fairly", as though he would lose caste if he were once to let himself go in reckless enthusiasm.

"Good-bye and thanks." Then in sheer mischief: "See you in the church to-night?"

"Good God, *no*."

"Aren't you coming?" innocently. "I thought you'd have been humanly curious."

Jonathan repudiated the idea that he was humanly anything.

"Lal's got it all written down," he volunteered, at the front door.

This was news to Ted, and he half-turned to inquire what it was that Lal had "got written down", and why? Then decided, no, dammit, I'm not going to keep on asking questions of this young lordling. Lal's bound to tell me himself.

* * *

Lal was on his way to the schoolroom, hoping Ted might be there, and anxious to hear what stirring events had been settled while he slept, when he met Terry . . . who said: "hullo." And *he* said: "hullo." And they both stood still, ready to die of shyness at the encounter. The last time he saw her, she was lying prone and vanquished on the chancel steps, not giving battle any more, not caring what became of her. She did not know he had stood there looking down at her flung body. The last she remembered of him was his mocking challenge ringing down the church, shattering hope, piling up the conditions of her surrender.

"Are you better?" asked Lal, with a supreme effort.

"Oh yes, thank you, I'm quite all right. I haven't been at all ill really." Then, forcing her tongue to emulate his timid politeness: "Did you — have you — did you sleep well?"

("It sounds so silly, but I can't talk, in case he thinks I'm still not talking to *him*.")

"Yes, thanks, once I'd seen off Uncle Ted to the Cock. It was I who let him in last night, you know."

Terry knew; Uncle Ted had told her that — and a little more; the little more was what lay behind her question whether he had slept well.

But now the tension was somewhat eased; both with sighs of relief leapt to the fact of Uncle Ted having come and how lovely it was, as their safest subject (if any subject were safe?). Together talking of Uncle Ted's arrival, they moved along towards the schoolroom.

"Cold in here," remarked Lal. The wood was crackling in the fireplace and the coals had not yet caught. "I suppose it's only just been lit."

They flopped down on the hearth-rug, close in front of the fender . . . as close as they had been when Terry had brought down Rosalind's Christmas present to show him. Not consciously remembering, but anxious to keep the ball rolling (only not any duck-ball) Terry plunged again into would-be careless chatter; she was a trifle better at it than Lal:

"Nanny's such an old ass, what d'you think she brought me last night for an idiotic sort of extra Christmas present?" And she described it, with all the detail that the simple chunky shape of one small toy lamb could carry. "And Major Lambert-King told Nanny it was made of some sort of composition and that's what made it shine. Funny though, I quite like it. Not that it's any use except just to keep, of *course*."

"I wish you'd show it to me," exclaimed Lal in such eager friendliness that his bad mistake was out before he could stop it . . . He rushed straight on: "Not now, of *course*. When we've got time."

Loving him for his clear state of remorse, but wishing she had not begun on presents (of all subjects), Terry remarked, to help him:

"I think sometimes, don't you, that the older one gets, the more one sort of likes babyish presents?"

He warmly assented, and began to tell her about how Uncle Ted had loved the clown-box . . . stopped dead and once more silently kicked himself for a clumsy idiot. But the girl's face was suddenly all alight . . . And Lal caught his breath: "Why, she's beautiful!" his body and soul mysteriously aching . . . drawn taut like wire . . . till her voice, childish and happy, set him free again:

"Then he *did* love it! Then Clare was as wrong as she could be! Oh, I'm so glad!"

For while Terry had still been offering herself to Uncle Ted in her interesting role of trying to rise from her bed of pain because "the play must go on", she had been a fraction too late to check at an effective quotation from Pagliacci, the Clown with the Broken Heart . . . Then a sudden agonised recollection of what Clare had spouted on broken-hearted clowns in connection with Uncle Ted. . . . However, she noticed that he seemed to be taking it with remarkable calm.

She and Lal now agreed, both loyal to Clare, that the latter loved Uncle Ted so terribly, she could never endure a thought of the least thing hurting him without a fierce desire to protect him at all costs:

"Like mothers."

"Not mine, thank heaven," declared Terry, with touching sincerity.

"And I expect if Clare had ever been a clown, *she'd* have minded being reminded, and so she thought he would too."

After a pause: "She's on her way back, you know. Uncle Ted phoned her because —"

"Yes, I know, he wants us to do it to-night, after all."

Shyness descended again, worse than ever. Speech had run easily while they talked of Clare, but here, here was the play.

With averted head and staring hard into the fire, Lal said: "Well, Uncle Ted got me to see it would have been a frightful shame to let down the Vicar when we'd promised him a silver collection for his dossal, and when he was looking forward to it and I expect not minding all his usual vicarish worries half as much as usual. He's awfully poor, you know; clergymen nearly always are."

"That's queer." Terry sounded a little perplexed: "Uncle Ted didn't remind me once about the Vicar and the collection and us promising —"(Oh bother, I shouldn't have mentioned promises — no, it's all right, I don't think he's noticed!) "What we talked about was doing just *that* play, a Nativity Play, not made-up but repeating a real thing that had happened, the biggest thing that had ever happened. Uncle Ted felt that by acting it again as though it were still happening, we meant a sort of courtesy to *them* at Christmas, because it isn't as though they didn't know or care any more like ordinary people who write plays and die — at least, perhaps they may care too, only not in the same way. And then I said: 'You mean if we started rehearsals of Twelfth Night, for instance, and then chucked it up, it wouldn't be so rude to Shakespeare as — as to *them*, because they're sort of living nearer'?"

"Just up the road," Lal put in, half laughing; but not a scoffing sort of laugh; she saw that.

"Yes, just up the road. And Uncle Ted said: Yes, that was just what he *did* feel, and it was awfully exciting I should be feeling it too."

Easier now to rattle on in their old free way; the barriers were down, and they could even recall their quarrel, still contrite but without flinching. Gravely surveying Uncle Ted's summing-up, Terry passed it on to Lal, confident that all three of them were in whole-hearted agreement: "To spoil a Nativity Play by having

293

our own small hot selfish little wars all over it, so that in the end we weren't able to get on with it at all — it's not good enough."

"No, it isn't nearly good enough." But then Lal's serious assent broke on a mischievous recognition of Uncle Ted's methods: "If you ask me, he knew we had to be hauled up to scratch again, and did it for each of us in a quite different way, the old ruffian! What worked best for me might not be as useful with you."

Terry inquired with deep interest: "What quite different way do you suppose he thought would work best with Clare?"

"Oh, he didn't have to bother to think up anything for Clare; he'd only have to say 'Come straight back, I want you', and she'd ask no questions but start off at once, out of pure love for him."

"Isn't ours pure?" in a very subdued little voice, acknowledging the truth of Lal's insight, but bothered at the idea of something wanting in their own response. Yet before he could reassure her, she saw in all humility that neither she nor Lal were capable of behaving with the essential single-minded humility of Clare. Self-defence, self-justification . . . the nightmare was happily past; but if Uncle Ted had not been Uncle Ted . . . For a moment Terry had a vision of him and St. Joseph as the same man, so her next remark was not entirely irrelevant:

"One can take anything from Uncle Ted, because it isn't as though he talked religion at us."

"Lord, no! He wouldn't do that." Lal dismissed the shocking idea.

294

"Oh, it's only *you* here," exclaimed Roddy, entering the schoolroom, followed by Erica. "Where's Uncle Ted? We've been hunting for him everywhere; I haven't shown him my magnetical blackboard yet."

"He's gone to fetch Jonathan."

"*Jonathan?* Why ever?"

"We're going to do the play, after all."

Erica's reaction to this startling news was entirely favourable. Once more in her ears sang the amiable refrain: "Who was that perfectly lovely child who played the Angel?" Soon she would probably be hearing it. So:

"It would have been such a pity if we hadn't, after learning the parts and having all the costumes here."

"Who's to play the Virgin Mary?" demanded Roddy. "You or Rosalind?"

Lal put in hotly: "Terry, of course. As though Ros would be any use!"

"I said at once she wouldn't be; I said it first; *I* said it to her herself."

At that very moment, Ted was being waylaid in the hall by Rosalind, who had been waiting about for him to return from his visit to Jonathan. For *if* his mission had succeeded, which she thought unlikely, but if it had and Jonathan were producing the play this evening, then she would not dream of being offended that he had sent for her yesterday and then had not needed her; she would be what she had heard Jonathan call an old trouper, ready for any emergency, willing to take up her part not merely at the eleventh hour, but almost at the twelfth . . .

"No earthly!" said Ted, anticipating her question. "He won't."

Rosalind was full of sympathy: "I'm afraid once one gives up the idea of doing a play — but I *am* sorry, Uncle Ted, for you and the children; it must be such a disappointment. I suppose Jonathan feels it really is too late?"

"Oh, we're doing the play. Jonathan's quitted for good."

"Well, you know, Uncle Ted, we can't blame him, can we? I can't think it right to do that sort of a play unless it has been perfectly rehearsed. In fact, honestly, I never really thought it a play for the children at all, though I was ready at once to help them by coming in at the very last moment."

Ted saw by her mode of abdication that she took for granted there was no other Virgin Mary on the cards, so to speak, except herself. No need, however, to disillusion her; Jonathan was the attraction, and without Jonathan producing, Rosalind would continue quite firmly not to think it right to do "that sort of a play."

"So you advise us to give it up?" with the air of a meek disheartened man, highly deceptive for those who did not know Ted through and through.

"Oh, I'm sure you should; certain things aren't so good when forced." She made "Christmas in the Market Place" sound like a mushroom out of season.

Odd, reflected Ted, on his way upstairs to the schoolroom; Orlo's flesh-and-blood; that girl! And a tinge of sadness invaded his thoughts. For he had been devoted to his friend, and could not console himself with any idea that Orlo lived on in his daughter. Doe, but not Orlo. It struck him as a mistaken choice for immortality.

Lal and Terry and Roddy and Erica were restlessly waiting for a lead to action.

"Oughtn't we to be rehearsing?"

"I think we'd better see what Jonathan — you know what he is."

"It feels like weeks, doesn't it, since we rehearsed? And yet it was only yesterday; no, we didn't rehearse yesterday, did we? We tried on our costumes all the morning; and in the church —" Erica stopped, and congratulated herself on her tact in not pursuing recollection of what had happened yesterday evening "in the church."

Suddenly, at the word "rehearsal," Terry was attacked by stage fright and first-night nerves: "I can't remember one line of my part. I'll have to learn it all over again." She made a mental grab for her entrance cue: "Everything's gone all white and blank inside my brain, like a sheet of paper. What *am* I to do? What *do* people on the stage do when they've forgotten their part? Jonathan won't believe me; he'll be furious; he'll think I'm still —"

Jonathan! — Lal discovered that he too was rather dreading the arrival of his great white chief. He and Terry were ashamed of not having come up to the standard of how a real theatrical company should behave. "A parcel of quarrelling kids" floated before them in letters of fire, as against their vision of a constant state of harmony and selflessness during professional rehearsals; which pretty illusion, had it been overheard by any theatrical producer, must have occasioned a burst of almost maniacal laughter . . .

"Here's Uncle Ted!"

"I'll try and break it to you gently," said Ted, when he could be heard through their enthusiastic welcome; "your producer has thrown us over; won't have anything more to do with the play."

"But we've got the costumes," objected Roddy.

"Well, that's a good thing. Are we down-hearted?"

"*No*," Lal answered for the rest. "Because honestly, I'm not a bit surprised."

Roddy suggested they should act "Pearl of Great Price" instead, tenacious of the idea he had mooted before he had resigned himself to a Nativity Play. This was a little too much for the original Ceddie Conway to keep a sober face; he collapsed into helpless laughter.

"I don't see why not," argued Roddy, objecting to such levity; but as he did more or less see why not, he let go, muttering: "Because then you could do most of the acting, and you're used to it."

Simultaneously, Erica, Lal and Terry caught up Roddy's notion, but on lines of sounder sense:

"Of *course*! Now you're here, you'll play Jonathan's part, won't you, Uncle Ted?"

"It'll be fifty million times better than having Jonathan."

"You'll be frightfully good as Old Melchior."

"And you're in the real theatre."

"You're used to learning parts at top speed, aren't you?"

"So that's all right, isn't it?" Terry summed up, a little anxious that Uncle Ted had not with his usual goodwill already pledged himself to take on all Jonathan's liabilities.

What a thrilling change to be made in the carefully written-out programmes: "Old Melchior" — and then not a mere Jonathan Reed, but the famous Ted Barnett, idol of the London public.

Ted himself had thought that this might be not only a thrilling change in the programme, but perhaps a little too thrilling . . . to an audience assembling that evening to see some children act a Nativity Play in their Parish church.

"Afraid it's quite out of the question," with a grave shake of the head. And he explained that according to the rules of his profession — "You've heard of Equity, haven't you, and how strict they are?" — his peculiarly sensitive Union would forbid him to appear as an amateur in any performance where money was to be taken; it involved breaking certain clauses in his contract, and the risk of being thereafter blackballed by every manager in England and the British Commonwealth and America too . . .

"You see how it is, don't you?" — yet at the sight of their solemn upturned faces, so disappointed and even appalled at the heavy implications involved had he yielded to their importunity and weakly consented to act, he felt a small pang at his own convincing account of a non-existent predicament.

". . . Would Uncle Nick do it, d'you think?" asked Terry, abandoning the greater name with a sigh. "He's a dramatist, isn't he, not an actor, so perhaps Equality wouldn't mind?"

"Uncle Nick can't," Roddy came in with a flat objection; "because he's not here. He and Aunt Tania have eloped."

Even Erica was not in on this startling piece of news, and shared astonishment with Terry and Lal:

"*Eloped?*"

"Uncle Nick and Aunt Tania?"

"When? Why?"

Roddy was not quite sure when and why. He had this information at second and even third-hand, from the staff.

"It's true, isn't it, Uncle Ted?"

Ted said no-one had told him anything about it and he had his doubts, for surely somebody would have known?

"That's just it about an elopement. They don't."

"Uncle Ted," put in Lal, rather impatiently discarding Nick and Tan for his far greater concern about the Vicar's silver collection: "if Jonathan won't and can't, what are we going to *do*?"

"Got the play here?"

Lal produced his copy of "Christmas in the Market Place," crumpled and covered with hieroglyphics. Ted rapidly looked it through, and declared that no actor alive could learn so much at the last moment; they would have to get in somebody to read the part.

"Dad?"

"Dad wouldn't. He never reads to us. Besides, he doesn't much like church."

Neither had Ted much hope of Anthony. After some cogitation, he suggested the Vicar might be persuaded.

300

It seemed to Terry and Lal, comparing notes afterwards, that the Vicar had played a very much more important part in the whole set-up since Uncle Ted's arrival last night. Until then, he had barely been remembered, half-contemptuously by Jonathan when formal permission had to be obtained. They were not used to so much Vicar in their daily lives.

The idea appealed to Erica:

"Mr. Crichton reads awfully well," she recollected. "Don't you remember, Roddy, we heard him quite a little while ago; and Nanny's always praising his beautiful voice."

"Yes, but he can't *produce* a play. Jonathan told Judy that *producing* a play was the most important thing. And that you can't do a play if it isn't produced by a proper producer." When Roddy once had a thing wedged into his head, nothing could loosen it.

"As a matter of fact," Lal volunteered very diffidently, "I've actually got all Jonathan's stage directions, the cuts and the exits and entrances and all that, copied out into my own copy of the play; so if it would be the slightest use — I mean, I know it's a terribly tough job and needs endless experience to do it properly, but during the last day or two before we — I mean, while we — I mean — Jonathan did find that he couldn't quite do without a sort of assistant, and as I was terribly keen, he let me be his; we went down the church together once or twice to have a good look at just where the stage would be and the lighting and everything, and so —" He came to a full stop, hoping to God he had neither been putting on side nor making a ghastly fool of himself?

But his uncle said: "Go on, Lal," with such an encouraging look that Lal felt better at once.

"Well, you see, I got hold of his copy of the play and wrote down in the margin everything he'd written down, and all his little drawings and maps and things. Not that I really thought I'd need it, but I'd got interested in that behind-the-scenes way of looking at it all, and it made mine — my copy, I mean — seem different from the others because one couldn't read it unless one had first heard Jonathan himself explaining; it's in short lang. Anyhow, as we're up against it and there really *isn't* anyone else and the play's to-night and it's now damn nearly lunch-time —? And if somebody better turned up, or Jonathan changed his mind, I could hand it over in a minute."

Before Lal spoke, Ted had been about to come to the rescue by reassuring the harassed little troupe that his Union (his Equality, as Terry called it) *might* consider allowing him to produce, as long as he did not focus the spotlight on himself by acting a single line. But liking the way things were turning out, he resolved to remain absorbed into the dun-coloured background, and only step out from it with an offer to carry round the plate for the Silver Collection, if the Vicar cared for him to perform this small service in which his popularity might work a few silver miracles.

CHAPTER
FOURTEEN

"If I hadn't been christened at the proper age," remarked Doe at lunch, in humorous recognition of her children's insistent "Mummy-will-you-go-and-see-the-Vicar?", "I'd have said that that's what they were after. All the years we've been living here, I haven't seen as much of the Rev. Mr. Crichton as during the last week; and unchaperoned too!"

"Mummy, I did offer to come with you, truly; I wouldn't have minded a bit, but Lal said he wanted me for a run-through."

"But there was no-one to run through." Roddy recognised this unpalatable fact aloud, so that the grown-ups could not possibly miss it. "Only me and Terry and Erica. Clare hasn't come yet, and nor hasn't Judy, and we didn't know if the Vicar was going to say yes, so he wasn't there either. And when we tried without them, Lal stood in front holding the play the same as Jonathan used to, to watch what we were doing, so it was only Terry and me and Erica acting. And if Erica had gone with you, there would only have been Terry and me, and that wouldn't have been enough for a run-through."

"Ten little nigger boys," laughed Doe.

"And when we skipped and got to where Lal couldn't settle whether we could find enough kings or be one too few for the Three Kings —"

"Auntie Doe," Terry interrupted, "was the Vicar nice about being in the play? Was he pleased?"

"What's he going to wear?" asked Roddy.

"Nothing, of course, Roddy."

"But —"

"You know. What he always wears. Vicars don't dress up."

"Oh."

Doe addressed the adult members of the party; "As now he won't be able to see to it himself, he asked me if I'd kindly look after putting people in their seats."

"You ought to say 'pews', Mummy," Erica primly corrected her. The word struck a chord of memory in Doe . . . Nick giving them the title of the plum of his Revue: "Take a Pew." Queer, with Ted actually here, sitting where Nick had sat . . . ("He's a born clown; when clowns feel they have a message to preach — God, it turns my stomach!") She wondered if Sorrel remembered too?

"Can any of the rest of us do something to help?" Sorrel inquired of Ted.

"Over to you, Lal." He noticed that Lal had eaten practically nothing; he had noticed, too, the instant and perceptible relief of the assembled cast of "Christmas in the Market Place" when Lal made his tentative offer to take on Jonathan's role of producer: here again was someone on whom they could throw the whole burden with trustful dependence, not any more obstreperous, but

304

glad to lean and lean heavily. (That's what always comes of offering to hold the baby, reflected Ted; poor Lal! I've seen it happen a hundred times.) So he suggested, *à propos* of Sorrel's offer:

"What about addressing a formal request to Mrs. Sorrel Maitland to take on the post of wardrobe mistress, Lal? You'll be lost without one, you know."

Sorrel readily consented. And Doe added mischievously: "And you, what about you, Ted? You're letting yourself off very lightly, aren't you? What's *your* contribution to the labour and heat of the day?"

"Oh, I'm offering to take the plate round, if your Vicar will give me the job. You're quite right, Doe my dear, I don't like hard work."

Anthony came out of his reverie: "If Ted's going to make the Collection, why not let him make it without having the play at all? Answer the purpose just as well; better, perhaps." And withdrew again into silence.

And Ted, successfully passing off this Roddyism as a huge joke, could have kicked Anthony heartily on the shins. After his own loving precautions that the children should not realise the magnitude of his star quality, for Anthony just to have gone and thrown it into plain words —

As though to emphasise his blood-relationship with Anthony, Roddy spoke across the table to Lal:

"If Clare doesn't come in time, is Ros going to be asked to act Elizabeth, like when Terry wasn't going to act the Virgin Mary?"

Appreciating swiftly that this conception of her daughter as general understudy to be picked up and thrown down at will, was hardly likely to appeal to

Rosalind, Doe intervened without appearance of undue haste:

"By the way, the Vicar's very kindly having Evensong early today, three o'clock instead of six; and he says that naturally he wants to read through your play before to-night, as he's deputising for Jonathan. I said that one of you would run round with a copy later on. Don't let them forget, will you, Ted?"

Ted laughed, as he promised; for he had seen on the face of each of the young actors that familiar tightening-up, that look which meant "Not *my* copy, whatever happens," that over-my-dead-body look . . . In this if in nothing else, they showed a marked kinship with every professional company he had ever known.

At this moment a major diversion occurred with the whirlwind entrance of Clare into the dining-room and into the arms of Uncle Ted. She did not notice she had been followed into the room by the young American, Dwight van Buren.

"Oh, Uncle Ted! Oh, it's *swell* seeing you! I thought I'd never get over. They were terribly sweet in the way they understood about the play and my getting back at once, only they simply didn't know what 'at once' meant. They kept *on* saying I couldn't possibly go till I'd had some lunch, and that this-aft would do just as well, as the show wasn't till to-night. I thought we'd never get off. If I could have driven the car myself I'd have just taken one. Oh darling, *darling* Uncle Ted, it was such bliss hearing your voice on the phone! And you do see, don't you, why I'm so dreadfully late? The van Burens kept on saying —"

"Well, they sure are terrible folk, the van Burens," her escort cheerfully agreed. And Clare flushed and gasped: "Oh, I'm sorry. I'm awful."

Dwight van Buren did not mind. He had caught sight of Rosalind. Naturally he accepted all Doe's offers of a seat at a table, coffee, dessert, beer — No hurry, he had plenty of time, no hurry at all over getting back; he could stay for ever if required.

"I say," shouted Roddy, interrupting the young man's manoeuvres to get seated not between Anthony and Sorrel, but on the contrary, next to Rosalind, and Who-cares on his other side, "I say, couldn't he be one of our kings?"

It may have been by combined wishful thinking or simply from the over-wrought state of the leading actors concerned, Lal, Clare and Terry, that when Ted visited the schoolroom shortly after Lal had swept them all off after lunch, nothing had as yet been done about sending the play round to the Vicar. Being Uncle Ted, Lal naturally stopped rehearsal to learn his pleasure; anyone else would have been given marching orders; not from any desire to show-off that he was now producer; he was long past that; but it was desperately important and desperately difficult to get some sort of a straight run-through without either Judy or Jonathan. (Damn Judy, why doesn't she *come*?)

And perhaps for the only time in his life, Uncle Ted made things worse, not better, by his appearance and reminder.

"Oh Lord, I'd forgotten! Yes . . . well . . . my copy's no good to him, it's scribbled all over; besides, I have to *have* it. Here, Clare, let's send him yours, you're not using it."

"Where is it?" asked Clare.

"I don't know. Haven't you got it?"

"No, I didn't take it away with me." She looked helplessly round the room as though expecting "Christmas in the Market Place" would rise up and leap forward at her call, saying "Mistress"!

Naturally someone said: "When did you have it last?" And tension increased . . . Clare had had it last when they all had had theirs last, at rehearsal yesterday in the church. The silence lasted long enough for the company to become aware that she had probably flung it down when she rushed off in high emotion after accusing Terry.

"Terry's got hers," Erica chimed in, not on what had been said, but on what they were collectively remembering; "because I picked it up and brought it home for her after — you know!"

Terry knew; they all knew. Lal very gently asked Terry if they might borrow her copy for the Vicar? Immediately and on the mere suggestion, it became her anchor, her life-line, her only hope:

"I *can't*. Oh please, Lal, I can't. Please, Uncle Ted, I can't let it go. I simply can't. I've *got* to read my part through before to-night. I don't know what's happened, but I can't remember a word of it. It's just as if I'd never learnt it. Please, *please* let me keep my copy, and perhaps if I hold it up to the very last minute —"

308

Uncle Ted patted her on the shoulder and spoke the same soothing words he had spoken to every seasoned leading lady or every young actress making her début, ever since he first went on the stage:

"There, my dear, you'll be all right. It'll all come back the moment you start. You'll be surprised afterwards that you could ever have felt like this. Bless you, it's as much a symptom as sneezing when you have a cold; no production's complete without it. Well now, Erica, something tells me *you're* not suffering from first-night nerves, are you? Be a sport and let's have your copy, and I'll take it to the Vicar and get rid of myself hanging round here and disturbing you all. Lal's been very patient so far; he knows rehearsals have a fatal fascination for me!"

Lal tried to grin back at him, but did not achieve much; for to own the honest truth, he *did* wish they could be left to get on with it; they were trying as hard as they possibly could to get back to form again, but they had all lost so much confidence; their quarrel had shaken them, and moreover there was a terribly over-polite conscience-stricken "after you" sort of atmosphere, a trying to compensate for past misdemeanour, just at an hour when a bit of stage bumptiousness would have been far more useful than diffidence. And he kept on thinking of things he ought to be doing and no time to do them: ("If only Judy would *come*! Damn her, where can she have gone?")

Roddy and Erica had been whispering together. And Erica said: "Of course I'd have given you mine at once, Uncle Ted. But I didn't have a whole copy of my own; I shared one with Roddy; and he isn't *quite* sure what he's done with it, are you, Roddy dear?"

Roddy shook his head, and for once looked as though he might be going to cry at any moment. For this was tangible wickedness, to have lost his copy of the play; something for which a small boy could rightfully be scolded; not just a fuss, like the silly things that had been upsetting Terry and Clare yesterday; though now Clare had lost hers too, and Terry would have if Erica had not picked it up in the church and brought it home. He hoped Uncle Ted would remember both those items on the charge sheet? For somehow Roddy did not want to point them out; somehow he thought Uncle Ted would like that even less than him having lost the book; though to a real actor and a famous actor with his picture on posters and things, that must seem pretty heinous. Roddy stared up at him miserably, awaiting judgment and the birch . . . till it occurred to him that Uncle Ted was not looking angry at all, just a bit bothered.

"I'm afraid we can't leave the old boy without one till to-night, you know, if he's taking two parts."

"But he's only going to *read* them."

"Yes, but all the same he'd like to *know* what it's about."

"But it's a Nativity Play. Wouldn't he *know* what it was about?"

"He might have a rough notion," admitted Ted.

"Uncle Ted."

"Yes, Erica?"

"If you went and got Jonathan's copy of the play to take to the Vicar —? As it's Jonathan's part he's going to have, he'll need it and Jonathan won't; don't you think that's the best idea?"

As a matter of fact, it was; and Ted conceded it; and Erica the Indispensable whispered of herself: "with a wisdom beyond her years." . . . And Lal and Terry and Clare and Roddy were looking so relieved, that Ted frankly took them into his confidence; they were nice kids and would understand how he was only human; especially if they had had much to do with Jonathan.

"You see," he confessed, "it's a question of who's to ask him for it. And I don't want to. He doesn't like Funny Men. And he seemed to think, when I talked to him this morning, that we were all bound to make a frightful mess of the play without him, and had much better leave it alone altogether. So I'd rather he didn't hear now that we were in a bit of a mess already."

At once they all felt passionately allied with Uncle Ted in a grim resolve that the last person to know of anything going wrong should be their ex-producer.

Stimulated by this, Roddy gave a sudden excited squeak:

"I *know* where mine is! I've remembered!" He rushed off in triumph to fetch it for Uncle Ted to bear off to the Rev. Mr. Crichton.

Scoring over Jonathan acted as an all-round tonic. Half an hour later Lal was able to say "Look, this isn't too bad. Not much sense in going any farther till we get Judy for her scenes. If I only *knew* where Judy was! But by now the church ought to be empty, for me to whiz along and make out a list on the spot of the things to be carted over."

Terry noticed that Lal spoke with none of the pleasure in his importance as senior producer which had inflated him when Jonathan first invited him in on the fun, fun with no direct responsibility; noticed too, that his Joey had lost nearly all its fluency and swagger and cheek which had formerly made it irresistible; while though his Joseph had gained somewhat in sincerity, it was handicapped by his new shyness and was still no star performance.

"But he's more like *being* St. Joseph," Terry reflected, with a queer little thrill at her discovery that Lal was giving all he had in service to the play itself, and sought to gain no reward in credit or in thanks. He carried the full burden now, with its multitude of selfless worries; but at no time did he let them jolly well know it so that they were jolly well to sit up and take notice. It was funny though — Terry gave a little inside chuckle — how he had automatically called on Roddy to come along with him in the capacity of Assistant Stage Manager (or errand-boy!), and how Roddy at once began to strut and put on airs, as Lal had done with Jonathan.

In the hall Lal ran into Dwight van Buren, who was being reluctantly escorted by Rosalind up to the "rehearsal room," as she called it, as sounding slightly better than "schoolroom."

"I say, did you want me? Wasn't there a part? — a King or something? I didn't come before, because I thought maybe I'd be in the way and you'd send for me when you were ready." And he might have added "and because I can't tear myself away from the most beautiful girl I've ever met."

312

Roddy accepted the reference to Caspar, Melchior and Baltazar as a compliment to his own earlier suggestion that the stranger might be cast for one of them: "Not the black king you can't be; that's the one Lal's wanted from the beginning."

. . . "Lord, I'd forgotten! I must have been mad," muttered Lal.

Rosalind bridled on behalf of the attractive young American so unexpectedly thrown into her lap. Why were children nearly always so rude to a guest?" I must say, Lal, considering Mr. van Buren so very kindly offered to step into the breach —" She flashed Mr. van Buren a bewitched smile.

But Lal meant he had been mad not to realise that blacking his face for Baltazar in addition to playing Joseph who was actually kneeling beside the Crib at the moment of the procession of the Three Kings, was utterly impossible now that he was himself producing the play as well. It would not in any case have been easy, for he did not know exactly how Jonathan had proposed to deal with the time lapse, and give him a chance to get off and reappear as Baltazar in their final decision to end "Christmas in the Market Place" on the Magi moving slowly towards the Crib, bearing gold, frankincense and myrrh. No doubt Jonathan would have provided something resourceful, if only to get out of having to do that long acting speech he detested, with old Melchior alone on the stage. But it was too late now for Lal to start thinking up fresh sequences — there was no time for anything — and Judy not turned up yet.

"I'm terribly sorry, Mr. van Buren, do forgive me, but I've decided we can't end the play that way, after all. And I say, I've simply got to rush off to the church." He glanced appalled towards the grandfather clock in the hall. "Hell, it's nearly four! And I'd hoped to cart all that stuff over before it got dark. I say, do excuse me."

Which should he do first? The lighting? Or call on Miss Cathcart who played the organ, for a rapid consultation about which carol to have at the end, for the audience to join in the singing? Yes, but "the end" — what end? The play had to end *somehow*. Should he first get that point fixed up with the others? Or settle where to get the screens to provide an illusion of more exits and entrances than they really had — Jonathan had been going to borrow them from his father's consulting room! And fetch the trusses of straw from the barn in good time; mustn't be damp if Terry had to sit on them (Terry was still looking white and transparent, and it had been his fault) . . . Oh, and the Vicar had to be shown the cuts for him to copy them in; would the old boy need his standing-desk thing to read from? And if so, wouldn't it be infernally in the way? Or could he do without it? Perhaps he could double reading with prompting; you couldn't risk doing without a prompter when you were on the stage yourself more than half the time . . .

Lal's brain reeled in all directions with the million things still to be done. Could brains actually crack, he wondered? He was tempted to throw it all up, not perform any play to-night, tell Uncle Ted it simply wasn't possible. No, that wouldn't do, either; no play meant no Silver Collection; you mustn't go on making promises and breaking them and letting people down; the Vicar had been looking forward to covering up that ghastly picture . . .

"I'll help cart over any stuff you like," van Buren volunteered, determined that even if he were not cast for a king, he would find some excuse and stay on. To sit beside golden Rosalind during the performance would be a whole heap better than mucking about behind the scene with the kids. For he visualised it as a play with orthodox curtain, scenery and wings.

A knock at the front door; Lal was nearest; impatiently he flung it open.

"Jonathan told me to come along," gasped Judy. "Am I wanted?"

. . . "They did their best, and there, you can't do more than your best!"

". . . Not raining, is it? Hope not, it's quite a stretch walking home. Fog? Oh dear! I'd never have thought, would you, that our Vicar could read like that? Ought to have been on the stage."

". . . Who was that perfectly *lovely* child who played the Angel?"

". . . They bit off more than they could chew, if you ask me."

". . . To think that Ted Barnett himself — d'you know, he stood in front of me for ages making his jokes — I'll never forget; I thought I should die, laughing."

". . . I must say, I was disappointed (wish people wouldn't push so!) — didn't seem to me to make sense at times."

". . . Got your torch? Nice to be able to use 'em again. Look, there's little Erica Maitland . . . Didn't she look lovely as the Angel? No, over there. She's the only one of them to come out, dear little mite; I expect she was shy and wanted to get to her mother."

". . . That tall girl — she'd a slight accent: American, was it? But such a pretty voice, it didn't seem to matter. I *liked* her scene with the Virgin."

". . . It all ended so sudden-like, didn't it? As if they hadn't meant it to end there."

". . . Didn't the Vicar read it *beautiful?*"

". . . I never dreamt I'd ever have the chance to give three-and-six to Ted Barnett himself. I meant only to give a shilling; wasn't worth more: a lot of children dressed up who didn't know half the time if they were coming or going — But it'll be something to tell about, now that Ted Barnett himself —"

". . . Look at our Miss Erica. Wasn't she a *lovely* Angel. There, I'm afraid she heard me."

". . . When he said 'Thank you', Ted Barnett called me 'my dear'; 'Thank you, my dear', he said. Made one feel generous, to be spoken to like that by him."

". . . Well, it was too ambitious for those children, but they all tried their best, and it might have been a lot worse."

". . . Wonder how much he collected? Five bob of it's mine."

"Is Terry —? Oh, here you are, darling — Come along, you're to be driven home in kind Mr. van Buren's car, with Grandpa and Rosalind — You'll like that, won't you? It was Rosalind who thought of it: 'Terry looks ready to drop' she said; and she's longing to tell you how well you acted. No, Terry dear, it's no good please-auntie-Doeing me with those pleading eyes in a white face; you were quite ill last night, and you've had a long exhausting day. Besides, you want to be well enough to go to the theatre with Lal and Clare on Tuesday night, don't you? You're to go straight to bed when you get in, and we'll bring you some hot milk. I told them to drive round and pick you up here at the vestry door; there are such crowds pouring out in front."

Lal thought he was the last to be left behind in the vestry. He was simply too tired to summon up energy to move. All that mess and litter to be cleared up — costumes and props and wiring and screens and straw. Where did one begin? And was it usually expected of the stage-manager and his myrmidons (in this case non-existent) to get everything looking normal again on the very same night, or be for ever blackballed by the profession?

Then Clare, pushing her way through a rapidly thinning audience, came in with a welcome message from the Vicar:

"He says we're to go home and go to bed and not worry about a thing. Plenty of time to see to it all in the morning."

"Oh, all right. Where's Uncle Ted? Did he say —"

"I couldn't get near him; he's all hemmed in and surrounded. Come on, Lal dear. I'm whacked, aren't you?" Her glance at him was wholly protective; she had already seen that her cousin was something more than whacked, and she purposely slowed up her own normal pace through the churchyard . . . so that by the time they reached the lane, it was all but empty; everyone had dispersed.

"You were *fine*, Lal. And I think you managed it all just wonderfully."

Lal's faintly mocking smile, not at her but at himself for a flop, was lost in the darkness. All he said was:

"Thanks. Yes, it didn't go too badly, considering. The Vicar stole the show; apart from him, your scene with Terry."

"Lal, I've had a letter from Mother. I found it when I got back to-day. They want me to start for home the middle of January."

"I say, that's in a fortnight. I thought you were to be over here for months."

"So did I — well, for three months anyhow, but it's because she's heard Mrs. Bosanquet will be sailing then, sooner than she'd meant, and Mother and Granny are afraid of not finding an 'escort' for me if they wait till later. *Escort!* As though I couldn't go alone. I wish you were coming, Lal."

"So do I."

"Mother says she expects you over for a real long stay with us as soon as ever you can. That would be grand . . . if you'd like it?"

"I'd love it. Your mother was awfully sweet to me that time she was over, and so was your grandmother, and I'm awfully fond of Uncle Ken; he reminds me of Uncle Ted." Lal carefully stopped here . . . with a mental reservation.

"Lal, did Uncle Ted like your present? I'm sure he did."

Lal hugged to himself a happy memory of Ted's rapt delight playing with the clown-box . . . And made careful reply:

"He seemed to, I think, unless he was pretending. You know Uncle Ted!"

Clare thought there might have been a disappointment — and quickly reverted to California:

"We'd have good times together, and our house — Granny's San Francisco house — looks out on the Ocean."

"I've heard it's terribly luxurious; I shan't know myself." He was making a strong effort to shake off those heavy clouds of sleep numbing his tongue, pressing him down at every step.

"Yes, it is; at least, you'd have your own bathroom. The other three, the little ones, Jack and Gene and Gay, they adore it and nothing would ever get them away. They're darlings, but they're more Mother's, and I belong more to Father. And somehow, Lal, you'll understand, I feel English and shabby and glad to be the same as you, the same as Uncle Ted and Terry and all of us."

Lal suddenly took her hand and held it tight for a moment.

"We've still got New Year's Eve to look forward to. I'm *longing* for you to see 'Pearl of Great Price,' and I'm glad it's just going to be you and me and Terry in the box."

"Yes, so am I. Terribly glad."

* * *

Meanwhile Ted and the Vicar were in the counting-house — in this case the vestry — counting out the money.

"Twenty-one pounds, eleven shillings and sixpence," Ted announced with a flourish.

"It can't be," said Mr. Crichton, awed at such a grand total. "Are you sure you haven't made a mistake? Let me count it again."

"No need for that, my dear fellow. If I've gone wrong one way or the other, it couldn't be more than sixpence."

"I hadn't reckoned on more than twelve pounds at the very most. It must have been you, Mr. Barnett; you charmed it out of their pockets. I — I hardly know what to say!"

Ted grinned happily, seeing that the Vicar was rapidly getting a little tipsy at the sound of coins musically chinking, and at the sight of those generous piled-up heaps of silver.

"Perhaps it ought to go for repairing the porch? It's in grave need. The dossal is a luxury —"

"Not on your life! The porch can sit on its hind legs and wait till your next Christmas collection. The children acted their play to get you a dossal, and a dossal it shall be; twenty-one pounds' worth of it."

"There won't be such a magnificent one in all Berkshire; in all England."

"Almost worth while having put up with the 'Sacrifice of Isaac' for so long?"

"I won't deny it was a trial, but as you say —" The Vicar broke off. "I gather I owe it to you as well, Mr.

Barnett, that the young people didn't throw up the play at the eleventh hour. I'd no idea, of course —"

"Their producer threw it up at the eleventh hour; these children are made of rather better stuff."

"Oh, Jonathan Reed. Yes . . . quite."

They exchanged glances of enjoyable understanding.

"He riled me more than a bit," remarked Ted. "That was one reason, not my best but one of them, why I was glad we pulled it off in spite of him."

The Vicar confessed that Jonathan Reed was somewhat in bad odour with him, too; "He didn't care a brass farthing for St. Crispin's, except when it suited him to use it for his convenience and to show off his cleverness. A bad upbringing; his mother dead, and Dr. Reed an atheist. Perhaps that may be what influenced me to say I would read a rather long part for the children; he had no right to let them down."

"He had some reason," Ted admitted, being a just man; "and between ourselves, I'm afraid they didn't cover themselves with glory —" He stopped for a moment, contemplating his own phrase. "Or did they, perhaps?"

"Even then," remarked the Vicar quietly, "it was far better they should do it than not. Quite apart from the Silver Collection," he added hastily.

"Yes, that's how I felt. Nobody's praised them, and the show didn't really deserve it; though I believe that wasn't because it was too ambitious for them; even Jonathan admitted they would have given a remarkable performance if something hadn't happened. To-night was probably a bit of a blow to their pride. But it wouldn't have been a good idea to have to remember for the rest of their lives that they'd promised to put on a Nativity Play and then left it lying in broken pieces all over the floor. Now — well, at least they managed to get it on; better than no attempt at all; lame and confused and halting as it was, somehow they scrambled through." Ted was silent . . . seeing that the Vicar, who at first had been listening attentively, had drifted off into a dream of damask brocade, soft yet brilliant, gold and deep purple and turquoise . . .

"Twenty-one pounds, *sixteen* shillings and sixpence!" Ted suddenly dived into his pocket and produced two half-crowns. "Clean forgot to put anything in the plate myself!"

EPILOGUE

"Why didn't I cry?" Tan handed Sorrel a stiff whisky and soda from the sideboard, and then dropped back in the other arm-chair in front of the fire. "I always cry at funerals and weddings, and when I hear a crowd cheer or see people standing silent and bare headed on the pavement in the rain. I'm that sort of emotional idiot. But I didn't cry to-day."

"Too like a bad dream?" suggested Sorrel.

"I don't remember if one ever cries or laughs in dreams? Does one?"

They discussed this listlessly for a little while. It was better to keep talking on impersonal topics. Presently they would be bound to stumble again on the unbelievable fact of Ted's sudden death in a car accident, four days ago. "If only I could have seen him just once —" for Tan, still a Chief Commander in the W.A.C., had been transferred to India at her own urgent request in the first week of 1947; given the job of investigating which were the most eligible of the personnel to be sent to an Officers' Training Camp in England. She had only returned within the last week.

Sorrel wondered if she had seen or heard it announced who was doing the Personal Appreciation on the radio after the News this evening . . .

"If you cry at weddings," carefully, "I suppose you'll be drenched at Rosalind's?"

Tan laughed (yes, that's fairly safe. Let's both talk hard about Rosalind). "Do you know anything of the bridegroom? What's his name? van Buren?"

"I've never met *him*, but his younger brother was at the children's play . . . the Christmas before last. He motored Clare back to the Manor."

"Clare? But she was *at* the Manor."

"She rushed over to the van Burens for the week-end . . . and that's how Rosalind met the family later on," Sorrel finished lamely. A chain of luck leading straight through for Rosalind, link after link, from a duck-ball to an eligible husband and the Voice that Breathed o'er Eden. Yet even this had not been such an invulnerable subject, after all. Nothing was. Suppose she had gone on: "No, *you* wouldn't have known, because you and Nick had already flung away in opposite directions — before the children had a final flare-up too; and the play was all to hell; and Terry collapsed into bed in my room after I'd said horrible things to Doe. And then Ted came down."

Put like that, how simple and bare it sounded to anyone who had not been there: Ted came down.

But Tan, her mind absent and in mourning, had not noticed the long silence.

"Will you be able to get down for it, Sorrel?"

"Oh yes; quite easy; they've fixed it for Boxing Day by Grandpa's special request. And I managed to get out of going at Christmas last year, so there's really no excuse. I had a very mellow letter from Doe asking if Terry would be bridesmaid with Erica?"

324

"Our little Erica will look like an angel . . ." But this was poor material for a laugh without Ted, without Nick, to join in.

A high gust of wind rattled the windows: then an angry spatter of rain. Tan pulled the curtains across.

"Doe wasn't there to-day, was she? I didn't see her."

"I'm not sure; one might so easily have missed anyone in that swirl of people. I had a glimpse of Anthony wedged right over on the other side, and I don't think she was with him. Thank God, Lal wasn't here."

"Where *is* Lal? I meant to ask."

"California. He went across on a long visit to stay with Ken and Louise. He and Clare have at least each other to hang on to; both of them adored Ted."

So they gave in now for a short spell, and talked of their friend, without outward signs of grief, but rather as though some great prince had died and been given a nation's funeral . . . Then a clock in the room chimed the half-hour, and Sorrel sprang up and exclaimed:

"Later than I thought! I must get home."

She did not mention what was the urgent need; and Tan did not ask, but thought: That's true; she's barely giving herself time.

"Good-bye, Sorrel. Thanks for fetching me to go along to-day. I usually prefer facing up to things alone, but not — not when — it would have been awful."

"Good-bye, Tan dear. It's nice you're home again and that one can get at you."

. . . And in less than half an hour she would be hearing Nick's voice talking about Ted. Last time she had heard it . . . he had also been talking about Ted. Had he volunteered to do this "appreciation"? *Could* he appreciate Ted, feeling all he did against "Pearl of Great Price?"

If he dares make one single criticism — Tan clenched her hands fiercely . . . Then relaxed; lay back in the armchair watching the fire's spasmodic flicker; glad the rest of the room was gathered into dusk; glad that she was too exhausted to keep on asking herself these perpetual questions with any hope of an answer: had Nick and Ted met, during the two years she was away? Had Ted seen Nick's Revue, heard "Take a Pew"? Hardly, since the long run of "Pearl of Great Price" was only broken by his death; and she still believed that Nick's cruel burlesque must have shaken any actor's power to continue playing the part of Ceddie Conway as Ted had played it.

Oh, Nick was utterly heartless; too damn sure of his infallible opinions on everything under the sun. Nick who always knew better than God, for *him* to speak presently of Ted, having neither understood nor loved him, was a piece of virtuosity she would never forgive!

Don't talk so big and windy, Tan my girl. You've already "never, never forgiven" Nick, nearly two years ago. You can't never forgive twice in the same place.

Only twelve minutes now — eleven — ten — perhaps she had better switch on to the Home Service to make sure it was working; you couldn't trust mechanical things not to betray their masters. That hellish car which crashed head-on into Ted's Humber!

Tan sprang up, impatient with her own futility. Funny, how even thought could be futile at a moment like this, when surely one's thoughts should be deep and strong and sad? But hers were little tadpoles, grey shadows with long tails darting to and fro in a stream . . . You lost a whole shoal of them under the roots along the bank . . . and when they came back, they might not even be the same tadpoles.

Here am I, meandering a long rigmarole about *tadpoles*, and it's twelve minutes past six, and for all I know, my clock's wrong.

And still, with her hand stretched out and touching the knob, still she could not bring herself to give it just that one twist which would bring Nick's voice into the room . . .

. . . Nick's voice, sincere and sorrowful, and not at all embarrassing as Tan had most feared, while he spoke of an unassuming funeral which before their very eyes, by the crying need of all human beings for the great laughter-makers, had spontaneously sprung into a royal progress along the crowded streets.

This was moving enough; and Tan, who had seen it for herself and had not cried, now found the tears were pouring down her face; she would have remained dry-eyed had Nick been appealing for effect, using beautiful phrases, doing an oration.

He had to speak, of course, for a little while — not long — on Ted's career; and especially on the sudden twist to his fame, bending it in a different direction, when over two years ago the vaudeville artist startled his critics and audiences, his critics grown uncritical, his audiences won to even more loving affection, by his playing of Ceddie Conway in "Pearl of Great Price." He had to.

Yet suddenly Tan sat up, incredulous, her heart thumping. Was it true? Could it really be true, or a fantastic illusion, that she was actually sitting here and now at this very moment listening to Nick make a public apology . . . though millions of his hearers could not have the remotest notion that he was doing anything beyond paying his simple tribute to the quality of a beloved friend:

". . . You see, perhaps we've never known anyone who could so naturally and so happily keep *himself* out of the way, all the time and whatever he was doing. It was like a glorious conjuring trick, only without a set of rules attached; and thank God, we know that it wasn't a trick at all, but the very essence of Ted Barnett.

"I'll give you an example of the amazing way it worked. A good many of you must have seen a burlesque that I wrote of 'Pearl of Great Price' in my Revue which you were kind enough to keep going till a few months ago. No effective parody can ever show the least compassion for its victim, and I'm afraid that as the author, I specially wanted this one to be effective. I've never been burlesqued myself and I dare say I should take it pretty badly, but when Ted came to see it, he shouted with laughter; I should have spotted any hurt pride, any outraged dignity hidden under his genuine delight in what had been done to him. There was none. I'd been warned that his own performance of Ceddie Conway was bound to suffer damage and bruises from its encounter with 'Take a Pew'; and indeed, anybody of

328

reasonable imagination would have thought so. So I went along the night after Ted had been to our matinée, wondering. . . . You'll hardly believe me, but though I'd read the play, I'd never seen it before.

"It was, they tell me, the same lovely performance he always gave.

"That's what I meant, you see, when I said that Ted never let himself get in the way; he hadn't got that sort of self; probably that's why he could do as he liked with us, and never knew his own secret or even that there was a secret. There was, and it's told now for good and all. For our undoubted good and for us all. I mustn't keep you any longer. Good night."

Tan dared not wait and recover breath in case he should leave the building at once. She switched off, went to the telephone and dialled the B.B.C. number.

"Hallo. When Captain Nicholas Hilliard comes down — he's just been speaking on the Home Service after the News — could you please ask him to ring up Kensington 41859? It's urgent. Yes, that's right. Thank you."

. . . He would not be surprised at her voice; the familiar telephone number would have got him over the shock. Tan could not have waited more than three minutes before the bell rang.

"*Nick?*"

"Yes, dear."

"Can you come round?"

"Of course. At once. Same address?"

"Yes. Not quite the same Tan."

ISIS publish a wide range of books in large print, from fiction to biography. A full list of titles is available free of charge from the address below. Alternatively, contact your local library for details of their collection of ISIS large print books.

Details of ISIS complete and unabridged audio books are also available.

Any suggestions for books you would like to see in large print or audio are always welcome.

7 Centremead
Osney Mead
Oxford OX2 0ES
(01865) 250333